'A captivatin

'A thrilling tale of love, lust and revenge.' *The Lady*

'A ri   el of a story, full of colour, desire and danger. I was
transfixed.' Julie Cohen, author of *Together*

'An exquisite read . . . will keep you engaged from the first page to the
last. This is historical fiction at its best.' Book Liberarti Reviews

'A beautifully-crafted novel . . ., by turns opulent and visceral. The
encroaching sense of menace was perfectly paced, as was the slow
reveal of the shocking truth underpinning the story. I adored it.'
Clare Harvey, author of *The Gunner Girl*

'Jack the Ripper meets *Pygmalion* . . . very creepy.' *Best*

'Marina Fiorato's latest novel will delight her ever increasing
number of fans.' Dilly Court

'A great summer read, I would highly recommend if you enjoy
tense, romantic thrillers, and have an interest in the
Victorian art world.' *Sixty Surfers*

Praise for Marina Fiorato:

'Captures the scents, passion and vigour of Italy.' *Books Quarterly*

'Entertaining and witty.' *Daily Mail*

'Fiorato creates her own masterpiece.' *Booklist*

'Captured in every character and locale is Fiorato's artistic flourish:
a true chiaroscurist, she renders her models not only with radiant
colour but rich meaning.' To The End Of Her Days

Also by Marina Fiorato

The Glassblower of Murano
The Madonna of the Almonds
The Botticelli Secret
Daughter of Siena
The Venetian Contract
Beatrice and Benedick
The Double Life of Mistress Kit Kavanagh

Crimson and Bone

MARINA FIORATO

HODDER

First published in Great Britain in 2017 by Hodder & Stoughton
An Hachette UK company

First published in paperback in 2018

1

Credit quote from Alexandre Dumas La Dame Aux Camélias (pp. 36-37)
Charles Dickens Hard Times (p. 75)
John Ruskin Mornings in Florence (p. 147)
Dante Alighieri La Divina Commedia Inferno (p. 226 p. 249)

A CIP catalogue record for this title is available from the British Library

Paperback ISBN 9781473610545
eBook ISBN 9781473610521

Typeset in Dante by Palimpsest Book Production Limited, Falkirk, Stirlingshire

Printed and bound in Great Britain by Clays Ltd, St Ives plc

Hodder & Stoughton policy is to use papers that are natural,
renewable and recyclable products and made from wood grown in sustainable
forests. The logging and manufacturing processes are expected to conform to
the environmental regulations of the country of origin.

Hodder & Stoughton Ltd
Carmelite House
50 Victoria Embankment
London EC4Y 0DZ

www.hodder.co.uk

For Charlie Rablin
a true gentleman

PART ONE

London

Prologue

London, 1853

They called it the Bridge of Sighs, because it barely passed a night without a suicide. That night was no different.

In the very centre of Waterloo Bridge, nine grim arches of new-cut granite arching over the freezing Thames, a figure climbed up onto the parapet. A young woman, and a slim one. The greedy wind snatched away her bonnet, and her red-gold hair streamed out behind her like a ragged pennant. She lifted her arms at her sides, like Christ on the cross. A passer-by, looking through the swirling mists at the figure with her raised arms and her halo of golden hair, might have thought her an angel. But she was no angel. She was a prostitute. Her name was Annie Stride.

Annie Stride looked her last on London with no regret. Her final breaths smoked before her face, the vapours swallowed by the swirling fog. Through the shifting ether she could see the water below – grey as steel and cold as charity, the reflected moon already drowned there. The jumpers did not last long, not in January. It was the cold that killed you, they said, never mind the water. Well, she was already cold. The one person in the world she'd given a damn about, the one companion who had spared her a kind word, shared a bowl of gruel, lent a bonnet, had stepped off this bridge three months past. And that, Annie reckoned, must've been about the time she got with child.

She'd thought at first that she'd missed her bleeding because of what had happened to Mary Jane – the shock and the policemen and the coroner and the pauper's burial. But then she'd started puking and thickening, and she knew.

She pressed her icy fingers to her stomach. You couldn't see the belly yet. She could still tie her stays. She could still make her money, when she wasn't too sick. But that wouldn't last. And then what? Sit under the arches of the Adelphi with all the women she'd seen there, ragbags with babies under their skirts, begging for coins instead of making money on their backs?

It had been a bad Advent and a worse Yule without Mary Jane. Shivering in their cold little loft above the Haymarket, Annie had been too sick with the baby to capitalise on the open-handed merrymakers – she could not buy a lump of white bread nor black coal. With the first of the month had gone the last of her money, counted into the landlord's greedy glove, and in exchange for the short rent he had given her notice to quit. She had told him she had nowhere to go, but that had not been true. She did have somewhere to go. She could follow Mary Jane into the Thames.

There was not, now, a soul to miss her, and she in turn would not miss this grim city. She would not miss the spiky form of the new Parliament, crouching like a dragon, where Big Ben had, just last night, rung the new year's peal; nor would she miss the Inns of Court or the Bank or the 'Change. These fine establishments meant nothing to her save as hostelries for her many clients, places for them all to go during the day when she left their beds. Even the lamplighter lighting the lamps along the river could not bribe her to stay with his string of pearls. Annie Stride closed her eyes and let herself fall forward into space.

For an infinite moment she tipped and fell – then a hand took her arm, hard, and pulled her back. Her battered boots slipped on the parapet and she would have fallen anyway had she not been lifted bodily down and set to her feet. A face below a smart topper looked earnestly into hers. She could see nothing but blobs for eyes, a smear for a mouth.

'Madam,' said the mouth. 'What are you about? Such a desperate action!'

She didn't think she had ever been called madam in the whole course of her life. She had sat dry-eyed these last three months from all the hardships, but now a simple word was enough to fill her eyes with tears.

He let her go at once, all manners, as if propriety did not allow him to touch her. But Annie was used to men's hands upon her, soft at first, rougher, hurting. And without the steadying hands, her knees somehow gave way beneath her and she fell against the cold stone of the balustrade.

'You are not well,' said the fellow. 'Hie! Cabman!' He hailed a passing hansom with his cane, and wrenched the door of the carriage wide. 'Please, madam. Take your ease inside for a moment. The night is cruel and you are half frozen.'

Numbly, Annie allowed herself to be handed in, and collapsed gratefully on the buckram seat. The gentleman took off his hat – for it was such a grand one he could hardly get in wearing it – and settled opposite her.

The cabbie leaned down from his box, his breath smoking. 'Where to, sir?'

'Hold your horse for a moment, would you?' said his passenger.

The cabbie settled into his greatcoat and tucked his hands into his armpits. The horse stamped and snorted where it stood. The traffic went around it and the cold Thames flowed silently below, and Annie studied the man who had saved her from a watery grave.

He looked much younger without the top hat – and lacking it she could see how handsome he was. He had thick brown hair with a curl in it, tamed with some pomade for an evening out, clear grey eyes, a fine aquiline nose and a curiously feminine mouth set above a strong jaw. His clothes were formal – tails and an opera cape. He looked as if he were on his way to a play or some such. Sometimes Mary Jane and Annie had played a little game between themselves to see if they could guess the profession of the men who came down to the Haymarket to stand them a drink in the public before other niceties took place. They became experts at this game, quickly spotting a banker or a man-at-law or a minor nobleman who had come to mix with the drovers and coopers to pick up a bit of tail. You could tell the toffs because they couldn't stop themselves speaking gentlemanly even to a common whore, so bred into the bone were their manners. They didn't forget them until the bedchamber, when they left them at the door.

This fellow opposite her in the hansom was one of this sort, a toff. You could see it in the way he took off his kid gloves, finger by finger, pulling them at the tip and easing them off. He laid one on the other and offered them to her. They were warm, as if an animal still lived in the soft skin.

'I will not ask you again what you were doing just now, for it has become clear to me. What has brought you to such a pass? Can nothing turn you from this terrible path?'

Not trusting herself to speak, Annie blinked her eyes and the tears dropped onto the gloves in her hand, darkening the light leather. She looked down at her bitten, dirty nails. She could not put the gloves over such fingers. She was not worthy to sit with this gentleman. She was nothing.

'What is your name?'

She shook her head. 'No point telling you that. I ain't going to be around long enough for us to get acquainted.'

'Do not say such a thing,' he reproached. 'Can I convey you somewhere? To your home?'

She gave a bitter laugh. An ugly sound. 'I don't have no home.'

Her voice, too, sounded ugly to her ears, her East End accent betraying her true home, her first home. The vowels of St Jude's Street in Bethnal Green. She'd lived there with her many brothers and sisters; her mother, who had a baby every year, and a father who put the babies in Ma and then blacked her eyes for falling pregnant again. By the time Annie was thirteen, she had eleven brothers and sisters and could barely remember all their names. That was when her pa had dressed her in her Sunday gown and taken her to the upper room of the Old George pub, where a gentleman waited. The gentleman told her he was her uncle and asked her to sit on his knee. Pa had been there, so she'd thought it would be all right.

It wasn't all right. Afterwards, she'd handed Pa half the money her 'uncle' had given her, and run away the same night with the other half. But she'd quickly discovered that there was no way for a girl alone to live in London except by doing what she'd done with the gentleman in the upper room of the Old George in Bethnal Green. She'd met Mary Jane, they'd worked the streets together, and she'd never allowed herself to look back.

'Have you no one to care for you?' asked the gentleman

'I did have a . . . companion. A girl like me. She died, here, three months ago.'

'At Waterloo Bridge? On . . . let me see, the first of October?' He seemed truly shaken by her revelation, as if it somehow affected him personally. As though it was his own kin, thought Annie. 'Gracious heavens.'

He seemed truly sorry, much sorrier than Annie had been when she'd learned that Mary Jane had been found drowned. Annie had been angry. She simply didn't know why Mary Jane had left her. They hadn't been happy, never that, but they'd made merry enough together, and dreamed of better lives. They would have a drink in the evening and put their coins together, and talk about their clients, those men who'd paid for it. They called them 'The Bastards', and laughed about them all: the criers, the talkers, even the hitters. Calling them names and laughing about them was all they could do – it was the only power they had. It made it all seem a little less terrible.

Mary Jane had been more of a sister to Annie than any of the sisters that shared her bed in St Jude's Street, with their sharp little elbows and their cold little feet. The two of them had always had enough to eat and drink, and a quart of ale or a posset at Christmas; sometimes a new bonnet, sometimes a feather pillow. At Yule, the bastards might buy them trinkets or gifts – not much, mind; things that were too mean for their wives but that would not cost so much money as to be missed at home from the housekeeping: tawdry brooches or cheap gloves. Yuletide was a profitable time for a likely girl, and Annie and Mary Jane had been readying themselves for a busy season. Mary Jane had seemed content – she'd been out most nights with a regular – and then one morning she just hadn't come home, and instead of the scrape of a latchkey there'd been a dawn knock at the door and a constable standing where Mary Jane should have been.

Unknowingly, Annie had crumpled the kid gloves in her hands. She straightened them tenderly and laid them on the seat beside her. She was suddenly impatient to be gone – gone from the carriage, gone from this world. This gentleman had changed nothing. His kindness had not improved things; he'd just postponed the end. She reached for the handle of the carriage door.

'Wait.' He laid his warm hand over her cold fingers. 'It distresses me greatly that you should despair of life, particularly as you seem so young in years. You are – forgive me – seventeen? Eighteen?'

She had frequently lied about her age. She was slim, and not tall, so she often shaved some years off, as some of the bastards – like that first one – seemed to prefer their girls young. Now there seemed little point in fibbing. 'I'll be eighteen in June.' She corrected herself. 'That is, I *would* be.'

She could see that he registered her slip and saw some hope in it. The grey eyes held a darting intelligence. 'I will not attempt to deter you. But if I could beg you . . . would you indulge me . . . could I ask for an hour of your time?'

Annie narrowed her eyes. She had little vanity, but she knew well enough that her looks were her living – did this gentleman really imagine she'd spend her last hour on her back? She raised her chin. She did not have to take offers any more; she would not eke out her life in some lodging house with this fellow, however handsome he was. She looked at him sharply.

He held up his bare hands before him, fingers spread. 'I assure you, there is nothing improper in my request. There is something I wish to show you. An hour is all I ask. And after that hour, if you wish to be returned to this place, I will have the hansom leave you here, and I will drive away and not look back.'

His grey eyes were earnest, pleading. Annie was not used to entreaty – men usually did as they wished with her, supposing that their payment excused them from such niceties. She was touched. An hour, after all, was not so very long – if she was to live a further hour on this earth, it might as well be with a man who treated her with kindness. 'All right,' she said. 'An hour.'

He smiled for the first time, and it gave his handsome face a charming, open expression. He leaned from the carriage window and called to the driver, 'Trafalgar Square.'

The driver took his hands out of his coat, touched the horse with his whip and the hansom bowled across the bridge to the north, leaving the river behind.

Chapter 1

Five years, six months and one day ago

I go down to the beach and stand looking at the dark hunch of the HMS Captivity out on the horizon. It is very windy, so I don't feel a fool saying what I've come to say; I know the wind will snatch my words as soon as they are out of my mouth. 'Goodbye, Dad,' I shout into the southerly. 'I'm off to London.' Then, in case by some freakish chance the wind carries my words to him, I add, 'It's your Mary Jane.' I can't see him, of course, but I know he's there, six deep in some ratty bunk on board the prison ship.

I wait for a reply, and the wind buffets me back; but there are no words carried upon it, and no echoes of Dad's Norfolk accent. When he gets back, in ten years, I'll be twenty-two. I'll be a woman. And I'll be a Londoner; I'll talk differently to him.

I could've stayed here in Holkham after Dad got sent to the hulks, if only Mum hadn't got herself hanged by mistake. And now I'm off to my aunt's in Battersea. I'll miss the Norfolk stars, but I suppose they have the same ones there. What I'll miss most is the water. At least Dad's got water, and plenty of it. I hope they have water in London.

The hansom cab bowled into Trafalgar Square, scattering pigeons as it went. Annie looked without interest at the newly built square with its column and fountains. There were to be four lions about the column and a statue atop, but there was no statue yet, and only one lion, crouching below the column in solitary splendour. In front of the vast porticoed gallery a number of carriages queued, and the way was lit by great torches, the tall column throwing crazy shadows like the gnomon of a sundial.

'Is this what you wanted to show me?' she said to her rescuer, dully.

'Wait,' he said. 'Just wait.'

As Annie idly watched smartly dressed couples descending from the carriages, the gentlemen in tails, the ladies in flashing satins, and wondered where she was bound, the hansom stopped in the queue and her companion spoke to the driver. 'You may go in front – they know me here.'

Annie was curious. 'Where is here?'

'The Royal Academy.'

Annie did not know what the Royal Academy was – as far as she took notice of such things, the new domed building in Trafalgar Square was an art gallery. *The Royal Academy*. Perhaps this place had something to do with the Queen? For one mad moment she pictured herself, just as she was, in her rags, bobbing a curtsey to Victoria herself.

She lurched back in her seat as the hansom pulled in front of the other cabs and she was handed out at the bottom of the broad marble steps. People turned to stare, and she shuffled behind her companion as he tipped the driver; but they were not looking at her. They were looking at him. They nodded and smiled, they whispered behind their hands, and one small knot of people gave him a little burst of applause. He nodded and smiled in acknowledgement, and crooked his arm for Annie. 'Come.'

'But . . .' It was enough to look down at her ragged dress – an old brown fustian, stained with God knew what. And the rest – no bonnet, her hair half unbound, dirty nails, and tear tracks down her grubby face.

'Ah,' he said, and tactfully unhooked his opera cape and swung it about her shoulders, covering the offensive gown. 'There.' He gave his ready smile. 'Now you are the Queen of Sheba.'

Annie took his arm up the steps.

Inside there were marble halls warm with crowds and candle-light, loud with echoing laughter and the tinkle of crystal. Servers with silver trays handed round little ranks of sherry glasses. Annie took one, drained it, set it back and took another, not caring for propriety. It wasn't gin, but it would do. Her companion took a glass and sipped it, regarding her watchfully. She smiled tightly; she needed the liquor, for the eyes were looking again, this time at her, peering down their noses at the tattered clothes beneath the cape, the grubby face, the raggedy hair. But now the alcohol warmed her empty belly – the belly with the baby in it – and she stared back defiantly, not caring what they thought.

'Is this what you have to show me?' she asked, suddenly brave. 'All these toffs?' She did not bother to lower her voice. Her companion shook his head.

'Wait,' he said again. 'Just wait.'

More steps, and then a vast room with almost every inch of its oak panelling covered with paintings. Some huge as a workhouse door, some tiny. At first Annie could see only colour: red-headed women in jewel-coloured velvets working at their tapestries and clasping flowers and reclining in meadows. The canvases were beautiful and placid, nothing to stir the soul. Then, in the far corner, away from the general throng, there were other, more troubling works – darker hues for darker subjects, subjects all too familiar to her.

Here was a painting of a woman starting up from the knee of a bewhiskered young gentleman as he sat at a piano, her eyes clear with sudden realisation, hands clasped with resolve. It was a picture of the very moment that a woman of easy virtue realised the error of her ways. Here was another, of a woman shrinking away with shame as her fond brother found her working the streets, collapsing against a wall with an expression of shame and regret. A third, which was itself in three parts, like an altarpiece, showed a scene that was anything but devotional. The first panel depicted a woman prostrate under the accusing gaze of her husband, who crumpled a letter in his hand. Her two little girls, building a house of cards, looked round at their mother as her adultery became known, their house collapsing under their little hands. The second panel showed the same girls, some years later, living in a shabby garret, gazing at the moon and the rooftops from the smeared window. In the third panel, under the same moon, their mother, her fall complete, sat under the arches of the Adelphi Theatre, ragged playbills fluttering over her head and a baby's feet sticking pathetically from under the skirts of her tattered gown.

Annie gazed at the three wretched scenes and knew she was making the right choice to leave this world. She knew why her saviour had led her here: he had wished to show her the error of her ways. But his design had not worked. It had only served to remind her of the way her life would end up if she chose not to end it. It was all very well for the woman at the piano to spring up and repent and take work in a shop or factory, to forget her low ways and make a good marriage some day, in a town far away where no one recognised her from the street corner or the gin shop. But the third painting, the one divided into three, showed her that there was no way back from disgrace for a woman with a child.

'It's no good,' she said to her rescuer. 'I know the life I've chosen. Why d'you think I want to leave it?'

'I did not bring you here to see those,' he said. 'But this.'

It was one of the largest paintings, a vast dour canvas like a door into the dark. It depicted a drear scene of Waterloo Bridge, swathed in freezing fog, just as it had been tonight. All was exactly the same: the lamps lit along the south bank like a string of pearls, the Thames grey as pewter, with the drowned moon floating in it, the new Houses of Parliament crouching like a spiked dragon. But where Annie had seen this scene from above, the artist had depicted it from below – this was a view from underneath the arches, on the filthy shore of the Thames. And in the foreground, half in, half out of the water, was a girl in white. She was large as life, but she was quite, quite dead. And she was Mary Jane.

Annie gasped, and took a step forward, gazing at her dead friend. She reached out as if to touch her face, to close the staring eyes. There were shadowy figures in the background, but Annie only had eyes for Mary Jane. Her first thought, ridiculously, was that she had never seen her look so clean. Her face had the grey sheen of an oyster shell, her brown hair was darkened further with the water, her arms were spread on the shingle as if she embraced her death. A Sunday-school phrase came back to Annie: *she was washed of all her sin.* Mary Jane had always been somewhat of a slattern, never one for the carbolic; but here, in her white muslin, she could have been an angel. Annie lowered her eyes, unable to look any more. And saw, there on the frame, a little brass rectangle etched with the words: *The Bridge of Sighs, by Francis Maybrick Gill.*

'You see,' said Francis Maybrick Gill gently at her elbow, 'I was there. I was passing over Waterloo Bridge three months ago, just as I was tonight. I heard the hue and cry. I went down the steps to the shore.' She turned to look at him. 'The mudlarks had found her. Just children. They called the constables to pull her out. The constables gave them a halfpenny. When the coroner's man came, the constable said, "Another one for you, Mr Brownlow." Just like that.' He shook his head. 'Another one for you. I will never forget it. I gave the coroner's man a guinea for a coffin, and they took the body away.'

Annie remembered the coffin of good hardwood – the coroner's man had not cheated the carpenter, then. She had wondered, at that terrible little parish burial at St Leonard's in Shoreditch, where the money for the coffin had come from. Working girls were usually buried in clapboard, lying together in rows like they'd been in life. She turned to the artist – she could have embraced him. She truly loved him at that moment, for the small office that he had afforded to a dead whore.

The painting made the blood beat in her head – the thudding of a dying heart, the rushing river. How could one picture conjure all that noise and drama, and at the same time capture the calm on the shore, the lapping of the water, the excited cries of the mudlarks, the world-weary constable greeting the coroner's man. *Another one for you.*

Francis spoke again; low-voiced but insistent. 'And when I crossed again today, and saw you on the parapet, well, I knew I could not let you jump. I was too late for her,' he said regretfully, 'but not for you. I did not know, of course, that you were acquainted with . . .' He nodded to the painting.

'Mary Jane,' she whispered.

'With Miss Mary Jane.' His deference to her dead friend made her love him once more. 'I was not able to forget her. I went home directly and took up my brushes. I abandoned my antique pretensions and my nymphs and dryads and painted something *real* for the first time. I could not let her be; I painted study upon study and then this canvas, as you see – and the result was that this is the first painting of mine to be accepted by the Academy. I owe your friend a great debt; and since I cannot pay it to her, I would pay it to you.'

Debt was a frightening word to Annie; it meant threats and bruises, cold fingers and toes, a grumbling belly, prison bars. She had often been in debt, but had never been owed one. 'How?'

He took both her hands now and stared fervently into her eyes. 'I want you to let me save you.'

'What do you mean?'

He took his case watch from his waistcoat pocket. 'Our hour is over. I am hoping that my work spoke to you as my words could not. So I must ask you: would you like to return to the Bridge of Sighs?'

She looked back at the painting. The paint swirled and swam before her eyes, and she thought she would faint; by some dark alchemy, Mary Jane was gone and it was a painted Annie who lay there on the shingle, her eyes as shiny and dead as pebbles, her hair water-dark, her mouth fish-wide. She blinked and the picture resolved itself: Mary Jane was back in place, but Annie was doused suddenly in a sweat as cold as Thames water.

'No,' she stammered, dry-mouthed. 'No, I will never go back there. But I don't know where I *can* go.'

'You can come home with me,' said Francis Maybrick Gill.

Chapter 2

Five years and six months ago
Turns out they do have the same stars in London. I'm looking at them now.

The stars followed me all the way here in the carriage from Holkham overnight, keeping pace with the horses. Our parson had put me in a brougham with three ladies coming to London. 'It is not seemly to travel with men, Miss Mary Jane,' he said, but he didn't explain why.

London is dirty and cramped. Every inch of it is built upon. My aunt lives in 'flats', but I don't think they know what flat means here. Norfolk is flat. London is high. Everyone lives on top of one another.

I miss air that is clean and doesn't choke you. I miss the space, the sand, the openness of the beach. I have stars but no water. I'm in a place called Battersea but I haven't seen the sea yet.

A different hansom cab took Annie and Francis north to Bloomsbury and the fine tall houses of Gower Street.

Francis tapped his cane at the driver and the carriage drew to a halt outside number seven, a handsome frontage with a black door and a brass knocker and a fanlight overhead. He handed Annie down and the door opened at their approach. Francis gave his topper and gloves to the butler who'd let them in, a man far too well bred to do more than fractionally raise one eyebrow at the lady accompanying his master.

'Bowering, have Mrs Hoggarth make some gruel – and make it thin, mark you. And a nice strong posset with three eggs.'

The butler nodded once and vanished, and Annie looked about her. The hallway was grand and long, the floor tiled with black and white like a chessboard. A broad staircase curved away around an unseen corner to the upper floors. A great mirror hung over an occasional table, and below it a silver salver sat upon the table, filled to the brim with overblown white flowers. Annie suddenly thought of Mary Jane – she'd looked as pallid as those petals in the painting.

Francis saw her looking. 'Camellias,' he said. 'They are actually the flowers of the tea plant.' He looked her in the eyes. 'Sometimes heavenly beauty comes from humble origins.'

She could have sworn he was talking about her, but then she caught an eyeful of herself in the mirror, a dreadful ragged creature. She had nothing to say to beauty tonight, nor beauty to her.

Francis led her into a small sitting room. After the stark black and white of the hall, it seemed a jewel box of a place, straight from Arabia. The walls were papered in oxblood red, with a golden filigree decoration. There were swags of midnight blue silk at the windows, and glowing lamps with panes of coloured glass. Francis placed her in a stuffed chair of topaz velvet with feet carved in the shape of elephants, next to a merrily burning fire. He drew up a carved stool to be next to her, and laid the back of his cool hand on her forehead. 'You will do, once you have warmed yourself through and eaten something.'

Annie could not quite believe her surroundings. She'd been in elegant houses before, when fine gents had wanted a bit of rough; but they'd been panelled in walnut and painted in eggshell grey, muted and expensive. She'd also been in low houses ablaze with colour, but they'd been hung about with cheap gewgaws and fraying silks. She'd never been in a place like this, a place that was so colourful, so exotic, but so costly. It gave her the same dreamlike feeling of unreality that she'd experienced in the gallery – she felt as if she was not really here. Just as there she had changed places with Mary Jane on the canvas, here she felt as if she had exchanged lives with some other confounded girl who now found herself on the parapet of Waterloo Bridge. She looked at the man who had effected this change. In his cloak and topper he'd even looked like the magician who played at the Hackney Empire, swapping girls between his painted boxes with a flash and a bang. She felt the same slavish awe for him that she'd felt for that magician.

'Thank, you sir,' she whispered.

'You may call me Francis. I think you know that is my name.'

The little bronze plaque on the painting. 'Francis Maybrick Gill,' she said.

'Yes.'

'An artist.'

'Yes. And you? Might we at last become acquainted, now that you will be in this world a little longer?' His ready smile warmed her like the flames did.

'My name is Annie Stride.'

'Then, Miss Stride, may I know something of your history? If I am to help you . . .'

'Sir . . . Francis, you're asking about something you might not want to hear.'

It was the right room for tales, this one, she thought; but all the tale-tellers she'd seen in etchings were dressed in big bloomers with bracelets up their arms and jewels hanging between their eyes, not in raggedy fustian with tangled hair and tear stains. They told tales about giants as big as houses, and elephants, and genies that lived in bottles, and golden palaces, not the shameful goings-on in St Jude's Street and the Old George and the Haymarket. They drank sherbet and ate Turkish delight; her stomach was as empty as a drum and rumbled loud as a tattoo.

As if in response to its call, the door opened and a little maid-of-all-work came in with a tray bearing a steaming bowl. She set the whole thing carefully down on a table that was not a table but a dark wood trunk inlaid with little triangles of brass.

'Thank you, Minnie. You may go. Oh, and Minnie: run a bath for our guest.' The little maid stared at Annie with round eyes, gave a bob and fled.

Francis turned to Annie. 'How long since you have eaten?'

She shrugged 'Can't remember.'

'Then better to take it little by little.'

He took the bowl of gruel from the tray, and picked up a silver spoon from where it lay on a snowy white napkin. He spooned the gruel into her mouth himself, and even in the colourful dream she was having, this seemed strange. It was not the gesture of a father to a child, but something else. Something about the spoon on her teeth, on her tongue, in her mouth, seemed overly intimate, so intimate that it almost seemed to belong to her old life, not this new one. Abruptly she was present in the here and the now, the dreamlike bubble penetrated by a silver spoon. The gruel slid down her throat, the warmth spread to her insides, and she forgot the strangeness of it as she began to feel full, a sensation she had almost forgotten. Then gratitude filled her up, too, almost to overflowing.

When the gruel was gone, he set down the spoon. 'Now, Annie, if you have the strength . . .'

She could not look at him. She took up the silver spoon and regarded her warped, smeared reflection. 'I'm afeared.'

'Afraid? Of what?' he prompted gently.

'That if you know what I've done, you will turn me out of your house.'

'Miss Stride. Annie. I know that you are a . . . working girl. And I am of the opinion that women of your class are victims more of circumstance than their own design.'

'I ain't following you, sir.'

'Francis. Tell me your tale, and I am sure you will prove my argument for me.'

So Annie told her tale, as briefly as she possibly could. She did not spin it out, or embellish it, as if she sat on silken pillows. Bethnal Green and Ma and Pa and all the brothers and sisters would not take her a thousand and one nights to tell. She didn't even want to think of it all, much less say it.

Francis let her talk, but from time to time he'd put in a question. 'And were you educated at all?'

'There was a school at the end of St Jude's Street. But I only went till Ma had her fourth, then I had to leave to help at home. Learned to read and reckon, but that's about it. And there was a Sunday school at St Matthew's church where we learned a bit of scripture. We wasn't holy, but Pa made us go 'cos he always had a heavy night on Saturday and wanted us out of the house Sunday so he could sleep it off.'

'St Jude's Street?' Francis asked.

'That's it.'

He smiled sadly. 'Patron saint of lost causes.'

Annie huffed out her breath. 'Reckon that's me, all right.'

'Not at all. Perhaps St Jude saved you tonight.'

'It weren't him that did,' she said to him fondly.

He seemed gratified. 'Go on.'

'When I was thirteen, I . . . ran away.'

'Why?'

Annie hesitated. She'd told plenty of filthy stories in her time to the bastards, who wanted to hear fantasies about being ruined by the parson, or some duke, while they fucked her. But this story, the filthiest of all, she could not tell. She could not tell a good man like Francis why she really left St Jude's Street and never looked back, no, not even to regret the smiles and the sticky handholds of her sweetest sisters. She could not tell him about what had happened when her father took her to the upper room of the Old George public house on her thirteenth birthday. She'd had a glimpse down the pit that night, and whatever she'd been forced to do since had not even approached the horror of it. She'd sworn even as she ran from the place that she would never tell a soul. So she lied to Francis. 'There was no room in the house. Like the woman in the shoe, my Ma, you know that story?' She was rattling on like a hansom, trying to cover the gap in her tale with another, but he did not probe her further.

'I know it. So then . . .'

'I took up with Mary Jane. She saw me wandering up the Haymarket. She told me I was pretty.'

Annie remembered the force of the compliment from the most beautiful girl she had ever seen, with hair so dark it had a blue sheen to it like a crow's wing, and a milk-and-roses complexion, and dark lashes so long they fanned her cheeks. Mary Jane had offered her a sugar mouse – the only one in the paper bag she held. Annie had been flabbergasted. 'The whole thing?' She remembered the undreamt-of delight of having a treat to herself – something that did not have to be painstakingly cut into twelve with a paring knife and shared with her siblings.

The sugar mouse made her Mary Jane's slave; it was the first gift she'd ever been given, the first kindness she'd ever been shown, and as such was incredibly potent. So when Mary Jane invited her to take a walk, she'd clutched at the older girl's hand as her sisters used to clutch hers. Annie remembered now that even the wondrous sweetness of the sugar mouse on her tongue was nothing to the sweetness of having a friend for the first time in her life. Even after they'd set up house together, she'd kept the little string tail of the sugar mouse for years in her trinket box, a precious relic in the worship of an older girl so certain, so assured. Mary Jane hadn't looked like that in the river. All her self-assurance had been washed away.

'Mary Jane taught me everything.' For a moment, the enormity of her loss threatened to overwhelm her. 'Reckon *she* was my education.'

'What did she teach you?' Francis leaned forward on his footstool, listening, interested.

'How to be with the bastards.'

'Is that what you called them?' His voice was gentle.

She nodded. 'She taught me how to do what they wanted but not to let them have *me*. She taught me how to take myself away, how you could do those things and not want to kill yourself.' Realising what she'd said, she hurried on. 'Mary Jane knew what it was like to be brought low – she'd been in the asylum and had a brand to prove it. It was on the inside of her arm and she wouldn't show no one. 'Shamed of it, she was – said the bastards wouldn't touch her if they saw it, but she covered it with bracelets or sleeves and she did all right. We done very well together – one blonde, one dark. Then, on the first of October, she stepped off the bridge.'

Annie swallowed. She knew then that Mary Jane had never managed to keep herself separate – that the feeling of worthlessness, of wanting to end yourself, never went away. And when Mary Jane had left her, the feeling had come rushing in on Annie, without her friend to hold it at bay. A crack in the dam, collapsing inward with a rush of water, and no Mary Jane to keep the water out.

'And you had no warning that she intended to . . . take her own life?'

Annie swallowed. Him saying it like that seemed to make it somehow real. A wave of sorrow rose in her throat and for a moment she physically could not speak. Then she whispered, 'Not a clue. She'd got herself a regular, she said, with a bit of tin to spend. Came home every night smelling of fancy perfume, waltzed in like there was music playing.'

'And did she say where she'd been? Or who she'd been with?' He seemed acutely interested.

'No. Said she'd tell in good time. Just seemed sort of like she'd done something clever. Seemed like she was going up in the world.'

'And how did that make you feel?'

Annie shrugged; she rarely examined her feelings, and much less often was asked about them. 'I thought, good for her, didn't I? I knew if she did well she'd take me up with her. I'd do the same. That's what it was like, her and me. Like sisters, see?'

'And then?'

'And then she didn't come home.' There was the wave again, rising, rising. She choked it down. 'Constable come instead.'

He nodded. 'And what followed?'

'Well, after the funeral, I was took bad. Thought it was the melancholy, you know?' She couldn't quite bring herself, yet, to mention the baby. 'We hadn't paid the rent in months – Mary Jane said it was no matter 'cos it weren't unchristian to do a bunt on Christ-killers.'

'Forgive me – Christ-killers?'

'Jews. Hebrews an' those.'

'Ah. The Children of Israel. And I assume by "doing a bunt", your companion intended that you were both to leave and find other accommodation with the rent unpaid?'

'You catch on quick. But so did Mr Haft – that's the landlord. He weren't to be caught napping; he must have sniffed that that was my notion, and he came in with his key one night and took all my clothes.'

'He took your *clothes*?'

'Every stitch save what I was sleeping in. It's an old trick, to stop you doing a flit. So, January the first' – her eyes widened; it seemed a lifetime ago – '*today* I had to give him my last shilling.' She'd put all her money into the landlord's grubby fingerless glove coin by coin, counting it out, seeing him counting it, too, with his sharp little eyes, knowing it wasn't enough. 'I gave him everything I had, but I still came up short, so he made so bold as to give me notice.'

'And he returned your clothes, I presume?'

'Not he. He's a crafty old stoat – he knew he could sell some of 'em; some nice bonnets and bits I had.' Including the trinket box with the gifts from the bastards and, much more precious, the string tail of the sugar mouse. 'He left me with this one old gown and one bonnet, and the wind took that. So having nothing else in the world, as you might say, I went from him direct to Waterloo, where you saw me on the bridge.'

Francis let a little silence fall, then shook his head sadly. 'Not quite Scheherazade,' he said. 'So let me understand you – you are all alone in the world? There is no one with whom I could make pains to reunite you? No other friends or acquaintances? I could make enquiries of the authorities, ascertain whether your family still reside in Bethnal Green . . .'

'No!' she said. After what Pa did – Pa, that first, original bastard – she would not go back under his roof, not for a thousand pounds. 'I ain't going back there.' She looked up at Francis through her lashes. So kind, so handsome, so gentlemanly, so *opposite* to Pa; yet she was about to end their acquaintance. She had to do it – there would be no hiding it soon. 'I ain't entirely alone. There's one thing I left out. I'm . . . having a baby.'

His face went suddenly still – not with anger or disgust, nor yet pity; it was an expression she could not define. He seemed to think for a long, long moment, during which she became as sure as she could be that his next action would be to turn her out of his house. But as he got to his feet he merely said, mildly, 'Very well, Annie. That is enough for tonight. You need your rest, especially in the light of the . . . of what you've just told me. Take your bath – I will have a room prepared for you, and Minnie will bring a posset up later. Minnie!'

Annie felt lighter than air as she rose, unburdened, and followed the little maid up the carpeted steps, and it wasn't just the thick, fluffy pile underfoot that made her step so light. Even though she'd kept the darkest secret of all from Francis, she still felt better for telling him part of her history. Even to speak of Mary Jane was to ease, just slightly, the dreadful burden of grief. At the turn of the stairway, she began to smell a delicious scent of lavender, obliterating the sickly smell of the fat flowers in the hall. Minnie went ahead into a doorway that was belching steam like a locomotive, and Annie followed.

The bathroom was worthy of – what had Francis called her? – the Queen of Sheba. The walls were panelled with onyx of varying colours, framed in polished copper mouldings. Chandeliers of rose and opalescent crystal hung from the ceiling, and a rich Oriental curtain, hanging from a golden rod, veiled a bath of rose-coloured marble with a roll top and the clawed feet of an eagle. At the opposite side of the room was a couch covered with a white fur of some beautiful dead thing sacrificed for the comfort of the bather. A rich Oriental peignoir, printed with silken roses, hung from the back of the door on a golden hook. A linen box holding warm Turkish towels stood next to an immense porcelain basin painted with designs of water lilies.

Annie stood in the midst of this steaming luxury in her dreadful dress, feeling like a stain on this spotless temple to cleanliness – a grubby smear in the centre of the room. She hardly dared move. She knew that with a touch she would ruin those snowy towels and gleaming mirrors. Even the maid, nothing more than a little tweenie in black and white, fitted here better than she. Minnie leaned over the bath and fiddled with the ornate hot and cold taps. As she turned them with an effort, a jet of boiling lava soaked Annie's boots.

It would have taken nothing less to move her from her rooted spot. Now she knew how to behave. She'd learned to fight like a cat on the street – to scrap, chin and elbows out, for every corner or territory, to rise to any slight, real or imagined. Men must be flattered and cajoled, but other girls – Mary Jane excepted – she could cut down with impunity. 'Mind what yer doing!' she cried, immediately on the attack. 'What the *fuck* are you playing at?'

The maid straightened up at once, crimson with the steam and mortification, wiped her forehead under her cap and spoke for the first time. 'I'm so sorry, miss. I've been here three months and I'm still getting used to that geyser – a right funny one it is.'

'Damn near boiled me like a chicken.'

The maid bit her lip and said quietly to the floor, 'You'll find everything you need here, miss. I'll wait till you're done.'

Annie found herself alone, and regretted her sharp words at once. What was she thinking, savaging that little slip of a thing? She was instantly sorry, and tears threatened to rise again. She wanted to beg the girl's pardon. She had not always been hard like this. Street work had made her dirty inside as well as out. Time to change.

Hurriedly she kicked off her sodden boots and stripped off her soiled gown; she could not wait to be free of them. Would she could slough off her foul character as easily. She did not know what to do with her old clothes, so she kicked the grubby little pile under a chair. She kept on her bodice and bloomers and stepped into the water, which was sprinkled with purple heads of lavender. She had only ever washed at the shockingly cold street pump in Bethnal Green, or had a bath before the fire in St Jude's Street on a Saturday, which, by the time the water got through eleven children to Annie, was almost as cold. In her lodgings with Mary Jane, there was never more than a washstand, or an ancient geyser if they were lucky, and they had to wash themselves piece-meal. There was never a full immersion; never, thought Annie with a shiver, till the end, and the Thames.

She sat in the water, her dirty linens soaking. She still thought in some confused way, even after all she'd done with the bastards over the years, that bathing naked was somehow indecent. Suddenly disgusted, she stripped the sodden clothes off with an effort, and threw them down on the cork mat by the bath. Now she lay back in the brimming tub, luxuriating in the lavender-scented warmth. Her hair spread about her, and lavender heads caught in it, and she thought of those girls with yards of red hair she'd seen in the Royal Academy, twiddling flowers and staring down from their gilded frames. She allowed the water into her mouth till she thought of Mary Jane at the end, then she spat it out like the spout of a fountain. She rejected the water in favour of air. She was going to live.

She struck a pose, just like those girls. 'I'm the Queen of Sheba!' she said to the chandelier above her head. 'Yah!' and the brilliants resonated faintly in reply. She let her hands travel to her belly: a little roundness under her touch, soft and springy like proving bread, despite her thinness. Her breasts, too, were tight and tender, and mapped with faint blue veins – belly and breasts both full with the baby. 'Not tonight,' she said aloud. 'I will think on you tomorrow.'

She rubbed the lavender into her hair, feeling all the grease and dirt lift away, then sat up, water streaming from hair and face. She rummaged on the little marble shelf beside the bath, where there was a little rank of inlaid boxes. Here were various kinds of soaps, boxes of starch, bags of bran, perfumes, pastes, cold creams, carbonate of soda. She frowned at them. There could not, surely, be a *Mrs* Maybrick Gill, else Francis wouldn't have brought her home. But there was everything here that a lady would need. Perhaps he had a sister. Or maybe – the thought made her laugh – he was a ponce. 'Only I don't *think* so,' she said to the carbolic. This tendency, too, she had learned to divine over the years – for Mary Jane and herself, men who liked men were a waste of time and effort, and they'd learned to identify and avoid them.

Annie proceeded to use every cream, paste and unguent she could find, until she was clean and oiled and smelling like an apothecary's shop. Only then did she get out and wrap herself in the steaming towels from the linen box. The bath water was Thames grey, the wilted lavender heads floating like flotsam. She felt ashamed of her grime – must she sully everything she touched? – so she hauled out the plug before the maidservant could see it, and put on the peignoir. Wiping her sleeve across the looking glass, she regarded herself – all eyes and cheekbones and water-dark hair. She looked like a corpse. Frightened, she huffed at the glass to mist it again and obscure herself.

Outside the door the little maid waited sheepishly, and would not meet her eyes. She conducted Annie down a grotto of a hallway, which was painted a rich cinnabar and hung with gilt frames of religious and pastoral scenes and little mirrors. A handsome cabinet clock ticked loudly, but when Annie looked into its face, she saw not numbers, but signs of the zodiac dancing a reel round a central sun. Minnie opened a door and stood back, and Annie walked past her into her room.

She had never seen a bedchamber like it – the walls were yellow gold and gave her the feeling that she'd shrunk to a sprite and entered the yolk of an egg. The bed was covered with a heavy silk coverlet of turquoise, and every lamp had fringing or crystal droplets clinging to it like dew. Francis's house was a house where colour lived, thought Annie – colours you did not think could be friends or even neighbours all dwelled together in this happy amity.

Minnie stood at the doorway, her hand on the handle as if for safety. 'Miss,' she said, 'I'm sorry about before. Please don't tell the master. If you leave your boots outside the door, I'll clean them for you by morning.'

Annie went to her and caught the girl's damp hand. 'Truth is,' she said gently, 'I ain't fit to clean *your* boots.'

Minnie almost smiled, almost nodded, then withdrew her hand and herself.

Annie walked to her bed, suddenly deathly tired. There was a hump beneath the coverlet and she put a hand upon it – the delicious warmth of a bedpan. Over the hump was folded a clean linen nightgown, its fibres warm from the copper. She'd always slept in her bodice and petticoat before, but could not face putting stained and crusted garments on her newly clean body. She supposed that she must wear this nightgown to sleep. It felt deliciously comforting as it slid over her body, and smelled of lavender. Before she had got with child it would have fitted her, but now her breasts were full and tender and stood forth like globes straining at the lacings. She squeezed out the long rope of her hair in the cotton cloth laid by the washstand and plaited it over her shoulder, damp as it was. Then she lifted out the bedpan and placed it on the floor, and got between the fine linen sheets. She did not want to be in the dark, not tonight, so she left the lamp burning.

She was almost asleep when there was a soft knock at the door.

'Yes?' she called, suddenly wide awake and not knowing what to say – privacy was a novelty to her. She expected the little slip-shadow of a maid, and hoped to make further amends, but it was Francis himself, holding a glazed posset pot, with a napkin over his shoulder.

'May I?' He stood at the threshold like a bridegroom, and she beckoned him in with a small smile. He drew up a chair beside the bed, averting his eyes from the fold of the covers that did not quite cover the portion of her bosom exposed by the nightdress laces. 'Take this all down,' he said, 'but slow. Small sips at first.'

Annie took the posset pot from his hand, threading her thumbs through both the handles and lifting the spout to her lips. The posset was warm and sweet; she could taste the hot milk and the nutmeg and the wine, and something else, another heady flavour that she could not place. The creamy concoction went right to her innards and warmed her from within.

'Good?' he asked.

She nodded, drinking still.

'It is a recipe of my mother's.' He watched her fondly. 'I want you to sleep well and lay your worries aside. In the morning we will talk about your future.'

'And the baby's,' she said.

He looked down. 'Yes, of course, the . . . that matter also.'

She soon drained the vessel, and he took it, still warm, from her hands. She looked up at him, full of posset and gratitude. He was a good man, and God knows she hadn't met many of those in her life.

She threw back the covers and raised herself on her elbow in a practised way. She knew how to lick her lips, and widen her eyes, and push out her tits to make a man harden. One of her full breasts fell forward against the lacings of her gown. His mouth dropped open a little, his eyes flared and he put out his hand. It was working. She was grateful, so grateful to him, that she wanted him to climb into the bed, and then she could show him her gratitude the only way she knew how. But he merely reached for the coverlet and pulled it over her body.

'Good night Annie,' he said softly, and left the room on silent feet.

Chapter 3

Five years, five months and seventeen days ago

There's a little place called 'the area' outside my aunt's house. It's surrounded by railings that look like iron bars. I hold the cold railings in each hand and look out through the bars, wondering if this is what it's like to be Dad on the prison ship. I can look up, though; he can't.

And when I look up, there are the stars, and I can imagine myself back on Holkham beach, where there is space, where I can breathe.

A man passes by, with a topper and a cane and a frock coat. He stops and tips his hat to me. 'Stargazing again, young miss?'

He seems friendly and well spoken. He is in his middle years, with a wide girth, and grey at his temples, about the same age Dad would be now. 'I like the stars,' I say shyly.

He smiles at me. 'So do I, and no wonder. My name is Starcross. So, you see, stars are part of my destiny.'

'Pleased to meet you, Mr Starcross,' I say, just like we do at home. 'I am Mary Jane.'

He can't shake my hand, for I am in my little prison of railings. But he does something funny – he puts his cane through the iron bars and I shake the silver top of it. We both laugh.

'You are not from London, I think, Mary Jane?'

I shake my head. 'Norfolk,' I say.

'Upon my word,' he says. 'One of my very favourite places. Do you know Hunstanton?'

'Do I?' I say, delighted. 'It is only a little way down the coast from Holkham, my home.'

'I spent many happy days there as a boy, sporting in the sea.' The middle-aged gentleman smiles fondly.

I swallow hard. There seems to be something in my throat. 'I miss the water,' I say.

'Then you are very fortunate. There is a river, the greatest river, just beyond those houses.' He points with his cane. 'There lies Old Father Thames. I'd be glad to take a turn with you to the bank; we'd be there and back in a quarter of the bells.'

I look at him. He reminds me of Dad. I open the little gate and squeeze through, and take the arm he offers.

When Annie awoke, the winter sun was streaming in through the shutters and the baby was all over the bed sheets.

She sat up, wide awake with horror, and the warm blood pooled between her legs. As she threw back the coverlet and pulled the sticky nightgown away from her groin, a bright V of red stained its whiteness.

She sprang out of bed, her innards cramping, and hobbled, knees jammed together, to the washstand. She found a napkin there and shoved it between her thighs, stripped off the nightgown and used it to wipe her legs. Then she put on last night's peignoir – mercifully red – and sat shakily on the bed to survey the mess.

She did not think of the baby at all in that moment, or what the blood might mean. All she could think of was how much trouble she was in. How much had that nightgown cost, or those sheets? Francis would call the constables on her. She stood and stripped the bed, poured water from the basin jug into the washstand and began to soak the offending linens. The blood only carmined the water and stained the rest of the sheet. She scrubbed frantically, feeling most peculiar, the focus of her eyes drifting in and out, her knees buckling and then snapping to.

She could feel more blood flowing into the napkin at her crotch when she moved.

She jumped guiltily at a knock at the door. Minnie entered. 'Miss, I am to tell you—' Her eyes widened at the gore, then, 'Jesus have mercy!'

Annie clasped her hands to her belly. 'My baby,' she moaned. 'Help my baby.'

Minnie's little hands flew to her mouth, and the gesture was the last thing Annie saw before she fell to the floor insensible.

She woke still in the egg-yolk room, in fresh sheets on a newly made-up bed. Francis sat on a chair drawn up to the bed head, and he had one of her hands in his.

She mouthed, 'The sheets.'

He made a shushing shape with his lips. 'No matter.'

'The gown.'

He smiled. 'Matters even less.' Then the smile died. 'The doctor has come and gone. You lost the baby, Annie.'

Lost the baby. Like the doctor, come and gone. She swallowed as if ingesting the news. She didn't know how to be, how to conduct herself. There was a large tranche of relief, flavoured with a tiny, wafer-thin slice of sorrow.

She'd never wanted a baby, never once. Ever since she was old enough to stand the blood and the screaming, she'd had to help her Ma every year in the little house in St Jude's Street. Hold her hand for hours till the bones cracked, and fetch water and linens for Peg from up the street, the midwife of Bethnal Green. She'd seen enough, *heard* enough of childbirth, half a dozen times, and that wasn't counting the ones that died. They'd broken her mother, those babies. Broken her body and spirit, etched more wrinkles on her face each time, literally drained her as if they were suckling her life force from her nipples along with her milk, until she was as sad and flat and deflated as her breasts. And for what? To raise not a prime minister or an explorer, but a succession of shrill, snotty nuisances – boys to go into the blacking factory and girls to go to the upper room of the Old George. Annie had never had the heart for a child till now, never felt for a child until it had run out of her onto the fine sheets in a trickle of crimson.

She did not know who had put the child in her belly – it could have been any one of the bastards. She did not think of the father, nor fantasise about being a family; but she did think of the child. And when she thought of the child, the sorrow waxed and grew and overtook the feeling of relief. This child of every father, of no father. She pictured him, now that he was a ghost, a boy of four or five in a little Norfolk jacket, a cap on his blonde or brown or black hair, chasing a hoop down St Jude's Street. The hoop running away from him, rolling and rolling down the street, him running after it until it was gone, and he was gone, too. Come and gone like the doctor.

'The doctor said you will be well again,' said Francis gently. 'You are strong and young, and can bear a child one day. Sometimes nature has her way.'

Annie kept to her bed for she didn't know how many days, listless and barely awake. She would be aware of Francis coming in and out, bearing bowls and books. She never saw a servant once during this time; it seemed Minnie had vanished, too. Francis assumed her care completely – he was physician, midwife, nurse and companion.

And at night he would read to her from a book – she never knew what book it was, nor thought to ask, but in her delirium it seemed to be the story of her own life, of a girl at the mercy of the bastards and a good man who tried to save her from her fall.

'"Her delight in the smallest things was like that of a child. There were days when she ran in the garden, like a child of ten, after a butterfly or a dragonfly. This courtesan who had cost more money in bouquets than would have kept a whole family in comfort would sometimes sit on the grass for an hour, examining the simple flower whose name she bore."'

She would listen to Francis's low, cultured voice, sure he was speaking of her. The notion that she was not a woman who had lost a child, but a child herself – the child she had never been allowed to be – was so comforting that Annie retreated into it completely. She had never been nurtured or nursed; if you were ill in St Jude's Street, you took to the only bed in the place but then had to shift for yourself – Ma would be too busy to spoon-feed, and besides, if Annie was sick, the chances were that half a dozen of her siblings would be, too. But here in Gower Street, Francis personally gave her soup and porridge, and now it did not seem strange to her that he would feed her with his own hand. For he'd assumed the role of parent, too; she was his child, and it seemed shameful and perverse that she'd once importuned him in this very bed. She was weak with gratitude and something akin to love; but not desire, not for now. She depended on him utterly, listening for his step on the stair and the scrape and turn of the doorknob more eagerly than she'd ever anticipated the approach of her mother.

In the hours that he was gone – painting, she supposed – she would become afraid, for then she would be visited by spirits. Mary Jane would come, with her oyster-sheen face and her water-dark hair, and tap pitifully on the window pane, her voice pleading, her eyes hollow with death. Annie would turn her gaze from the window only to see the little boy in the Norfolk jacket sitting on her bed, so real that she could almost feel the dip of his weight on the mattress. He would reproach her with hazel eyes just like hers, reproach her with not wanting him. At such times, under those accusing eyes, she would close her own, only to be haunted by dreadful dreams of swirling fog and freezing water, and an alternate fate on the Bridge of Sighs, where she tilted forward and fell. She would wake from the fall with a jolt and long for Francis to return; she had come to depend upon him so greatly that she felt he was her talisman; he protected her not just physically, but spiritually. The shades who visited her would not share their ether with Francis – it was as if his very presence kept them away.

As her health improved, she learned not to look at the window or the coverlet when she was alone, but would fix her eyes instead upon one particular prism of glass hanging with its brothers and sisters from the bottom of the bedside lamp. For the middle hours of the day the sun struck it in such a way that the light split into a rainbow arcing across the golden wallpaper, a rainbow of all the colours that lived in this room, and in this house. She would watch it creep, inch by inch, across the wall, until it receded altogether at sunset. Then the weather turned, as it always did in London, and there came a succession of dull days. Annie missed the rainbow, and even though the spirits came to her no more, she sank into a gloom.

And then one day the sun shone again, the rainbow returned, she could suddenly sit up; and Francis Maybrick Gill offered her a job.

Chapter 4

Five years, five months and ten days ago

Mr Starcross and I have been walking out for a week now, and my aunt does not know a thing about it.

Every day we go a little further, and we talk about Norfolk and the places we both know, and London, the places only he does. We've seen the Thames at Battersea, and the common at Clapham, and the huffing trains at Victoria. I know London at night very well, and at breakfast I am tired and dead-eyed, but my aunt cannot guess why. You mustn't think me stupid. I know I can trust Mr Starcross, for the first night, when he took me to the river, he brought me back directly as he had promised.

Tonight is different, though. We've walked further than ever and by the moonset – remember I am a country girl – I can tell that it is late. 'Mr Starcross,' I say, interrupting his account of one summer at Cromer. 'I think we must go back.'

He takes his pocket watch from his waistcoat. 'Goodness,' he says. 'You are right. I had hoped to show you the gardens at Vauxhall, but it has taken us longer than I'd thought. Here: what about this for a notion. I have an acquaintance who lives nearby – a very respectable elderly lady. Let us call there and have her order a hansom cab. Have you ever ridden in one before?'

I shake my head. 'No.' I am doubtful. I've seen the quick little carriages all over London, but remember what Holkham's parson said about travelling in a carriage with a gentleman.

But Mr Starcross is already leading me down a little side street – 'Silverthorne Road', reads the sign. 'A hansom will have you home in a trice,' he says. 'We are on an adventure, Mary Jane.'

'A model?'

'Yes,' said Francis. 'I want you to sit for me. I will pay you, of course.'

Annie shifted a lock of hair that had fallen over her eyes. 'Why me?'

Francis uncrossed his legs and sat forward earnestly. 'I want to save you. I want you to take gainful employment. I want to lift you up. I am aware, of course, that there are those who would not consider being an artist's model respectable employment, but compared to your . . . previous occupation, it is a step along the right path.'

Annie eased her hands beneath her behind and sat up straight. She'd thought herself no good for anything but whoring, and she'd seen what happened to old whores. 'Gone grey,' she and Mary Jane had called it, with the confidence of youth. *Sal's gone grey. Peg's gone grey. Saw Lally in the Strand – she's gone grey.* And they didn't just mean the hair. They meant everything: clothes, skin, teeth. Once you'd gone grey, there was little option open to you but to become one of the park women; a degraded creature with no shame, who would wander in Hyde Park or Green Park in the winter, before the gates were closed but after dark. They would haunt the by-walks like wraiths, shunning the golden pools of light cast by the gas lamps, for they were no longer handsome enough to tempt a man by daylight. The men who went to the parks at night had the darkest desires, and knew very well that these low wretches would consent to any humiliation for the sake of a few shillings. To go grey and become a park woman seemed to Annie a fate even worse than Mary Jane's.

But she had a little pride left. She lifted her chin and fixed her eyes on Francis. 'So I'm to be your charity case?'

'No,' he said, deadly serious. 'There is another reason.'

'What's that?'

'You are beautiful.' He spoke it as a bald statement of empirical fact.

She had been told this before by the bastards, many times and in many ways. *You are an angel. You are a stunner. You make my prick pain me.* Always before bed; they never bothered after. She'd had no reason to disbelieve them – they did not have to sweet-talk her; they were paying. They said it to make themselves feel better, not her. Men liked to feel that they had made a wise choice, a fine bargain, a good deal – but that did not make it any less true. She had never doubted it till now, now that the salute came from the lips of this kind, disinterested man; she could not, she thought, possibly be beautiful after losing Mary Jane and the baby and having so many days in bed – she could feel the grease on her skin, the knots in her mass of hair. She'd not been near a brush and comb, nor a pot of rouge, since her landlord had taken hers off her.

Francis filled her thoughtful silence. 'You are, if I might say, at the very height of your powers. Such beauty should be captured as it is, preserved, rendered immortal.' He echoed, eerily, what she'd just been thinking. One day, she would grow older, and men would not turn to look at her when she passed. Maybe all women went grey – whether a washerwoman or a countess. But if Francis painted her, she would live forever.

She took hold of a hank of hair and inspected it doubtfully. 'You sure? I mean, maybe I was handsome a few months past. You ain't seen me done up, with me best bonnet and a lick o' paint. Would've knocked your eyes out then.'

He smiled readily. 'I am rather glad I did not see you then. I like you now. And I will like you even better when my maid has had her way with you. She has some skill – she dressed my own mother's hair in Norfolk so is quite au fait with the toilette of elegant females.' He paid the compliment delicately, and stood to ring the bell pull.

The maid entered – but it was not Minnie. This was a long streak of a girl, dark and sallow where Minnie had been all fair hair and peaches and cream.

'This is Eve. Eve, give your greeting to Miss Stride.'

Eve bobbed but remained silent. Francis said, 'Eve, you will come to Miss Stride this afternoon and help her with her toilette, and those various creams and unguents that ladies use upon their skin and are a mystery to we men.' It was said with a smile. 'Most importantly, you will dress her hair. And then, this evening before dinner, I will try a sketch or two, if you are agreeable.' This last to Annie, but she was not attending. She sat up a little straighter, frowning.

'Where is Minnie?'

Francis's eyes flickered. 'Thank you, Eve,' he said.

The maid bobbed again and vanished.

Francis sat once again by the bed, and did not quite meet her eyes. 'Minnie is gone.'

'Gone? Gone where?'

'I found her another position. At my father's estates in Norfolk. As I said, Eve was my mother's lady's maid. I sent them Minnie, they sent me Eve.'

Father's estates. She had known he was gentry; that bathroom alone must have cost a fair old pile. 'Why?'

He leaned forward and took her hand between his. 'Annie. You are . . . were . . . a woman of the world. And I, as what you might call a bohemian, also dissimulate.'

Annie was certain she had never called anyone a bohemian in her life, not being perfectly sure what it meant. He caught her look. 'We both live outside the norms of society,' he explained, 'and even morality. Your work brought you into contact with . . . low things. My work also can expose me to things my fellow man may regard as indecent – I find my models everywhere: the criminal, the delinquent. I think I told you that before I painted your departed friend, I found myself studying the classical subjects repeatedly; thus I have painted the nude a thousand times, and I may tell you, it is easier to recruit my subjects from the gutter with a promise of a shilling or two.' He looked down. 'But Minnie, a girl of a respectable home and upbringing, what she saw, the blood . . . what the blood meant . . . what you said . . .' He sighed and looked at her candidly. 'She knew you were not married. She was upset.'

Annie thought for a moment of how she must have looked to that child of a maid, half naked, covered in blood. 'Shocked her, did I?' she said, defensive.

'No. I fancy she was upset because she liked you.'

'She *liked* me?'

'Yes.'

She was touched. The little maid, whom she'd sworn at and belittled, had been concerned for her. She felt a warmth, a sisterhood, that she'd not felt since Mary Jane; followed by a sharp sorrow that Minnie had gone. 'Oh.'

'Now that Eve is with us, we'll make a fresh start.'

Annie flopped back on the pillows. 'Reckon that's the right name for her then.'

'What is?'

'Eve.' She remembered those Sunday-school etchings. 'First lady on this earth, weren't she?'

Francis looked at her as if his hound had just spoken to him. 'Yes. Yes, she was. And you know, Annie, you have a perfectly good intelligence beneath . . . well. What if . . . ?'

She laughed, surprising herself – she had not thought she'd ever laugh again. 'Blow me, Francis, you might've finished those ol' paintings, but you ain't too sharp at finishing a sentence.'

He laughed, too, and took her hands, both of them this time, and looked at her, eyes shining. 'Let us make an Eden. Here. I will make you anew. Never will there have been such a woman. The first, the original, the *only* woman.'

She did not know what he meant by this, but he said it like he was God and she was not sure it was quite Christian. She caught herself thinking that, and laughed again. Was *she* to become a prude now? Her merriment had tired her, and she could feel her eyes closing.

He saw it. 'Time enough for that,' he said, and he rose and trod softly to the door.

'Francis?'

He stopped with his back to her, his hand on the handle.

'What was the book? The one you was reading to me?'

'Oh, nothing in particular.'

She was almost asleep, but she had to know. 'Was it a romance? A love story?'

She could not see his face, but his voice had a smile in it. 'Yes,' he said. 'A love story.'

Then he was gone, and she wasn't sure if it was her or something else that had amused him so.

Eve, the new maid, so silent and sullen, nevertheless effected a change in Annie. She helped her to another of those boiling, fragrant baths in the handsome bathroom, and then opened the little boxes and inlaid chests and used all the creams and ointments and oils on every part of Annie's body – even down to rubbing a little rose salve into her lips, a dusting of rouge to the cheeks and a slick of palm oil on her eyelids. Then, once Annie was dried and wrapped in a dressing gown, Eve steered her back to the bedchamber, sat her before the crystal triptych looking glass on the dressing table and set about her hair with the brushes and comb.

Annie had never had her hair cut. Her little sisters had regularly had their mouse-coloured hair shorn for fine ladies' hairpieces and wigs, but Annie had inherited her mother's strawberry blonde. Ma's hair had become thin and grey, but Annie's hair had brilliancy in every filament, and was allowed to grow to her knees. She had wondered why her hair alone was spared – until she was thirteen, and Pa took her to the Old George. Then she understood.

And when she'd begun to work with Mary Jane, their looks had gone well together – Mary Jane a true brunette, with dark brows and red lips, her hair straight and shiny, and Annie with her reddish-blonde mane with a curl in it. Day and Night, they called them down the Haymarket, as they took turns with their gentlemen, one out and one in.

Now, Annie looked at herself in the glass as Eve took a handful of bright tresses at a time, attacking it from the ends with the silver-backed brush, moving closer and closer to the scalp. The weak winter sun streamed through the windows and kindled in her hair, which fell about her like a red-gold cape. The peignoir could no longer be seen – she was clothed in fire. Annie watched her own expression as she tried not to wince at the snags and tangles; she would not let Eve know that the comb hurt. She played a game with herself, pretending that she was indeed the Queen of Sheba, practising a serene expression so *they* wouldn't know, looking at her then, that she wasn't a queen; that she was just a common dollymop from St Jude's Street.

She caught herself thinking it, and knew that *they* were the patrons of the Royal Academy, with their expensive faces, looking down their long noses at her. They wouldn't look at her like that now. Her skin was like African ivory, her lips full and pink, her cheeks rosy with rouge, her hazel eyes, with their orange centres, in this light as fiery as her hair. One of the bastards, a hunter returned from Africa, had taken her on a tiger-skin rug in his drawing room, a room with four walls pinned with the severed heads of his other victims. She'd half expected him to keep on his pith helmet and boots – he had not, but he'd taken her like an animal on all fours on the prickly pelt, his trophies watching them from the walls. 'Don't look at me,' he'd said to the back of her head as he spent himself in her. Afterwards she'd been putting on her boots and had looked into the rug's orange glass eyes. 'You can see now,' the hunter bastard had said, 'why I didn't want you to look at me. Your eyes are just like the tiger's.'

She looked at herself now in the glass, eyes afire. I'll look where I like, she said in her head to her reflection, feeling suddenly powerful with her tiger's eyes and her mantle of hair and her lady's maid. *A lady's maid.*

'You come from Norfolk?' she asked Eve.

'That's right, mum.' The girl spoke exactly like Mary Jane; it was like a blow beneath the ribs.

'Do you know Holkham?'

'I do, mum. It's hard by the big house.'

'By Francis's . . . Mr Maybrick Gill's . . . estate?'

'That's it.'

'Big, is it?'

'Oh yes, mum. Take you a day to walk from one end to t'other, and another day to go over t'house.'

Annie nodded. 'I s'pose his ma must be a very great lady. The one you did the hair of.'

'That I dunno, mum. I never met her.'

Annie in the mirror frowned a little, forgetting she was supposed to be the Queen of Sheba. She must've took Francis wrong – she'd thought this girl had done his ma's hair. No matter – Eve certainly had some magic in her fingers, for she had coaxed the waves into the fiery tresses rippling down to her knees.

When she was finished, the sullen girl smiled a little at her handiwork, and even ventured a remark. 'Looks a treat, it does, mum. Like the picture papers.'

Annie lifted her chin a little and tried to speak like Francis. 'Yes. Yes, it does. Thank you, Eve.'

Back in her chamber, Annie found a grass-green gown on her turquoise counterpane, and clambered into it. This, she supposed, was the uniform for her new employ, like a maid's frock or a factory girl's chemise. She fastened the gown, an odd thing with no stays or structure but a square neck, loose waterfall bodice, tight sleeves tapered to a point at the knuckles and a deep V at the waist. The long skirt had a train, sewn with water-white crystals. The crystals clattered and whispered along the polished floorboards as she walked down the hallway to Francis's studio, a room she'd never seen before. She knocked and entered.

The studio was big and airy and suffused with the sunset, the dying light pouring through great ecclesiastical windows that arched to a point and were glazed with lead quarrels in the design of lilies. The windows were white and the light was golden, but the room itself was entirely papered in vivid green from floor to ceiling, rich and verdant as Eden and figured with delicate gold wreaths of tiny leaves.

She had seen such wallpaper before – the colour was called Scheele's green, a name she would never forget. A bastard who picked her up in the Ten Bells had taken her to his fancy house. He was trade, not a gentleman; she could smell trade – and she could smell, too, that he had once been poor. He took her in his drawing room, and seemed to take almost as much pleasure in telling her what everything there cost as he did in what he was doing to her. While they were in the act, he told her, memorably, that his Scheele's green wallpaper cost more per yard than she did. She remembered walking home to the Haymarket, and even the coins in her pocket were no consolation for the fact that she was worth less than paper.

She did not feel that way today. She fitted here in this dress, in this rich and gorgeous room with its fancy wallpaper and its churchy windows. She was so busy drinking it all in that it took her some moments of gazing at the wonder to realise that Francis was already in the room. He stood before an easel, with his paints and pots and paraphernalia around him, a vast Arabian rug beneath his feet. He was informal in breeches and boots and shirt and waistcoat, his shirt slightly open at the neck to show wisps of curling dark hair and the dip of his throat, golden in the light. He wore his perpetual smile, and looked very young and very handsome and very eager as he greeted her. She smiled back, liking him very much at that moment. She was someone else now; she had shed Annie Stride, and she had been varnished and decorated and reupholstered. Now she was worth more than the wallpaper and she owed it all to him.

He came to her and put a hand out, as if to cup her cheek, but he did not touch her. 'Perfection,' he said, like a prayer. 'I knew you were beautiful. Your hair! And your eyes . . .' He lifted his hand to them. 'My mother has a ring of topaz. Your eyes are just like that.'

She preferred topaz to tiger, would rather be the ring of a lady than the trophy of a bastard. Francis lowered his hand to take hers and led her forth. She was unaccustomed to such long skirts and lifted them to watch her footing – then gave a little cry and jumped back a pace. There was a snake on the rug, the diamonds along its back mimicking the pattern. It was a green adder; that hunter bastard had had one in his drawing room, though his was in a case, hidden behind glass and grass and some cock-and-bull story about strangling it with his own hands.

'It won't harm you now,' said Francis, smiling again. 'It is long dead.'

She peered at the serpent and saw that he spoke the truth – it was no more real than the snake in the glass case had been. It was stuffed artfully to coil into an S shape, as it presumably had in life, writing through the grasses of some distant savannah.

Annie skirted the snake carefully and Francis seated her on a tapestried piano stool set in the centre of the huge rug. Politely he asked, 'May I?' before he arranged her skirts in a swirling pool about her, and brought all her hair forward over her shoulders. Then he handed her a perfect apple, round and glossy as a little planet. It was as green as the dress; as green as the snake. 'I want you to hold this in your hand,' he said, 'almost as if it is appearing from your hair – your arm should be hidden in your locks. Perfect. Put your foot on the snake – no, the other foot.' Annie obediently placed her bare foot on the mummified snake – she'd expected it to be cold and slimy; it was neither. 'And now look towards the windows.' She turned; her skin heated like a blush, and tears sprang involuntarily to her eyes. 'Ah, there,' he said. 'Can you feel it? When you feel the warmth on your face, and are so dazzled that you can hardly see, that is when you have found the light. It takes some girls years to do it – you have the instinct, like a sunflower.'

He stood behind the canvas, pencil in hand. He described a number of sweeping circles, then stopped and took a step back, regarding her. 'A model must also be an actress. I want to see in your eyes how much you want that apple. Have you ever really wanted something, Annie? Something you couldn't have?'

There had been so many things, in her short life, but what came to her mind, ridiculously, was a meat pie. She'd been in Clare Market, one bitter Yule, begging with her brothers and sisters, and a pie man had walked past her with his tray. A heavenly waft of buttery pastry and rich meat gravy had drifted to her nose, making her stomach contract with hunger. Each pie was a penny, and there was one sitting on the top of the pile, calling to her. She did not have a penny – she could have grabbed the pie and run, but she was too afraid. Her Pa had told her over and over again that if she got caught stealing, she'd go to the Beak – he'd told her this as if the getting caught was a worse crime than the thieving. It had taken her years to realise that the Beak was a judge; she'd always imagined a great stooping vulture who would peck out her liver and lights. So she'd run from the pie man and gone back to St Jude's Street, and eaten the thimbleful of thin gruel her Ma had prepared. Then she'd gone to sleep with hunger still clawing her stomach, and dreamed of the pie.

'Yes,' she said to Francis. 'I've wanted something.' But she did not tell him about the meat pie – she feared it would not be quite poetical enough for Francis.

'Show me.'

She looked at the apple in her hand as she'd once looked at the pie; Francis said, 'Perfect,' and took up his pencil again, working in quick, broad strokes. He talked as he drew, his eyes flicking constantly to her. She was used to men's eyes on her, but she'd never been regarded like this, in a dispassionate way, as if she was an object.

'Never fear,' he said, 'we will not work for long today for two reasons – one, the light is only perfect like this for a short time in the winter, and two, as a novice, you will tire easily. Modelling is an onerous task, I'm afraid, however easy it may look.'

He spoke the truth. She began to tire; her neck and back aching with the twist of her body, the hand that held the apple beginning almost imperceptibly to shake. She gritted her teeth, and said nothing. She wanted to keep her dignity about her, like the Queen of Sheba or whoever the lady in the green dress was supposed to be.

Just as she thought she might scream with discomfort, Francis stretched as she longed to do, and put up his brushes. 'That will do for today. The light thickens, and you are tired.'

She began to protest – she had thought she was doing so well.

'No, I can see it in the expression. You will be a fine actress –

your features are transparent, your soul shines out. You will never be able to lie to me, Annie.'

It was said lightly, and Annie answered in the same spirit. 'Reckon I wouldn't want to.' She stood, and stretched gratefully like a cat; like the tiger rug. She watched him as he cleaned his brushes.

'Thank you for your patience, Annie. Go and change. I except you will be needing your dinner, after your afternoon of hard work.'

There were many answers to this; uppermost in Annie's mind was the remark that it wasn't nearly so hard as making a few pence on your back with some fella you could hardly stand to look at, much less have inside you. But she remembered that Francis had compared her to the Queen of Sheba, so she merely replied, 'I wouldn't say no.' She was suddenly ravenous – dinner could not come soon enough; but there was something she wanted to see first. 'C'n I look?'

Francis made a courtly gesture to the enormous canvas. *Of course.*

It was a miracle – it was her, but not her. They were just pencil lines under a transparent white ground of paint, but it was as if she was looking at herself in a dusty looking glass, and that other self lived in the reflected room somewhere, bleached of colour and quite, quite still.

'Why is it white?'

'It is the way I work,' Francis said simply. 'I prepare my own undercoat paint, from bone meal. It's a type of gesso called bone white. I lay down the bone first. If you reflect for a moment, you will conclude that bone lies beneath everything – under your clothes, under your skin. When I lay the colour on top, I can work back to the bone, and it's like a light shining from within.'

'Who is it?'

'It is you.'

'No . . . I mean, who is it meant to be?'

'Come, Annie. You were at Sunday school. The apple, the snake?'

The maid. 'Eve,' she said. 'It's Eve.'

He nodded. 'Well done. The original fallen woman. Eve was the first of your kind.'

She didn't know if he meant women or whores. But she liked it when he said *well done*. She wanted him to think her clever, and not just a gutter creature. She thought about those Sunday-school lessons, and the priest's voice, and had a flash of recollection. 'She were made of bone, too.'

'Who was?'

'Eve,' she said. 'The Lord made her from Adam's rib. So she were made of bone.'

Francis looked at her as if he'd had a revelation as well. Then he touched her face with his hand, like he wanted to see if she was real. 'Yes, Annie,' he said. 'Yes, she was.'

Chapter 5

Five years, five months and ten days ago

We find the door half open when we arrive at his acquaintance's house, and Mr Starcross remarks how careless his friend has been to leave the street door open so that anyone may get in. Inside I am relieved to be received by a quite old lady, who is talking to several young women draped about the room. She tells me that the girls are her daughters, whereat some of them laugh. The old lady gets mad at that and orders them out of the room. I do not like the place at all, and ask to get a cab; the lady is all kindness and sends for one, and invites me to take some refreshment while I wait. I refuse wine as I think it would not be proper, but agree to take a dish of coffee, and while I drink it the lady talks to me agreeably. It transpires that she knows my aunt; although she does not call her by name, she gives her own name and asks to be remembered to her.

The cab takes an awfully long time coming, and I get ever so drowsy. The lady suggests I take my ease on the couch, and suddenly I am lying down. Mr Starcross comes closer, his face looming and swimming, then his mouth is on mine. I open my own mouth to protest, and his tongue is inside. Choking, I struggle, but my arms are rope. I appeal to the ladies for help, but my voice makes no sound. All the same, they approach me where I lie, and I learn to hope; but the old lady pulls up my skirt and the girls hold my arms.

Then he does it to me.

Over the next weeks and months, Annie Stride settled into her new life at number seven Gower Street. It was so markedly different to her previous life that she could hardly countenance it. It was the small, inconsequential things that set her back on her heels – the things Francis would do without thinking twice. In her idle moments she would wander from one room to another, crossing and recrossing thresholds, for in the Haymarket, and at Jude's Street, too, her home had been a single room. Space itself, and these numberless rooms and floors all belonging to one resident, was a boon she had never dreamed of. Here, too, the casements were secure, and her skin was never chilled by draughts. Here the roof did not leak, the icy drips waking her in the small hours. Here she undressed to go to bed, instead of huddling under the coverlet fully clothed. She could go to the bathroom and hot water would pour out of the tap, instead of having to walk half a mile to the dirty fountain at Seven Dials, and more often than not break the ice on top of it before she could fill her pail. And – *and* – she could pass down the hallway without being accosted by a greedy landlord, or being spat at by the 'respectable' lodgers, or having her tits grabbed by the chandler who lived opposite. Ah, that was the finest thing of all; she had her *person* to herself – she'd gone from being constantly handled, fondled, fucked, to no one touching her at all, from her rising in the morning to her going to bed at night. Of all the everyday luxuries, this was the most wonderful of all.

But soon these novelties became commonplace as Annie felt herself changing. She marvelled at how adaptable the human spirit must be, for soon she did not find it remarkable that hot water poured from the wall, or that no one assaulted her on the way down the stairs. She was no less thankful, and no less grateful to her benefactor, but she quickly became accustomed to the good life.

She became used to the servants, too. As well as Eve the maid, there was Bowering the butler, and Mrs Hoggarth in the kitchen.

Annie became accustomed to dealing with them, and modelled her manner on Francis's. He was always polite, but never friendly, keeping a distance between himself and the servants – they were on two different sides of the river, and she preferred to be on the north bank with him.

She ate well, and the way Francis kept his table convinced her more than ever that he was a man of great wealth. There would be pig's feet and pudding and conserves and custards, and her favourite, Mrs Hoggarth's game pie. Francis's father would send game from his estate, and now and again Annie would see Bowering opening the door to a basket full of feathers or fur – a brace of pheasants, their heads dangling, or a pair of hares curled up as if they slept – and her stomach would rumble, knowing that by nightfall these poor creatures would be plucked and skinned and roasted and would be sitting upon her plate.

She could see her looking-glass self filling out – the hollows in her face and at her collarbones and under her eyes disappearing. She would never be fat, but she was less gaunt, her skin creamy and lustrous, the violet shadows under her eyes gone. Her arms grew rounded, and dimples dipped her cheeks.

She was warm and well fed and safe; the Holy Trinity of needful things that she had chased all her life. But now she had more, much more. For the first time in her life she had pride in her work, and enjoyment, too. She had never enjoyed the work she'd done with Mary Jane – even when she'd escaped the dark alleyways for an evening and had been with a handsome captain in his barracks, or a young aristocrat in his town house. She'd never taken pleasure in it – she'd never had the moment that the bastards had every time, the moment that they paid for; the moment when their bodies shuddered and burned and burst asunder. Of course she feigned pleasure, if that meant they'd pay more, but she was used to that. All her working life she'd had to play a part, to be what she was not.

From her very earliest days she was at work for her father on the streets of the East End. At that time she did not have to face the dark horrors that awaited her in the upper room of the Old George, drumming their fingers with impatience as she lived out her childhood. But she was still, to all intents and purposes, acting. Her father would place her in a doorway and direct her to fall back on the step and pretend to be half asleep or half frozen with the cold. She was naturally thin and pale, compared to her more robust and ruddy siblings, who fought with their rude words and sharp elbows for every crust at home. Annie could be relied upon to look half starved, for that was what she was. Any charitably inclined gentleman passing by the sleeping child would be moved by her pitiable appearance to touch her on the shoulder. Then her father had trained her to 'waken', to move slowly and rub her eyes. The man, thoroughly deceived, would give her alms and pass on, and little Annie would compose herself again to wait for the next chance. Sometimes the rougher hand of a constable would descend on her shoulder; and then Pa would grab her by the arm and lift her bodily – hard, hurting – and drag her round the corner to try again elsewhere, away from the bobby's eye.

Years later, when she'd joined up with Mary Jane, she'd had to act again – she'd had to be Alice or Betsy or Evangeline, whatever the bastards wanted to call her, their sweethearts' names, their wives' names, women with whom they'd never dared to do what they did to her. They were names of girls they'd lost or girls they couldn't get – one had even called her by the name of his dead dog. Some of them wanted you to play a role – a workhouse girl, a fine lady, the wife of a friend. She'd done it all, anything to kindle the working girls' alchemy, to get the copper coins to turn to silver ones and, if they were well pleased, the silver to gold. And now she had the satisfaction of discovering that her years of acting had not been in vain; she could play all the different roles in which Francis cast her, and play them well.

She realised very quickly that Francis was good at his work, too. She'd admired – if that was the word amid the cold douse of shock – the sheer *reality* of *The Bridge of Sighs*, the painting of Mary Jane she'd seen in the Royal Academy, but as she worked with Francis she began to realise that his genius lay not only in the finished painting but also in its creation. From that very first day when she'd seen him draw her as Eve, she knew he had a rare skill; and in the days that followed, she would, in her breaks, stretch, and walk over to the canvas, to see the painting come, by stages, to life.

His method was singular, and not at all how she'd imagined a painter would work. She'd assumed, if she'd ever given the matter any thought, that an artist had a palette of paints and coloured in his outlines using each pigment in turn. The reality was somewhat different. On the first day, Francis sketched directly onto the canvas with a graphite pencil, drawing the design to absolute completion – the background, her figure, every last detail. Then, on the next day, he would entirely cover the area he intended to paint with bone white, mixed with a little varnish, so the paint was opaque and the faint pencil lines could still be seen. The covering film would be allowed to dry so that it was slightly tacky, then he would paint a single colour on softly with sable brushes. Annie could see that he must work lightly – so lightly – else the bone white would be worked up into the colour and it would be muddied and blurred, its purity destroyed. He used strong, jewel-like hues – vivid reds for her lip and greens for her gown and fiery oranges for her hair – and the effect of the white ground shining through was to give the painting a particular luminance, like the stained-glass windows she remembered from St Matthew's church – the only beautiful things she had seen in the whole of her childhood.

Francis's colours were not just transparent but seemed fatter, richer than any colours she had seen – she believed that the sleeve of her dress was full of the flesh of her arm, that her bodice was full of bosom and that there was a beating heart beneath. The paintings in the upstairs passageway, by other, lesser artists, looked thin and poor in contrast. They did not live, nor breathe, those fat cows in their fields and those skinny racehorses with spindles for legs. They were as flat and lacking in innards as a tiger-skin rug. Francis's colours were intense, they were solid, they were *real*.

And then, when he had laid down his colour, he would coax back the bone white through the layers, to bring a spark to her eye, a sheen to the silk of her gown or her hair, a slick gloss to her lip. Annie stood looking at Eve when she was completed; the woman who was made of bone. He had painted her not in some biblical past but here in this room, before the Scheele's green walls, the golden filigree leaves and the verdant paper creating a new Eden for her. The snake, just as he was, was half camouflaged by the diamond pattern of the rug, waiting to effect her fall, but Annie took no note of him. She gazed and gazed at her own face, her lips wet and parted, her – what had Francis called them? – topaz eyes looking at the apple with naked desire.

She felt stirred. Even though she'd seen how he'd painted her, step by step, she still could not understand how he'd done it. She had once gone with one of the bastards to see a conjuror in the Argyll Rooms, and the fellow had pulled a dove from his hat. She'd jostled close enough to touch the bird, and felt the wind of the wingbeats on her face. The dove was real. The hat was real. She'd seen the conjuror perform the trick with her own eyes, but simply did not know how it had been done. This was the same.

'It's magic,' she said now, still thinking of the hat and the dove.

Francis stood with her, peering over her shoulder, as if they were looking in a mirror in which only she was reflected, and did not demur. 'She is the forerunner,' he said grandly, 'for what will be my greatest cycle of work. I will take as my subject the Fallen

Woman, and you,' he placed her hands on her shoulders, 'will be my muse.'

Annie took no offence. She was used to plainer speaking than that, and had no argument with being called what she was.

Having begun with the Bible and that original sinner, Eve, Francis continued in the same vein, thumbing the Old Testament for references to the oldest profession. For his second painting of Annie he transformed her into someone whose name was very familiar, someone by whose name she had often been called.

For this sitting she once again put on a dress that had been left on her bed by an unseen hand. This time it was a gown of bright orange satin slashed to the waist; at her throat, ropes and ropes of turquoises, heavy and cold, which clicked together smartly as she walked. Once again there was no corset, no stays, and when she went to the Scheele's green studio, Francis wordlessly arranged the gown himself, open to the waist so that a wanton half-moon of breast showed each side of the necklaces. He pushed the mass of her hair behind her shoulders and down her back, and pinned up the front with turquoise combs, placing them several times until he was happy. Once again she had to share her tableau with a poor stuffed creature; this time it was a large black dog that had been immortalised in a sitting position, with bared teeth and a vicious look in its glass eyes.

Annie herself was placed in a grand throne-like chair, gilded and carved with curlicues and spindles. Francis asked her to gaze forward, chin high, with one hand on her jewels and the other on the head of the dog. 'Look like him,' he said. 'Look like the dog. Hard eyes, and fight in your belly.'

'Who am I today, then?'

'You are Jezebel,' he said, looking only at his canvas.

Annie smiled to herself.

Francis noticed – he noticed everything. 'Why do you smile?'

'Because I've been called that before,' she said drily.

He did not stop drawing, but he flicked his grey eyes up at her. 'Where?'

'Oh – in the Ten Bells in Spitalfields when I couldn't pay for a drink, outside the meeting house on Commercial Road where even the godly temperance lot used to say it and spit. Some of them even called me it while we was . . . at it – it seemed to excite them. I been called Jezebel all over London, Francis.'

'I beg your pardon,' he said handsomely. 'I meant no offence.'

''S all right.' The name had no power here, when she was dressed in this gown and these jewels, in the Scheele's green room. 'Who was she, then? Never thought she'd be a toff.'

'She was a queen.'

'Queen of Sheba?' she said, sharp as anything.

'No,' he smiled. 'Queen of Israel.'

'She weren't a working girl, then?'

'No. Her only sin was that she wore fine clothes and jewels, and made up her face and dressed her hair. And she only did that when she knew her time was up.'

'How come?'

'Her husband died in battle and his killer came for her. Jezebel knew he was coming.' He scratched his nose with his pencil. 'That is what I'm painting – her last moments. She was a stag at bay – no, a dog in a corner. I want you to almost bare your teeth.'

She imagined the cornered Jezebel, and her killer riding nearer. It was as good as the music hall. 'What happened in the end?'

'She knew it was over. She put on all her finery. She wanted to go out of this life a queen.'

Annie thought of Mary Jane then, all dressed up to go out that last night, smelling of perfume, done up to the nines in her best white muslin. She had a sudden notion. 'How'd Jezebel die?'

'She was thrown from her window, and the dogs ate her,' said Francis briefly.

She shivered at the very idea of it; a fallen woman indeed, to tumble from her fancy court to be a dog's dinner in a ditch. She forced a smile and patted the brittle fur of the stuffed dog's head. 'Reckon I'm safe from 'im, anyways.'

Now Francis glanced up. 'Safe from everyone here, Annie.' He looked directly at her. He seemed to be waiting for something, his pencil hovering in mid air. Suddenly it came to her what he wanted.

'*Thank you*, Francis,' she said fervently.

He nodded, smiled, and busied his pencil again.

After Jezebel, it was another Bible story: Rahab, the Harlot of Jericho. 'One of the four most beautiful women the world has ever known.' Francis touched her cheek as if transferring the compliment to her. Once again he arranged her gown himself – a simple cream homespun banded in stripes of red. Her hair was loose like a bride's and Francis hung a single red cord about her neck. He went behind an ornamental screen and brought forth a stuffed kid goat with slabbed orange eyes, holding it as if it was still alive. 'He will be peeping through the open door. And you will be carrying these.' He handed her two bundles of wheat as golden as her hair, and arranged the prickly bunches in the crook of each arm as if she carried twin babes.

'Rahab was brave as well as beautiful,' Francis explained as he drew in long, sweeping movements. 'She lived in the walls of Jericho and hid Hebrew spies in her house under barley and flax to keep them safe from the enemy within the walls. The red cord about your neck symbolises the cord that hung outside her house to identify it as a safe house to her allies.'

This Annie understood. 'In Whitechapel, the curtains are green if it's a cathouse. They light the lamps in the evening, when the girls are in, and the green glows out through the fog. Cathouse – cat's eyes.'

His charcoal halted. 'Did you . . . work there, too?'

She nodded. 'Oh yes. Got to go somewhere, haven't you? They

give you a room by the hour. Then you can stay on and take another man or two, if there's anyone about.'

'You'd do that?' he said, in a tone she could not define. 'Have one after another, all in succession?'

She shrugged. 'It's money, ain't it?'

He came to her then, knelt before her as if he prayed, and took her face in his hands. He spoke deliberately. 'You will never, *never* have to go back there,' he said. 'That world is behind you now – those men will not touch you again.' He looked at her imploringly.

Annie had been reading men for years and once again got the feeling that he was waiting for something. '*You* saved me,' she said, and she slid the hands that cupped her face to her mouth and kissed them gratefully, charcoal dust and all.

Francis seemed touched. He smiled and returned to his canvas.

After a week or two of being courageous and homespun as Rahab, Annie was wanton in purple and scarlet as the Whore of Babylon, with a ring on every finger and a gold cup in her hand. She had learned, now, to look for one of God's creatures in each tableau, and this one was no different: a lamb lay curled on the ornamental rug at her feet, strewn with leaves, the glass eyes painted closed. 'A sacrificial lamb,' explained Francis. 'In the days of Abraham, lambs were highly prized. It was thought that if one was killed, it would make God look kindly on the people.'

'So the lamb died for everyone else.'

'For the common good, yes.'

Annie looked at the curled creature. 'Daft bugger.'

Francis frowned a little. 'You think such sacrifice foolish? Is there no nobility to be found in helping others? No chivalry?' His tone was playful, but she detected a deeper meaning. By now she knew what to say.

'I've only met nobility once, and that is in *you*, dear Francis – my knight in shining armour.'

As the weeks passed, the light moved round in the church-like windows, finding new brightness and longevity with the coming of the spring, and Francis left the Bible behind for Rome, and cast Annie as a woman called Lucrece. Lucrece was Annie's favourite character, for she could lie down on a chaise longue for the entire day, clad in a loose white Roman toga and gold sandals, and had to do nothing but recline, her hair tumbling from chaise to floor, her eyes closed and her lifeless hand clasped loosely around a dagger. Her demise was watched by a stuffed owl perched on the antimacassar above her head, to represent, Francis said, the wisdom of Minerva. Annie didn't see much wisdom in letting yourself be raped by a fellow called Sextus and then making away with yourself; but she blessed the Roman matron for her sacrifice, which meant that she could often fall asleep in the spring sunshine.

But as always, Francis wanted to talk. 'Has anyone ever . . . taken you against your will?'

She was so drowsy that she did not really register the probing nature of the question; she was too comfortable to mind. 'Not exactly. That is to say, if they pay, they get what they want. But I've had bastards ask me to pretend that I don't want it – to pretend I was being attacked, to act scared, to fight them off.'

He seemed oddly interested. 'Why do you think they did that? Those men? Why did they want to feel as if they took you against your will?'

'I think they wanted to feel powerful. I think they liked the fight.'

'But why?'

She had to make the effort to think. 'Well, I s'pose because if you know a girl doesn't want you, you don't have to ask yourself so many questions.'

'What questions?'

'Whether she likes you. Whether you're any good. I s'pose . . . I s'pose you don't have to please her.'

'So men still felt they had to please you? Even when they were paying?'

She stretched – he wasn't painting anyway. 'Some. You'd be surprised. Some take you and don't care. Some want you to tell 'em they topple the mountains and move the earth.'

Francis tapped his brush on his teeth. 'And were they really powerful? The men who played at rape?'

Now she didn't have to think. 'No. It was always the weak ones as wanted to do it.'

He seemed to consider this. 'And how did you feel? About these . . . violations?'

She turned her head a little. No one had ever asked her such a question. 'When? During?'

'No,' he said. 'No. Afterwards.'

She breathed in a long breath through her nose. 'The same. I felt exactly the same as ever.'

Spring warmed to anticipate summer, and Francis left the ancient world for more modern times. Now Annie wore clothes that were old-fashioned but familiar in line – a grey figured gown with a tight waist and a milkmaid shawl of snowy lace. This time she had to kneel, holding a stuffed white dove poised for flight, three-quarter face looking towards one of the pointed windows.

'Am I in church?' she asked.

'You are in a chapel of sorts,' said Francis. 'A prison chapel. You are Gretchen, from the play *Faust*. Faust, her lover, had sold his soul to the Devil; Gretchen murdered her mother in order to be with him, but confessed her sins, made atonement and was saved from prison by the angels of heaven.'

Annie considered as she knelt. She was used, by now, to the fact that being with Francis was a bit like being with a bastard, but without the fucking. She knew what he liked, and knew she could give it to him; he wanted to know about her life and he wanted her to be grateful. She knew nothing about him except that his father had an estate in Norfolk and his mother had a maidservant. She sensed, too, with a wisdom she had not known she possessed, that his probing of her past life was not particularly because he was interested in those incidents – they did not seem to titillate him; he did not harden and pounce as she might have expected. No; he wanted her to recount her past only to throw her present into sharp relief. The worse the past was, the better the life he had given her. Underlying it all was the sense that he was her saviour, that he had reached out his hand to her and raised her from the gutter.

She racked her brain – there was little she could think of to say about St. Matthew's church that would interest him: the Sunday attendances, the Bible stories, the confessional. They were not high church, the Strides – she did not know that they were any church at all – but the other children confessed, so she did, too. Mostly she made things up, so her subsequent atonement was as fake as her confession. No, there was no sin in her when she went to church, but Annie had the perfect prison tale for Francis.

'I went to visit a lord in the Marshalsea, a viscount who had gambled his estates away. This bastard was down to his last shilling, but seemed more able to live without food than a girl, and he decided to spend this final coin having me brought to the jail to kneel before him and take him in my mouth.' Her knees remembered the cramped position, and she made some comparisons between that day and this, and thanked Francis, and praised him, as she knew he required. She sensed that he was never as gratified by references to nobility or chivalry as he was by the title of saviour. He could not hear enough that he was her salvation; and for all her native intelligence she could not divine if he was a philanthropist, like those wearisome pamphlet-wavers who descended on the East End on the Sabbath, or was paying some private penance. They were back in the confessional again, and she thought of Gretchen's atonement, of her own. Was this his? If so, for what?

A fortnight on her knees, then she was elevated to a sitting position. 'Manon Lescaut,' Francis said, seating her at a gaming table before a precarious-looking house of cards. 'A young nobleman gave up his inheritance for her, then had to keep her as his mistress by cheating at cards.'

As Manon she was dressed in a shiny satin gown of the black and red of the cards and a pair of black lace fingerless mittens. Her hair was dressed in a style most familiar to her – the black and red feather cluster of a working girl. A stuffed black cat peered from beneath the card table with his green eyes, and Francis scattered a number of cards at her feet. He arranged the rest in her left hand, save the ace of hearts, which he put in her right, directing her to pose as if she were placing it on the very roof of the card construction, completing the house.

As ever, Annie had a story for him – she told him of the time she'd worked a card house where the girls crawled under the tables to titillate the gentlemen while they played. As she spoke, she kept her eyes on the house of cards as she had been instructed; they looked so unsteady that she was careful not to touch them. She felt the strain of the pose, and registered the similar strain of her strange friendship with Francis. She had the feeling that if she said the wrong thing, their delicate balance would collapse. Once she dozed a little and jerked awake as her fingers touched the house of cards. Her eyes flew open and she threw out a hand to steady the structure, but discovered the cards were stuck artfully together.

'You see,' said Francis, and she turned to see him smiling at her. 'I thought of everything.'

At the beginning of true summer, Annie posed for what Francis announced would be the last of his Fallen Woman series. She watched him mix his bone white, in what had become a familiar ritual before each painting. He always needed lots of white, as it was the base for all his figures, but he seemed to be mixing more than ever. Annie liked watching him. It reminded her of watching her mother bake, one of the only calm and comforting rituals of her life. Baking meant two things – that they could afford flour in St Jude's Street that week, and that there would soon be bread to eat. Now she watched Francis pour the bone meal into the oil and turpentine, the bone rising in a choking, chalky dust.

'Where'd you get all that bone meal?' she asked.

He didn't look up. 'Plenty of bones to be had in London,' he said.

She knew what he meant – at Smithfield market, where they sold meat, bones were ten a penny. There were great chalky mountains of them, like a charnel house. You could buy them to make soup. Sometimes in St Jude's Street her Ma had fed the whole family from one bone in the pot, a thin, unsatisfying soup as clear as water, but it was hot and wet and it stopped your stomach rumbling. She watched, fascinated, as Francis stirred the mixture in the vat, and thought how many families it would feed. There were plenty in London so hungry they would drink it down just like that, oil and turpentine and all.

'Why don't you make the other colours, too?'

'You need a good colourman for that,' he said. 'Someone who knows his hues and his pigments. I buy the colours in. But white is uncomplicated, it is no colour at all, so I make it myself.'

'That's a deal of white this time,' she observed.

'Yes,' he said. 'I will need a lot of it for the gown.'

And so he did, for her costume was a gown of figured white muslin, in which she stood simply, facing forward, hair flowing to her waist.

'No dead critters today?' she asked.

'None,' he smiled. 'Just these.' He handed her an armful of white flowers. They were bloated and many-petalled, and had a sickly-sweet smell.

'Who am I to be today?' she asked, a little wearily.

He heard it. 'Just yourself,' he said. 'The end of the cycle,' and he fell silent.

This was odd – he was usually happy to talk. She felt oddly unsettled and tried again. 'Will this one have my name?'

'No. We will call her . . .' He seemed to think for a little. '*The Girl with the White Camellias*.'

Camellias. The same flowers that were in the salver in the hallway.

Over the hours that followed, she grew to hate the camellias. The sickly smell rose to her nose and made her stomach lurch, and she had no idea why, since it was not particularly strong or noxious. The blooms did not make her eyes stream or coax sneezes from her nose; she just hated their company and would watch them wilt hour by hour, willing their death. Despite the relative comfort of the pose, the camellias made this sitting worse than kneeling for a week as Gretchen, or holding the chalice as the Whore of Babylon.

Besides this, the dress she wore was not comfortable. All the others had fitted so well, they could have been made for her. This one felt very much as if it had been made for someone else. The sleeves were tight, and it pulled across the bodice and bit under the arms. The skirts had very faint but very large patches of brown staining, perhaps from rain or travel, and the cloth felt stiff, as if it had been overly starched – the new maid, no doubt, finding her feet.

Annie willed Francis to tell her a tale, as he had done for all the other women, to take her mind off the discomfort of the white dress and the rotten white flowers; but he worked in silence. Something seemed to have gone wrong. This picture was bleached and pale; gone were the jewel-like hues; bone white was the only colour on his palette and on his canvas. Francis seemed to have gone, too, leaving a blank of a man. He had withdrawn as suddenly as the sun goes behind a cloud, and she longed to feel the warmth of his conversation again.

Her mother wit told her that Francis's mood had something to do with this pose, these flowers, this dress. At length she tried again. 'How did you come by this gown?'

He paused. 'It belonged to a lady I knew.'

'Was she a whore, too?'

His face was suddenly still with anger. The house of cards teetered. 'No,' he said shortly. 'She was an angel.' He forced a smile. 'Let us stop for today. Take your ease until dinner.'

She put down the unbearable flowers and fled the room. They were all of a piece with her sadness, the horrible grief and void that Mary Jane had left, the sudden loss of Francis's regard.

When she reached the door of her chamber, she pressed her hot cheek against the cool fingerplate, hesitating with her hand on the doorknob. She would go back; she would apologise – for what, she didn't know, but it did not matter. Her whole existence depended on Francis and she could not have him vexed at her. She turned and trod back to the studio on silent feet, as if even her footsteps might irritate him.

She was about to open the studio door when a sound made her check, a tiny breathy gasp or cry. She was not yet the lady Francis wanted her to be, so she felt no compunction in falling to her knees and applying her eye to the keyhole. A little draught puffed at her eye, as if the frenzied activity within had disturbed the air. For Francis sat, his breeches disarranged, handling himself, his breath coming fast, his eyes staring fixedly at his painting of her as the Girl with the White Camellias.

She watched him, frozen, until the final moment; then tiptoed away. The scent of the camellias followed her down the hall to her chamber.

Chapter 6

Five years and five months ago

Now I've stopped crying all the time, Mother tells me I'm pretty enough to be a dress lodger.

I should explain: the bawd at the whorehouse in Silverthorne Street wants me to call her Mother, like all the other girls do. It means that if she's out on the town with us, and the bluebottles question us, we just say we're with our mother. She says that if we call her that at home, then if we're out, and even if we're scared, we'll blurt it out natural-like. She says it'll be second nature soon, but it might take me a while. It sticks in my throat a bit, seeing as my own ma was only lately hanged – by mistake.

Mother's looking after me now – I haven't seen Mr Starcross since he did what he did to me. I'm glad; but I bet he's out there collecting girls for Mother, girls like me.

A dress lodger, the others tell told me, is a girl who wears a special frock that Mother's bought from the finest tailor, an investment, so to speak. She puts on the frock, and a hat and a muff, too, and that means she can streetwalk in the smart parts of London, north of the river, because she doesn't look like a ragbag. A fellow watches her in her finery, then approaches her, and they go to his club or his town house or some such. Mother follows her at a distance, to make sure she doesn't do a bunk with the dress.

The dress was the nicest thing to happen to me since I came to Mother's. All silk and embroidery and dark blue like a starless *night. When I put it on, I could imagine I was a lady, and not what I really am: Mary Jane the whore.*

The girls said I was lucky. They said the gents are nicer – that they give you presents, and if they do, Mother lets you keep them, as long as they're not worth much. They said that the toffs are gentler – they don't take you like a dog like the carters and chandlers of Vauxhall do. They said it don't hurt so much north of the river. They were wrong. None of them are pretty enough to be a dress lodger, so they didn't know.

The gents are worse.

Annie still did not know for sure whether Francis wanted her.

On the night she'd come to Gower Street, she'd offered herself to him, guiding his hand to her breast, and he'd drawn it away. He'd seemed appreciative of her body as he'd painted her, but only as he might have admired a still life – a vase or a bowl of fruit. She'd never seen that candle flame of desire in his eyes that she'd learned to recognise over the years. He'd never seemed titillated by her stories of her past life, however depraved they'd been.

Annie had never before been moved to examine her relationships. Her past life, though squalid, was at least simple. She knew that men wanted her because they paid her coin. It was implicit in the transaction – no more complicated than the purchase of a pie on a street corner: appetite, desire, transaction, satiation. But now that she had the measure of Francis, now she had seen him spend himself before her image, she knew even less. It was almost as if it was this particular painting that had moved him. He had not seemed enflamed by her as Jezebel, when she'd shown her half-moons of breast, or as the Whore of Babylon, with a dark shadow of hair at her groin. He'd not been moved by the wanton expression of Eve, nor the luscious lips of Manon, painted red and parted like a cunt. No – he had spent himself over the picture of her in bone white, demure with flowers and dressed in sprigged muslin.

But despite the fact that her image, at least, seemed to please him, there was still the very real risk that he would send her away. His work seemed to be over; the mysterious Girl with the White Camellias marked the end of that intense period of months when she'd played all those fallen women for him. What he'd done in front of her painting was the shattering culmination of that time. She was very afraid that he would now turn away from her like the bastards did after orgasm – their desire gone, their eyes never meeting hers, their countenance ashamed.

Yet he seemed to have no intention of doing so. 'You and I have only just begun,' he said.

His strange mood forgotten, they talked and laughed just as before, and the sun shone again. Now that he'd stated his intention to keep her at Gower Street, and now that she'd seen what she'd seen, she fully expected him to make his move, to take her to his bed. But he did not. Annie felt that their union was inevitable – a when, not an if – but he seemed to be waiting for something, and as time passed, she began to sense what it was.

When he'd said they'd just begun, he did not mean that there was more to paint – although he spoke from time to time of further canvases he planned in the future. He meant chiefly that there was more work to do on the re-creation of Annie Stride. He wanted to remake her completely – to create a new Annie for himself who was entirely his creature and who would slough off her old skin like that of Eve's green serpent. And when she was re-created in his image, fresh and new like the first woman to walk the earth, like the woman made of bone, then, she thought, he would take her. The thought made her shiver with both unbearable excitement and revulsion, which could not be separated.

There was much to do. Francis had approached her like one of his paintings. He had given her a background – the water-white tiles of the bathroom, the Scheele's green studio, the Arabian Nights drawing room. He had worked upon the broad strokes first – the long sweeps of graphite – cleansing her body, her hair, feeding her stomach. Then he had blocked in the colour, giving her peignoirs and dressing gowns and bonnets and shawls, all in the jewel-like hues that he favoured.

And now, only now that she had form and colour, he proceeded to the finer strokes – the detail. He began to correct her speech. 'Not "I ain't got no", Annie. "I *haven't got any*".' And 'Instead of "I reckon that", try saying, "I *think* that".' He looked at her fixedly. 'What *do* you think, Annie?'

''Bout what?'

'Anything. Everything.'

'I hardly know.'

'Why don't you know?'

'Well.' She laughed suddenly. 'It's a big question, ain't it?'

'And you don't have any answers?'

'No, reckon I don't.'

'Why?'

She sighed. 'Reckon it's because I ain't been told what to think. I always wait for *them* to tell me.'

'Who?'

The bastards. 'Well, I s'pose, *men*.'

'Ah,' he nodded. 'Well. That won't happen here. I want to hear what is in your mind. And in order to form opinion, you must be educated.'

He would read to her from the newspapers. 'The notion that a woman may not understand politics is an old idea,' he declared. 'A man does not want a dolt for his companion.'

'Am I your companion, then?' she said, looking at him through her lashes with some of her old coquetry.

'Don't you care for that identification?' he asked gently.

'I been called many things,' she said. 'But that's a new one on me.'

'But you have no objection?'

'Not likely. That is,' she tried out one of her new phrases, 'on the contrary.'

Companion seemed to mean friend, but more fancy; this new status led her to hope, so she listened and learned eagerly.

'The United States has a new president,' Francis announced over breakfast, 'by the name of Franklin Pierce.' He looked at Annie sideways over the paper. 'Whom do you suppose he succeeded?'

She screwed up her eyes and nose. 'Millard Fillmore?'

He smiled. 'That's right,' he said. 'Next time without the facial gymnastics.'

He went on to read that India had a new railway from Bombay to Thana, and she had to inform him that Thana was in the province of Maharashtra; and on hearing that Giuseppe Verdi's new opera *Il Trovatore* had premiered in Rome, she was obliged to name another two of his operas.

Some headlines, though, were apparently not for her ears. Now and again Francis would frown, stop reading and fold the paper away, tucking it down between the cushion and the arm of his chair. There it would stay, forgotten, for the rest of the day. Once, when he had gone out in the evening to his club, she ferreted it out and read the offending page. She wished she had not. A working girl had been found in the Thames under Waterloo Bridge. Annie's skin chilled.

She felt many things on the reading of this story, but in the myriad of feelings that swirled beneath her corset, two were uppermost. Firstly, she was thankful; so thankful that she was no longer within the reach of the dark waters of the Thames, that if Francis had been at home, she would not only have thanked him, she would have kissed his feet. Secondly, she felt a spreading warmth that he would seek to protect her in this way – once, she had lived this life; now, she was not even to hear about it.

Francis, having ascertained that Annie knew her letters ('No thanks to Ma and Pa – it was the priest at St Matthew's as taught us'), encouraged her to read for herself – not books to begin with, nor the newspapers with their sensational headlines, but a periodical called *Household Words*. She worked her way through articles about improving society, or developments in science, but her favourite bits were the serials, stories chopped up into little pieces. In the evening, after dinner and before the fire in the Arabian Nights drawing room, Francis would encourage her to read aloud to him. She would do so with increasing confidence, while he gently corrected her as she stumbled over the more challenging words.

'"*How could you give me life, and take from me all the in . . . ina . . ."*'
'Inappreciable.'
'"*. . . inappreciable things that raise it from the state of con . . . con . . ."*'
'Conscious.'
'"*. . . conscious death? Where are the graces of my soul? Where are the sen . . . sentiments of my heart? What have you done, oh, Father, what have you done with the garden that should have bloomed once, in this great wilderness here?" said Louisa as she touched her heart.*'

Something in the passage reminded her of her own story, and of her Pa and the upper room of the Old George; and of Mary Jane and her dad sent off to the hulks and her wandering off with that seducer who reminded her of him. And now Annie Stride from Bethnal Green was here in Gower Street being looked after like a flower by this man who fed and watered her and encouraged her to blossom. But Francis was no father figure. He was young, he was handsome, he was . . . *what* was he? A friend, maybe; perhaps a schoolmaster, for he seemed to play that part more than any other. Sometimes under his correction she felt stupid, and became offended; but most of the time she took his tuition well, for she harboured a strong determination to better herself.

She developed a curious two-tier process of speech: she would frame phrases in her mind, rehearse them silently, and then speak. It gave her a very measured way of talking, slow and deliberate, so unlike her real passionate, staccato self. On the street she used to string words together like necklaces, never stopping in her continuous rosary of speech, a trick she'd caught from Mary Jane with her thousand-words-a-minute Norfolk drawl. Now she was delighted with the change, feeling that every polished vowel or clipped consonant took her further away from St Jude's Street.

Francis seemed very well pleased with her circumspect way of talking, and her vocabulary, which had fattened but shed 'unsuit-able' words. He did her the honour of never patronising her – he used long words and complicated ideas in order to train her, expecting her to rise to his level rather than lowering himself to hers. If she did not know a word, he assumed that she would learn it. And she did. 'All moves,' he said, 'in the right direction,' and Annie would smile to herself indulgently and think, with the aid of her grand new lexicon, how conventional he was for a bohemian.

He was also very insistent upon manners. He taught her not just how to talk, but how to walk, how to shake hands, how to put on her gloves, how to take them off again, how to carry a fan. She was given not a morsel of food until she'd said 'please', and could not leave the table until she'd said 'thank you'. 'Ingratitude,' he would say, 'is the most heinous of sins.' Annie could think of plenty that were worse, but she kept her peace and did as she was bidden. After all, she did owe Francis everything, and did not ever want him to withdraw his regard.

She was a quick study and learned in very short order when her thanks were required. She uttered them blithely and readily, quite happy to give Francis his due. No wonder he required her gratitude – he was giving her not just a new life, but a new self. And for her part, she was entirely happy with her rebirth. There was nothing of Bethnal Green that she valued enough to keep.

Now that their prolonged sittings for the Fallen Woman series were at an end, Francis took his tuition of Annie outside the home. 'You are quite the actress,' he said, 'and have embodied for me all those unfortunate ladies from the Old Testament to our modern age of science. Now I would like you to see another actress of note. Adelaide Neilson is giving her Isabella in Shakespeare's *Measure for Measure* at the Adelphi, and I have managed to secure tickets.'

Annie knew little of Shakespeare, even less of the play, and had never heard of Adelaide Neilson; but the Adelphi Theatre she knew very well, or at least the arches under it that gave onto the fetid river, so she was curious to see it again from her new perspective. She was ripe, too, after her weeks of confinement in Gower Street, for a trip out on the town. She had not been abroad since the dreadful night on the Bridge of Sighs; she felt like a different girl to then, and would like to see how the world had gone on rolling like an old barrel since she'd stepped off it.

On the appointed evening, Eve brought her a gown to wear that Francis had chosen himself. It was a lovely thing of golden silk – no, she corrected herself, topaz, the colour of her eyes. She allowed Eve to help her into it and tie her stays. The crinoline was voluminous, and held the burnished skirt out wide as if fanned out by invisible fingers. There was figured gold lace upon the stomacher, and a filigree of the same lace at the bodice and sleeves. Eve dressed Annie's hair low on the nape of her neck in a great roll, and pinned the heavy mass with combs set with tiger's eyes. The hair on her crown was parted severely in the centre and dressed close to her head. And just above her ears and on her forehead the maid turned the stray strands of red-gold about the poker till tiny curls sprang away from her fingers like watch springs.

Annie smoothed the dress over her body as she peered in the looking glass. She remembered when she had been a dress lodger with Mary Jane, paid to wear fine clothes and parade the Strand, luring men into the lodging houses. Those dresses had been cheap and tawdry; although they'd appeared fine from a distance, and to a girl from Bethnal Green they had seemed the stuff of Solomon, she knew now that they would bear no scrutiny, with their gewgaw gems and sloppy seams. This topaz dress had more fine embroidery in an inch of its fabric than the gaudy dresses she used to lure the bastards in.

The looking glass told her that she was a lady. She had been told how to speak and how to act, and now she looked the part, too. She peered at herself more closely. Who was this looking-glass girl? Would she know how to behave in society? It was all very well to play the lady in Gower Street with Francis; their own private parlour game. But now she was anxious to make him proud, not to let him down in public; and she must begin by being prompt – he was waiting for her. She took a last doubtful glance in the glass. Where was Annie Stride?

She put on a tobacco-brown theatre cape and muff, pulled on her gloves finger by finger as she had been taught, and went to meet Francis at the foot of the stairs. He was ready for her in his tails; his hair tamed, his topper in his hand. Perhaps she had become accustomed to him, but at that moment, seeing him in his dress clothes, she was struck by the extreme potency of his good looks, and she hurried down the stairs too eagerly for elegance. As she took his proffered arm, her excitement was only tempered by the ever-present bowl of camellias on the hallway table, emanating their sweet malign scent.

London on that summer evening looked different to Annie. Perhaps she herself was different, or perhaps the London you saw from a hansom cab was different from the London you saw from the streets. It was easy to ignore, from a carriage, the wretches in the shadows and the women under the arches. The streets Francis took were clean, broad thoroughfares, the districts decent and well lit. But when they reached the Adelphi, she was on more familiar ground. She was no more than a spit away from the Haymarket and her old haunts – she could have taken him, in less than a moment, to Sam's or Lizzie's or the Burlington Rooms, there to spend the evening in far less exalted company than the glittering theatregoers crowding the pavement.

That other London, beneath the skin, was so close; Annie looked sideways at Francis as he armed her into the glittering foyer, and wondered if he knew. She thought of the girl in the looking glass, and the thin skin of silvered mercury that separated that smart lady from her real self. She squeezed Francis's arm gratefully. But for him, Annie Stride could so easily have been there and not here. He was the difference. They were mere yards away from the gutter, but so far above that desperation, out of the darkness and in the light.

An usher dressed in red and gold conducted them up a marble staircase marked by a sign that said, bizarrely: 'To the gods'. Annie was aware, as she climbed, that with every step she left behind those women under the arches. They were shown into a private box, and as she walked forward to the lip of it and put her gloved hand on the balustrade to peer over, the gilded theatre was spread out below her. The gods indeed – she was as high as heaven, and could have spat on the heads of the bejewelled ladies seated below. They were fancy, but she was fancier.

'You like it?' Francis asked.

She nodded. 'Whitechapel don't go to the play in kid gloves and white ties.'

'You are not in Whitechapel now,' he said.

'No,' she replied, 'that I'm not.'

As she settled herself into her red plush seat, she realised anew just how rich Francis must be. She thought of the Scheele's green wallpaper, the bathroom, the game pie, the estate in Norfolk. It had never once occurred to her, over the last few months, to clear him out and go. She did not want to be that sort of girl – she wanted to go up, not down; she liked it here in the gods, at the top of the marble stairs. She thought of the girls that stole – they ended up either in front of the Beak, or floating in the Fleet, that secret underworld river where bodies were dumped and rarely found.

Francis turned to her as the lights dimmed. 'I do hope you will like the play,' he whispered, as courteous as if she were the Queen herself. 'I think its subject might be of particular interest to you.'

Annie did not like the play. She liked the costumes, and the stage sets were very cunningly painted. But she found the drama dull; there was so much bally *talking*. She enjoyed the interval, when Francis bought them sherbets and some little chestnuts from the theatre bar. Her hairpins hurt her; her hair was heavy at her nape, and seemed to give her head a downward tendency. In the second act, she found herself falling asleep in the warmth of the theatre and the comfort of the plush chair, her head lolling on Francis's shoulder. She woke with her cheek against his stiff shirt front, and sat up dazed. In her past life she might have expected a backhander across the cheek if she'd fallen asleep on the job; but Francis only smiled at her and nodded toward the stage. She sat up straight, blinked and tried her best to take notice, straining her ears to penetrate the language, thick as London fog.

The scene taking place seemed to be in a prison cell, evidenced by the bars on the windows and the strong light artfully shining through. A brother had been imprisoned, and his sister – a nun – was visiting him. The sister's name was Isabella, and Francis gave Annie a great nudge when the lady entered. This, then, must be Adelaide Neilson, the famous actress he had brought her to see. Annie did not think much of her. She was handsome enough, in a mannish way, but not beautiful at all; her voice recalled the women bawling the price of fish in Billingsgate; and her girth was such that she did not seem to fit into her habit. Yet from what Annie could make out from the dense language, Isabella was a great object of desire for some duke. Her brother was trying to get her to sleep with the Duke in order to save his own life, and Isabella was refusing.

Miss Neilson, her strong features framed by the nun's white wimple, did a fair job of defending her precious innocence and steadfastly simpering her refusal. But Annie thought her performance too *much* somehow – like the smell of those dratted flowers Francis favoured. Her Isabella was much too sweet. Annie had been pretending to be an innocent since she had ceased to be one, and she knew that you mustn't put too many eggs in the pudding. A simple sweep of the eyelashes, a downcast glance would do, not all this screeching and weeping. But perhaps the truth was that she knew nothing of the theatre, for the audience thought it very fine, and rose to their feet with a great cheering and clapping and stamping of feet.

Annie clapped politely, too, until Francis handed her her wrap. But Francis, as she was beginning to learn, didn't miss much. 'I fear the evening bored you,' he said.

Annie felt mortified. 'No, Francis, you mustn't say so. I had a lovely time.'

'I had thought you might identify with the themes of the piece.'

'I couldn't really make head nor tail of it. The only thing I got was why the nun one didn't do what her brother asked.'

'Well, Isabella felt very strongly that if she gave in to the Duke – Antonio – then she would be damned. And that if her brother – Claudio – persuaded her to give up her honour, he would be damned, too.'

'Oh.' Annie subsided. 'Turns out I didn't get that either, least-ways not how you've just explained it.'

'Why did you think Isabella refused to sleep with the Duke?'

''Cos it's her body, ain't it?' She struggled to express herself. 'Do it for yourself, do it for money, but don't do it for a man. It's like the lamb.'

'The lamb?'

'The lamb in the painting. That old Whore of Babylon. You said the lamb on the floor was a sacrifice, something that had to die for the good of others.'

'You are quite right.' He looked pleased with her. 'Isabella *was* exactly like the lamb.' He opened the gilded door of the box for her, letting in a gale of chatter and laughter from the stairwell. 'Am I to take it that you would not sacrifice yourself for your brothers?'

Bethnal Green surfaced. 'Garn with you, Francis. I wouldn't give them a penny to piss. They was nothing but a peck of bother. Some of the girls was all right.' She remembered small, sticky hands in hers. 'But so far as I can tell, I wouldn't sac . . .'

'Sacrifice.'

'. . . sacrifice myself for anyone or anything.'

He was so interested, he forgot to correct her lapsed speech. 'Wouldn't you? Wouldn't you really, Annie?'

'No.'

He gave her his arm back down the marble stairs. In the general din, they had to lean close, so even in the midst of the crowd their conversation was strangely intimate. 'What if there was someone you really loved?'

She considered. 'I couldn't say. I ain't never . . .' Suddenly she could not look at him.

'Yes?' he prompted gently.

'Well, I ain't never felt that way.'

He nodded slowly. 'Then let me put it another way. What if there was someone who'd done you a great service – perhaps many services? Would that person merit your sacrifice? Could such a person, for whom you felt regard – let us not call it love – could they expect your *gratitude*?'

The word was a trigger. She was expected, she knew, to make a gesture. 'Dear Francis,' she said. 'You are the only person who deserves such loyalty from me. And for you, of course, I would do anything.'

With this he seemed satisfied, but Annie still felt it was necessary to divert the conversation back to the play. As they entered the glittering atrium of the theatre and passed below the chandeliers, she asked, 'So how did she get out of it?'

Francis frowned a little, as if his thoughts were elsewhere.

'Isabella,' she explained. 'How did she get out of having to sleep with the Duke? She refused him, but her brother still got to live. I didn't get that bit.'

'Well, they persuaded another young lady, Mariana, to sleep with him instead. She was already a . . . lady of easy virtue, as you might say.'

Annie snorted. 'S'pose it didn't matter about *her* being damned, then.'

They emerged onto the street and Francis hailed a carriage. 'I think the notion was that Mariana's would be the lesser sin, since there was no . . . ahem . . . virginity involved.'

'Well,' she conceded. 'I c'n see that. Once you break the seal on a bottle of gin, you might as well drink the rest, eh?'

'As you say.' A cab slowed to a stop before them, and the cabbie touched his hat. 'My abiding question about the play,' Francis said, 'is how the Duke does not know that the lady in his bed is not the lady in his heart.'

'All cats are grey at night.'

He laughed and handed her into the carriage. As they settled Annie's skirts, and Francis's top hat, he said, 'Perhaps you prefer another breed of entertainment?'

She did not want to disappoint him, and tried to communicate something of her earlier thoughts. 'I think Mr Dickens could take Mr Shakespeare in a fight, if they was to square up.'

He smiled. 'It might be better to say that you prefer contemporary literature to that of the Renaissance. Would that be fair?'

She ducked her head. 'Mr Dickens writes about the London I know. Cheapside, Cornhill, the Marshalsea. And St Giles churchyard; the souls that hang about there ain't exactly righteous. He knows it, 'cos he must've seen it.'

'What were your diversions before you met me? Could you tell me?'

She looked up. 'I could *show* you.' Suddenly, abruptly, she missed the entertainments of her former life. She forgot the hapless women crouching beneath the arches. Surely she was safe now, now that she was a lady. Surely it would be all right to give Francis a glimpse of low fun from the distance of prosperity?

'Show me?'

'Yes. I could show you something that would knock yer eyes out. Tell the driver to take us to Vauxhall Gardens.'

Francis raised an eyebrow. She knew what it meant – Vauxhall Gardens was by no means a respectable place, but all the same, gentlemen *did* go there, not only for the girls, but also for the entertainment. She tried to reassure him. 'Don't worry, it was a royal place once, and I seen royalty there myself.'

It was true – she'd seen the Duke of Clarence there; not close up, but the whispers of his presence had rolled around the gardens like a pea on a drum. She had seen no more than a tall figure with a patent-leather sheen to his hair and the watchful stance of a heron. Francis, however, perhaps convinced by this royal reference, leaned from the window to give the instruction to the driver.

Annie sat forward urgently. 'There's somethink else.'

'Yes?' he said indulgently.

'Could I take me hair down? These pins is killing me.'

The ready smile came again. 'Well, we are crossing the river – it will not matter now if you sport a more . . . transpontine style.'

After three months in Francis's jewel box of a house in Gower Street, the Vauxhall Gardens were much shabbier than Annie remembered. Hansom cabs crowded the little square outside, and by the pay place was a huge peeling transparency of a master of ceremonies bowing, with the words 'Welcome to the Royal Residence' on a faded ribbon about his head. There was nothing royal about the look of it; despite her protestations to Francis, the place looked like the aristocracy had long since departed.

She would have turned back, but Francis was already paying their shilling apiece at the gates. Beyond the entrance, matters improved, for the gardens were artfully lit with limelight and flares. Burning torches marked the night walks, and fire-eaters further illuminated the night. It was very pleasant, yet Annie could not escape the thought that if the marble stairs of the Adelphi had elevated her to the gods, she was now descending into hell.

It was the first time she'd been to the Vauxhall Gardens for leisure, not work. She'd never come accompanied, for mostly she'd arrive alone and leave on the arm of a gentleman. She banished all thoughts of hellfires and allowed herself to feel superior and safe with Francis. She spotted at once all the sallies lolling by the lake like a flock of gaudy waterfowl. Now she could look at their bright petticoats and their circles of rouge high on each cheek, and feel nothing but indulgent pity.

Francis followed her eyes. 'Would you have been among them?'

'Last time I was here, that's exactly where I was,' she said; and before he could hint, 'I am much better off now, thanks to you.'

He kept them at a distance, skirting the gaggle of girls. Annie was interested in his reaction to seeing others of her kind; he regarded them with a wary fascination and seemed reluctant to go near enough to attract their catcalls, but he was as chivalrous as ever. 'They make a fine show,' he said.

'In the night, yes,' she said, 'with their paint on they look well enough; but in the daytime, coo! It's a different matter.'

They walked a good few steps before Francis spoke again. 'The garden, too,' he said. 'She's a cunning old whore.'

Annie understood at once – she'd been here at dawn when the cracks showed and the paint faded, and the stark light of day penetrated the shadowy corners. For now, though, all was colour and gilt. They passed a dwarfish man in full evening dress walking hand in hand with a giantess in a blue pelisse and bonnet. There was the Moorish tower, all yellow and crimson like a barber's pole, with a fellow painted up as a blackamoor breathing fire at the top. There on the rotunda, beneath the peeling papier-mâché chandelier, a boy balanced on a vast blue ball pricked out with golden stars walked himself up and down a ramp by the action of his feet. He seemed unnoticed by all about him, for in the supper boxes and arbours with their flowers, gentlemen brayed and girls lolled against them. Everything in the rotunda was pretend – the flowers were cut from paper, the ladies were not really ladies, and the gentlemen were not really gentlemen.

Deeper into the gardens now, where comic singers sang their popular songs from rickety stages, and a Nassau balloon, brave in yellow and green silk, rose above their heads, the gas lamps roaring like lions and the ladies shrieking from the basket. A hermit in a plaster grotto, with a beard as false as his cave, called out to them and promised to tell their fortune. Francis waved him away, but tossed him a coin. The old man bit it, then fixed them with his bright eyes and said, by way of thanks, 'Stick to the path, young sir; young miss!'

Deeper still, and deeper; the travellers needed refreshment and shared a cup of rack punch and a plate of ham cut as thin as paper. An open-air orchestra played with more enthusiasm than skill; French clowns cried 'Houpla!' as they somersaulted across their path. At length they came to a firework ground cunningly knocked out of sounding board to resemble long arcades of arches and a jade-topped tower.

'It is meant to be Venice,' said Francis, with amusement in his voice. 'It is the Piazza San Marco in Venice.'

Annie heard the warmth in his tone, and saw his face in the torchlight, the starbursts of the fireworks in his shining eyes. 'Look.' She pointed to where an acrobat announcing himself as 'Joe Il Diavolo' made a death-defying descent from the clapboard tower with squibs and crackers in his cap and heels.

In search of other diversions, they wandered the long covered arcades, sawdust-strewn and lit with coloured oil lamps, peering in at the sideshows. They watched a spinning zoetrope of a racehorse, running and running in an eternal steeplechase against itself. They peered into a stereoscope machine, and watched slide after slide of a fat woman taking off her clothes; more flesh was revealed with each photograph, click, click, click, and they laughed when in the final frame she was obliged to hide behind an aspidistra.

'Now then,' Annie said triumphantly. 'Weren't that something? A woman is clothed, and in a few clicks she's as naked as Eve in Eden.'

'It is a clever trick, I grant you,' said Francis as they walked into the night. 'But I must fight Mr Shakespeare's corner and claim that although the Vauxhall Gardens may have more to delight the senses, the play might better feed the mind.' He turned to her under the firework sky. 'Shake upon it?'

She took his hand with a smile of her own, then he folded it under his arm and they continued in perfect amity to find the way out.

But they took a wrong turn, to a place beyond the arcades, where no little coloured lamps lit the way, and darkness reigned again. Annie felt suddenly cold. She would not have turned a hair finding herself on the nightwalks a month ago. Now she felt almost afraid. She heard again the counterfeit hermit saying, 'Stick to the path, young sir; young miss,' but whether he spoke to another couple or in her memory she could not divine.

As they turned a corner by a small coppice of trees, Annie almost jumped from her skin as a dreadful, shambling baggage emerged from the dark. The woman, if woman she was, was reeking and ragged, her head without a tooth in it, her face mapped with a thousand wrinkles, her gown slashed to the waist to show two pendulous flaccid breasts, sucked dry long past. The horrid crone extended a claw and grasped Francis by the forearm.

"'Ere, I know you, don't I, dearie? Stay a while, 'andsome, like you done before.'

Annie caught a glimpse of Francis's stricken face. 'Madam,' he blustered, 'you are mistaken. I . . .' Hearing the fear in his voice, her own fled and she felt suddenly fiercely protective. He had helped her so much; very well, it was her turn.

She pulled him aside and set herself in front of the woman, chin out, hands planted on hips. 'Fuck off back to your shadows before I cut you,' she hissed. 'You ain't seen a decent man for so long, you don't know when you trip over one.'

The crone laughed mirthlessly. 'There ain't such a thing as a decent man,' she declared; then she drew nearer, and peered at Annie, her currant eyes flaring with a glint of recognition. 'Why, if it ain't Annie Stride, got up like a toff. You remember me, dearie? It's Mother. You remember old Mother? I kept an eye out for you when you was a dress lodger; watched you like you was one of me own. Go on, Annie,' she wheedled, 'go splits with me for old times. Time was you wasn't above sharing, you and that Mary Jane.' She reached out a hand to chuck Annie's cheek, but missed by a long way and stumbled a little, the gin fumes emanating from her crabbed mouth giving good reason for her unsteadiness.

Annie flinched as if the woman had succeeded in touching her. 'Leave me be,' she hissed, 'or I'll slit you from chin to cunt. I ain't one of your kind, nor shall be.'

As she backed away, she bumped into Francis; she'd all but forgotten him during this dreadful reminder of her old life, but in her flight she grabbed his arm and hurried him towards the fireworks and the light. Above the whistles and bangs she could hear the bawd shouting: 'You *are* one of us, Annie Stride. Don't matter how fancy your frock is. I remember you when you was a dress lodger, and you're still a dress lodger now.' And then she receded into the shadows, cackling with laughter.

Annie was shaking so hard with rage, it took her some moments to realise that Francis was shaking, too. She led him directly and unerringly out of the gate and into a hansom cab, handing him in as he had once handed her. Even in the lamplight she could see how white his cheeks had become.

'Don't take on, Francis,' she said. 'It's an old trick, saying they know you. She was just trying to draw you in, get you to talk to her. Make you feel obliged, like. Most times the likely young fellers that go down the nightwalks don't know who they've 'ad before and who they 'aven't.'

He tried to smile, but she could see he was shaken. For some moments he could only look from the window silently, biting his lip, consumed by some private emotion, as the carriage took them ever northward, across the Vauxhall Bridge to the right side of the river, to safety. She regretted more than ever the impulse that had led her to take him to the Gardens. What was she thinking? She had begun the evening walking marble stairs to the gods. She'd sat in the painted heavens among the cherubs, higher than all the folks below. What had possessed her to climb down the stairs again to the mortal world, and then descend lower, to the underworld she used to inhabit?

'Annie, you were . . .' Francis faltered. 'Your manner, your speech, I hardly knew you.' He shook his head slightly as if reeling from a blow. 'Was she really your mother?'

On another day she might have laughed; but just at the moment she had no laughter in her. 'No. You know I told you the story of Mary Jane? That baggage was the bawd at the cathouse. She used to get all the girls to call her Mother.' She sighed. She had thought of this period of her life earlier in her chamber – could it have been only a couple of hours ago? That moment of reflection before the glass seemed a lifetime distant, as if she had stepped though the silvered surface to another world since. She could lie, but she didn't want to. She took a breath. 'Me and Mary Jane was dress lodgers for a time. You'd parade the pavements in a pricey frock, greeting the young men and trying to get them to take you to some rough house. There's always a bawd following you, to see as you don't decamp with the dress. The watchers, as they call 'em, are always too old to work, always badly dressed. The men don't see 'em; 'cos their eyes are on stalks for the peacock, they don't notice the sparrow.'

'And that . . . *person* . . . she was your watcher?'

'Mine and Mary Jane's. Yes.'

She could see an unspoken question in Francis's eyes. She boldly took his hand. 'I don't want to go back there,' she said forcefully, 'not never again.'

He looked at her, and now he could smile gently, as if every furlong they travelled from Vauxhall put him more at his ease. 'Back to the Gardens? Or back to your old life?'

'All of it,' she said forcefully. She was desperate to convince him, but had not the words. She thought of the theatre; of the gods, and the cherubs holding up heaven. 'I want to climb the stairs,' she said. 'Only upward from now on.'

He could not possibly know what she meant, and she could not explain; yet he seemed to understand. He squeezed her hand. 'Only upward,' he agreed.

Chapter 7

Five years ago

I've got an idea of how I can get away from Mother.

I don't say anything, because there's no one to tell. I'm friendly enough with the other girls, but there's no one I'd trust. I've learned the hard way not to trust. I trusted Mr Starcross, didn't I, talked with him, walked with him, and got in a carriage with him, and look how that turned out.

No, I don't tell anyone, but in bed at night I practise a new voice. I remember back in Norfolk, there was a big house in Holkham, with a squire and a missus and a son. I remember the missus reading the lesson in church at Christmas, with a voice like crystal. I practise her voice, removing all traces of Mary Jane from Norfolk, mumbling to myself until the girls either side dig me with their elbows and tell me to stow it.

I bide my time until Mother asks me to put on the midnight dress again and go with her to the Strand. It's a fine evening and I walk up and down as I always do, with Mother following me like a shadow. I smile at all the gentlemen who look at me, but I don't let anyone take me home. I am looking for one man and one man only – a man wearing the same midnight blue as me, with a tall hat on his head and a nightstick at his side. A bluebottle.

Now, I usually avoid bluebottles like the typhoid. But tonight I march right up to him and pluck his sleeve. 'Excuse me, my good man,' I say in my best Lady Holkham voice, 'I think someone is following me.'

The policeman looks me up and down. I hold my breath, heart hammering, but when he's finished looking, he touches his hat. 'You just point him out to me, miss, and I'll tan his hide for him.'

'It is a lady, of sorts,' I say. I turn and point straight at Mother, where she's skulking in a shop doorway.

His moustaches bristle. 'Leave 'er to me, miss. You wait here.' He blows his whistle and takes his nightstick from his belt. Mother looks from him to me with poison in her eyes, as if she can't decide what to do. Then she runs, and the bobby chases her.

I have no intention of waiting here. I pick up the midnight skirts and run, as fast as I can, in the other direction.

After the ill-fated night out, when they had briefly glimpsed each other's worlds, Francis and Annie kept at home for a time.

Annie took the air in the handsome little square at the end of the row, and in the smart streets surrounding, but other than that she was happy to stay in the house. She would read and write, and even paint a little. After she had slipped backward in the pleasure Gardens, she vowed that her darker character would never be allowed to visit again. Whatever Mother had said, she was different now. Or she very soon would be.

She turned her mind to improving herself. Francis gave her leave to read in his little library, a room at the top of the house walled with books, with a domed ceiling painted in a dark blue pricked out with gold stars. The design gave Annie an uneasy jog of memory – then she remembered the balancing ball at the Vauxhall Gardens, the boy clown lurching and righting himself, walking the starry ball under his feet, never falling. She needed to stay atop the ball, too, and not fall again. She graduated from periodicals to books; she studied the moral heroines in the books of Mr Dickens and Mrs Gaskell, and found in the demure and sweet behaviour of every Dorrit and Mary and Nell a model for her own.

Sometimes, reading of these paragons, she wondered if that unguarded moment in the Gardens had tarnished her in Francis's eyes beyond redemption. But he seemed as friendly and solicitous as ever. In time she began to realise that it was *he* who had been put out of countenance; that his bohemian credentials had somehow been damaged by his reaction to the underworld. He had laid claim to that underworld as his inspiration, but his first real encounter had left him terrified. She saw him now for what he was: a deeply conventional young man from a good family, from money. He could not function in her world, and no more he should. She felt more affectionate towards him than ever. He never referred to that evening, and she was more than happy to leave it behind, to leave all of it behind. She wanted to live in Francis's world. So she kept to the good streets and the good squares, and if she ever saw a beggar or a drab, she crossed the road.

During this time, she saw a little less of Francis, for he was still working on his paintings – there was much to do, she learned, in the finishing of them: framing and varnishing and engraving, all of which he seemed to do himself. At last, though, they were finished, with Francis's name and the names of all the parts she'd played etched into little copper plates affixed to the frames. There they were, all the faithless ladies, immortalised. And every one with her face.

Then her days were her own for a time, while Francis took the ladies out one at a time, shrouded in thick felt as if they wore their travel cloaks, and handed carefully into a hansom as his escorts for the evening. She felt, foolishly, jealous of those ladies – she felt dull at home, missed her excursions with Francis and envied the fallen women who were taken on the spree in her stead. She did not know where he took them; she assumed to dealers and galleries. They always returned, and were disrobed and sent back to the Scheele's green studio with the others of their kind, a sorority of the fallen.

Then one night Francis came back with shining eyes and hauled her from her fireside chair, waltzing her round the drawing room. She danced with him till they were both breathless and collapsed together on the chaise. 'We are in, my Annie! A whole exhibition at the Royal Academy! Let us find you something to wear – this time you really will be the Queen of Sheba.'

Francis was most particular about what Annie would wear for the private view at the Royal Academy. 'You must be stunning,' he said. 'There will be other models there, but every eye must be trained upon you.'

She was surprised, then, on the appointed evening, when Eve helped her into quite a plain dress of teal shot silk, with a square neck and tight sleeves tapered into points just above her knuckles. It was a style Francis would call medieval. She glanced in the glass, a little disappointed. She looked striking, and her strawberry-blonde hair clashed becomingly with the teal, but the overall effect was a little dull. The floral wallpaper and the drapes at the window looked more ornamental than she.

There was a light tap on the door, and Francis entered, almost hidden by a bale of bright trailing cloth. He held it high.

'You gave me the idea,' he said, 'when you said that every eye followed the peacock and did not note the sparrow. Tonight you shall be a peacock.'

Annie walked forward and weighed the material in her hand. It was heavy figured silk, artfully embroidered with peacock feathers in shining threads of the brightest turquoise and emerald, and the blackest black for the eyes touched with a nacreous highlight of blue. The whole shimmered in the lamplight with an oily sheen, just as feathers might. As Francis placed the mantle round

her shoulders, she realised that it was a kind of coat, with voluminous sleeves that fell almost to the floor, terminating in crystal
tassels. The same crystals trailed from the train, giving the coat a
sparkling hem.

'No jewels,' Francis said, 'and your hair down like a bride. Let
your beauty speak.' She looked at herself in the glass. Over the
plain dress and beneath her tumble of hair, the coat was stunning.

She turned this way and that. 'Where did you get such a thing?'

'It was my mother's,' he said.

It was uttered regretfully, in the past tense, as if he missed her
– no: as if he *mourned* her. Annie was puzzled at this. She knew
little of Francis's family, but she could have sworn that his mother
still lived, with Francis's father the squire, in the big house in
Norfolk; had Eve not come directly from his mother's service there
to this house? But she did not pry, for she could not expect everyone
to leave their mother's side without a backward glance, as she had
herself.

Once Francis had gone to dress, she and the silent Eve busied
themselves with those special arts of which men know nothing.
The coat was so strong and bold that her features needed a little
definition, so Eve added a fingerful of shimmering blue turnsole
to each of Annie's eyelids, a rose blush to each cheek, a red salve
to her lips and a little charcoal to her brows.

Annie's entrance to the Royal Academy of Arts was very
different from when she had first been there some months ago.
It was now early summer, so in the balmy evening Trafalgar Square
was still light and resplendent in its fresh-cut snowy marble. She
noticed that there was another stone lion now, crouching above
the fountains as if he would take a drink. Where the cabs stopped,
in place of torches there were horns of plenty overflowing with
summer flowers.

When Francis handed her down from the hackney carriage,
every eye turned to look at her, just as they had six months before.

This time, though, they did not look to judge but to admire; they stared, they drank in her beauty, eyes wide, mouths agape. She felt the power running through her like blood. She knew now how the Queen of Sheba had felt; the queen she had never portrayed. She had known it, just as Francis had known it; the importance of making an entrance. She heard, in her head, an orchestra playing a fanfare. She climbed the steps on Francis's arm, his consort, his equal, his better. The peacock coat trailed up the steps with each tread, the crystal beads whispering behind her along with the crowd.

She saw, amid the gathering, more models, sometimes with artists, sometimes not. They had, for the most part, red hair – as was the fashion in art at that time – but theirs was gathered up or plaited demurely. There was one stunner who nodded to her from the arm of a dark gentleman with a slight complicit smile, as if conceding the game. *Well played*, said the smile.

Annie smiled back. 'Who's that?' she whispered to Francis.

'I do not know the lady's name,' said Francis. 'But she is the model of Mr Rossetti, on whose arm she hangs, and is soon, they say, to be his wife.'

Annie stopped in her tracks. *To be his wife*. This was a new turn on things and no mistake. That man was a gentleman, by his looks and bearing, just like Francis, and the redhead no more than a model. A new dream, unlooked for, unhoped for, dawned in her mind, and she had to press her lips together from the sheer secret glory of it.

In the great chamber where she'd been with Francis that other evening a world before, Annie met herself. She was everywhere, peering out from every wall, as if caught in that world between two dressing-table mirrors where the self is multiplied many times over. She was Eve in her green gown holding her apple. She was Jezebel with her braided hair and her turquoises. Then Rahab, in her simple homespun with her hair loose as a bride's.

There she was as the Whore of Babylon, the only picture in profile, her white hand holding that blasted golden chalice, the sacrificial lamb curled at her feet. And there, Lucrece, a huge horizontal canvas; she reclined in a white toga, her strawberry hair tumbling to the floor. There was Manon at her fatal card game. Then the kneeling Gretchen in her prison, a tremendously moving painting; Annie marvelled at Francis's skill, for in this grey ground of a prison cell, in the simple grey frock, he had made her hair sing in the slabbed light from the barred window, the mass of it glowing like carnelians. And yet, she must remind herself, there had been no cell, there were no bars, that was all Francis's conjuring trick – just Annie Stride in the Scheele's green room, kneeling and clutching a stuffed dove. But the dove in the painting now lived, its black-bead eyes given life by some magic of a single white catchlight of paint.

All the dead creatures – Eve's snake, Jezebel's dog, Rahab's kid, the whore's lamb, Lucrece's owl, Manon's cat and Gretchen's dove – lived again; they breathed as she did, or else were as dead as she. They were there in all canvases but one; in the painting Francis had entitled *The Girl with the White Camellias*, Annie stood in solitary state, in the bone-white dress, alone save for the noxious, beautiful bundle of dead flowers in her arms.

She squeezed Francis's arm. 'There's no creature.'

'I beg your pardon?' he said from the side of his mouth.

'No bird nor beast. In *The Girl with the White Camellias*. It's the only one with no dead creature. Why?'

Just as Francis made to answer, two men appeared at his elbow, coughing for his attention. One was elderly, tall as a maypole and jocular; the other smaller and younger, with the serious air of a clergyman. The elder spoke first. 'Francis. I congratulate you on your latest work. Wonderful, man, wonderful.'

Francis wrung them fervently by the hand in turn. 'Sir Charles, I am by no means ignorant of the fact that you have been my

champion in lobbying the Academy to accept work on these . . .
difficult subjects.' He turned to the younger man, crouching in
Sir Charles's shadow like the lion under the column. 'And you, Mr
Ruskin, have my heartfelt thanks for your kind letter to *The Times*
in my cause. I am indebted to you also for the part you played in
my being allowed to exhibit here.' The serious young man bowed.

'If *I* were to write to *The Times* and take Francis as my subject,'
boomed Sir Charles, 'I should write that Mr Maybrick Gill long
since found his technical competency, but now he has found his
passion.' He turned to Annie and bowed. 'Perhaps that has to do
with finding the right muse.' It was said with old-world gallantry.

Francis seemed to recall his manners with a start. 'Forgive me
. . . this is—'

'Oh, I know who this is,' interrupted the old man.

Annie froze and felt Francis doing likewise. She peered closely
at the old gent, with his lamb-chop whiskers and his rheumy eyes.
Had she? To her shame, she couldn't recall. She couldn't be
expected to know every bastard that had been at her over the
years; there'd been too many, old as well as young. If he'd paid
her for bed, though, surely he would not announce it in *this*
company.

'This is Eve,' said Sir Charles. 'This is Manon. This is Gretchen.
My dear, from this night forth, you are famous. You are known
to us all.' He dipped his white head to kiss Annie's hand, and
when he straightened, his eye held a twinkle.

Annie was equal to this; despite her youth, she'd spent years
sharpening her instinct as to how best to make herself agreeable
to a man. This old gent did not outface her. Her smile thawed
with relief, and she bobbed a little curtsey. 'I can't take any credit,
your . . .' She chose her words carefully, but had to stop herself
calling him Your Honour, as if he was the Beak. '. . . sir, for it was
all Francis's doing. In truth, it is less to do with my face and more
to do with his brush.'

Now the clergyman-looking fellow spoke, not as if he wished to, but as if he could not stay silent. 'There I must agree. Charles, this young lady has expressed it absolutely. Art lives in the artist, not the subject. Francis can paint a woman or an apple with equal skill and dispassion, and he has done it here.' He gestured to the great canvas of Eve and the green globe of the apple that had made Annie's hand shake and cramped and curled her fingers into a claw for an hour after each sitting. 'What has passion to do with the case? What has passion to do with art at all?'

'Everything,' interjected Francis with a short laugh.

'Precisely, dear chap,' agreed Grey Whiskers.

The younger man shook his head. 'Art is about nature, observation, truth. Passion merely muddies the water.'

'My dear John,' said the older fellow, 'you are such an old stick for one so young. Wait till you reach my age and you will learn that passion *is* truth . . .'

Forgetting all but their own argument, the three men disregarded Annie. As they talked on, she heard a low whisper at her ear. 'And what do *you* think?'

It was the girl with the red hair, who was soon to be someone's wife. She, too, had been abandoned by her consort, who'd joined the debate at full pitch, gesturing wildly like a foreigner. Close up, the redhead's skin had a sheen like the inside of an oyster, and there were violet shadows beneath her luminous eyes. She was beautiful, thought Annie, but her skin was, well, *shallow* somehow. You could see her skull beneath it.

'They don't care what you think. Not they. Not high-and-mighty Sir Charles Eastlake, nor low-and-mighty Mr Ruskin.' Annie warmed to the girl; she could hear the East End twang, and divined that her origins were perhaps no greater than her own. 'Tell you why they don't care: you ain't *you*, you're *all* these gels . . .' she waved a thin white hand at the vast canvases on the walls, 'and they can't listen to all of 'em at once, can they? What a clamour that'd be, eh?' The girl smiled – her teeth were small and white as daisy petals. 'I've not been plain Lizzie Siddal since I left my father's house. I've been Ophelia, Beatrix, the Lady of Shalott, even the Blessed Virgin 'erself.' She counted the ladies off on her long white fingers. 'Singular, ain't it? They all want you to be someone else.'

Annie smiled back. 'I'm Annie Stride,' she said, for the first time that night.

Red-headed Lizzie peered at the paintings on the wall with narrowed eyes, then turned back to Annie as if she found her more interesting. 'If you ever find somebody who knows you through and through, and still wants to be with you, stick to that somebody like glue, you hear?' Her restless green eyes settled on Francis and she jerked her head towards him. 'Does 'e know you through and through?'

'Oh yes,' Annie said, ''e knows me.' And as if she had summoned him, Francis was by her side, and the girl was gone.

Annie took her cue from Francis for the rest of the evening. When a succession of young men came to her side, all with faces shiny with soap and hair flat with pomade, but fingers stained vermilion or alizarin or some other word in the strange language of paint, he introduced her as Eve, or Manon, or Rahab, never plain old Annie Stride. With the growing mystery of her identity, her power swelled and grew like a peacock's tail. The young men lined up like courtiers. Could they get her a punch, a sherbet? Could they leave their card with her? Would she hear tell of their new idea – a series of paintings of Shakespeare's heroines, of the saints, of rural shepherdesses? The room buzzed like a hive of bees. Who was Francis's new stunner? Where had he found her? Could she be prevailed upon to sit for anyone else?

The wine flowed, the candles were lit, and with the warmth of Francis's approving eyes upon her, she beguiled the room. Three months of education united with a lifetime of charm meant that she was more than equal to every sally, returning every witticism, laughing at every joke and then going one better.

Sometime later, she did not know how late, she saw Lizzie leaving with her man. The redhead turned at the door and sought Annie's gaze over the crowd, then raised her hands. For a moment Annie thought she was praying, but then Lizzie pressed her two long forefingers together till the fingerprints blanched. *'Like glue,'* she mouthed, and then she was gone.

At home in Gower Street, Annie could not contemplate sleep, despite the lateness of the hour. She took off the heavy peacock coat at once; she did not know what to do with it, so she left it crumpled on the floor like shed skin. She put on her lavender nightgown and sat at the dressing table before her triple image. Her eyes seemed enormous, shining and wide, her cheeks rosy and hectic. She pressed cold hands to her temples. She looked like a loony.

She was not the littlest bit tired. She rose again and put on her peignoir, ready to go downstairs and find Francis – he would, she knew, be having a glass of porter and she could do with one herself – but he was nowhere to be seen. She padded about the house in her bare feet. She opened the door to the drawing room, but the fire was ash and Francis's glass was empty on the mantel. Could he have gone out again, so late? The servants had gone to bed; not even Eve was abroad, and no wonder, thought Annie – she'd looked done in when she'd answered the door not half an hour ago in her nightgown, with a candle, a long plait and a yawn.

Annie mounted the stairs again, and opened the door to the studio. The Scheele's green walls were silver in the moonlight, the crystal windows stood sentinel, the fresh canvases slept in their dust sheets, and there was no one within. Disappointed, Annie walked down the hall to her own chamber, past the ticking cabinet clock. With the sound of the pendulum in her ears, she noticed a thin rectangle of gold floating at the very end of the passageway.

An outline of a door, lit by a lamp within, a door to a room she'd never seen. Heart thudding in time with the pendulum, she walked to it and laid her hand on the cool handle.

As she opened the door, she was greeted by a cohort of staring eyes, some large, some tiny, all glass. They belonged to creatures of feather and fur, poised to peck and pounce; but – she laid her hand on her heart as if to still it – they were not predators but her old friends. Snake, dog, cat and all.

The room itself was a sort of large shelved cupboard, big enough to walk into. A gas lantern in a style she had come to recognise as Arabian burned overhead. In the gaslight, which she had seen nowhere else in this modern house, the animals' eyes seemed animate, alive. Behind the shelves, the walls were papered in an elaborate print. The ground was the deep, profound pink of raspberries, with a satin sheen. The pattern was of black-throated geese flying over camellia blossoms. The flowers made her shiver – the flowers and a memory. Now when she looked back at the creatures, it was not their animation that struck her, but their lifelessness. All of them, from the big black dog to the white dove with her button eyes, were dead, quite dead. There was a smell of death, too, some nameless chemical that had been used in their preservation but could not hide the charnel odour of decay.

She'd been had in such a cabinet once, by a doctor who kept his collection of medical curiosities in it. He had lifted her skirts, and pressed her face against a bell jar in which floated a baby with two heads. The motion and urgency of the coupling had made the little monster dance about. A cabinet of curiosity, the doctor bastard had called it. That had been a fearful place. This . . . well, evidently Francis had a cabinet, too, and in it he had stored the animals from his paintings. 'They are on loan,' she remembered him saying, 'from a friend who curates the new Museum of Natural History in South Kensington.' He must not yet have sent them back. She told herself, sternly, that there was nothing sinister here;

just storage. So why did her heart beat like a drum, why did she want to slam the door and run, and not stop till she was behind the door of her own chamber?

She steeled herself to stand her ground, and speak. 'It was a good exhibition,' she told the animals softly. Her voice sounded most peculiar. 'You all looked proper. You should all shut them eyes now. G'night.' She closed the door softly, as if they slept.

Chapter 8

Four years, eleven months and three weeks ago

It is a long way to walk to Battersea just to have the door slammed in my face. My aunt gives herself time to say that she is a respectable woman, and that I am not, before she shuts the door. I stand there for some moments, wondering what to do next. I cannot go back to Norfolk; I must make my way in London, but honestly. I make a vow to the closed door that I will never again give my body to a man for money.

It takes me seven days to give up. By that time the midnight dress is slashed and tattered; the heels have come off the fancy boots; the hat with the little net is a bird's nest. I am sopped, and freezing, and I haven't eaten anything all week except cabbage leaves from the cobbles of Covent Garden market. I looked for work; of course I did; I tried the shops first, while the dress was still nice. Then the factories as I became more ragged. But the only work I was offered in those seven days was the same work I ran from at Mother's – men offering me coin for my services.

So I give up. I take another long walk, this time with no hope in my heart, all the way to Blackfriars. You will see I know London well by now, and can find my way from one ward to another. There's only one place I will never visit again: 17 Silverthorne Road, Battersea. Mother's house.

At Blackfriars I make my way to St George's Fields, and there, hard by the church, looming large, is my destination; a place I *heard about from the girls at Silverthorne Road but have never seen. A dreadful place, but better than Mother's. Above the iron gates, spelled out in more iron, are the words MAGDALENE ASYLUM.*

At the door is a stern nun with a ledger who asks for my name. God knows my family name is nothing to be proud of: father on the hulks, mother hanged by mistake, daughter a whore. So when she asks me, I simply say: 'Mary Jane.'

It was almost as if Francis was not an artist any more. He did no more painting at this time; he never laid his hand upon a brush, and only picked up a pencil or stick of charcoal when he was teaching Annie. He had expressed a desire that she learn to draw, for not only was it one of the accomplishments that a young lady should have, it was the best way to appreciate art, to try to achieve it for oneself. But his own artistic passion had quite gone. He was like the electric, thought Annie – he had burned bright and steady, without a flicker, creating all those vast canvases in a matter of months. Then a switch had been turned, and his light had gone off.

He was happy enough, though – he did not seem to suffer any dark nights of anguish, or days of self-doubt in the wilderness, or any of the torments that she had known of when, from time to time, she had come across artistic types who had done well enough to spend a few shillings in the brothels. He was content, and polite, and equable, and his ready smile was always upon his face. One thing was for sure, thought Annie: he did not paint for money, for he always had bundles of it. No, something else drove him, and whatever it was, it was now absent.

She was a little chastened – she had hoped that *she* was his inspiration. Still, it was pleasant to know that he did not just need her for his model; that she was there for some other reason. He had not yet taken her to his bed, so he was not in her thrall sexually, but even without this enticement she seemed well ensconced in Gower Street as his companion. Nor did he seem to be seeking gratification elsewhere. On occasion he would go out alone, to his club or the Academy, but she never had the inkling that he had other romantic attachments in his life. She had never suffered from jealousy; she had, on occasion, seen a bastard take Mary Jane while still warm from her own bed. But at the very thought of Francis with another woman she burned with fury, and she was very glad he gave her no cause for such envy.

Summer had come to London, and they were at their leisure to enjoy it all. Not for them the seamy pleasure gardens of what Francis called the 'transpontine' – the world across the bridge. They stayed north of the river and enjoyed everything the best society had to offer. Francis seemed to have many acquaintances but no friends, and she wondered very much at this; that someone so handsome, urbane and agreeable should have no intimates. She could only conclude that his separateness was of his own choice. They went to many public entertainments, but kept no company – they gave no dinners, nor attended any. Francis was never seen at a companion's house, nor invited any fellow to his. Wherever they went there were nods of acknowledgement, even respect, and many greetings by name. But that was as far as their social intercourse went. They went about skimming the surface of the pond like nacreous dragonflies, but whenever an acquaintance promised greater depth, or a further engagement was suggested or an invitation given, that friendship was politely terminated.

Annie and Francis were enough for each other – they needed no one else. They would talk to others in company, but only to savour the moment when they would be alone together again. They were both absorbed in the re-creation of Annie Stride, and time spent in salons and assembly rooms seemed time wasted. She was hungry for words and would devour books as she would food; they nourished her now far more than Mrs Hoggarth's cooking. She became as obsessed as he with the eradication of the East End from her speech; she would sit for hours with the *Complete Works of Shakespeare* heavy in her lap, pretending she was a famous actress, affecting long vowels and declamatory tones. She would sit in the parlour promising her revenge on the Roman Empire or declaring love for a man dressed as an ass, with little or no understanding of what she said, only how she said it. She would happily tolerate Francis attaching a clothes peg to her nose to correct her nasal drone, or filling her cheeks with marbles to sharpen her consonants. For a while she sounded strange to her own ear, but in time she became familiar with her new voice.

She began, too, to recognise herself in the glass – she and her reflection were acquainted, assumed similarities, became one. She was as delighted as her mentor at the disappearance of Annie Stride. On their evenings out, Francis would never introduce her by her real name, ruthlessly maintaining her mystery. He received compliments on her behalf, and some of them gave her glimpses of his past – *You always have the most beautiful women in your company . . . I never see you without a stunner on your arm . . . this lady is the most beautiful of all* – but such hints seemed to have no relevance to her. She did not expect Francis to be a monk. She did not know what she expected him to be. They went about like they were betrothed – no, as if they were married. But there their conjugal illusion ended. He never behaved to her in a less than gentlemanly manner, despite their close bond and constant company. He never even so much as kissed her on the cheek. In town, he was as solicitous as a husband. At home, he was a brother. In the studio, he was her employer, and in the drawing room a benevolent schoolmaster. He was every man, but still not a lover.

She thought she understood him now. When she was reborn, when she was perfect, he would claim her. And in the meantime, she thought his forbearance made him superior to other men. He was not a slave to his animal passions, but in control of them. But at the same time she had seen a little corner of passion in him, the contorted desire on his face when he'd spent himself in front of her painting, and the memory made her shiver with anticipation of what was to come.

There was no doubt that Francis adored her. He would gaze at her when he thought she wasn't looking, as if drinking in her beauty; he would gather up great bundles of her red-gold hair and twist it round his hands as if it were as precious as spun gold. He would treat her with great affection; he was solicitous if she had a cold in her head. He would buy her trinkets, and even give her money of her own. She had never before been given money that she had not earned – by feigning sleep on a doorstep or feigning passion in a bed. He did not count it into her grubby hand like a bookkeeper – and not a penny more – nor throw it at her to pick up off the cobbles, ashamed of the act he'd just bought. He gave it to her in a little embroidered purse, a gathered bundle of tapestry with a unicorn stitched upon it. He begged her not to be offended, but to accept it should she need some trifle: pins, or ribbons, such things as ladies might sometimes find themselves in need of. But she did not buy pins or ribbons. She did not touch the money, but kept it always at her waist as a reminder of how far she had come.

She only bought one thing, and that was for Francis. They were at the Cremorne Pier, taking a promenade after dinner in Chelsea, and out of curiosity entered a small black-iron gazebo lit from within like a lantern. There sat a fellow with a screen and a candle, snipping silhouettes with a small pair of scissors. A lady also sat there, with the candle throwing her shadow onto the screen, her beau watching her. She giggled so much that she wriggled around on her chair and her shadow blurred until the artist was obliged to beg her to be still. Annie looked on with fond contempt; *she* would not have moved a muscle, such a model was she now. As if he had sensed her watching, the artist swung round in his chair and beckoned her with an inviting hand. 'Miss?'

Annie shook her head. 'Not I,' she said. 'Him.' She squeezed Francis's arm. 'Go on,' she said. 'Sit for him.'

The giggling miss rose, clutching her shade in her hand, and pressed it into her beau's glove; he gazed at his lover where she lay in the palm of his hand and promised fervently to have it framed. While this touching pantomime played out, Francis took her place on the stool before the screen with a faintly quizzical look.

'Sir,' said the artist, 'be good enough to face the parakeet there.' There was a sad-looking blue bird wired to one of the struts of the gazebo, so the subject would present a perfect profile. 'And if you please, smooth your hair back a little from your forehead.'

Annie crossed her arms and smiled. 'That's it, Francis,' she teased. 'Nice and still. Boot's on the other foot now.' She could see his silhouetted lips on the screen bulge and flatten, as if he smiled, too, then he straightened his face.

She had thought he might fidget and complain, but he was an ideal model, sitting as still as stone, looking at the stuffed parakeet, the parakeet looking back at him with black-bead eyes. She admired his profile – he was without doubt, she thought, one of the finest-made men she'd ever seen, and she'd seen plenty. The artist's cutting hand was a blur, the little scissors flashing as he worked. It seemed just moments before the shade was finished and the artist handed it to her. It was a perfect miniature, Francis to the life: the curl of his hair, the tilt of his nose. She paid the shilling from her own purse, and pressed the image into Francis's glove, just as he had seen the giggling miss do.

'It's nothing for one who has given me so much,' she told him.

He looked at the shade in his hand and smiled at it. 'But Annie,' he said, 'it is everything. You have given me back myself.'

He looked oddly intense, and she was not sure of his meaning. 'Were you lost, then, Francis?'

'I think so. But now I have you to inspire me,' he said seriously. 'A painter is nothing without his muse.'

But it was now full summer, and Francis still showed no sign of picking up his brush. If Annie had just made his acquaintance, she would not even have known that he was an artist. The door of the Scheele's green studio remained closed. No colourmen came to the back door with pigments, no carpenters arrived with wooden struts. Francis Maybrick Gill might have been any ordinary gentleman.

They continued to go out in the daytime, to the parks, or the regatta, or the tennis, enjoying the delights of the season. Francis cultivated the mystery that surrounded Annie. He would take her out to see the world, and took the phrase to its most literal extremity, for that summer there had been constructed an enormous globe in Leicester Square, built to represent the earth, with painted plaster casts of every country. This miniature world was nonetheless so vast that patrons could go inside it while comfortably keeping their toppers on their heads. A fairground of helter-skelters and trapezes sprouted in the shadow of the plaster globe, and Annie, from the giddy heights of a swing, felt that the world was at her feet.

Francis took her to the assembly rooms, to hear concerts, and she was spellbound by a piece called 'The Arrival of the Queen of Sheba'. The music rose in her throat like tears, and she thought of how she'd walked in to the Royal Academy that second time, in the peacock coat, and felt like a queen. He took her to the theatre again; 'No more Shakespeare,' he joked, and they went instead to the new productions at the Lyceum. Once, when they were in the audience for Mr Planché's *The Mysterious Lady*, the lights went up at the interval and the audience turned around with a hubbub of chatter, craning to see something, shading their eyes with gloved hands, peering through their opera glasses. Annie, in the stalls, turned round, too, to see what they were staring at. Had royalty entered unannounced? Then they began to clap, and she realised that they were applauding *her*.

Francis sat back in his chair, smiling broadly. 'Strike an attitude, Annie,' he said. 'Give them what they want.'

So she stood and struck a pose and kissed her hand, at which a great cheer went up. She sat again, perplexed and gratified.

So much for the world of theatre, but Francis and Annie moved in the art world, too; Francis's world. Annie saw Lizzie Siddal again and thought she looked more dead than alive. She and Miss Siddal were two faces of the moon; and as she waxed, Lizzie waned, wan and thin. 'I think Miss Siddal is unwell,' she said to Francis, feeling oddly guilty, as if she was responsible for the diminishment. 'Really? I thought she looked remarkably well. But,' he added rapidly, 'there is only one woman to delight my eyes.'

Annie kept her ears and eyes open and learned a little of this world of Francis's, of the politics between the artists and the Academy, between the Academy and the establishment. She learned of the movement that was on everybody's lips, the Pre-Raphaelites, words that seemed to her as complicated as the concepts they represented. The movement was exciting and contro-versial and Francis was considered to be at the leading edge of it. And if he were, then she was there with him at the vanguard, the most famous model in London and yet unknown in essentials. Calling cards would pile up on the silver salver in the hallway at Gower Street like playing cards on a gaming table, but Annie never returned the calls. Out of loyalty she sat for no one but Francis. Her fame grew; she would hear herself talked of wherever she went.

'You must see this miraculous girl of Francis's . . .'

'Who is she?'

'A stunner, that's for sure . . .'

'Yes, you must see Francis's stunner . . .'

'Where did he find her?'

'Christ knows . . .'

Annie would look at Francis, and Francis would look at Annie, and they would share a smile. Sometimes a photographer would approach her and ask Francis if he could take an image of her, as if she were his possession. She would stand still for the exposure with a serious expression, and was never impressed by the resulting dour monochrome image, which seemed to bear much less relation to the reality of herself than the portraits that Francis painted of her. The photographs appeared to be curiously dead, the image of a moment passed. She never liked the things; but Francis bought a few of the plates and brought them back to Gower Street. Annie never saw them on display, and supposed that he tucked them in his cabinet of curiosity, with all the other dead things.

Sometimes they would walk home from their evening entertainments, in the light summer evenings, on the broad, well-lit thoroughfares of Regent Street or Russell Square. Once, when they passed Euston station, they saw an advertising hoarding lit by lamplight. Annie took a second look – she could have sworn at first glance that it was Francis's painting of herself as Eve. There was the vivid green background and figured dress. There was an approximation of her face, graphic and formalised, and her red-gold hair swirling about her head in a stylised pattern. But in her hand, in place of an apple, was a green bar of soap.

Below, the ornamental lettering shouted: 'Give In To Temptation!' and went on to extol the virtues of Pear's soap. Annie took a sideward look at Francis, fearing that he would be angry – his Eve was now so famous that even the soap-peddlers mimicked it – but he only laughed. Nothing could displease him at present; the whole world amused him. 'Well, it is art of a sort, I suppose,' he grimaced, 'and however it might offend our sensibilities, it proves one matter beyond doubt: that you, my dear Annie, are the toast of London.'

The toast of London. Annie had begun by thinking she was special, that she had some purpose on the earth. Her father assisted this impression when he picked her out to con the gentlemen on the doorsteps of the East End with her red-gold hair and her angel's face, leaving her plainer siblings to beg for coin. Then he'd procured her ruin in the upper room of the Old George and she'd thought herself mistaken. There was no mark of destiny on her; she was fit only for the gutter. Now she'd been raised up again, and felt exceptional, and extraordinary, and all the long words that Francis had put into her mind and her mouth.

She was passionately grateful to Francis. She had come across, from time to time, those who had offered her redemption – do-gooding ladies who had thrust pamphlets into her hand, pamphlets that half the girls couldn't even read; dodgers in dog collars who'd sermonised at her. She'd never worried about her soul like some of the Irish girls did, never yearned to give up being a working girl – she'd just wanted to clamber up the ladder a bit. She and Mary Jane and just about every girl they knew had dreamed of a man to set them up in their own house – a captain of the guard, or a minor noble – so they could stay at home, safe and warm in their jewels and their gowns, just waiting to be visited.

If Francis had asked her to be his mistress, she would have jumped at the chance. But he did not ask. She had the benefits of a kept woman without having to give of herself in return. He never preached at her, like the priests in the street; he would hold forth in a general way about the ills of society, but he would never judge. Nor was he a hypocrite – some of the priests, she remembered, would hold her arm a bit high and rub their hand against her breast, all the while telling her she was no good and should repent. She presumed that Francis had some scruples that prevented him from taking her to bed. It seemed that he was that rarest of things – a decent man. And just as he was schoolmaster and patron and friend to her, likewise she seemed to live as many personas for him as there were women hanging on the green walls of the studio. Pupil, chaste mistress, quondam wife; whatever she was, she was his.

They might have continued thus forever, but for an unexpected visit.

It was late at night, after the servants had gone to bed. Annie heard a knock at the door and came awake suddenly, because the sound reminded her not of polite society taps, or the tradesman's knock and whistle, but of the times that old Hebrew landlord of hers had come for the rent. Rapping and loud – it was the knock of trouble.

Bowering opened the door in his nightcap. There was a brief low-voiced conversation on the doorstep – she could hear none of it but knew that the butler was attempting to refuse admittance to such a late visitor. Then she heard the visitor's voice, commanding and immovable, and she knew that he would win the day. Sure enough, he was conducted into the hallway, and in the light of Bowering's candle she caught a glimpse of the latecomer: a giant of a man with a bristling moustache, fine leather gloves and a coat of discreet ginger check. He took off his bowler as he crossed the threshold, revealing a lion's head of blonde hair. He was closely followed by another man, younger and darker and thinner, dressed in much the same way.

As if he were a man who knew when he was being watched, the blonde giant looked up and saw her on the stair. She froze where she sat, heart leaping, feeling inexplicably guilty; but the giant only nodded grimly and followed Bowering into the drawing room with his man at his heels. Her heartbeat subsiding, Annie sat and listened, straining to hear. She did not dare creep down to listen at the door, but at this distance she could distinguish no words, only sounds. A booming, low voice, questioning, probing. Then Francis's voice, smoother and higher, solicitous and soothing. Convincing? She never heard a third voice at all – the small, slight man was presumably only listening, the same as she.

She waited for perhaps fifteen minutes, her joints stiffening in position and her feet chilling on the stair. The sickly smell of the camellias on the hall table rose to her nose and turned her stomach. At length the drawing room door opened once more and the blonde giant emerged, taking his bowler and gloves from Bowering without a word. He looked up at Annie again, this time with an oddly sympathetic expression. He opened his mouth as if to speak to her, then shut it again and left, the smaller man following him like a shadow.

After a long, long moment, Francis appeared and walked across the chessboard hall. He looked, she thought, oddly checkmated, as if he had found himself in a corner. He, too, saw her concealed on the stairs, and his footsteps stuttered. Then he ducked his head and mounted the carpeted steps, passing by her without a word.

Annie felt as though she had been slapped. It was the first time in their acquaintance that he had ignored her, and she felt cold without his regard, as if the sun had gone in. It was how the bastards used to look at her after the act, as if she wasn't there. She got up and mounted the stairs, slowly.

Francis went into the studio and she followed him, hesitating and unsure. It took her a moment to realise what he was doing. He was touching his brushes for the first time in weeks, collecting them up in his hands like spiky bushels of wheat. What she'd thought was an occasional table lay open with a gaping mouth – it was a trunk with brass bounds, lid thrown open, and he was filling it, rapidly, with his brushes and pigments and palettes.

'You're leaving?'

'I'm going to Florence,' he said shortly.

'Who's Florence?'

He laughed, much more like the old Francis. 'Florence, Italy,' he said to the trunk as he packed.

Her heart contracted. 'What about me?'

She saw her life in London without him – she would not, of course, be able to stay on in Gower Street. Could she model for others, after the sensation she had created? Perhaps she could get a job at a milliner's or a costermonger's. Or would she inevitably slide back into the life she knew best and hated most? She had nothing here without Francis – he had raised her up like the trapeze they had seen at Leicester Square so she could see over the top of the world. She did not know what they were together, but she did know that without him she would be back down in the gutter.

Francis stopped what he was doing and came to her. 'My midnight visitors helped me see what I need to move forward in my work,' he said slowly.

'Francis, who were those men?'

'That was Sir Charles Eastlake and Mr John Ruskin. They have been my patron and sponsor respectively at the Academy. They advised me on how to begin painting again. They counselled me that I have my muse; now I need the right canvas to throw her beauty into relief. Italy, Annie, where it all began, centuries ago, before Raphael.'

She tried to unpick this. 'What are you saying?'

He took her by the shoulders. 'My dear, *dear* Annie. I am saying that you are coming with me. If you will?'

His eyes clouded briefly with doubt. She looked into his handsome face, and her heart bloomed. It was not right that he should look so anxious. She had to make him smile again. Of *course* she would go with him. 'Yes, I will.'

And the smile returned. He was all fire and enthusiasm, like a child at Yuletide. 'Go and collect your things.'

'Now?'

'Now.' He laughed aloud with the fun of it. 'We must catch the boat train in the morning. I will order Bowering to bring the packing cases, and send Eve to you.'

Many hours later, after she and the yawning, dead-eyed maid had folded and tissued her gowns, her peacock coat, her muffs and bonnets and pelisses, Annie fell on the bed, fully dressed and ready in her travel cloak, for a brace of hours' sleep before the hansom came to convey them to the boat train. In the half-land between sleep and waking, she was back at the Academy in the peacock coat, talking with Lizzie Siddal. The red-headed girl was walking towards her, but her hair was floating as if in water, spread around her like sunrays, flowers tangled in the strands, swimming, drowning, like Mary Jane. Annie's train rose up behind her like a peacock's tail and spread high and wide, and everyone turned to look.

Two men approached her. The old one kissed her hand, grey moustaches tickling. 'I know who you are,' he said.

The redhead with the floating hair said, 'They don't care what you think. Not high and mighty Sir Charles Eastlake, nor low and mighty Mr Ruskin.'

An old man, tall like a column; a young man, small and in his shadow. Then she saw the gentlemen from downstairs, the midnight visitors: blonde and dark, two moustaches, two bowlers. Both the same age.

Suddenly Annie was wide awake, cold with certainty.

Whoever those men downstairs had been, she thought, they were not Sir Charles Eastlake, nor Mr Ruskin neither. She pressed her hands to her stomach below her stays, from where the feeling seemed to emanate. She might not know who Francis's midnight visitors had been, but she did think she knew, after all those years on the street, a couple of policemen when she saw them.

PART TWO

Florence

Chapter 9

Four years, eleven months, two weeks and three days ago
The first thing the nuns at the Magdalene home did was to mark
me as one of their own. I went into a hot little room where a small
nun was poking the fire whilst a tall one looked on. I was warm
for the first time in a week, so I almost didn't mind when the tall
nun grabbed me and tore the sleeve from my left arm.

The second nun approached me with the poker. I wriggled and
screamed like a sow, but the tall nun simply clamped her hand over
my mouth, and as the red-hot tip came nearer, I saw that the poker
had a little glowing M on the end. It was a brand.

The tall nun's grip was like iron and there was nothing I could
do as the smaller nun pressed the M to the top of my arm. The
pain made me bite down on the nun's hand until I tasted blood.

For the first few days the brand was so painful I couldn't bear
clothes on my arm. It bled, and wept, and the M puffed up an
angry red.

On the fourth day, the scab came off, a perfect little M in my
hand. I assumed the brand was my initial, until I saw that all the
women had the same one. They couldn't all be Mary Janes. I real-
ised it had to stand for Magdalene, whatever that word meant —
maybe the founder of this fell place had been a Mr Magdalene.
Then one of the women pointed to the M on her own beefy arm
– well healed; she'd been here years. 'M is for Malefactor,' she said.
'It means you've done wrong.'

Annie leaned over the parapet of the Ponte Vecchio, the warm stone pushing her stays into her ribs. Perhaps the stone, and the stays, and the ribs would stop her heart from rattling in her chest like a pudding in a copper. Sweet bells sang from every tower and seemed to ring in her blood. She could not quite believe that a mere six months ago, on a freezing January night, she had stood thus on Waterloo Bridge, before she'd climbed up on the parapet, and looked out at the steel water, the silver moon, the pewter buildings. The cold metals of London seemed not just a season away but a world – they could be outposts on a cold star. How could it be that in a brace of days – a boat train, a boat, a night train – she could be in this place, that the world could be so changed?

The sun itself was too bright to look at, but it gilded everything below like a smith. Florence was made of gold, the same summer gold they wrought in the little shops Francis had showed her as they'd crossed the bridge. The old bridge was made of stone as yellow as sunflowers. The cathedral had a burnished bell for a dome, St Paul's through the looking glass. The riverbanks were lined with ochre palaces, and the hills about studded with little villas and churches like nuggets of amber. Even the water below – which even the most poetic heart could not describe as crystal, being as it was at a summer low and the colour of sand – glittered brightly with borrowed light.

And there was a greater difference than all of these. Then, on the Bridge of Sighs, she'd been alone in the world. Now, she was not. Francis Maybrick Gill stood beside her, carrying her parasol, for she'd wanted nothing between herself and the Florentine sun.

'This is where we fit. Exactly,' he declared. 'We have come home.'

She turned to look at him. He was leaning on the parapet, too, his hat dangling perilously from his hand over the river. He was wearing a suit of cream-coloured cloth, with a loosely knotted silk tie the colour of summer lawns. A lock of his hair had been blown from its fellows by the summer breeze, and fell over his clear grey eyes. While she had been looking at the view, he had been looking at her.

'You are a Florentine, Annie, not a Londoner. You have a *quattrocento* look; you are a veritable Botticelli. I was so right to bring you here. This is your canvas.' He looked from her to the view. '*Here* is the Eden we sought. It will be as if the Bow bells never rang and the rain never fell.' He waved his hat to the old city, as if in greeting. 'Here are more musical bells! Here is more clement weather!'

He squeezed her hand and her new ring bit into her finger. He'd given her the ring on the boat, as they'd watched the white cliffs recede and England with them. The weather was grim, the winds howled and the grey seas boiled, but Francis's mood, which had been dour and silent on the boat train, had lifted as the cliffs slid from sight, and with a new freedom he'd slipped the ring over her glove. 'We are to travel as man and wife,' he'd cried against the wind. 'In France, at the customs house, you will see that you are listed on my papers of conveyance as Mrs Maybrick Gill.'

Annie's heart had thumped – she'd thought of Lizzie Siddal, the model who was all set to marry her artist beau, but Francis had soon deflated such expectations.

'I want to assure you that this deception does not proceed from any motive of mine besides expediency,' he'd bellowed in her ear. 'Once the notion of bringing you to Florence had seized hold of me, I felt I must accomplish it as soon as I may – I could not countenance the thought of the summer slipping by while we waited for your travel papers. This ring is nothing but a bit of theatre; nevertheless, I want you to know my regard for you. See, the ring itself expresses it.' He'd lifted her hand between them, held it tight against the wind and pointed to each stone. 'Ruby. Emerald. Garnet. Amethyst. Another Ruby; and a Diamond. R. E. G. A. R. D.'

She'd turned the ring on her hand and smiled. 'It's lovely,' she'd yelled into the tempest.

'It was my mother's.' The wind had snatched the words and thrown them away as soon as they left his mouth, so it was hard to hear his tone. Was there affection there, nostalgia? The howling gale drowned out all nuance. But Annie had been jolted, once again, by the fact that Francis spoke of his mother as if she was in the past. He'd said many times that she lived in Norfolk. One thing was for sure, she must have been a generous lady, to give first her peacock coat, and then her ring, to a girl who was nothing but a common bangtail. She wondered then if Lady Maybrick Gill knew to whom her bounty was given, and was sure she didn't.

In the charming painted café of the Gare de L'Est in Paris, Francis had spoken more of their new relationship. 'The Channel was the dividing line,' he'd said. 'Now that we are on the Continent, there is an opportunity for both of us to make a new start. You must make an especial effort with your bearing' – she'd sat up a little straighter – 'and your elocution now that you are travelling as my wife. Florence nowadays is as full of English – and, I'm afraid, Americans – as it is of Florentines, and it would not do to give yourself away.' Annie had looked up at the frescoes above the tinkling café tables that depicted the train travelling to wild landscapes that had been painted above the teacups of civilisation. Then she'd looked at Francis fondly, and nodded, hiding her smile in her cup. In London he'd thought himself quite the rebel; perhaps travel made folks more like themselves.

And now here they were, man and wife, standing on an old bridge in their new Eden. But with the Florentine citizens bustling at their back, the boys pulling handcarts piled high with bright fruits, the beggars, hands out, babbling their droning rosaries of unending pleas, Annie wondered briefly if the two of them would be enough. They were very *English*, Francis and herself. They were strangers, alone together.

'D'you know anybody here?' she asked.

'You mean, do I have any acquaintance in the city?' Francis asked. She was so used to his correcting her that she had long since ceased to mind. 'No. But I have been here many times. It is the city I love; the architecture, the art, not the people. In Florence, everything of interest is dead,' he declared. 'And there's nothing so wonderful as death to make one feel alive.'

Annie thought of Mary Jane, and thought she understood what he meant. 'Where will we live then, if you have no kin here?'

He turned his back on the river and crooked his arm for her. 'I have found just the place. Let us return to the carriage. I will show you.'

How different was their carriage from a hansom cab! It had an open top, but was more like a haywain than a brougham. The sun beat down, and their legs were entangled in their trunks, piled in all anyhow. A driver in shirtsleeves and braces in place of a Norfolk jacket, and a battered straw hat in place of a bowler, conveyed them up the hill with not one word of English. Annie was mightily impressed, but not entirely surprised, that Francis seemed to have a command of the local language; and while the two men conversed in the well-rehearsed roles of master and servant, she was free to look about her.

They were climbing out of the city on a steep road of ochre dust, curving in an S shape and lined by tall trees the shape of spearheads and so dark green as to be almost black. The houses and churches receded to leave only green hills, with the occasional building appearing for a moment behind silvery trees, only to disappear again like children playing hide and seek. One house was so beautiful that she gave a little cry, and Francis smiled at her delightedly. 'You like this one?' he said. 'Let us take a look.' He spoke in dialect to the driver, and the carriage turned up a little driveway; the house disappeared for a time, as seemed the habit of the buildings hereabouts, then revealed itself suddenly in all its glory. It had a handsome marble façade on three floors, with an arrangement of fine arches on the lowest level and seven square windows set high along the frontage. There were garden terraces, shady groves, and lilac flowers growing on the face of the stone. Annie clapped her hands as the carriage slowed.

'I am glad it pleases you,' said Francis as the cart stopped. 'Shall we go in?'

He handed her down and walked her up the gravel path. Close up, Annie could see that the frontage of the house was half devoured by ivy. It was the most attractive building she had ever set eyes on, even when she'd been up the Burlington or down the Mall. This was a new idea of what houses could be – big, certainly, but not grand. Beautiful, but not imposing. It was a place that could be a home.

She paused at the threshold. 'Is this *your* house?' she asked, wide-eyed.

'It is,' he said, smiling. 'I acquired it for its happy situation, but also, I admit, the name.'

By the door was a wooden plaque, with dark ornamental letters burned into it like a brand. Annie made out the words *Villa Camellia*.

She pressed her hand to her stays. She suddenly felt a little queasy. Perhaps it had been the long travel, the winding drive, the hot sun; but she could not escape the notion that it was the flower's name that had turned her stomach. She shook off the idea with her bonnet. It was ridiculous to think that a bloom could harm her – not even the flower itself, but the mere name, writ down. She took Francis's proffered hand and followed him towards the doorway. This was a home – her home.

The big oak door was studded like that of a castle, and Francis opened it with a huge iron key straight from a fairy tale. The interior could not have been more different from Gower Street.

In place of an entrance hall was an airy atrium, with white and terracotta tiles on the floor. The walls curved in, as if corners had never been heard of in Florence, and a bright chandelier with crystal brilliants hung high over a three-legged table set about with white and gilt chairs. The walls themselves were remarkable; seeming to be made of white porcelain decorated with tiny enamelled flowers connected by figured golden leaves. Annie felt as if she was in an upended china teacup.

A few steps led down to the very different world of the kitchens. Here there was rough white plaster on the walls, from which Annie could swear she saw filaments of centuries-old straw poking out. The bricks of the house were exposed in attractive arches, and there was rough grass matting on the stone floors. There was a long table with a dozen wooden chairs, and a big rough wooden bowl upon it filled only with lemons. On the wall, wide wooden shelves held a collection of fat pottery jugs, in every shade of cream and brown, from huge stone cider jars to tiny porcelain creamers. Here, too, was a collection of shining copper kettles and large brass cans. A wooden stove lay ready piled with logs, and a candelabra that seemed to be fashioned from a cartwheel hung above the table.

'Yes,' said Francis ruefully, following her eye, 'I am yet to determine if there is a geyser for hot water. They don't, I think, have the electric either. But we will make do admirably.'

Annie wondered who, exactly, would be making do, and badly wanted to ask if there were servants; but she heard herself framing the question, and laughed. She had come a long way from St Jude's Street.

The drawing room was a comfortable room at the bottom of the house with broad terracotta cross ribs, painted with faint frescoes that seemed to have rather a lot to do with grapes and wine and little to do with religion. There were white porcelain reliefs on the walls and thick cinnabar rugs on the floors; easy chairs and settees upholstered in tapestry, and oil lamps with burnt-orange glass.

Compared to the well-appointed rooms of the lower floors, the stairway was simple, not even as grand as Gower Street. The steps were rough-hewn stone, and there were no banisters, just a handle of rope. The staircase was not enclosed, but open to the rest of hallway. The skull of an ibex hung on the wall at the turn, eye sockets staring, curly black horns against the plain white plaster mimicking the spiral of the stair. Annie eyed it with suspicion, thinking she would not like to pass it at night, but Francis chucked it on its bony cheek as he passed, in a friendly fashion.

On the first floor was the bathroom, a place of great interest to Annie, for now that she was used to regular bathing, she was sure she could not go back to her grubby old self. The tub of white marble was placed right in the middle of the room, the walls were white, and the ceiling between the wooden beams was painted a bright cerulean blue. On the walls hung a collection of pictures, all different, a blur of subjects in different-sized gilded frames. Two dormer windows opened out onto the vista, and Annie anticipated, with a little leap of excitement, that she would be able to see the copper dome of Florence's cathedral while she was taking her bath.

Along the halls was an airy morning room painted duck-egg blue, with map chests enamelled in blue and white, plenteous floor space and two big south-facing windows. 'My studio, I think,' said Francis, 'and here a place to rest from my labours.' 'Here' was a large divan as big as a bed, with a dark gold canopy. Annie eyed it longingly, for the bed on the wagon-lit from Paris had been hard and narrow, and she had been unable to sleep well from excitement and the rocking of the train.

She wondered where she would be sleeping – a house like this must have dozens of bedrooms to choose from – but did not have to wonder long. The very next room was a bedroom as simple as the stair had been; the bedding was costly, but plain and white, and the dark-wood bedposts terminated into spindles like chair legs, and had not a canopy. Above the bedhead hung a dark icon of a pallid Madonna. Perhaps the Florentines thought there were more important things to do than sleep – by the look of the house, eating and entertaining were matters considered to be more worthy of decoration. Still, the room was bigger than the one she'd shared in St Jude's Street, with twelve siblings sleeping in one bed.

She felt Francis's hand on her arm. 'This will be your room,' he said.

Your room. There it was – the answer to the unasked question that had been hanging in the musty, hermetic air of the unopened house. Your room. So they were not to be man and wife in the bedroom, too. Annie was perplexed. She walked forward and trailed her fingers over the white cambric coverlet. There was a chill feeling of discomfort just below her ribs – could it be disappointment? Francis had given her his mother's ring on the boat, he had said they would live as man and wife, even that she would take his name.

'My room?' she asked. 'Am I not to . . . be with you?'

He looked at her fondly. 'It is usual in the upper reaches of society for a man and his wife to have separate bedrooms,' he said gently.

Annie knew he spoke the truth – she had, on occasion, been with a bastard in his room while his wife slept next door. She thought of that simple animal act that seemed so necessary to all the bastards in London that she and a thousand other girls had made a living from it. The act that could compel a man so strongly that he would spend himself in a Haymarket whore just a wall away from his sleeping wife. But now it seemed she'd happened upon the only man in the world who could live without it; and of course, in the weather-vane way of life, he was the only man she'd ever wanted.

Did the fault lie with her? What more must she do before he would claim her? How could she improve further to be worthy of him? She wondered what he was waiting for, and wanted more than anything to ask him. She had been used to plain speaking in her former life, but here and now she could not bring herself to ask the question. She was afraid that if she forced him to express his reasons out loud, this Florentine dream would pop like an insubstantial iridescent bubble in that Pears advertisement, and he would send her away. So she held her tongue, straightened the coverlet where it had been depressed by the touch of her hand, and followed him from the room.

Francis led her down the stairs again to a dining room with plastered walls the colour of sand, a vast oak table with too many chairs for just the two of them, and a candelabra made of inky wrought iron hanging low over the table from the vaulted ceiling.

As they acquainted themselves with the Villa Camellia, Annie learned that the beauty of the house lay not just in the architecture and the decor, but in the details. It was clear that Francis had prepared the villa personally for his retreat from London; his hand was all over it, and his face, too: a tiny miniature of his silhouette hung in a gilt roundel on a vivid purple wall. Closer inspection showed that it was the shade she'd had snipped for him at the Chelsea pier. There were other touches as well. A goblet of bright blue glass sat on a windowsill, reflecting and rivalling the sky. An onyx bust of a bearded scholar stood by an open window, facing not the room but the view, and favouring the residents with the back of his head. And the view was definitely worth looking at, thought Annie, Florence spread out below like the magic carpet she'd once seen at the Whitechapel Empire, all glittering and glowing and seeming to float above the valley floor. But for the moment, she, too, turned her back on it.

'Francis,' she began tentatively. 'When did you purchase this villa?'

His grey eyes flickered. 'About a year ago,' he said. 'It has been a long-held dream of mine to come here and paint.'

'And you furnished it yourself?'

'Yes,' he said, running his finger along the casement. 'I had to prime the canvas on which I was to paint my muse.' *But you didn't know me then*, she wanted to say; but once again she kept her peace. He touched the same finger to her cheek. She and the villa, both his property.

Last of all, he showed her the largest room she had yet seen. Here was something to rival the view, for every inch of the wall was covered in books. Wooden shelves stretched from floor to ceiling, with slim dark-wood ladders to reach the volumes. Halfway to the ceiling was a balcony with a walkway, holding more shelves, as if there were not enough books already in the place. In the centre of the parquet floor was a desk with a topper of tooled leather, and a pile of scrolls with legal seals of oxblood wax. The ceiling was the teal of twilight, picked out with gold quatrefoils, and a pair of large glass doors opened onto a garden that stretched as far as the eye could see.

Annie walked about the room and, because for her to see was to touch, she trailed her fingertips over the bound spines. If the Florentines did not care about their sleeping quarters, here was where their hearts beat strong. Francis followed her on silent feet.

She said, wondering, 'I ain't never . . . *have* never seen so many books in one place.'

He placed his fingers reverently on the spines, where hers had been. 'Yes. This library is another reason why I took the place. Mind, the Florentines did not always set such store by books as they do now. In medieval times, they made a great bonfire of books in the Piazza della Signoria; the plume of flame was so high you could see it from this house.'

Annie was shocked. 'Why would they burn books?'

'They did not like what they said.'

Now she stroked the spines sympathetically. Books were the principal delight of her new life, and she hoped to continue her love affair here.

'Are there English books?' she asked hopefully. 'Mr Dickens made some journeys here, I think. Remember, in *Pictures from Italy*? I read some at home. That is, in London.'

He caught the slip. 'Annie; my dear Annie. *This* is our home now.'

It was uttered with such finality. 'Are we never to return to Gower Street?' She'd been happy there; granted, it was a world away from that other London in which she'd been born and raised, but it was still London, still England.

'Not for the foreseeable future,' he said decidedly.

Francis had been planning his departure for a while, had meticulously furnished his villa, but for Annie it was a shock; she felt like a flower uprooted and replanted in sunnier climes, struggling to find a footing in the foreign soil. She could not have been part of his original plan; *a year ago*, he'd said, he'd taken the villa a year ago. Had it been her arrival in his life that had prompted such a precipitate departure? But she'd been with him for six months before they'd left.

'Francis,' she asked. 'Why did we leave London so fast? Was it to do with the men who called?' Would he tell her, this time, who those night-time visitors really were?

'It was,' he said. 'Sir Charles and Mr Ruskin suggested that I have a change of scene, to develop my work further. They proposed that I paint my next series in Italy, and explore the art of the Renaissance, before Raphael.'

She had caught him in a lie once, and now he had lied again. His reasons might be valid, but whoever had told him to come here, it was not Eastlake and Ruskin. But he was frowning, and once again, she got the sense that she should leave well enough alone.

'Then Mr Dickens should stay in London, where he belongs,' she said.

Francis brightened immediately. 'Him and all the other home-spun authors. Ah: here.' He mounted one of the little ladders, pulled down a book and blew a plume of dust from its spine. 'I knew there would be a copy. At the time of that Bonfire of the Vanities, it was forbidden to own one. Now it is practically against the law not to.' He leafed through it. 'Here's something with more meat to the tooth than your Mr Dickens. A work that survived the fire – it was singed, but was plucked from the flames by a courageous hand, then reprinted, and translated, thank the Lord.' It was the first time she'd heard him invoke the Almighty. 'A Florentine writer for our Florentine sojourn.'

He handed her the battered book. 'Dan-tay,' she sounded out. '*The Divine Comedy.*' She looked up. 'Is it funny?'

He laughed. 'Not even slightly. Read a little of him. There are three parts: *Paradise*, *Purgatory*, and the *Inferno*. I will hear you tonight.'

He sat at the great desk, now unquestionably the squire of the place, and began snapping the seals on the indentures with rapid fingers. Sensing that she had been dismissed, Annie laid her hand on the handle of the glass door leading out to the garden. As she crossed the threshold, Francis called; 'Start with the *Inferno*. Everyone does.'

She walked out across a broad terrace where four chairs sat about a little iron table. The arrangement was completely shaded by glossy leaves and delicate wisteria trained over an arrangement of ropes to form a living canopy. There was a walkway with three elegant arches open to the view, and under their shelter lay two basketwork chaises longues, draped with Chinese shawls. From the arches led the garden pathway, and she walked down it, the gravel crunching beneath her feet, the Dante under her arm. She settled on a low wall to read, but the sunshine dazzled her, the view enticed her, and she was up and wandering the alleys. There could be nothing in the book Francis had given her more worthy of attention than that which was around her.

The house had been a wonder, but the garden amazed Annie even more. She had been raised in cramped streets, and wondered how different she might have been if she had been brought up here. This garden was the size of a London park; but there were no broughams driving, no couples promenading, and no boys sailing their wooden boats on the lake. It was just for her. The sheer space of it was, besides its beauty, the most striking feature. That a man could own such a place in Florence, and a place like Gower Street, too, that he was disposed to leave empty indefinitely, was staggering. She wondered, not for the first time, just how rich Francis was.

A grove of silver-leaved trees grew by the house, with hard green fruits that were cool to her touch. Terraces with low walls enclosed formal gardens with tended paths; crumbling urns stood patiently on the corners while green lichen devoured them. There were no flower beds here, such as Annie had seen in the London parks; everything was green, with herb gardens and trees and shrubs in pots and planters. Formal statues stood in graceful attitudes, some of the ladies striking poses Annie recognised from her own sittings. She supposed that artists were magpies, borrowing what they liked the look of. The stone ladies were all peaceful, beautiful, serene; the men were the same, standing happily, gazing off into the distance, not seeming to notice they were naked. These nameless men and women, some carrying harps, some grapes, some gourds, were the gods and goddesses of this land. She did not know any of their names, but she knew they had nothing to do with the Almighty she had met in St Matthew's Sunday school; the God of Bethnal Green.

A delicate fountain plashed in the centre of all, the cascade falling onto lily pads as big as dinner plates. There was no drama here – everything was gentle and peaceful and beautiful – but beyond the fountain, down the hill, the garden turned a little wilder. Here the flowers that were absent from the formal gardens flourished unchecked. Mossy steps wound up and down and round, half covered by turf, having been worn down over hundreds of years by hundreds of feet.

Annie walked in the footsteps of the long dead, the sun heating her back, the pads of her fingers bubbling with sweat on the buckram cover of the book she still held. Alien insects chirruped in a rasping rhythm, as if the garden had a heartbeat. Here, too, there were statues, but in stranger forms than the polite deities of the terraces: a massive stone foot, a torso overgrown with ivy, the curl of an outsize ear propped by a ruined arch. And most beautiful of all, in a little bosky dell lay a stone face overgrown with rock roses, nose to chin only, with the upper half cracked away. The fragment was bigger than Annie herself. She ran her fingers over the vast contour of the mouth – she could have seated herself comfortably on the bow of that lip. Here angry giants had been and gone, she thought, and broken the little humans, or turned on each other and left their own massive features decoratively scattered about. And now they were harmless, dismembered – even the tiny shoots could bring them low, and even a giant's foot could not outrun the ivy or the snails that left silver trails over each toe.

Beyond the broken face lay a little wilderness of tangled trees, and Annie ventured inside, seeking the welcome shade, and walked a mossy path to a natural arch formed by twined branches. At the end of the path was an old stone bench; the wilderness stopped abruptly and Florence was spread below her, taking her breath away. She sank down on the bench and gazed and gazed. If she listened closely, beneath the buzzing of the bees and the birdsong, she could hear the bells. Francis had called it Eden, but Annie knew different. This was Paradise.

She laid the Dante beside her on the warm stone bench, breathing in deeply. And there, suddenly, in amongst the foreign, was the familiar. The view still glittered below, but it was now tarnished, as a scent rose to her nose. She was in a strange land, but there was something she knew, something unpleasantly familiar, something sweet and deadly. She turned and found a branch of blossoms curving towards her, curling about the stone like a man trapping a girl at the bar. She recognised the fat blooms, some red, some white; too many petals, too sweet a scent. It was as if the sun had gone in. They were camellias.

Chapter 10

Four years, ten months and one day ago

The Magdalene Asylum is hell on earth.

The nuns are as mean as demons and beat us with blackthorn sticks if we don't work fast enough. We launder all day until we are asleep where we stand. It is as hot as hellfire in the laundry. All the women cough from the steam, or worse, from the lye we use on the stains. Some of them cough up blood on the white linens, and are beaten even harder for that. And after a day of work, there is no bed to fall into; at night we sit on chairs sleeping against each other, held upright by a rope.

At least Mother would check our teeth for holes and our hair for lice, and would dose us if we were ill. And she would feed us well – the clients liked plump, healthy girls, it was why we got good money. At the Magdalene Asylum we are on starvation rations – a ladle of watery gruel once a day. And at Mother's there was at least a bed to rest in, even if there were a few of us sharing.

It's when I start to look back at Mother's all wistful-like that I realise how bad the asylum is. One day a woman dies right next to me, and is taken away by the coroner's man like a bundle of laundry. 'That's the only way you'll leave here,' says the woman on the other side of me. Then I become frightened, frightened for my life, and if I hadn't been, I never would have done what I do next.

When the laundry carts come in the morning to collect the washing, I get in and pull the sheets over my head. The linens are piled on top of me and I think I'm going to suffocate there and then, and the *coroner's man can have me directly. But just as my lungs are bursting, the wheels begin to rumble – we're leaving the cobbled yard. As soon as I reckon we're outside the gates, I burst forth like a spirit from the tomb, scattering my winding sheets on the cobbles, and before the launderer's man can whip me, I run as fast as I can over St George's Fields, right over the grass where the cart can't follow. And then, when I can't run any more, and with a heart like a stone, I walk back to 17 Silverthorne Street, Battersea.*

There were only three intruders in Francis and Annie's paradise.

The driver who had brought them up the hill on the first day always seemed to be at their disposal; he would sit and snooze and smoke under the shade of the cypresses. He was obliging and grovelling and always on the lookout for a tip, his eyes bright as two coins. He was called Michelangelo, a name that seemed to amuse Francis. 'And the gardener, I suppose, will be called Leonardo.'

The gardener was not called Leonardo, whatever Francis's suspicions might have been, but Gennaro, a silent ancient who was Michelangelo's father. The trio was completed by the old man's wife, Nezetta, who seemed to be cook, housekeeper and maid-of-all-work combined. This lady, who must have been as ancient as her husband, walked up and down to the nearby market in Fiesole with her string bag laden with bright produce. Her smoking son never seemed to oblige her with the cart, nor did she seem to mind the walk. Despite her age, she was a tireless worker, for as well as cooking three meals a day, she washed the linens, made the beds and cleaned the villa. Nezetta was as voluble as her husband was silent; she talked all day, in a nonstop stream of dialect, whether there was anyone present or not. At nightfall, which was well beyond dinner time in these summer months, the three of them departed in the carriage, unless Francis required Michelangelo for some evening's entertainment; in which case the old couple would hobble down the road, leaving their son to smoke in the twilight.

During the sunlit days, Gennaro crept round each path and flower bed achingly slowly, like the hour hand of a clock, stopping frequently to lean on his rake. Annie never heard him speak, and he did not acknowledge her presence except to fix her with his rheumy eyes and touch two gnarled fingers to his straw hat.

But she was not lonely; Francis was all the company she needed. Besides, she had a new adventure to preoccupy her, for every morning, after breakfast and before the sun became too fierce, Francis continued her cultural education by introducing her to Florence.

Michelangelo would drive them down the ochre road, the cold morning mists that lay like a shroud over the golden city lifting in the bright sun, the sky a hot high arc of stinging blue, the city glittering below. Annie learned to identify the copper dome of the Duomo, the lantern tower of the Palazzo della Signoria, the little white church at San Miniato. Florence tugged at her heart in a way London had never done. She loved it, she truly loved it.

On their very first morning as residents, Michelangelo drove them not to the old bridge, but to the great stone square of the Signoria, and deposited them at the foot of the very lantern tower Annie had seen from the Fiesole road. It was early; the pigeons fluttered in the cool morning shadows, and giant stone statues half emerged from the dark. The citizens of Florence rushed about with their carts and barrows and crates, but the tourists set a more sedate pace, wandering about in twos and threes, clutching instruments of leisure, not work: easels and watercolours, postcard prints, guidebooks. 'Look at them,' cried Francis. 'I have never seen so many copies of Murray's guide to Florence, not even in a pile at the bookseller's.'

Annie smiled at them; she was disposed to like everyone at present, even these hapless English. 'We're no better,' she remarked.

'Oh but we are, Annie. We *live* here.'

She looked at him. Florence suited Francis; his clothes were lighter, his hair was lighter, too, in the sun, his skin was darker, his grey eyes brighter. He laughed and smiled even more than he had in London, if that were possible. He was impossibly handsome; but he looked just as English, to Annie's eyes, as the other tourists. She wondered how she looked; Francis had said that she fitted here, but in her new sprigged muslin with creamy lace flounces and duck-egg blue ribbons, and with her hair bound behind her head as befitted a gentleman's wife, she felt very English, too.

Francis took her arm, and they skirted the stone bowl of a fountain. 'We are to become part of this city; not just as residents, but to join with centuries of artistic tradition.'

There was an odd permanence to the statement, and Annie wondered again how long they would be here. Francis had never spoken of London unprompted since they'd left, and seemed to have forgotten that they had ever lived there. But she did not mind. He had already given her so much; and now he had given her Florence. At that moment she did not care if she never saw London again.

'Show me,' she said. 'Show me *everything*.' She turned about like a child, laughing and scattering pigeons. 'Where do we start?'

'That is an easy question to answer.'

The Uffizi gallery was not yet crowded, and they were practically alone with the painting. 'This,' said Francis, 'is where all the trouble began.'

Annie gazed at the canvas. She could not see anything troublesome about it. A serene-looking Madonna, blonder than she, was seated with a book. At her knee, the Christ child played with a cherub, or a baby saint, the same age as he, passing a little golden bird between them. The trio were placed under a milky blue sky, with feathery trees behind them untroubled by wind, and fluffy white clouds in the sky.

'Look at the sweetness of the face, the triangular composition, the softness of the colours, the intimacy between the group,' said Francis with palpable distaste.

'Why is this painting so bothersome?'

'It is by Raphael,' he replied.

Light dawned. So this artist, this very one, had given birth to a movement. The Pre-Raphaelites, those clever young men who hung about the Royal Academy, as ever-present as their canvases, in velvet coats the same hues as their colours.

'It was not this painting necessarily, but this artist, what he began and what came after.' He turned to her. 'What do you think?'

She considered. 'I think it's charming.'

'Charm,' he said. 'Precisely. I could not have said it better myself. Charm: gentle, placid, moderate charm. The most damaging word in all of art. If a man tells me my paintings are charming, he might as well spit in my face.' He shook an admonitory finger at the Madonna. 'Do not mistake me. I was seduced by charm myself in my younger years. Do you remember, I told you I used to paint nymphs and dryads, in a style a little after this. But I woke up,' he continued, his voice growing louder. 'Art must bleed, and for that we have to go back, before Raphael. Come.' He strode away, in such a passion he almost forgot to wait for Annie.

She half ran after him, down more painted corridors, and for the rest of the morning was taken from painting to painting, the little bronze plaques on the frames scrolling back and further back like a time machine, from fifteen-something, to fourteen-something, to thirteen-something. She saw what Francis meant – the compositions were simpler, less realistic, flatter. 'The drama here is not found in the composition, but in the execution. For the Mannerists, those who came after Raphael, composition is king. They forgot how to *paint*. Here you are in the dark days of medievalism, Annie; ask yourself how *these* paintings make you feel.'

The answer was simple. The early paintings made her feel frightened. They reminded her of the stern icon at the head of her bed. She knew they were Christian, but they seemed heathen with their bloody gods. The colours were earthy, immediate; the bright red of blood and muscle and sinew jumped forth as if in relief from gold backgrounds. There were no more tender Virgins and babes, but bleeding Christs hanging from their crosses like the carcasses in Smithfield market. To Francis they were clearly superior to the later paintings they had seen, but Annie had liked the pastels and the swirling veils, the pretty cherubs and snowy doves. Whatever Francis said about valuing her opinion, she did not want to give it. She did not want to differ from him to the extent that he might lose respect for her. She tried to frame something diplomatic to say about this butcher's shop of a room, but could think of nothing; one painting (by Duccio, Francis told her helpfully) was so visceral that she had to turn away from it; and it was then that she saw someone watching her as intently as Francis studied the painting.

He stood at the end of the long gallery, utterly still. The hour had grown later, so more people populated the gallery, standing between the watcher and Annie. He was tall, at least a head taller than Francis, with long dark curls that fell about his stern face. He was wearing a military-looking jacket in dark cloth, double-breasted and buttoned. He seemed to carry a sword at his side, as English gentlemen had long since ceased to do. One hand rested on the hilt, and the other . . . wasn't there. The man had only one arm; the other was absent, the empty sleeve pinned up at the elbow.

Annie was well used to being stared at by men, and a little of Bethnal Green surfaced. She stared back at him hotly, more directly than any lady would ever do. He was not outfaced, but nodded his head a little in greeting. Annie's hand groped for Francis's arm. She whispered, '*Francis.*'

'My dear?'

He turned to her, and she to him, then back to the one-armed man. But, like a phantom, he had gone.

'Annie? Are you quite well?'

She shook her head a little, scanning the people in the gallery, desperately looking for the man. She smiled weakly back at Francis. 'I am a little tired, perhaps.'

He took both her hands and carried them to his lips. 'You are quite right. Please forgive me. We have seen quite enough for our first morning. We will continue tomorrow.'

The square outside the gallery was now in full sun, and she took a huge breath of the fresh air, almost a sigh of relief. Her mind felt overloaded with images: all those crucifixions, all those weeping women, the Marys by the cross, the Thomases thrusting their hands into the bloody gash at Christ's side, the five wounds multiplied so many times over in dizzying arithmetic that she could not reckon however hard she tried. And somewhere in that crowd on Calvary, that strange one-armed man, tall and stern and dark, watching her.

'Let us walk a little,' said Francis, 'and take the air.'

In the bright daylight, all dark thoughts of staring strangers fled into the shadows, receding like a nightmare in morning. Of course, thought Annie, a ghost could walk in that bloody Smithfield of a gallery, but in this heathen city he had no powers. For despite the great churches and the constant bell song, Florence, she felt, was not a Christian city. There were other, secret gods here. It was a place of symbols and signs – the whole city was a grand cipher giving sly clues to its own history. They worshipped a bronze boar, the Porcellino, which was enthroned in the holy place of the gold-loving Florentines, the market. And as they walked, Francis would point out other heathen graven images: the stone balls of the all-powerful Medici, the leaping dolphins of the Pazzi, the moons of the Strozzi, the lilies of the city herself. Annie saw the stone balls as often as the cross, as if city and church played each other at a hand of cards, and the city was winning. She began to look for the symbols on her own account, and point and pull on Francis's coat like a child when she spotted one.

The statues that stood sentinel in the Piazza della Signoria were gorgons or Greeks; they had nothing to do with Christ either. And of the stony figures who stood sentinel in the niches outside the Uffizi – well, thought Annie, there wasn't a bishop nor a parson among them. They were all writers, painters, thinkers. It struck her, suddenly, why Francis fitted here. In London she had only seen him comfortable in a room – in his own studio or parlour, or the grand salons of the Royal Academy. Here he fitted in the very streets themselves; here a painter could be king. As for herself, she was not yet sure. As Francis had said on their very first day here, she resembled the models she'd seen in the Uffizi, with these very stones and towers as their canvas. But in some corner of her heart she was still a Bethnal Green bangtail, and she didn't see any painted girls lolling in doorways, or leaning bare-breasted from windows. Either the girls all collected in some distant district, or Florence had no room for the likes of her and Mary Jane.

'Look,' said Francis. 'There's our old friend Dante.'

Annie stared up at the man who had written the book that Francis had plucked from the thousand-and-one on the shelves of his library. Dante had a long face like a shovel and a nose that curved down above a mouth that did likewise. On his head he wore a cowl and a wreath of leaves. The strong sun etched deep wrinkles into his face.

'He don't look happy.'

'He was heartbroken,' said Francis. 'His great love, Beatrice, died.'

Annie looked at the stone face with new eyes. She'd thought

Dante a frightening schoolmaster, but now she saw grief in the stern landscape of the face. 'Poor fella.'

Francis seemed so consumed by an idea that he forgot, for once, to correct her. 'Yes; and no. His loss prompted the greatest work of his life.' Now she looked from the stone man to the flesh-and-blood one, and not for the first time, she wondered if Francis's inspiration was not love, but loss.

They waited for Michelangelo in a shady café under broad canvas awnings. The Florentines had evidently discovered that it would benefit them to know how to make tea, so Francis's desire to drink something more typical was foiled. 'What did you learn this morning?' he asked over the cups.

Annie thought carefully. She knew by now that she must offer an opinion, but she decided to speculate upon his. 'I think you liked Jesus when he was dead better than when he was alive.'

He gave a little bark of laughter. 'What can you mean?'

'Well,' she stirred her tea, 'you preferred the pictures of the crucifixion to the babe in the stable.'

He thought about this for a moment. 'Perhaps you are right. Perhaps there is more to be said about life when a person is *in extremis*.'

She frowned a little.

'Perhaps there is more truth in death,' he explained, only making her more confused; but she was not to be confounded for long.

That first morning was the beginning of the next stage in the education of Annie Stride. In London, Francis had honed her speech and her deportment – the outward shows of respectability. Now came the last but most significant step in her re-creation: he improved her mind. She was certain, with a sick anticipation, that once he had remoulded her completely, he would take her to his bed and consummate what he had made. She was the most perfect expression of a muse, the logical conclusion for a man whose very profession was to create a masterpiece out of raw materials – something from nothing. One of the first words she had learned in Florence – Renaissance – seemed to fit perfectly. Francis was reimagining her, stage by stage, moving to the completion of the process he'd begun when he'd first set pencil to paper to draw her as Eve. Now she was being fully coloured, with three dimensions and five senses. She was being reborn.

Francis took her to see another embodiment of the Renaissance: the milky, towering statue of David in the Piazza della Signoria. Annie gazed unashamedly at the stern, handsome fellow. Used to nakedness, there was nothing to shock her but his size. 'If that is the David,' she said remembering her Sunday-school days, 'how big is the Goliath?' And Francis laughed.

Then they walked to the cathedral ('*il duomo*,' said Francis) to inspect, close to, the vast dome that she had seen from the hill. The dome had been designed by someone called Brunelleschi, who had solved the problem of how to build it. Up close, it was not copper like a bedpan, but a series of tiny terracotta tiles rounded by white marble, while the church itself was a startling multicoloured coffer of red and white and green. She gazed at the doors of the baptistery with its reliefs cast of pure gold, and wondered how many sovereigns they would make. They went to the convent of San Marco to see, as best as they could in the incensed gloom, Fra Angelico's *Annunciation*; and to the Medici palace to admire the much more dazzling colours of the *Procession of the Magi*. At the Ospedale degli Innocenti they saw Luca Della Robbia's china babies floating on their blue roundels, like little white Christs lying on their mother's cloak. And they went to Santa Croce, which, Annie had come to realise, was something of a place of pilgrimage for Francis.

There at the old church, revolving under the frescoes of the Bardi and Peruzzi chapels, she learned the difference between

Giotto and Ghirlandaio. She listened while Francis explained that master and pupil had begun and then completed the break with Byzantine art, effecting a move towards realism. She did not understand everything that he said, so she looked discreetly in her reticule for Ruskin's *Mornings in Florence*, and read instead his opinions of what she was seeing. *You shall see things as they are,* she read. *Easy or not, it is all the sight that is required of you in this world – to see things, and men, and yourself, as they are.*

Annie was a fair judge of literature by now, and a niggling thought, unwanted and left over from London, intruded in her mind. She struggled with the notion that the author of this personable and immediate prose could be one of the blunt bowler-hatted men who had come to Gower Street the night before their departure for Florence. Yet Francis had insisted, not once but twice, that the author of this very guide book had been one of those midnight visitors. For just a moment, she was conscious of a darkness as creeping and choking as the London fog, something sinister that had chased them from London to be consumed in that tempest in the English Channel. But there was too much to see, too much to do, to trouble herself overmuch; Florence consumed all of her five senses, and left no room for her to wonder whether, and why, Francis had told her the smallest and whitest of lies.

Francis was a good guide, shifting, as ever, between companion and schoolmaster. He always sought her opinion, and demanded that she give him one in return, however ill-formed she might think it. His own opinions were very decided. He would rage about Raphael and his followers, and invite Annie to see the realism of Giotto and his school. In the Capponi Chapel, he fumed against Pontormo's *Deposition from the Cross*, with its swirling lines and pastel colours, until the sacristan shushed him. But in the church of Santa Maria Novella he stood respectfully before Masaccio's *Holy Trinity* as at a shrine, and praised the stern straight lines of realism in a voice as low as prayer, so that she had to strain to hear him. In the Palazzo Pitti he loudly rubbished Raphael's whimsical *Madonna della seggiola*, making the tourists stare, but Giotto's *Ognissanti Madonna* in the Uffizi, depicting exactly the same grouping of Virgin and child, soothed him into silence. Annie reflected that she had never seen him as angry at anything in life as he was at a painting, and wondered, with a sudden chill, what it would be like to have such rage directed at her.

Her education was not a trial to her, as she might have expected; in short, Annie took to art. In this world that she'd always thought belonged to the toffs of the Royal Academy, she found so much that was familiar. She would look into the eyes of Botticelli's *Primavera* and see an expression well known to her; a working girl's look, half bare-faced cheek, half promise. This world belonged to Annie as much as to anybody else. She knew little – though she was learning fast – of composition, or chiaroscuro or character, but she felt a kinship with the paintings that she felt no one else in the crowded gallery could share. Ever since that first visit to the Royal Academy, the night that Francis had pulled her back from the brink, she had felt a connection with those girls of canvas. She looked on the models as she would the sallies on the street – she might size up their clothes or their hairstyles with a friendly rivalry, but essentially she was one of them. And of course for those who told darker stories she had an extra empathy – she felt the same for a biblical woman punished in some street in Jericho as she had upon reading in the newspaper about the noseless prostitute found in the Fleet. There was always heartfelt sympathy coupled with an inglorious nugget of relief that it wasn't her.

She also felt for those models a physical connection that spanned the ages. She wondered if the Madonna of the Goldfinch had found it odd to hold a dead bird in her lap, as she herself had done as Faust's Gretchen. She wondered if the pagan Venus, rising naked from her shell, had strained her hip to stand in what Francis called the *contraposto* style, as Annie had as the Whore of Babylon. She wondered if Parmigianino's Madonna of the Long Neck had, in the third hour of a sitting, inwardly screamed with pain as she held her head at that crooked angle, and thought only of sundown, when the light was gone and she could stop and stretch that famous throat of hers.

In front of the earlier paintings, those dark and bloody medieval panels, Annie forgot the models and was lost in the scene. Before Duccio's Christ she did not even consider the male model who might have been tied to a yoke to give the right placement of his arms. She thought only of the agony of the Christ and the five bleeding wounds, and the weeping women. This proved Francis's point more effectively than all his ranting. These older gods were real to her, just as they were to him.

Chapter 11

Four years and ten months ago

Mother examines the brand at the top of my left arm. M for
Magdalene. M for Malefactor. M for Mary Jane.

'Don't show it to anyone, you hear?' she orders. 'It marks you
out as one of the rightless. The fellas will do up their trousers and
leave. That M means you're no better than a slave, and no one is
obliged to pay a slave.'

She has no need to tell me. I'll show the bastards anything – all my
holes if they want – but never the top of my left arm. Never again.

'No matter.' Mother takes my chin in her hand. 'You're as pretty
as ever – or you will be when you've been fed. We'll have you back
in a dress tomorrow. I'll keep you, but you'll have to work off the
other dress you took before you get a wage again. And Mary Jane,'
she calls me back, 'whilst you are out, look for likely girls. We lost
a couple when you were gone. Went on jobs and never came back.'
In explanation she draws a grubby forefinger across the folds of
her throat. 'Pretty ones we need, and young, too.'

I find a girl on my very first day back on the job. She is walking
up the Haymarket like an angel come to earth; a skinny angel with
a cloud of red-gold hair, looking from side to side with her huge
amber eyes – tiger eyes. She is running from something – I know
that look; it was stamped all over the faces of the women in the
Magdalene Asylum as surely as the brands on their arms. She is
running from a man. Close to, she looks ravenous – I watch her

gazing at the pie man as if she'd eat all his pies and the arms that
hold them, too. I can't buy her a pie, for Mother keeps me short;
instead I buy her a sugar mouse. She looks at it like it is the Crown
Jewels and me as if I am the Queen.

'What's your name?' I ask.

'Annie,' she replies. 'Annie Stride.'

Annie saw the one-armed man everywhere she went.

At first, she saw him in the Uffizi, day after day; in the Vasari corridor, on the stair, in the loggia. She was aware of two things: that he was watching her, and that she felt a marked reluctance to tell Francis about him. She was not afraid of ridicule, but she was afraid of the man, as if there was some dark complicit secret between them. She looked for him, unconsciously, whenever she entered the cool halls of the gallery, with something suspended between hope and dread. She never failed to see him, he never failed to bow to her, and when she looked back, he never failed to disappear.

After the first few days of their summer in Florence, which she and Francis spent only in the Uffizi, she talked to herself sternly. The fellow was not following her. He must work at the gallery. There were countless priceless artefacts and paintings there; perhaps he was some sort of guard for these treasures, which explained the military-looking uniform. She put him out of her mind until she and Francis began to visit other churches and galleries, and he was there, too, and she began to doubt the workings of her own mind.

At the Ospedale della Pietà he lurked beneath the black arches and the white babies floating above like cherubs. In the Baptistery he leaned on the mosaics like a relief of some Byzantine saint. In the Piazza della Signoria he stood as still as the statues. She even saw him at the Belvedere fortress, high above the Boboli Gardens, standing like a sentinel, and watching, always watching. At last, in the Palazzo Medici, she resolved to speak to him; but as she approached, he vanished once more.

Much as she loved Florence, Annie began to feel palpable relief when Michelangelo came with his cart. She felt she could evade the gaze of the one-armed man on the drive into the hills; he could not follow her to the villa. She experienced a lightness with the breath of the hill breeze, for the midday sun in Florence was oppressive, and up here it was a little cooler. She would always take down her hair in the carriage, letting the mass of it stream behind her like a pennant. Francis would raise no objection, but would regard her with what she remembered from London as his 'painting eye'. He had not painted a jot since they'd arrived in Florence, and never spoke about why, but she sensed the time was at hand when he would actually pick up a brush again.

Back at the villa, they would pick at one of Nezetta's delicious lunches out on the loggia, for the heat was fierce enough just then to melt away appetite, and only the faintest of breezes stirred the wisteria that shaded them. After their fill of sausage and cheese and wine, when the faint bells sounded the Angelus in the distance, they would rest, as was the way of the Florentines. Annie would sit on the loggia with a book. She found the Dante hard going, and even the shortest stanza had the power to send her to sleep. She would doze under the pergola, undisturbed by the whispering olive trees, while Francis would stretch out on the golden divan in his studio.

And in the afternoon, Francis began to paint again, just as she'd known he would. The fire that she had thought doused in London burned in him once more. His fingers twitched all morning as he looked at the varnished canvases, the frescoes, the panels, as if he could not wait for the afternoon. It was those Magdalenes that did it, thought Annie. When he saw those Magdalenes, he was compelled to paint his own.

Annie first met the Magdalene in the Uffizi.

There she was, at the foot of the cross, a girl with red-gold hair, a girl just like her. It was hours, perhaps days after the crucifixion. Everyone else had left, that cast of characters she'd seen at every crucifixion and every deposition from the cross. Jesus's grieving mother, that other Mary, had long since shuffled away on the arm of her son's dearest friend John, to take the apostle into her home and live out her days with him, tending him and feeding him and trying to find in him the son she had lost. Martha and Mary of Bethany, the sisters of Lazarus, had stayed long enough to assure themselves that their particular family miracle was not about to happen twice. The priests, too, assured that the King of the Jews was no longer a danger to anyone, either in person or ideology, had gone back to their rituals. Even the soldiers, their grisly work done, had returned to their dice and their whores. They would look among those camp followers for their favourite, the pretty one with the red-gold hair. But she would not be there – she was carrying out her lonely vigil at the feet of the only man she truly loved.

For once, Francis did not ask what Annie thought. She knew he could see how moved she was. He did not recount to her the story of Mary Magdalene, the whore who had anointed Christ's feet with priceless ointment from a white alabaster jar, and dried them with her golden hair; who had fallen in love with those feet and then the rest of the Lord; who had followed him for the rest of his short life, and had been the last to leave him at his death. She remembered the story from Sunday school in Bethnal Green as well as if it was her own. The Magdalene's story *was* her own.

'Would you like to see more?'

She turned to him, eyes afire. 'Yes.'

From then on, they sought out every Magdalene in the Uffizi, he as keen as she. It was a treasure hunt – they were looking for every skein of red-gold hair, every crimson cloak, every alabaster jar. Annie was seized by a quite violent excitement. If a woman who had been a common whore could be revered like this, depicted by great artists and immortalised on the walls of the Uffizi, why couldn't she? She followed eagerly as Francis led her to the Magdalene of Lavinia Fontana, who had painted her kneeling in ochre; of Sandro Botticelli, who depicted her standing in blue; of Carlo Dolci, who showed her seated in cinnabar. She did not know the names of the artists, nor trouble to remember them. They meant nothing to her; only the Magdalene mattered.

She became fascinated by the differences, the similarities. Sometimes the Magdalenes carried the alabaster jar, sometimes not. Even the jars were different – long like a goblet, squat like a pot of cold cream, as many different shapes as the Marys themselves. Sometimes the women reached out to touch Jesus; sometimes he warned them off and told them not to touch. Sometimes Mary had dark hair and red lips, and then she reminded Annie of yet another Mary, in both appearance and occupation. But almost every time she wore a crimson cloak, the badge of the profession they shared.

They left the Uffizi then, and walked through the golden city to the music of the bells. The Virgin Mary was ever present, built into the corners of the alleyways, looking down from her shrine, shielding her precious baby from the fierce sun with the crook of her arm. Annie, feeling thankful for something she could not quite define, took a marguerite from her hat, and laid the yellow bloom on one of the plaster shrines with a careless hand. But the flames of the votive candles were invisible in the glare, and she felt the hairs singe on her arm between her muslin sleeve and her glove. She felt as if the Virgin had burned her on purpose, because she wasn't pure enough to lay the flower. She wrung her wrist and glared accusingly at the mother of God; that lady looked blankly back with a cool stare as blue as her cloak. Annie turned her back. She wasn't interested in Jesus's ma. That other Mary, now, in the crimson cloak, *she* would not have singed Annie's sleeve in judgement. Annie would have lit a candle for the

Magdalene; she would have lit a whole bonfire of them, and gladly burned her arm off doing it. Because that other Mary would have understood her.

Francis was just as excited as Annie about their new discovery. At the end of the day, he took her back to Santa Croce and walked straight past the Giottos, stopping instead in the large cloister to gaze at Rosselli's *Jesus and the Magdalene in the Garden*. There, in that peaceful place, he came at last to the conclusion that Annie had reached directly after breakfast. He turned to her and cupped her cheek. 'It is you,' he said. 'They are all you. All the Magdalenes. I have found her, Annie, the next great subject of my work; I will invite her in from the shadows, from the bottom of the cross or the corner of the tomb. Let us put the Magdalene in the centre of the frame.'

Today they could hardly wait for Michelangelo's pigeon-scattering arrival in the Piazza della Signoria. They sat hunched impatiently in the carriage, blind to the peerless views of the hills. They ate their lunch too quickly for good manners, drumming their fingers on the table as Nezetta served them agonisingly slowly, chattering all the time. Neither one of them could contemplate rest. Instead they went together to Annie's dressing room, and ransacked the wardrobe for something crimson.

But of course crimson was not a respectable colour, and Annie, in her guise as Francis's wife, would not wear any such thing. In the end, Francis ripped a silken curtain from above the garden door, and Annie, as swiftly as when she used to work, wriggled from her gown and ruffled out her hair. His creature, she waited, heart beating strongly, as he unlaced her petticoat a little at the bosom and wound the crimson silk about her body so that the folds fell to his satisfaction. He bundled her mass of hair over one shoulder, so that her throat was clear and bare.

Then he walked away from her, unlocked a corner cabinet and

took out a white object. For one moment she wondered if he had some strange sexual fetish that required an instrument of chastisement, but he carried the thing to her as if it were as precious as the Crown Jewels and placed it in her hands. It took her a moment to realise what it was: a white alabaster jar, cold and smooth and heavy.

He drew frantically all afternoon with broad, sweeping strokes until his snowy shirtsleeves were covered in charcoal. He opened the shirt and rolled up the sleeves. He ran his hands through his hair, swept the back of his hand over his forehead until he was covered in coal dust like a navvy. His hair was awry and fell in his eyes, but she had never seen him more handsome. She fixed her eyes on the white jar, on the heavens, on whatever points he told her to. She exposed more breast or less, moved her arm or her foot, swept stray curls away from her face. She was his slave for that afternoon. She would have done anything he told her. What they were engaged upon that afternoon was a kind of consummation: her modelling, his painting. She wondered if they would be one before nightfall, if the time had come when he would take her body as well.

In the meantime, they were bound up in a joint endeavour to honour the Magdalene. For that afternoon, Annie was the Magdalene, the Magdalene was her. She was all the women since the Bible began who had been subject to the bastards for their livelihood until they found one man who was merciful; one man who mattered.

Annie's limbs ached – Francis had forgotten to let her rest – but she did not care. At last, when the light was failing and Nezetta had called them for dinner three times, he laid by his charcoals and came and knelt in front of her, almost reverently, holding her face in his filthy hands. 'I must wash and you must dress,' he said, with an attempt at lightness, as if jolted by what he had awoken in himself. 'And then, we will dine as a respectable couple.'

And they did, but as she looked at him across the table, clean and lovely once more, his hair combed back and his tie knotted properly, she smiled a secret smile. Everything was the same as it had been at lunch, the food savoury, the wine sweet, Nezetta chuntering in Italian as she clattered the dishes and ladles; but something had changed.

Taking her cue from Francis, she took the Dante out to the loggia after dinner with their wine, as was their custom. The night was as warm as a summer day in London, and Florence was lit below by a thousand candles and gas lamps, a golden constellation. But Francis, on the other basket-weave chaise longue, was looking in the opposite direction, to the hills behind the house. 'She is watching over us, the Magdalene,' he said, 'and blessing our endeavours.'

Annie followed his eyes to a pinpoint of light, high in the hills above Fiesole. 'What d'you mean?'

'That,' he said, pointing to the golden star, 'is the convent of Mary Magdalene. The nuns pray and do their good works in her name.'

She looked at the burning light, well pleased with the thought that Mary Magdalene was still making a difference in the world.

Later, she read to him, and thought that he slept after the exertions of the day; but after a time he sat up and closed the book, removing the volume from her lap and replacing it with his head. Was it, she wondered, a sign? She stroked his hair tentatively, feeling the weight of his heavy head in her groin. Her heart began to beat faster, with something like fear. 'Let us go to bed,' he murmured. In the shuttered dim of the passageway outside her door, he leaned close and she readied herself for a kiss. But he merely murmured a chaste 'good night' in her ear and went to his chamber.

In her room, the dark was warm and oppressive. Annie stripped off her clothes impatiently, with no care for the garments, and left them on the floor like a shed skin. Naked as she was, she went to the open window, her body burning like the Bonfire of Vanities that was once seen from this house. Her room looked on to the hills, and there, high up, she could see the convent of Mary Magdalene, a bright pinpoint. She stared at the light till her vision blurred.

Chapter 12

Four years and four months ago

Me and Annie Stride are going into business for ourselves.

We've been dress-lodging for Mother for six months now, and made her more money than all her other girls put together. One dark, one fair – Day and Night, they call us. When one is resting, the other is lively and keen. We are closer than kin, Annie and I; she is like the little sister my mum and dad never bothered to give me. We are both of the same mind – why give half the pie to Mother when we can keep the whole pie for ourselves? I've found us lodgings in the Haymarket with a mean old Jew landlord. The last bastard Annie was with beat her black and blue. We need a better class of bastard. We're going up in the world.

When I tell her, Mother rages for a whole hour by the parlour clock.

Then at the end she gets all sad, and says she does not know what will become of her. Without the shillings from me and Annie, she might be on the streets herself, or else in the parks. I hear her unmoved. 'Don't ask me to pity you,' I say. 'To me you will always be the bawd who sent Mr Starcross out to fetch me in, to condemn me to a life on my back.'

'And who took you in when you ran from those she-devils at the Magdalene Asylum?'

'You did,' I say, 'but only because you knew you could make more money out of me than they.'

Mother cannot be self-pitying for long. The venom always returns, like the spit of a viper. 'You're no better, Mary Jane,' she shouts after me. 'You brought Annie Stride to me, and now you've made her into a bright little whore, showing every sign of taking to fucking like a duck to water. Now you're carrying her across the river, to make you a fortune in the Haymarket. Who's the bawd now?'

I walk out on her at that, but her words stick under my flesh like burrs. I vow then, as I take Annie's bundle for her and lead her over Vauxhall Bridge, that if I can ever be the betterment of her, I will.

Over the next weeks, Annie became the Magdalene.

She'd been called a Magdalene before, as it happened, as a shorthand for her profession; Mary was the patron of two millennia of prostitutes, right up to all the tuppenny bangtails of the Haymarket. Mary Jane had told her that the Magdalene Asylum in St George's Fields claimed to help the raped and the ruined. But Mary Jane had told her other things about the asylum, too, things so dark that by the time Annie had got with child, she had not even bothered to take the long walk to Blackfriars to ask the nuns if they would take her in.

But now she felt a sense of ownership over the Magdalene. And it seemed that Francis felt it, too. There was a marked difference in this phase of his work to the work he'd done in London. There Annie had only sat once as each fallen woman, but here Francis painted many versions of the Magdalene at every stage of her life. He worked Annie harder than ever before, and although she was happy to comply with his demands – better, as she'd often thought, than being on her back – the work was tiring in its own way.

Once, after a particularly long sitting, when she stretched her aching arms, the lid slipped from the white alabaster jar and fell to the tiles with a sharp crack. She stooped to retrieve it, mortified, but Francis beat her to it. He picked up the lid, examining it feverishly for cracks. 'For Christ's sake, Annie! Have a care!' he shouted.

She snatched back her outstretched hand, shocked. He glared at her then; and the look of rage and hatred in his eyes was enough to make her flee. She ran down the stairs and out onto the loggia and into the gardens, past the lake and through the wilderness. She collapsed on the stone bench, looking at the view, which always gave her solace, trying to understand. He had never raised his voice to her before. Why had that slip, a lid falling from a jar, raised his temper so? Yes, she'd had worse from the bastards, much worse; been called a bitch and a whore and a cunt, words that had no place in her new civilised life, her new civilised lexicon. She'd been struck, too, a thousand times, a stinging pain that was surely much worse than words. Francis had only invoked the Saviour, but he'd never looked at her like that before. He had created her, he had moulded her as surely as a potter into her current lovely form; so his small slight to her was more painful than any dreadful curse.

She held her hands to her heart. She felt a keen pain there, as if she herself had been broken. And if there was indeed a hairline crack in her heart, would this fault line spread and shatter her beautiful new life?

She did not know how long she sat there, gazing at the distant terracotta rooftops and listening to the muted song of the bells, but eventually she heard the crunch of footsteps on the path, a warm presence at her back. She would not look at him. *Fuck* him, she thought, the word giving her power, *fuck* him and his old jar.

Then his arms were around her. She stiffened, but he pulled her back against his chest and she relented, relaxed. He kissed the top of her head, as if she was a fractious child. 'I am so sorry,' he said. 'I was wrong to raise my voice to you; no better, you must think, than those unhappy men who importuned you in your former life.'

As this was so exactly what she had been thinking, she could not reply.

'I have no excuse, except to say that that jar is very precious to me.'

He sounded so forlorn then that she consented to look at him; and this time it was he who looked away, distracted by some private pain she did not understand.

He stood abruptly and brushed his breeches down – Francis was not a man for the outdoors. He was not a man of tweeds and walking sticks; he belonged in velvets with a silver-topped cane. His presence jarred with the soft colours of a flower bed, but among the strongly painted Pre-Raphaelite blooms of the Royal Academy, he'd blossomed, too.

'Shall we go back?'

His ever-ready smile had returned; he held out his hand to her and hauled her to her feet. Together they walked back into the house and up the stairs to the studio in fragile amity, and she sat for him silently for the rest of the afternoon, holding the white alabaster jar as tenderly as if it was a child, the child that she had once lost. She wondered, for the rest of the day, why such a cold, plain thing meant so much to Francis. She knew him well enough to know that he must control his universe utterly, and that everything in this house had been chosen by his eye and placed here by his hand. So why, in a house full of beauty and ornament, had he found a place for the alabaster jar? At sunset when he briefly turned his back to clean his brushes, she peeped beneath the lid, expecting the jar to be full of diamonds or sovereigns at the least, or maybe incense or something holy. But it contained only ashy grey dust.

Just dust.

Chapter 13

Four years ago

Annie and I have settled into the Haymarket. We work well together, and are making a good life for ourselves. We are not rich, but we are not cold, or hungry, and no one tells us what to do. We take the clients we want, but we have a pact – if one of the bastards frightens us, or wants something too dark, we let him go by. We know, by now, the bad from the good; by their appearance and their manner. Not their clothes, though – the clothes tell you nothing.

We didn't always know a good man from a bad. Not when we were younger. I tell Annie about Mr Starcross, who stole me away from my aunt and ruined me at Mother's. She tells me an even sadder story: that her own father took her to a public house called the Old George, where a bastard was waiting for her. She tells me what that bastard had her do; she tells me, too, that she's never told anyone else, nor ever will.

I feel as if she has given me a great gift, and I want to give her something in return. I show her my shameful brand, the M on my left arm, and I tell her that hers are the last eyes that will ever see it. We embrace each other fondly. Now that we know what to look for, we won't be fooled again. We can recognise the ones who mean us harm.

It's something in the way they look at you.

Francis was so passionate and prolific in his work that he soon began to run out of paint. Crimson was his particular problem; it was the Magdalene's colour, and whatever Annie wore to represent her, she would always have the scarlet drape twisted around her, the curtain that he'd torn down from the garden door that first day. He still could, and did, mix his own white paint – she assumed that Florence, like London, must have its butchers and its bones – but crimson was in short supply. And the Magdalene's crimson cloak, with its tricky folds and its singing carmine hue, drained his tubes and palettes of its reds like a bloodletting.

He began to travel into Florence without Annie, in order to find a colourman. When he was from home, she would spend much of her time in the garden. Francis took no pleasure in the grounds and always skirted the fountain with as much suspicion as a cat; but Annie adored the outdoor space. She took the Dante with her, with honourable intentions to read it, but spent much of the time gazing at the beloved view of the distant golden city. Yet even so much beauty can only sustain the soul for so long, and soon she began to feel lonely. A few days passed, and uncomfortable suspicions ticked through her head hour by hour like the workings of a watch. Was she not quite polished enough for Francis? Was that why he was hiding her in his hilltop castle like some medieval damozel?

She taxed him with her suspicions at dinner. 'Are you too ashamed of me to take me into Florence?'

Francis laughed. 'But I've taken you into Florence a thousand times!'

'To see paintings,' she said. 'Not *people*. Mary Magdalene and all the apostles don't count.'

Francis laughed again, and patted her hand. 'Dearest Annie. Certainly I can take you with me, if you would come.'

But still he did not; and still she sat in her lonely garden. She began to suspect that there was something he was not telling her;

some reason why he was not taking her into Florence in the evening. It was as if the place changed with the nightfall; that she was only allowed there when the sun was gilding the buildings. When the smith had damped his furnace and gone home, and shadows owned the streets, it was a different city. She would watch Francis's carriage light disappear as Michelangelo drove him down the hill, then wander to her favourite bench and gaze out as night fell over the city, until she became too cold and strangely afraid, and fled inside.

In the afternoons, Francis could only draw now, for he had no paint at all save his own bone white. He laid great swathes of white on his canvases, and then drew over it in a desultory fashion, slowly and sleepily, with none of his former passion. White was his bone, but crimson was his blood, and without it he seemed pale and wan. He drew Annie piecemeal, making scrappy, unfinished studies of hands, eyes, lips, hair, dismembering her on various scraps of paper to be pinned around the studio. They were fractions of a female, like Eve when she was just a rib; a small, sad curving bone instead of a living, breathing woman in Eden.

Annie could feel his frustration, for he had been in mid flow. 'Imagine if God had been obliged to stop on the third day,' he said with no trace of grandeur. 'If the Almighty had completed earth and time and space and light, but there were no stars to hang in the heavens and no animals to walk on the land. I have so much more to say about the Magdalene. The mountains and the oceans are yet to come. For the love of Christ, I need some *colour*.'

Annie was in the garden on the day that his angry prayers were answered and colour, finally, came up the ochre road to find him.

She was sitting on her favoured stone bench, gazing idly at the road below, not really seeing, until something came into view that jolted her from her daydream. A tall figure was walking up the path, his figure shimmering in the heat. At first he was just a shadow; in the burning afternoon, with the sun behind him, he had no more features to him than the silhouette she'd had snipped for Francis on the Chelsea pier. But as he came closer, she could see that it was the one-armed man from the Uffizi.

Despite the heat of the day, her blood seemed to freeze in her veins. She wanted to cry out for Gennaro, the ancient gardener, or to fetch Nezetta from the kitchen, or Francis from his divan. But she could not move. She felt that her doom was coming for her; the man who had stalked her through the ancient streets of Florence had risen up and come to seek her in the hills now that she no longer visited his dominions. She watched, rooted, as he came on purposefully, his feet kicking up the red dust. By the time he reached the fork in the road, she could only hope that he would pass by, that he was a Florentine citizen on some business here who would go beyond their gates and up the hill, perhaps to the convent high above. But of course, he turned in at the gate, as she'd known he would, and walked up the cypress path of the Villa Camellia.

When he was out of sight, in the curve of the path, her limbs found their sense again and she moved as fast as a lizard, back through the undergrowth and past the broken statues to the house. She watched from the loggia, hidden behind a column, as he passed close by. He was tall, and reminded her of nothing so much as the David from the Piazza della Signoria, dressed and animated by some dark magic, the white marble made tanned flesh, the snowy curls dark, the blank white eyes black. The face was the same, the flare of the nostril, the bow of the lip. But where the David was naked, this man was clothed, and that in a singular fashion.

He was no longer in the dark military coat, double-breasted and gilt-buttoned, that she recalled from the Uffizi. Instead he had on a full-skirted coat made from patches of different colour. The patches were not regular, but shreds and snippets, all sewn together like a rag mat. Some were iridescent like a magpie's wing; some were dull and rough. But all were brightly coloured, the colours that Francis loved, that Duccio and Giotto and Cimabue had loved. They were strong colours, stained-glass colours – no gentle hues of rose and primrose and duck egg, but stinging hues of blood and jade and egg yolk.

Yet the coat was not even the most noteworthy thing about his appearance. He was wearing a dark-wood yoke, like an ox, with stoppered bottles hanging from it on lengths of twine. The bottles were different shapes and sizes, but all as clear as day, showing the colours inside them – strong, vivid pigments, just like the patches on the coat. The effect was bizarre. His height and the bottles made him a sight to see, but he had a sound, too. She'd once seen a man by the door of the Whitehall Empire playing a table of wine glasses filled with water with a wet forefinger, in exchange for the pennies of passers-by. He'd called his instrument a glass harmonica, and she remembered now its eerie song. This man sounded like that – like the glass harmonica. The bottles sang their song as he walked to the front door, and as he stopped and looked, they tinkled and settled. Then he walked directly around the side of the house without checking, as if he knew exactly where he was going. He went down the steps to the kitchen door, ever open because of the heat, and rang the tradesmen's bell.

Annie crept to the doorway and listened, heart thudding, sure he had come for her. She no longer thought he was there to take her to some dark realm, but still she felt a distinct unease, mixed with curiosity. What did he want with her?

Nezetta was talking, as she always did, loudly and volubly. Annie could not decide if she was being angry or friendly. The one-armed man spoke, fast and low. Then familiar sounds – the scrape of a chair, the drawing of a cork – followed by an unfamiliar one: Nezetta laughing. When she summoned up the courage to peer round the door jamb, the visitor was sitting at the scrubbed wooden table with a glass in his hand, his yoke set down on the floor, the twine slack, the little bottles upright.

She leaned back against the plaster wall, heart thudding, gathering courage. *I am the mistress of this house*, she told herself, not really believing it. Then she swung around the corner, chin high. The one-armed man stood at once in her presence, with perfect propriety; unmoved, unsurprised, as if he had been expecting her. He towered over her, and fixed her with those olive-black eyes that she remembered; eyes that, she now realised, had watched her in her nightmares.

She did not speak to him, but to the cook. 'Nezetta,' she demanded, 'who is this?'

'*L'uomo arcobaleno. Ecco che arriva l'uomo arcobaleno.*'

'Nezetta. I know you speak a little English. Who is this man? And what is he doing in my kitchen?'

'*Si. Capisco. Ti sto discendo che è arrivato. È qui per vendere i suoi colori.*'

Annie would not look at the ghost. She took Nezetta by the shoulders. 'Nezetta. Who. Is. He?'

The one-armed man took a step forward. '*L'uomo arcobaleno,*' he said. Then, in perfect English: 'The rainbow man.'

She looked in his eyes and was suddenly back in Florence, in all those galleries and churches, where his gaze had the power to chill her to the bone. Her voice, when she could summon it, was no more than a whisper. 'I have seen you before.'

'And I you.' He was perfectly calm, his speech measured.

'What are you doing in this house?'

'I was invited by the owner.'

'My husband is the owner.' She was still not used to saying it.

'Then I was invited by your husband.'

He held out his hand – his proportions seemed massive, again like the David. Between his fingers was a cream-coloured card, stamped with a tiny string of embossed letters. She took it from him without touching his skin, and narrowed her eyes at the little rectangle. It was Francis's calling card.

'I met your husband in the Brancacci Chapel. He was in desperate need of paint, he told me. I sell colour, so here I am.'

'May I see *your* card, please?' Now she felt braver. As the mistress of the house, she would interrogate the tradesmen. In Gower Street Francis had trained her to speak to the butcher, the chandler. Why should a purveyor of paint outface her?

But he seemed amused. 'I don't have one. My colours are my calling card.'

'What is your name?'

'I told you. I am the rainbow man.' He spoke as if to a child, and she became angry.

'That's not what you said before.' She indicated Nezetta, who was watching beadily, wringing her apron. 'That's not what *she* said.'

'No. I'm known as *l'uomo arcobaleno*. It means the rainbow man.'

She was suspicious. She did not believe him, or his story. She was not letting him go upstairs to the studio until she was satisfied; Francis was all she had, and she felt fiercely protective of him.

'In England I would be called a colourman. I supply paint and pigments and varnishes to artists.' His accent was pronounced, but his voice was low and clear and musical.

Annie narrowed her eyes. 'Tell me about colour then.'

'What do you want to know?'

'Tell me what *you* know.'

'That would take too long.' He stated it like a fact, not a boast.

'Why? Because there are so many colours?'

'No. There are very few.'

'How many?'

'Seven.'

'*Seven?*'

'Yes,' he said simply. 'Have you never seen a rainbow? The light splits into seven colours.'

She did not remember many rainbows in Bethnal Green, although there must have been some – the rain fell and the sun shone there as it did everywhere else. Instead she thought of the time when she'd been in bed at Gower Street after she'd lost the baby. In those listless days when she had lain flat and turned her face to the wall, the one light in her darkness had been the little crystal prism hanging from the bedside lamp. Day after day it had conspired with the sun to create a rainbow on the wall for her, a rainbow that had moved from wainscot to dado rail over the course of the afternoon, only to vanish with the sunset. There she had become acquainted with all the colours, from hot red to cool blue, passing by the oranges and yellows and greens on the way.

'I have seen a rainbow,' she said.

'And which is your favourite colour, of the seven?' He asked questions as Francis did, expecting an answer.

She considered. It was not something she had ever been asked before, and she did not quite know what to say. She caught sight of the sleeve of her Chinese gown. 'Blue.'

'What kind of blue?'

'How many kinds are there?'

'Veronica blue, Prussian blue, ultramarine, Antwerp blue, cobalt. And they are just the ones I have with me.'

'Very well. What is *your* favourite?'

'That's easy. Ultramarine.' He bent to tug on a string at his feet, which sent one of his little bottles flying up to his hand. He caught it easily and unstoppered it one-handed. He tapped the neck of the bottle on the table, shaking a little heap of vivid blue powder onto the desk. Then he gestured to one of the chairs and pulled out another. Nezetta hovered, ostentatiously polishing the coppers, so Annie felt quite safe. She sat down slowly, and he sat, too, the little pile of blue between them. He waited until she was settled, then placed the tips of his index finger and his middle finger on the wood and walked them across the tabletop to the little mound.

'Hundreds of years ago, a man was walking through the mountains of Afghanistan.' The fingertips trampled on the little blue hill. 'He stopped to rest on a rocky outcrop and discovered patches of vivid colour that he called "bluestone". He thought the sky had fallen to the earth and turned to rock. He scraped a little into his pack, went down the mountain again and sold it, thus becoming the first colourman. He got good money for the fallen sky, but he did not really know the true price of what he had found.'

The fingers walked away from the ruined mound, leaving little blue prints on the wood. *L'uomo arcobaleno* held up two vivid fingertips to Annie's face. 'By the time of the Renaissance, lapis lazuli was more valuable than gold. This little pile costs as much as that ring you wear.'

Annie twisted the glittering Regard ring so the jewels were hidden in the palm of her hand.

'But I imagine your husband is a rich man, if he can afford a house like this and a wife like you.'

She raised her chin. 'I can't be bought, nor kept in a bottle.'

The stranger fixed her with his black eyes again, and she lowered hers first. There was a silence long enough for her to remember that she could indeed be bought, and had been all her life, and here she was bottled up in this beautiful villa, no longer allowed beyond its bounds. She spoke first. 'My husband could buy all your old bottles if he chose. But this isn't paint. It is only powder.'

'Yes.' He reached into his pack and produced a little stone mortar and pestle. He said something to Nezetta, who placed a white tallow candle in front of him.

'Now, watch.' He scooped some of the powder into the mortar, and unstoppered another bottle. 'Linseed oil,' he said, and began to mix the oil into the powder.

Annie wrinkled her nose. 'It smells,' she said.

'Yes,' he replied, unmoved. 'The rock is sulphurous. This is what hellfires smell like.'

It was said with great certainty, as if he had been to the inferno and back, and was allowed to wander in and out like a regular at a public house. As though he was indeed acquainted with hellfires, he produced a tinderbox and deftly struck a light for the candle, dripping wax into the mixture and hammering at it until it stiffened. He lifted the pestle and she saw a vivid blue, as blue as the Virgin's cloak.

'This is what they wanted, all those Renaissance painters,' he said. 'Without this blue, they would not have had sky; sky over the manger, sky over the Holy Family, sky over the crucifixion. So the sky that fell, and became rock, became sky again.'

Annie was struck by the idea, and could think of nothing to say. Instead she stared and stared at the vivid blue. It was the exact blue she'd seen in the Uffizi, and above the hills outside her door. She could only think that if the Holy Land shared a sky with Florence, the Almighty must have run out before he got to London – somewhere over the Channel, the blue heavens must have been patched with grey like a quilt. The visitor interrupted her musings.

'Well? Do I pass your test?'

'So you know about blue,' she said grudgingly. 'What about the other colours?'

'We will do them another time. I will teach you about all the colours before we're done, if you like.' He spoke oddly, as if there was a set time for their acquaintance that was already determined. But Annie was not yet convinced.

'So you go around like this, in that coat, and sell your paints?'

'Yes. And not only myself – there are many rainbow men.'

'How can you all make a living at it?'

'Very easily. Everyone in Florence paints. Even those who can't paint, paint.'

She looked at him sharply, sensing a joke, but his face was entirely serious. 'How do you know English?'

He shrugged. 'Florence is stuffed with English people. Most of those who can't paint are English.'

'Francis can paint,' she said defensively.

'I know he can. I have seen his work. He brought a picture to show me; a picture,' he said, 'of you.'

The fellow seemed genuine – she knew that Francis had taken examples of his work into Florence, all those times he had gone into town without her, to show tradesmen and dealers. But she still wanted to know why this man had dogged her around the city. 'You were at the Uffizi. And San Marco, and the Cappella Medici. And Santa Croce, and the Forte Belvedere.'

'Of course. I must do my research.'

'You were following me.'

'Not at all. I was following others.'

'Who were you following?'

'Giotto, Cimabue, Duccio. I am quite new to my profession. I have made it my business to become a student of art. I study colour and composition. I follow these Englishmen in their Norfolk jackets and I see what they look at, who they admire. If this year Giotto is the fashion, I need a lot of red. When they flock to Raphael and Portinari, I need rose madder to make pink. When they stand in front of Ghirlandaio, I stock up on gold leaf.'

'But when I saw you, you looked like a soldier.'

'I *was* a soldier. But all wars have to end sometime.' He held aloft the sleeve with no arm in it. 'I only spar now with the wives of painters.'

She felt, briefly, ashamed; she had entirely forgotten, in their alter-cation, that he only had one arm. But he did not have the demeanour of one damaged or winged, and spoke up for himself very decidedly; he did not seem to be asking for sympathy, so she gave him none.

'If you were there for the art, why were you watching me?'

He fixed his dark, fathomless eyes on her again, just the way she remembered. 'Am I the first man to look at you?'

'You are the first man to look at me like *that*.'

He tilted his head on one side. 'How do I look at you?'

'Like you have come to take me to the underworld.'

The black eyes blinked. 'I cannot help my appearance. Colour, you see, is so important. When you saw black hair and black eyes and a black soldier's coat, I was some demon. Now, in my harlequin garb, am I as terrifying?'

She looked at the rainbow frock coat. 'No,' she admitted.

'No. I have not the good fortune to look harmless. Your husband, white as milk, sea-grey eyes, light hair, he looks exactly as a good man should.'

Annie ducked her head, waiting for more – the sentence seemed strangely incomplete – but he fell silent.

Eventually he stood and picked up his tinkling yoke. 'May I see the good man now?'

She stood, too. The man had Francis's card, he had described him adequately, he had seen his work. There was no reason to keep him down here; Francis would no doubt be thrilled to have his colours again, thrilled to be able to paint.

She inclined her head slightly, and the rainbow man whisked his hand over the table, funnelling the vivid blue heap back into its bottle. As she escorted him out of the kitchen, she could see that, even though it had rested on the scrubbed oak for so short a time, the lapis had left a stain like a little bruise.

She led him to the stairs and up to the studio, the image of the perfect hostess. She knocked at the studio and entered alone at first to wake Francis, and have him arrange himself, and see his expression kindle when he heard that the rainbow man was here. Then she showed the colourman in and closed the door behind her. Here her perfect housewifery deserted her, for no one had told Annie that a lady did not listen at doors. It availed her nothing, though, for she could only just make out the murmur of conversation, although she could hear, quite clearly, the tinkle of bottles.

Chapter 14

Two years, three months and five days ago

Sometimes, very rarely, Annie and I are both home at night, in our own bed. Usually, as Night and Day, we take turns; or we're in bed with some gent till morning. But on the nights when we are there together, we pull the sheet over our heads and talk. The lamps are still lit, the fire still in, so we feel like we are in a tent from the Arabian Nights, full of shadows and light.

'What do you want, Annie?' I ask her.

'Enough food to eat. A good fire. Fine clothes, and a good man.'

I snort. 'A good man? I'm not sure such a creature exists.'

'Me neither.'

'How will you know him when you see him?'

Annie strikes a pose, placing the back of her fingers against her forehead. 'By his deeds,' she says dramatically, as if speaking of a knight of old.

I smile; then I sober. 'And what about love? Do you ever think about love, Annie?'

'Fuck, no,' she says.

I laugh and hug her. I love the way she speaks, so direct and dirty.

I hope she never changes.

Francis did not share Annie's reservations about the one-armed man. 'A capital fellow, that rainbow man,' he said. 'He had everything I needed, even my mummy brown.' He brandished a fat tube at her.

She laughed. 'What is mummy brown?'

'A special brown paint, not dull like the bitumen-based brown. It is made of mummies. Genuine Egyptian mummies.'

Annie knew what Egyptian mummies were. All of London was a-twitter over the recent exhibition at the British Museum; Egyptian jokes and fashions had even reached down as far as the Haymarket. One bastard had even asked her to pretend to be an Egyptian goddess come to earth to service him. Annie had found it all ghoulish, and still did.

'*Human* mummies?'

'Humans sometimes. More commonly cats.'

She made a face, and now Francis laughed. 'My fellow Academician William Holman Hunt shared your reservations. When he found out the origin of mummy brown, he buried his tube in the garden, with full ceremony.'

'And what will you do with yours?'

He looked faintly surprised. 'Paint with it.'

Francis was alive once more, his eyes bright, his fatigue gone. He painted her again, this time for a series of canvases about the crucifixion and resurrection. He worked her so hard that she began to miss the garden and the hours of leisure she had formerly found such a burden. But he seemed more devoted to her than ever, as he always did when he was painting her. It was as if she took on the attributes of his subject along with her own, and was more of a person, brighter and more vivid, like stained glass washed by rain. She wondered for the first time who it was that he really loved: a dead whore or a living one.

Their life at the Villa Camellia had a new aspect to it, for the rainbow man came to the house on Monday, Wednesday and Friday morning at Francis's request. Annie wondered at the strange coincidences of life, that the man who had dogged their steps in

Florence, appearing at every turn as if he were a thousand men instead of one, should now be inside their very door. They knew so little about the man, save that he sold paint, a fact that she could not dispute. She and Mary Jane used to pride themselves on their ability to divine the good men from the bad – or rather the bad from the worse – and she'd hoped that that instinct had carried over into her new life. But the rainbow man was one fellow she could not quite fathom. She would watch him when, in the afternoon, he walked back down the ochre road to Florence, his coat swinging about his calves, his yoke of bottles tinkling.

As if sensing her reserve, the rainbow man never sought Annie out. Once he had seen Francis and sold him whatever he needed for his palette for that day and the next, he kept to the kitchen, where Nezetta would give him victuals before his long walk back down the hill. But Annie's loneliness drew her to the kitchen door, where she listened to them talking, just as she'd done on that first day; and she learned as she listened that she was guilty of judging by appearances. She would never have guessed that this man, tall, dark and as severe in the face as an avenging angel, would have a runaway tongue to rival Nezetta's.

He would sit at the kitchen table, tradesman that he was, and gossip while he prepared the colours that Francis had ordered. Annie would cross the threshold and walk tentatively forward, attracted by the sounds of company like the warmth of a fire. She would draw up a chair and sit watching him mix and measure the pigments, listening to the incomprehensible music of the Tuscan language. To begin with, cook and colourman would ignore her, not from cruelty, but from a benign confusion, not sure what to make of their little mistress's presence. She would listen carefully, and bit by bit she began to understand a little of the great struggle for the unification of Italy that had been raging over the last year or so – that Italy was not a country as foreigners thought, but a loose muddle of states; some ruled by a king of

Sicily, some by a duke of Austria. A fellow called Mazzini, of whom both Nezetta and the rainbow man spoke as if he was the Messiah, believed that Italians should unite together and rule themselves.

Slowly, day by day, she learned a little of their tongue, recognising words and phrases, and even, tentatively, joining in. Then Nezetta, delighted, would draw her into the conversation, and the rainbow man would translate, and in a short time Annie had made her first female friend since Mary Jane. She learned of Nezetta's childhood in Montepulciano, her long marriage to Gennaro, her despair at her son Michelangelo, who would not go for a soldier, and her pride in her older son Gianfranco, who had gone and not come back. She learned that Gianfranco had lost his life in the same campaign as the rainbow man had lost his arm. 'It was during a street battle,' he told her. 'We Italians called it a Revolution – a very great name, to aggrandise our cause. The Austrians called it The Tobacco Riots – a very small name, to belittle us.'

Nezetta spat neatly on the tiles. 'Austrians,' she hissed. 'They are dogs.'

The rainbow man shrugged, an odd, incomplete gesture with his single arm. 'In truth, it was just five days in Milan.'

Annie watched Nezetta, on her knees, assiduously cleaning up her own spit with a cloth. 'What happened?'

'The Milanese have always been the allies of the Florentines, for they are ruled by Austria as we are here. So when they rose up against their Austrian oppressors, a group known as the Young Italians put on their red coats and travelled north to join in their struggle.'

'Heroes,' said Nezetta, straightening up as if in salute. 'My Gianni among them.' She dabbed the corner of the cloth to her eye.

The rainbow man let a respectful silence fall, then continued his tale. 'We began peaceably, by refusing to smoke tobacco or buy tickets for the lottery. Gambling and smoking, the two great Italian vices, were also the two great Austrian monopolies. Then their general, Radetsky, sent the soldiers out in the streets smoking cigars.'

'Radetsky,' said Nezetta, like an echo. 'He is a dog, too.'

'I remember it was a hard winter, and their smoke hung like fog in the streets, the aroma provoking the crowd. Some of the street orphans pelted the Austrian soldiers with stones, giving the troops the excuse they needed. They charged the unarmed people with their bayonets. When the Austrians attacked, the Young Italians armed themselves to defend the citizens.'

'Before long, the streets were thick with smoke once more, rifle smoke where the cigar smoke had been.' The rainbow man raised his head and breathed in through his nose, as if he could smell it still. 'Five were killed, including Giovanni.' He put his hand over Nezetta's where she had gripped the back of his chair as if to support herself. Then he stood and steered her into his seat, his hand now on her shoulder, speaking just to her. 'You are right about him. Your boy was a hero; I have never seen such bravery. If it were not for him, I would not be standing here now. He was too good for this world.'

Nezetta put the cloth over her head and sat there heaving. The rainbow man found himself another chair, and went on.

'Many others were wounded, including myself. My arm was shot clean off, my sleeve hanging like a pipe. My fellows carried me out of the fray and got me back to Florence on a cart. The monks of the Misericordia looked after me. I woke to a circle of hoods around me, black as crows. I thought I was dead. When I realised my arm had gone, I thought they'd pecked it off.

'I have never smoked a cigar since,' he added, 'but I use tobacco in my pigments. And every time I smell it, it takes me back to the north, and reminds me that the struggle is not done.'

'Never.' Nezetta rose, tidied herself, and began to bustle about again, muttering 'dogs' and 'heroes' to the ingredients she prepared.

Annie thought about the dogs and the heroes. All men fell into these two camps; and she had met many more of one than the other. Francis, she thought, was a hero. She looked at the rainbow man, drinking deeply from his cup, thirsty from his tale, and wondered which he was. Nezetta, it seemed, was in no doubt: the colourman's part in the tobacco riots on the side of her son had made her his slave. Nothing was too good for him. She pressed on him delicious morsels of cheese or sausage, cups of wine, or her special little almond biscuits that melted on the tongue with a burst of sweetness. The rainbow man returned the favour with a kindness of his own. Nezetta needed herbs from the *orto*, the kitchen garden, and he offered, obligingly, to gather them for her.

Annie wandered the paths with him, reluctant to leave off their conversation – because he had such a good grasp of English, she could converse with him much more easily than with Nezetta. But to begin with they walked in silence through the green and flowerless kitchen garden, as if he'd used up all his conversation for the day. Wordlessly, skilfully, he stripped the herbs from their bushes with one hand. When they reached the stone water trough, he stopped to wash the leaves in the jade water, and Annie watched him. She no longer thought he was death's harbinger, or some ill omen. He was not cursed, nor unlucky because he had lost his arm. Rather, he was lucky to be alive. Perhaps he had the flavour of the grave because he'd come so close to it. Nezetta's son had not been so lucky.

'Poor Nezetta,' she said aloud.

'Yes,' he replied grimly, and she could not quite read his tone.

She sensed there was more to tell. 'It must be a comfort to her to hear tell of her son's bravery.'

'That was my intention.'

'Then . . . he was *not* brave?'

He straightened. 'He was as keen as a puppy. He'd come up from Florence on a hay cart with a quart of ale to see some sport. He and his fellows put the rest of us in danger.'

'So he did not save you?'

'No. Quite the reverse. I tried to shield the young idiot and it lost me this.' He waved his sleeve at her.

Annie's mouth fell as wide as his cuff. 'But . . . you told Nezetta . . .'

'Would you have me tell her the truth?' he asked softly. 'The boy is gone. Let her have a fond memory of her feckless son. There is no one left alive to contradict me.' He shook the glittering herbs dry and deftly rolled them up along his thigh into a green cigar.

Annie did not blame him for the lie. He was kind, truly kind, and as they moved into the sun again, she warmed with it, inside and out.

'But that is the end of it, surely?' she asked. 'The Austrians rule in Milan still, and here, too?'

'For now,' he said grimly. 'It was not the end but only the beginning. The day is coming when Italy will be unified, with a liberal government, and all men shall stand as equals.'

She had never really considered a world laid out on such terms. In London the classes were well defined. She had been in the gutter, and there she would have remained without Francis's hand to lift her out. She looked at the house. Even from the back, it looked impossibly grand in comparison to her origins, with its loggia and its six square glazed windows along the penthouse floor. She wondered, for the first time, about the inequalities of society.

'*Can* such a place exist, where everyone is the same?' she asked doubtfully. She began to understand a little of the colourman's freedom with her. There was no tradesman's deference; he thought himself equal to her. (Little did he know, she thought with a secret smile, that she was lower than him by a long, long way.) He certainly always spoke to her as if they were of equal standing, and did so now. Was it one of the reasons why she sought his company? With Francis she always felt inferior – it was one of the evils of obligation.

'I am surprised you don't know of these things. In England, too, there are those who think that the advantages of privilege have reached too far.'

She frowned. 'In what way?'

'In London – where our leader Mazzini exiled himself – those of high birth, those connected with the establishment, they can . . .' he searched for the phrase, 'get away with murder. There are Masonic societies who protect each other, those in the House of Commons protect the wealthy, those in the House of Lords protect the titled. But no one is above the law; that is, no one *should* be.' He glanced at her. 'Though perhaps English gentlemen keep such affairs from their wives.'

The truth was rather different – she had not been shielded from such things so much as excluded from them. She knew just enough from her dealings with young parliamentarian bastards hot with argument straight from the House that politics was one of the privileges of the rich. Annie had been too busy surviving to think of the wider picture.

'Perhaps they do,' she said cautiously. 'Certainly Francis and I never discuss such things. I have no notion of what is happening in Britain and still less of events in Italy. Surely foreigners do not care about the affairs of other nations.'

'They do, though. How do you think it is that I come to speak English as you speak it?'

'You told me that your clients, the artists, are English; and I assumed that you learned it in the schoolroom.'

'So they are; and so I did. But I learned the English of a Londoner on the battlefield. There were good Tuscans at my shoulder, but many were from other nations who believed in what we were doing. One such became like a brother to me. A man called Charlie Rablin. He came all the way from London, where he had been inspired by Mazzini's speeches to join the Young Italians. He believed in the kind of society Mazzini described and fought bravely. By the campfire he taught me the language of your streets and a lot more besides. He was a mountain of a man; a strawberry-blonde giant with ginger whiskers. He cut a comical figure, for even in the fray he wore a bowler; we laughed at him, but it saved his head from the cosh a dozen times.'

Annie stopped walking suddenly. A mountain of a man with strawberry whiskers and a bowler. Such a man had come to Gower Street the night before Francis had taken her to Florence. It could not, of course, be the same man, but the remembrance of him was enough to make her feet stutter.

The rainbow man looked at her strangely. 'Is it possible that you know him?'

'London is a vast place.' She allowed herself a private joke. 'I cannot be expected to be acquainted with *every* man in the city.'

'He went home to fight another cause. He believes in the law, as I do. He went to be one of Sir Robert Peel's Metropolitan Policemen.'

She froze, and swallowed. Then she dismissed the thought – ridiculous to think that the rainbow man could somehow know, of all the fellows in London, the very one who had come to her door. She said, rather tartly, 'If he is indeed a policeman, I can say with some confidence that we would not be acquainted. I am a decent woman.'

He looked at her oddly. 'That I know.' They began to walk again, and she had the strange feeling that some moment of indefinable danger had passed. 'No one who has spent time in your company could think any different.'

He bowed his head, then took her hand, carried it to his lips, and kissed it. It was the first time he'd touched her, and the first time he'd shown her any gesture of deference. They walked back to the house in perfect amity, and she cradled the hand he'd saluted in the other, still feeling the imprint of his lips on her finger, as if she wore a second ring.

Chapter 15

One year, eight months, two weeks and four days ago
I think I've found the good man that Annie and I once dreamed of.

It is not the handsome captain who took me to bed last night, though, that's for sure. This morning, putting on his regimentals at sun-up, he refuses to pay.

Not in so many words, of course. As he buttons his scarlet jacket, he pats all his pockets in turn. 'Dashed nuisance,' he says. 'I haven't got any tin.' He flicks a glance at me where I'm tangled in the bed sheets. 'Tell you what. Come to the barracks on the King's Road after luncheon and ask for Captain Tuesday. I'll give you a bank-note then.'

I wasn't born yesterday; I know what this means. It's an old trick. The regiment are shipping out today on a lunchtime move-ment order; if I go to the barracks in the afternoon, the cupboard will be bare and 'Captain Tuesday' will have had a free fumble. The soldiers always give their name as the day of the week – that way the colour sergeants know that the women who come are not family members, and may safely be chased from the gates with a whip.

The captain is already halfway out the door, but no one gets dressed as fast as I do. I follow him down the grand staircase of the Athenaeum Club, and through the morning room where the gents are taking their breakfast. I'm not fool enough to make a fuss here; it might lose me future customers. But I follow him into *the street, and once I'm in Piccadilly, I start shouting at him.*

Quite often, when you start a ruckus in the street, they pay you just to go away. This one marches on, bold as you like, for all the world as if he's on parade. But just as we reach the Burlington Arcade, a man stops him, putting his cane across the captain's chest like a sabre. He is smaller than the captain, well dressed, with a soft slouch hat on his head. Under the hat he has brown hair with a wave in it and clear grey eyes.

'Sir,' he says. 'I think this lady is addressing you.'

Captain Tuesday curls his lip. 'She's not a lady; she's nothing but a tuppenny whore.'

'Your language,' says the gentleman, 'hardly befits the coat you wear. I suggest you pay her her tuppence.'

'More'n that,' I say. 'He knows how much he owes.'

A small crowd of passers-by have gathered to watch. The gentleman turns to the soldier. 'Well?'

Cursing, Captain Tuesday gets out his pocket book and passes me a note. I take it, disbelieving. He did not owe me as little as tuppence, but he certainly didn't owe me as much as a pound. He shoves past me, barging me with his shoulder. I hardly feel it, but the gentleman rights me onto my feet. Once I am steady, he says, 'Good day to you, madam,' and touches his cane to his hat.

And then the only good man I've ever met vanishes into the crowd.

Despite their differences of class, Francis and the rainbow man spoke a common language.

That language, spoken upstairs in the studio, was even more difficult for Annie than the Tuscan downstairs. She would recognise the odd phrase; but in the main, the conversation was unfathomable. She would hear words like alizarin, cinnabar, zinc, porphyry and haematite. This was not Italian, she thought, but the language of colour.

The rainbow man always spoke in terms of colour. The monks of the Misericordia had black hoods. The Duomo had a dome of copper. The road was ochre. He'd sit at the kitchen table after he'd been upstairs to the studio and tell Annie about colour as if he spoke of fond relatives. 'Black is not a colour,' he stated. 'Black is an absence of colour.'

'Francis told me white has no colour either,' said Annie. 'That's why it is the only paint he can make. It has no hue, so it's the easiest.'

'He's half right,' agreed the rainbow man. 'It is the easiest paint to make. But it does have a hue. Black is no colour; white is all of them.'

'What do you mean?'

'White is every colour at once.' He demonstrated by taking a pinwheel from his coat, painted with seven colours like slices of pie. He spun it on the kitchen table, and the colours disappeared into a blur of snowy white.

Each time the rainbow man came, he kept his kitchen promise that he would tell Annie about all of the seven colours; and every one came with a story. 'Why do you care so much about colour?' she asked.

He gave his strange lopsided shrug. 'It is my profession.'

'I thought you were a soldier.'

'I was. But I was a colourman before that, and now that the battle is done, I am a colourman again. Like my father before me and his father before him. Why, my ancestors likely tapped their bottles for Leonardo and Raphael.'

She seemed made, Annie thought as she listened, for men to tell her stories. The bastards used to tell her tall tales of their exploits: trips up the Amazon, or down the Congo, Bills they had passed in the House, or railways they had built. Until, anxious to speed the business that was sometimes quite literally in hand, she suggested gently they had no need to impress her, for their coin bought them freedom from such obligations. Then, in her new life, Francis had told her about the women she was pretending to be, regaling her with cautionary tales of Jezebel's grisly end or Gretchen's imprisonment, as if there were a chance that, without these parables, she would lapse back into her former existence. And since his education was the only thing that separated her from her old life, it was he who kept her elevated: he had raised her up; he could drop her, too – she was in his power.

The rainbow man did not moralise. She felt, talking to him, that he thought well of man; that man could do anything. She knew that Francis was not a lover of the company of other men; but she also knew that in his artistic tastes he preferred the men of Duccio, flayed or crucified and bleeding in biblical squalor, to the shining and muscular Renaissance mortals of Michelangelo. The rainbow man, on the other hand, placed himself firmly in the world that came after Raphael. Colour, though so simple – just seven rainbow bands, only seven – was infinitely complicated, and connected deeply to the earth sciences, sciences that had been studied and harnessed by man.

Some colours were friends with each other. Orange, the only colour to be named for a fruit, was close to yellow, both in hue and in chemistry. Indigo, the only colour to be named for a country, was so close to violet that some of their pigments were almost indistinguishable. She learned that to a Chinaman, green and blue were one word. Her own vocabulary widened as she began to learn, alongside her Italian, how to speak colour. She became drunk on the poetry of the hues – Persian indigo, Tyrian purple, midnight blue.

Colour could be royal. In medieval Florence, only the Medici family were allowed to wear purple. In ancient Rome, emperors wore it for their triumphs. In modern London, queens were crowned wearing it. Colour could be dangerous. Chinese yellow was so toxic that the artist who used it made his placid profession as perilous as soldiery. Some colours destroyed others. 'It was Leonardo da Vinci himself who warned artists not to use verdigris,' said the rainbow man, 'as it could ruin other colours with which it came into contact.'

At dinner each evening, Annie shared what she had learned with Francis. But he was no more than momentarily interested. She knew he cared not a jot where the paint came from, so long as it sat on his palette ready to load his brush.

With the rainbow man, Annie enjoyed a much more equitable friendship than she had with Francis, for he answered far more questions than he asked. True, he had less to conceal than she; but he seemed entirely open with her. He had none of Francis's reserve. Despite his serious demeanour, and his noble appearance, the colourman was a chatterbox after the fashion of most Italians; very soon she knew every detail of his childhood and every branch of his family tree. Like many of his countrymen, he seemed to live in the pockets of his kin. 'My Nonna and Nonno Cilenti live in Careggi. My Nonno and Nonna Graziani live in Sieci. My parents live in Florence. I have four sisters: Cicilia, Buona, Lisabetta and Tomasia. Buona has two boys, Enzo and Rafi. Lisabetta is having a child in the autumn.'

The conversation had Annie wondering; enough for her to question Francis. It seemed strange that she knew more about the rainbow man, whom she had known for a mere calendar month, than her own 'husband'. While sitting for him that afternoon, her hands curled around the cool white alabaster jar, she asked him the question that, she now knew, had long been at the back of her mind. 'Francis, may I meet your parents?'

He froze momentarily, his brush, loaded with the red of her cloak, poised in mid air. 'Should you like to?'

'I *would* like to, very much.'

He smiled regretfully. 'It would be a little difficult at present. It is more than a hansom ride from Florence to Norfolk.'

'Are we *never* to return to England?'

'Don't you care for Florence, my dove?'

'I love it,' she said with perfect truth, troubled, as she often was, that she had been caught in the sin of ingratitude, the deadliest sin of all for Francis. 'I could never have dreamed of even visiting such a wonderful place without your kindness, much less living in such a city.' She might have said more – she might have said that she loved Florence so much that she wished to be allowed back within its bounds – but now, with the rainbow man's visits, such excursions did not seem quite so urgent. If she could not visit company, at least company had come to her. The old city would wait. But in the matter of Francis's parents . . . She tried again. 'Perhaps they might come to see us. Here at the Villa Camellia.'

He studied her; not as the Magdalene now, but as herself. She could see the sea change in the grey eyes. 'It is an idea,' he said, his mouth starting to curl with the notion. 'My mother would fit perfectly in Florence. I should like, very much, to see you two together against such a canvas. I will write directly. Now, hold the jar a little higher.' He was speaking to the Magdalene again, and she obediently cradled the jar against her breast.

She daydreamed, for the rest of the afternoon, of talking walks with an elegant figure in lace in the Boboli Gardens, arm in arm under the same parasol; a figure with the same brown hair and upright carriage as Francis. She saw herself, in her mind's eye, conducting the figure along the Vasari corridor, and into Santa Croce; then taking tea at Fiesole, in one of those elegant cafés on the hillside, talking and laughing gently, and seeing the figure smiling as readily as her son, faint lines bunching at the corner of the grey eyes they shared.

Over the next weeks, Annie asked several times whether he had had an answer to his letter; but Francis dampened her expectations with warnings about the Tuscan poste restante, the perils of a summer crossing of the Channel, the state of the roads between Dover and Norfolk. 'It might be autumn, at the earliest, before we even hear from Holkham, let alone expect a visit.'

With that she had to be content; and she *was* content without further visitors for now, for she had the rainbow man to divert her. She sometimes asked herself if Francis was aware of their association, and, if he was, if he minded it. She was not used to such reflections. She was not accustomed to belonging to a single man; her time was paid for by many, and she belonged to a man for the hour or the night or the quarter-o'-bells that he'd paid for. Since Francis was keeping her around the clock, she supposed she owed him her loyalty; but she saw no breach in it from talking to a tradesman while he slept. The rainbow man was not taking anything away from Francis; without him she would merely be idling like a lapdog in the sun, waiting for her master to wake and whistle.

The house was happier for the colourman's presence; a paradoxical change, since he never actually smiled. Francis smiled all the time, but did not make her laugh half so much as *l'uomo arcobaleno*. It was most perplexing.

She taxed the rainbow man with this discovery one day in the garden. 'You never smile.'

'Rainbows do not smile either. See.' He described a downturned mouth in the air with his finger.

Annie was much struck by her new realisation that someone who never smiled could be amusing. From observation, she concluded that the rainbow man must be smiling with his eyes. Although his mouth kept that stern natural bow that she had seen on the David, his black eyes had a little catchlight in them, like the dot of bone white that Francis always used to give life to her own eyes in his paintings.

He seemed unsettled by her scrutiny. 'Smiling is not the most perfect weather-vane of a man's character,' he said. 'Does not your own bard say that one can smile and smile and be a villain?'

Annie could not make comment. 'Bard?'

'Shake-speare.' He gave the playwright two syllables.

Now she frowned. 'I don't rate Mr Shakespeare,' she said, suddenly all Bethnal Green. 'I saw *Measure for Measure* once and it was the longest night of me life.'

She could have sworn he was amused. 'I do not like him either,' he said. 'Dante, he is the only poet. And he gave birth to our new nation. Mazzini said that we should all speak Tuscan, for Tuscan is the language of Dante.' He sighed. 'In Florence, English poets are almost as plentiful as English painters – they clutter up our streets with their bad fashions and bad verse. But the English have no passion, no poetry.'

Annie felt moved to defend her nation. 'There I can't agree. Mr Dickens, now. He can turn a phrase like a chair leg.'

'I do not know this Dick-ens.' The black eyes twinkled. 'I do not know this chair-leg.'

Annie laughed. She was easy, now, in the company of the rainbow man – a man with a patchwork coat, and a family, and a profession: what was there to fear? She felt she knew him through and through – she knew the names of his sisters, of his dead dog, of his ex-regiment. She knew his opinions on everything from the Grand Duke to the weather. The only thing she did not know was his real name. Yet still she knew him, she thought with a shiver, much better than Francis. She wished, with another pang very like the first, that he could know her as well. Everything she had told him, including her name, had been a lie. She was no Signora Maybrick Gill, nor anything that that lady represented. She was a phantom, Francis's wife; an illusion as effective as the moving pictures she had seen once at the Vauxhall Gardens, and just as false. And yet there was a kinship between herself and the rainbow man, something that she sensed, with an instinct beyond her years, but could not define. Perhaps the reason for her ease was that with him she did not have to be grateful. She was tired, *so* tired, of being grateful.

She was relaxed in his company, for his foreign ear did not hear her accent, and he did not correct her Bethnal Green idioms. After all those months playing the fallen women of history, then Signora Maybrick Gill and Mary Magdalene, she was herself again. Despite the fact that she had lied to the rainbow man again and again, in his presence Annie Stride was reborn.

He reached her old self in a very particular way. Still they spoke of colour, but this time it was she who talked. He had done with his schoolmastering; now he wanted to know, in the manner of a smitten swain who craves to hear his beloved spoken of, what the seven colours meant to her.

'Our old friend blue, signora,' he said, strolling one day down the lavender walk, 'what does blue mean?'

That was easy. It was a peerless morning, the sky a hot blue arc above, the swallows darting. She pointed up.

He shook his head. 'Everybody has a sky,' he said. 'What does blue mean to *you*? Did you have a ribbon for your hair as a child? A silken gown?'

Now it was her turn to smile. There had not been many hair ribbons and silken gowns in St Jude's Street.

'Try closing your eyes,' he said. 'That is when we really see. Colours are like smells; a certain hue recalls a past experience or a childhood memory, just as a smell does. When I smell my nonna's pomodoro sauce, I am five years old again.' He steered her onto the old marble bench set in amongst the lavender, the stone warm beneath her skirts. 'Now, close your eyes, and look for blue.'

Smiling slightly, diverted, she did as she was bidden. With her eyes closed, the villa and the garden disappeared, and she was in the mist and murk of the East End, the fog as thick as porridge. A form loomed out of the mist in a blue coat and bright buttons.

The rainbow man's voice. 'What do you see?'

'A bluebottle,' she said. 'A policeman. Blue means his coat.' Blue meant fear for her because of policemen. She'd been a miscreant all her life, from her days 'sleeping' on doorsteps as a child, to her time as a dress lodger and those nights when she was hungry and sold her body in an alleyway at the back of the Ten Bells. Policemen always made her afraid, even in her respectable life at Gower Street.

The voice came again. 'Why do you fear him?'

His voice, and his probing questioning, possessed a strange power. Annie had seen magicians at the Exeter Street playhouse gulling audience members into thinking they had past lives, always famous or the noble, strutting around as Napoleon or Guinevere or Caesar. But the colourman had invited her back into her own past, with no crowns or laurels or thrones, but a cold seat on a stairwell, and a sharp rap on a door. The colour blue was the conduit to a memory so strong that she felt as if she were actually back there, living it.

'He might catch me,' she whispered.

'Why should he catch you? What have you done?'

She did not reply. In the world behind her closed eyelids, she was at Gower Street. She was safe. But no: a midnight knock.

'Now they are at the door.'

'Who? Policemen?'

Her eyes snapped open – she realised she had said too much. The rainbow man was looking at her intently with his olive-black eyes. She glanced down at her hands.

'No,' she said, laughing a little. 'I was wrong. They were not in uniform. They wore Norfolk jackets and bowler hats.'

'Who?'

'The men who came to Gower Street. Francis's . . . our house in London. The night before we left.'

He seemed much interested. 'They called for you? Or for your husband?'

She realised they were no longer talking of colour. She turned to him. 'They called upon Francis. They were not policemen. I don't know why I spoke of them. They were patrons. Critics. Friends.' She looked at him. 'You were wearing a uniform when I first saw you.'

Now it was his turn to look down. 'It is possible.'

'Yes,' she insisted, 'in the Uffizi. A black uniform, with many buttons.'

He shrugged his odd lopsided shrug. 'A remnant, perhaps, from my soldiering days.'

But he'd said they fought in red; and he was not, she thought, a man to mistake a hue – colour was his creed.

The next day, wandering the yew walks before lunch, they talked of yellow. Yellow was lucky. Yellow did not make her feel afraid; it made her feel fortunate. Yellow was Nezetta's butter, the sun of Florence, the gold coins she'd earned once or twice in her life from open-handed bastards – gold meant food in the belly, coal on the fire. The rainbow man made her close her eyes again. She was not sure this time, reluctant to lock out the sunny present and plunge back into the past.

'Yellow,' he said. 'What does it mean?'

'My hair,' she said, surprising herself. 'My hair is lucky.'

'Why?' he breathed in her ear.

Annie was silent. Her hair was tangled up with her childhood, and she could not go back to Bethnal Green.

'Is it what drew your husband's eye, when he first met you?'

She remembered the freezing January wind, her hair streaming out behind her on Waterloo Bridge like a golden pennant. 'Perhaps,' she said. 'But that is not the luck of which I spoke.'

'Tell me,' he urged, as if it was important.

She wanted to, so much. Her childhood, unloved and cast away without a second thought when Francis re-created her, was nonetheless a part of her. She let out a long breath. 'It marked me out. My hair marked me out.'

'How?'

The summer breeze blew in her face; the shadows of the olive leaves darted like fishes across her closed lids. She felt none of it. As before, the rainbow man's questioning had somehow transported her back in time. She was back home in St Jude's Street.

'It is a Sunday afternoon. We are all sitting round the table.'

'All?'

'My brothers and sisters. Twelve of us. Ma has the shears out. She's cutting our hair.' She remembered well the whisper of the shears, the long swags of brown and mouse hair being laid end to end on the scrubbed tabletop.

'Why?'

'For wigs and hairpieces for fancy ladies. By teatime, all of them are shorn as short as the lunatics in Bedlam. The girls look like the boys and the boys look like the girls – you can't tell between them. Pa's in the corner on the rocking chair, swigging from a clay jar. There's no food, but he's always got a drink.' Her lip curled. She could barely say his name. 'My ma gets to me and holds my hair close to the scalp, hard, hurting. Then my pa finishes the bottle and throws it at her. It clonks her on the head a treat, and she stumbles and drops the shears. He gets up and pushes her back from the table. "Leave that one be," he says. He barely knows my name. "That hair is worth a fortune."'

'And was it?'

She nodded. 'Not *my* fortune, you see, *his*. And not for a wig or a hairpiece, no – it is worth more living and growing and attached to a pretty child. I can make money for him as a slumberer, they call it. He takes a hank of yellow in his hand and calls me the Angel of Bethnal Green. It's the only nice thing he's ever said to me.'

Now she must open her eyes – if she kept them closed, more

memories would follow, of exactly how Pa had made a fortune from her; memories of a gentleman in velvet and the upper room of the Old George. Her eyes filled at once with tears. She realised that she had given herself away; now the rainbow man knew that she was no fine lady. But she didn't think he had tricked her, nor did he seem to think of her any differently. There was no judgement in his eyes as he studied her, only sympathy. He offered her his pied kerchief. She shook her head and smiled. 'It is the sun,' she said. 'Just the sun.'

The next day, orange was easy: a fruit she'd been given for Christmas – nothing but sweetness and happiness bursting on her tongue. And the day after that, green was obvious – it was Francis's studio, a colour from her new life, not her old one. It was safe to speak of green as they sat on the fountain's lip among the flashing dragonflies. Here, for that colour, she might have chosen the tails of those dragonflies, or the jade water of the fountain bowl, but in London, she'd never been to the country, never so much as seen a green field. The Scheele's green studio in Gower Street was a place where she'd felt safe, a place where she had found a profession she liked. A place where she was not hungry or cold or ill, where her body stayed untouched, where she wore beautiful clothes and ornaments in her hair.

'How do you feel?'

She kept her eyes closed. 'Safe.' No danger today. None. 'Francis keeps me safe. In a room of Scheele's green.'

When she opened her eyes, he said: 'Scheele's green killed Napoleon. What a legion of armies could not do, a lick of paint did instead.'

She frowned a little. 'What can you mean?'

'When he was imprisoned on St Helena, Napoleon was kept in a room that befitted his majesty. It was painted with Scheele's green, but Scheele's green is made from arsenic. Napoleon breathed in the arsenic for every day of his imprisonment, and it gave him a canker in his stomach. They wanted him alive; they kept him safe, to live out his life in exile, but they ended up killing him.'

Annie ceased to breathe. 'You think Francis is in danger?'

The rainbow man shook his head emphatically. 'No. He is here, breathing the Florentine air of sunshine and thyme. I meant to say only that even when you think you are safe, you are not.'

It seemed an odd thing to say; but his next utterance was even stranger.

'Do you ever leave this place?'

'No.'

'You do not go to Florence? Even to Fiesole? That takes less than a quarter of one hour.'

She shook her head. 'I told you; he keeps me safe.'

'Napoleon thought himself safe. Has your husband given you a reason?'

'No. He hasn't.'

He seemed to think for a moment, and she could hear only the fountain plashing at her back. He got to his feet. 'Look. I am going to Fiesole now. It is market day, and I must buy some spices for my pigment. I promised to run some errands for Nezetta, too. Why don't you come with me? It is just over the brow of the hill.'

'I cannot.'

'Why not?'

'It would not be seemly.'

'For the lady of the house to go to market? For her tradesman to show her the way? It is far more seemly than to go unaccompanied.'

'What would Francis say?'

'Why don't you ask him?' he said pertinently.

'He sleeps till noon.'

'And it is not yet ten; so how would he even know?'

'I cannot keep things from him.'

'Nor should you. But he may easily see your path,' he pointed out. 'Six fine windows overlook us here at the back. Seven at the front. We are concealing nothing; he may watch you go. Has he explicitly told you that you may not leave the house?'

'No,' she admitted.

'Are you a prisoner on St Helena?'

'No.' She laughed. 'No.'

'Well, then.'

The truth was, she *wanted* to go to Fiesole. The old Annie Stride would have gone anywhere with a man. Surely Francis would not mind? He would sleep the morning through, as he always did; she would be back before he woke, and he would be none the wiser. What difference if she walked with a man in the garden or with the same man a mile south in Fiesole?

She suddenly felt a bubble of excitement rise in her chest. Before she could change her mind, she rose, too, and led the way down the path and out of the gate, the windows at the front of the house burning at her back like eyes, and her brain ignoring the certain knowledge that Francis would mind very much indeed.

Fiesole was as near as the rainbow man had promised. It was a pleasant wander down the hill, and every cedar tree and turn in the road was a delight to Annie. She knew the Villa Camellia so well by now, and the gardens, that everything new was a treat. Fiesole was a golden little town, perched on the edge of a hill, with her favourite view of Florence spread below, as if someone had spilled a treasure chest. The Duomo was an upended grail, a bronze cup gilded in the sunlight.

The rainbow man gave her his arm around the old golden stones of a Roman amphitheatre set into the hillside. As she climbed the proscenium, her eyes kept wandering to the view, and she wondered aloud how those ancient audiences could have given any note to a bunch of posturing actors when there was such wonder to be seen below. Then the rainbow man took her to morning refreshment in one of the genteel cafés, where tea was served in long glasses instead of china by voluble waiters with patent-leather hair. They were not mistress and tradesman, but two anonymous tourists. They did not speak of colour here, but of nothing – those pleasant, meaningless nothings of small talk that go so well with tea. Then they walked beyond the amphitheatre into the hills, and found a field of crimson poppies with a view that stole the breath.

Collapsing down in the long grass in the midday heat, Annie felt free and happy – there was no need to sit up straight or remember her manners. She curled up, chin on knees, arms wrapped around her legs, and drank in the view. Here she could see another Florence, a different aspect from the villa's vista, but just as perfect. She had begun to think that her relationship with the city was connected with the Villa Camellia, that that view, now she was forbidden the city itself, was all that it could mean to her, perfect and immutable as a postcard on a wall. But here was a different one, and just as beloved. Did that mean the city was not connected to Francis either? Could she live here without him?

She realised how long she had been silent. 'What a day,' she said.

'Not for long,' said the rainbow man ruefully, sitting down beside her.

She looked where he pointed, to the puffs of cloud gathering on the horizon, brushstrokes of purple. Doubt clotted in her mind. She should not have stayed this long. 'I should go back.'

Perhaps he had not heard. 'Indigo and violet,' he said. 'Where have you met them before?'

The next colours. She closed her eyes readily this time. Orange and green had given her good memories. On this peerless day, in this beautiful meadow, surely no demons could stalk her.

But they did. To begin with, she could just see Mary Jane, her face registering shock, eyes and mouth round. Then she could see herself. They were both in a mirror, the speckled, pockmarked mirror in Mother's house, Mary Jane behind her, untying the stays of her frock, shocked at what she saw. And Mary Jane's voice, saying the Saviour's name over and over and over again. 'Jesus, Annie. Jesus, Jesus, Jesus, Jesus. What did he *do* to you?'

Something hurt. Her whole body hurt, all of her skin, as though she'd been flayed. The dress slid to the floor.

She was naked, but she looked as if she was still dressed – she was clothed in a dress of bruises, her body coloured from neck to wrists and feet in indigo and violet, livid, terrible bruises; everywhere, everywhere.

Arms around her then. Arms around her now. She'd spoken it all aloud, and the rainbow man had heard every word. 'Who did it to you?' he asked, into her hair.

She was shaking, despite the heat. 'I never knew his name. I think he was a Member of Parliament, in the government or something.' He'd taken her to some panelled room in Westminster. He'd stripped her first, then gone to town on her; beating her with his fists and feet. She could see him getting harder and harder with every blow. Then, and only then, when she couldn't move, did he do it to her. And compared to the beating, it didn't hurt at all.

She looked at the view through a curl of the rainbow man's hair, holding him tight under the gathering clouds, as if he and Florence together could take the pain away. She might as well tell it all now. 'Whoever it was, he had enough money to pay. Mother – she ran the cathouse – she let him do it to me. She just told him, "Not the face." It was the last straw. After that, we decided to set up on our own, my friend Mary Jane and me.'

'So you were both . . .'

'Yes.' So now he knew. And now he would go.

But he put his hand to her face and, as gently as if she were still bruised, drew her to him and kissed her.

No clash of teeth. No insinuating tongue. None of the ravenous, devouring tricks of the bastards, who kissed as if they wanted to climb inside her and eat her from the inside out. Just a soft, incredible kiss on the lips.

She drew back and looked at him, and he looked at her, his face calm, beautiful. For a moment, everything in the universe was aligned, and everything was all right. He had done it. He had taken the pain away. But then the wind picked up, and the crimson poppies waved around her, signalling wildly. The storm bunched and bruised over the city, and the first fat drops of rain fell on their skin.

The bells of the noonday Angelus rang out a distant warning. Flashes of lightning streaked like golden lizards from clouds to ground. The moment broke with the weather and Annie was frightened, no longer by the memory, but by what she had done. Francis had saved her from that world, the world where indigo and violet meant bruises, and brought her to a place where they meant summer storm clouds over Florence. Although her body had been a playground for the whole of London, she was as sure as she could be that that single chaste kiss in a poppy field was the greatest betrayal she could offer him.

She could not look at the rainbow man. She felt as guilty as if they had slept together. 'I must go,' she mumbled, breaking away from him. 'I'm sorry.'

She scrambled to her feet and ran all the way, racing the storm, the indigo and violet sky oppressive above her, the smell of the rain on the road bitter in her nose.

The seven windows of the Villa Camellia's frontage watched her return. She felt, as she passed the gatepost and came safely within the grounds, an odd combination of relief and shame. She ran through the garden without a backward glance and raced up the stairs to Francis. He was prone on the golden chaise longue, undisturbed by the storm outside. His eyes were closed, his face peaceful in repose. He looked like a little boy.

She felt remorseful, and sank to her knees beside him. He opened his eyes and looked at her sleepily. He blinked. 'Annie,' he said. 'You've come back.'

And she knew then that even though he'd been asleep, Francis was somehow aware that she had broken faith with him, and that their relationship was changed. The rainbow man was not the sorcerer; it was Francis. Francis knew that Annie had broken the bounds, not just of the villa's environs, but of their unspoken contract.

He reached for her and she sank into his embrace, and his silky brown hair pressed into the cheek still imprinted with the dark curls of the rainbow man. He buried his head in her neck, and she felt his lips on her throat, then his teeth. He sucked at her flesh as if he fed – half kiss, half bite. And into her neck, as if speaking to her flesh and not to her, he murmured, 'Don't ever betray me again, Annie.'

She examined herself in the looking glass later. An ugly little bruise, indigo and purple, flowered on her neck. There would be no hiding it; it was too high for a collar, too low for a choker. She knew then, before she turned away, that Francis had not meant it to be hidden. The bruise was a badge of ownership.

Chapter 16

One year, eight months and two weeks ago

I'm crossing Waterloo Bridge when I see the good man again, the man who made the soldier bastard pay me.

He is no longer wearing the slouch hat, but as you'd expect in my profession, I have a good eye for a face. And his is a handsome face, with the same grey eyes and brown hair that I remember from the Burlington Arcade.

He stops in front of me and bows, as if I were Victoria herself. 'Good day. Lady Burlington, isn't it?'

I smile my own smile, my Mary Jane smile, genuinely pleased to see him. 'It is,' I say, and I drop a curtsey. 'I owe you my thanks for your service to me that day.' Then I put on my work smile. 'P'raps I can do something for you in return?'

He frowns a little. It doesn't suit him; he seems made for smiles. 'What are you proposing?'

'That you take me home with you.'

'That sounds like a capital idea,' he says; and despite the business, I'm slightly disappointed. I thought he was different. I suppose none of them are.

But he goes on. 'I will not,' he says, 'be troubling you for your usual services, if I may make so bold. I ask nothing of you but that you sit and let me paint you.'

'Modelling?' says I.

'It pays,' he says.

I take his arm at once, and we walk over the bridge towards the north bank.

Annie was as sure as she could be that after her trip to Fiesole, Francis would send the rainbow man away. But quite the reverse happened.

He was to paint a triptych – a massive triple panel – and for the first time he was to work on wood instead of canvas. From his many solitary trips to Florence he had had made and delivered three huge panels of fragrant poplar wood, anchored with sturdy hinges of shining brass. Annie had watched the thing travel up the ochre road from Florence, the same road she'd walked with the rainbow man, the telltale red dust clinging to her boots. Francis had appeared at her shoulder, watching, too, his arm proprietorially around her shoulder, his bruise still fading on her neck. He'd been more attentive than ever, but the balance of power had changed subtly. She had been caught out in a transgression, and was now less of a wife and more of an errant child; anxious to please, desperate not to offend.

The panel was roped to a haywain, with boys running beside the cart to steady it in return for coin. 'What a vast thing!' she said lightly, a foolish woman impressed by the labours of men.

She had judged the mood correctly; Francis dipped his head and kissed her shoulder. 'They'll have to use a winch.'

He was right. The screen was so large, it had to be hauled up to the studio through the window, and the local boys stayed to watch this piece of theatre, screaming and whistling when the heavy poplar seemed destined to fall. Despite their hopes and fears, the panel now stood in the middle of the studio, plain as a stable door, waiting to be adorned.

Francis stood shoulder to shoulder with Annie, gazing at the wood, as if he saw great possibilities amongst the grain and the knots. 'It will be my greatest work,' he said. 'Fit, I hope, to be displayed in one of the churches here in Florence. What an honour, Annie, what a great honour to be part of the artistic and religious traditions of this city; the city of art and death.'

He planned to paint the Magdalene in her three famous encounters with Jesus. First, on the left leaf, she was to be depicted anointing his feet with the priceless unguent from the alabaster jar; in the largest, central panel, she was to be at the feet of Christ crucified. Lastly, on the right leaf, she was to encounter the risen Lord in the garden, to capture the famous moment when he told her that he could not be touched; *noli me tangere*.

Francis was ready. He had his Magdalene. He had his paints. All he needed now was a Jesus.

The rainbow man was reluctant at first. Annie watched him warily, standing in the shadow of the great panel. It was the first time she had seen him since the kiss, and her heart beat hard; but he had been courteous and deferential to her in Francis's presence, just as he had always been. There had been no opportunity to meet alone, and she was determined that there would not be again. But if Francis prevailed in this new scheme, they would be thrown together as models in the studio day after day.

For now, though, the rainbow man did not look at her. He fixed his troubled glance on Francis from his greater height. But the smaller man was in control.

'Come on, man!' commanded Francis. 'For one of the panels I only need some feet. You have feet, don't you?'

The rainbow man raised one dark eyebrow. 'It is my arms that are in short supply. Feet I have.'

Francis seemed irritated by his own gaffe. 'Don't drag them, then.' The colourman did not move. 'I'll pay you.'

The dark eyes flickered. 'You're already paying me.'

'Then I'll pay you more.'

'That won't be necessary.'

'It is a pity I am not painting Joseph and his multicoloured coat,' said Francis, walking all around him like a horse dealer. 'But perhaps another time. You have a good look. An *exceptionally* good look.' He stopped pacing and looked the rainbow man in the eye. 'Besides, you *owe* me this.'

Annie ceased to breathe; she was sure that Francis was talking about the trip to Fiesole. The rainbow man had taken a liberty; now he must pay.

'I am sorry, signor. The answer is no.'

Francis dropped his head and sighed shortly. 'Then I'm afraid we must say goodbye.'

Annie, involuntarily, gave a little gasp.

The rainbow man blinked, as if he'd been struck. Then he said, slowly, 'What about your paint?'

Francis met his eyes. 'I have enough, I think, for the triptych. I don't need more paint – what I need is a male model.'

The two men stood facing each other like combatants. Annie had no doubt that Francis would prevail; he was absolutely implacable when it came to his painting – nothing could stand between him and his needs. Her innards squirmed, whether with pride or shame she was not sure. Without looking away from the other man, Francis said to Annie pleasantly, 'Say goodbye to *l'uomo arcobaleno*, my dear.'

The rainbow man hesitated, then stripped off his coat, as if for a fight. But it was a gesture of acquiescence, not aggression; the exchange of one job for another. 'Very well,' he said.

Life changed at the Villa Camellia. The rainbow man would come up the ochre road every morning directly after breakfast, and pose with Annie all day, breaking off only to take his luncheon in the kitchen with Nezetta, Gennaro and Michelangelo, while Annie would take hers on the terrace with Francis. Sometimes, during a lull in conversation, she would hear snatches of voluble

Tuscan from the kitchen, and sometimes laughter, and feel oddly displaced.

The first sitting was chosen so as to be the easiest on an inexperienced model. 'We will begin with the end,' said Francis, 'with the panel of Jesus and the Magdalene in the garden after the resurrection – the last time they ever met.'

Now that he had his way, Francis was all amiable solicitude. His smile never dimmed and he could not have been more obliging to his new subject. He had found a length of rough cream cloth, which he draped over the breeches and white shirt that the rainbow man habitually wore beneath his coloured coat. 'Here is your shroud,' he said cheerfully. The colourman had to remove his boots. 'No hobnails in the afterlife,' said Francis. 'Imagine your feet are on cool green grass in place of this Turkey carpet.'

Annie had to kneel in her red cloak, her hair down her back in a loose golden sheet, almost brushing the floor. The white alabaster jar was behind her, forgotten. She held her hands in front of her, clasped together, reaching towards her Lord, imploring him to embrace her. The rainbow man stood with his hand high, palm out, face stern, forbidding her to touch him. Francis had asked him to grow a beard for the duration of the sittings. By the second day he had an ashen shadow on his chin, by the third a scatter of stubble, and by the time Francis, who had begun with his feet, had painted up to his face, he had a full beard. It gave him, thought Annie, the look of a mystic or a visionary; both of which, she supposed, Jesus was.

Perhaps it was this physical resemblance to the Christ that made the rainbow man now seem more distant; for although she saw him more, she felt she knew him less. It was hard to imagine that they would ever again be as intimate as they had been in that stolen moment in the field of poppies above Fiesole, for although they were permitted to talk during sittings – unless Francis was painting their mouths or other facial features – the rainbow man seemed to retreat in the presence of the artist. It was as if, having formed a relationship of servant and master with Francis, but an acquaintance of equals with Annie, he could not reconcile the two in the same room. Francis, though, would not let him withdraw; rather he drew him out, as if he were the parlour host at a particularly uncomfortable tea party. In very short order, Annie recognised the discomfort of having the only two men she knew – albeit in very different ways – in the same room. Francis alone seemed at ease, almost playful, and she began to realise that they were indeed in the parlour, but they were not having tea. They were playing a game.

Francis toyed with the rainbow man with a velvet paw. He asked him questions about his family, questions to which, he was well aware, Annie already knew the answer. She soon realised that the two of them were being punished for their intimacy. Francis might not have known about the clandestine trip to Fiesole, or that stolen moment in the poppy field, but as time went on, she realised that he was trying to divine if she had shared her past with the rainbow man; whether the carefully moulded Mrs Maybrick Gill had been dismantled, piece by piece.

He probed their intimacy in a subtle way; with conversation. He would never stray from polite discourse, and would flatter them both as if he spoke of great men and heroes, but his utterances were calculated to expose their intimacy. 'Four sisters! My! Did you hear that, Annie? Almost as many as in your illustrious household.' 'The son of a colourman, and the grandson, too! Oh, the sons of toil, to whom we artists owe so much!' 'A little house by the Arno, you say? Only think of it, Annie! So many souls in one little dwelling!' She felt then how much she had hurt Francis – and under the shame she felt sitting stubbornly in her solar plexus burned the warm and stubborn flame of his regard.

Only when Francis asked the rainbow man about his romantic attachments did he inflict significant damage, for here Annie learned that which she did not know.

'And what of Romance?' asked Francis archly, giving the word a capital 'R'. 'Is there a Signora Arcobaleno?'

Annie held her breath. Know him as she did, she had not asked the rainbow man this question, a question, she now knew, to which she desperately wanted to know the answer. She and Francis waited, now united in their curiosity, their two against the rainbow man's one. She could see the rainbow man's deep reluctance to answer, but knew, too, that Francis held all the cards; if the rainbow man wanted to remain in this house – and for some unfathomable reason she was sure he did – he must comply with the rules of the game.

Eventually he spoke. 'There was someone once. She loved me before I went to Milan. When I came back, she did not.'

'Why?' asked Francis interestedly. 'Had you formed some attachment with a beautiful Milanese?'

Annie stiffened, but again she waited for the answer as eagerly as Francis did.

The rainbow man's face was unreadable. 'No. It was a simple matter of aesthetics, something I am sure you understand. When I went to Milan, I had two arms; when I came back, I had one.'

'Show us.'

The rainbow man turned his head slowly and looked at Francis. Annie, from her kneeling position, cocked her head a little, thinking she had misheard. But the two men locked eyes, and Francis repeated his command.

'Show us. You are a handsome fellow, tall, well favoured. It must be a blight indeed to turn a lover's eyes away. We want to see.'

We want to see. He had made her complicit in his request – they were two against one again. *Show us*, he'd said, not *show me*. And she did want to see, however much her new manners rebelled. Francis knew it – he knew her well; he knew humanity well. Everyone loved a freak show, and she was no different. They were back in the Vauxhall Gardens.

'Come on, man,' Francis cajoled. 'We will see it soon anyway, for in the final panel you must strip.'

There was a long, long pause, a pause of brinksmanship. Then, without taking his eyes from Francis's, the rainbow man stood and removed his shirt, his gaze only briefly interrupted by the garment passing over his face.

Annie stared in sick fascination at his body, so like a statue's, so broad and finely muscled, but with a terrible lack. Her eyes travelled inevitably to the place where the missing arm should have been. She had seen many damaged individuals in the dark corners of London: men who had come back from the war in Afghanistan in half and pushed themselves on little wooden trolleys, their arms overdeveloped like an ape's; children who had been born without a limb and so were worth less to mankind, but worth so much more to an unscrupulous parent. She found the rainbow man's stump fascinating – a powerful shoulder, which shrivelled to nothing; the skin at its termination pale and taut here, puckered and rosy there. She gazed at it, wondering how his lover could have rejected the whole man because of the lack of one arm. She wished that she could explain to him that the rest of him was still perfect; if the David had had his arm lopped off, they would still, she was sure, show the statue; the galleries she had seen were full of maimed stone but the sculpture was still revered. But she could not imagine beginning such a conversation.

Francis, too, showed no revulsion for the sight, but his reaction was somewhat different: he seemed positively attracted to the peculiarity. He walked right up to the stump and stooped close, examining it like a physician, as the rainbow man watched him warily. 'It has a strange beauty of its own,' he declared. And then he did something extraordinary. He leaned in to the stump and kissed it, like Judas, right on the termination. For a moment the three of them were completely still, frozen in a tableau, as if they all posed for a painting, as if none of them could believe what had happened. The moment seemed to stretch for an eternity, taut as a piano string. Then Francis said, 'You may dress.'

After this, even Francis was silent, and Annie wondered if he realised he had gone too far. She looked at the rainbow man's set expression, even more like the David in its stern strength. He was angry, she thought, really furiously angry. As the late-afternoon light faded, she found herself wondering why he had allowed himself to be humiliated like that. Whatever Francis was paying him, it was not enough.

At the end of the session, Francis put up his brushes and announced, 'It is done. Panel one is complete.' The rainbow man moved at once; he shrugged on his multicoloured coat and left without a word. Francis, whistling a jolly air, began to clean his brushes, and Annie, suddenly unable to bear another cheery note, followed the rainbow man to the garden and took hold of his arm.

'Why stay?' she said. 'Why let him toy with you so?'

He had a wild look in his eye, half desperate, half pleading. 'Don't you know?'

She shook her head. 'No.'

He freed his arm gently. 'I will tell you soon. But not yet.'

And he walked back down the ochre road, the way he had come.

Strangely unsettled, Annie wandered back to the studio. Francis was gone and the panel stood alone. She wondered what the end result of this squirming discomfort would be; how it would translate upon the face. She walked around to the front and looked at it. The right-hand panel was finished: Mary knelt on the green sward to beseech the standing Christ. The painting was exquisite, the colours strong and jewel-like, the brushwork masterful. But it was their expressions that carried the painting into another league; they were exactly right. She and the rainbow man looked suitably agonised, skewered with not physical but social agony from Francis's questioning. And now another layer of doubt was laid over their relationship like a varnish: had Francis engineered this discomfort in order to achieve the best results for his painting? A week ago, she would have asked him. Now she could not.

The next panel, depicting the Magdalene anointing Jesus's feet, brought Annie and the rainbow man physically closer. In this painting he was seated, in comfortable homespun robes, while she knelt with her hair tumbling forward, his foot in her lap. It was the first time she had touched his bare skin. He was no longer a statue, but a mortal man; the foot was heavy, and warm, and made of flesh and sinew and muscle and bone.

'Take your hair in your hand and wipe his foot,' commanded Francis.

She took a great hank of red gold, and pulled it over her bare shoulder, looking down at the foot in her lap. It was paler than the rest of him, as if it had always been in a boot – a soldier's foot, she reminded herself. It was hard to think of him as a fighter now, so meek was he, so powerless in Francis's war of attrition.

Cradling the foot for the next weeks, never once looking at its owner except to exchange an awkward glance when they broke for a rest or lunch, was a strange experience. It was an odd inequality in what had always been such an equitable relationship. She had been the mistress of the house, he a tradesman, but they had always spoken on a level. Now, for the first time, she felt below him. If the rainbow man was subservient to Francis, she was now subservient to the rainbow man. She did not understand how she must be, how she must look, and it showed; Francis was twitchy and unhappy and kept stepping back from the great panel and shaking his head.

'What is it?' he asked at last, laying down his brush. 'Why can you not find the right expression this time? Can you help me understand?'

She rubbed her hands over her face, as if she was washing it, as if she could erase her expression for him to paint it anew. 'I feel like a footstool.'

He laughed, a short canine bark. 'Explain.'

'I feel . . .' she searched for the right word, '*demeaned* by it.' She could not give words to what she really felt – that, oddly, anointing someone's feet seemed in some ways more degrading than some of the humiliating acts she had performed for the benefit of the bastards.

Francis considered, and then said, 'You are missing the point. She washed the foot because she *loved* it. It was a part of the man she loved so dearly, but at that time she could not show it. It was almost a separate entity, a creature all of its own. Imagine,' his eyes glittered, 'that it is your own babe. Can you *imagine*, Annie, what it would have been like to have had a *child*, and loved it, and cradled it in your lap thus?'

She could bear no more. She got up from her pose and hurried into the garden, fists clenched. She did not know if she ran from the memory of the little blonde boy in the Norfolk jacket that might have been, or for the wanton callousness with which Francis had spoken to her. She could not believe that he would have been so unfeeling as to forget her lost child, nor could she believe that he would be so cruel as to use the secret to wound her. In either case, his behaviour was plain wicked.

A single tear escaped each eye and dripped from her chin, but she still didn't know if she was sad or angry. Then there was a presence at her back and an arm around her shoulder – he had come to make amends. But it was not Francis; it was the rainbow man. He held her tightly, talking to her in his own language – *non piangere, non piangere* – gentling her as if she was a child herself. 'Signora . . . Annie . . . don't,' he said. She felt his breath in her hair, and she looked up through her tears. 'Don't cry,' he said. 'Not for him.'

'It's not for Francis,' she said, her voice thick with tears. 'It's for *him*. I can't explain.'

'I know,' he said. 'A child you lost.'

She had not thought he would understand so much.

'Don't let him see. You must go back. We both must.' He wiped her tears away with his thumb. 'Hold your tongue. Turn the other cheek.'

Like Christ, she thought, recognising the biblical reference. It was as if the Sunday-school Jesus had stepped down from his woodcut and was here speaking his parable to her personally.

'Ignore the goading,' he urged. 'See it through.'

'How can I?'

'You *must*. Just a little longer, and then it will be over.' And all of a sudden this was not Jesus speaking; this robed and bearded man was a different rainbow man, a man she had not yet met. He had, all of a sudden, a forceful, professional manner; he spoke with command, almost as if she were a soldier in the field and he her captain.

For a moment, she felt as if he was not talking about the painting – something else was in train now. She was suddenly sure he had some other purpose in being here, a mission or a penance that would soon be over. She wanted, badly, to know what it was.

'Don't ask any more,' he said warningly. 'Just come back, with me, and pose, and let him paint. He is nearly finished.'

There it was again. For a moment she thought he meant that *Francis* was nearly finished. And the moment passed; surely he meant the painting, just that.

She dried her eyes and went with him. As they entered the studio, she saw the rainbow man change again, back into the deferential tradesman who would not, now, say a word until he took his leave at the end of the day. The man who had spoken to her outside was no man's vassal. He was a commander. Then she realised that he was playing a part; he had been all this time. Just like his beloved colours, he had as many hues as the spectrum – a very chameleon.

The rainbow man looked up at the crucifix. Hewn from olive trees and erected in the studio, it loomed over the three of them. 'Signor, we may have a problem.'

Francis looked up at the cross, too. 'You are speaking, I suppose, of your religious sensibilities? I might venture to suggest, my good fellow, that your God would be better served by your agreeing to pose than your refusal. If I assure you that this piece will glorify your Saviour, would that help you to put aside your scruples?'

The rainbow man stroked his new beard. 'My scruples are not religious but practical.' Wryly he held up his empty sleeve. 'Where would the Romans put the fourth nail?'

Francis waved the sleeve away. 'Do not trouble yourself, man. I will paint your missing arm with reference to your remaining one. For this panel you must strip again, of course.'

Once the colourman was undressed, his modesty covered with a brief loincloth, he draped himself over the wooden cross according to Francis's instruction – his single arm looped over the crossbar, his feet crossed at the foot, his head looking down. Francis did not salute the maimed arm again; he stood back from it, narrowing his eyes, and Annie knew that through his strange artist's alchemy the limb was growing back in his mind's eye like the branch of a tree, the hand and fingers sprouting and extending, the iron nail driven through the brand-new palm.

'And what is my instruction?' she murmured, suddenly weary, and unable to keep the tiredness from her voice.

'A simple one,' he said, his eyes shining with some strange excitement. 'You must look at him as if you love him.'

She shifted a little, anticipating an uncomfortable few days ahead. 'And will you ask the same of him?'

'There is no need,' said Francis, not troubling to lower his voice. 'He's already in love with you.'

Annie gave an involuntary gasp. She looked up at the rainbow man upon the cross. He did not look at her but at Francis, his face utterly still and stony. She did not believe Francis's assertion for a moment; it was another rather feeble kind of tease, another goading prod. But for some reason this barb had hit home more than any other – the rainbow man was not Christ at that moment, but St Sebastian, another doleful figure she had seen all around Florence, peppered with arrows, a martyred look upon his face.

Francis followed one shot with another. 'Well, it's true, isn't it? You are in love with my wife.'

She could not take her eyes from his statue's face; waiting for the answer, once more complicit with Francis.

'Yes,' said the rainbow man simply.

To Annie, the room seemed to upend itself. The rainbow man in love with her? She looked at him sharply, sensing a trick; waiting for a tiny nod of the head to tell her this was part of a bigger clandestine scheme, a twitch of the full lips to betray a joke; but he did not even glance at her. He just looked, steadily and levelly, at Francis.

Even Francis seemed startled, as if such a bald admission was not what he had expected. 'Very well,' he said falteringly. 'Then look at her with that love in your eyes. And you, dearest . . .' He cupped her cheek, and she almost flinched. 'Now, I know you do not love my colourman – how could you love a one-armed paint-hawker? Besides, you are too clever for that, my Annie, aren't you? You are the mistress of self-interest,' he continued pleasantly. 'You would know, my wise little owl, that to dally with this tradesman would be to throw away everything you have with me: this house, the fine clothes. You would know that to entertain such a thought would be to end up back in the gutter. Of course you do not love him. But you are a fine little actress, and you would oblige me greatly by looking at him as if you do.'

Annie listened to this speech, the blood thrumming in her ears. She heard her own character related back to herself, by turns angry, then afraid. By the time Francis had finished his pronouncement, she felt flayed – skinless, like those unfortunate saints in the Uffizi, completely exposed for what she was. She tried to answer in her new persona, clinging to the receding skirts of Signora Maybrick Gill.

'Dearest,' she said, the proper wife now, not a model. 'What you ask is not appropriate. Only fancy what—'

'Go on,' interrupted Francis. 'Love him back. I want to *see love*.' It was his master move; the endgame. His eyes glittered with enjoyment, such as she had seen only once before, when a man had watched another man couple with her. She had seen this indecent, vicarious enjoyment when she was thirteen years old, in the upper room of the Old George.

Francis was master of the situation. He seemed entirely confident that they would comply, and they did. She met the rainbow man's dark eyes for the first time since Francis had said the terrible thing, she looking up, he looking down; and in a very few moments she realised that Francis, far from being the victor in this little game, had defeated himself again. In those brief seconds, as she looked at the rainbow man and he looked at her, she made a startling discovery. And once she'd made it, she could not look away.

Annie began to dread the completion of the painting. She and Francis lived politely, even amicably, the surface of the lake unruffled, while below were dark waters with rip tides and eddies of emotion and dank, choking weeds of hope and doubt. The rainbow man loved her; Francis, as far as she could tell, did not. And this made her frightened. True, she was his wife in all but fact, and despite his flaying of her character in the presence of the rainbow man, in private he behaved to her with probity and affection, much as he ever had. But now there seemed to be some distance, as if he was punishing her for another man's feelings. He no longer attempted to improve her; as if she was, in some way, finished, a work he had completed ahead of the triptych. He no longer, in fact, seemed very *interested* in her. She tried hard, so hard to rekindle his regard, feeling suddenly the horrible insecurity of her situation.

Francis had been perfectly right about her: she was the mistress of self-interest, and had been since the age of thirteen, when she'd run from the horrors of the upper room of the Old George. Everything she had, everything she was, depended on him. She thought, sometimes, that he had another woman; he seemed preoccupied, and not by the painting. He would still go into Florence in the evening, kissing her fondly on the cheek before he left. *Good night, my dear.* Then he would return late, and she wondered then if he had been in another woman's bed. But the thought did not trouble her as much as she might have thought; this, for all she knew, was a modern marriage.

She wondered how many other Victorian wives lay alone in bed waiting for the click of the latch as their errant husband returned at night. Thousands, she thought, millions. She herself had taken what was theirs, those wives: their husbands' money, their sweet words, their sweat, their seed. She had *been* the other woman, and was sanguine, now, about being the wife. If she thought of another woman in Francis's bed, she could not bring herself to care. But when she thought of another woman in her place at the Villa Camellia, eating with her silver-plated knife and fork and sitting on her chair at the head of the table opposite Francis, her breath would become short and her skin would prickle with fear.

At the same time, the thought of the rainbow man sleeping with someone tortured her. The dark and deep undercurrents of the lake pulled her inexorably towards him. She would imagine him beside her, on top of her, inside her. She remembered every detail of their kiss in the poppy fields of Fiesole, how his lips had felt on hers, the touch of his fingers on her cheek. And now she treasured every receding minute of the sittings with him, their silent, expressive look into each other's eyes, hours of the same unbroken gaze in which everything was said, and nothing. They could not, of course, speak to each other; she could not ask him about his feelings or intentions. But she dreaded the end of this time, the day when their connection must break.

Annie could tell, as they finished each day at sunset and stood in their little trio to look at the panel, that they were nearing completion. The three of them knew that they were part of something great. Then, and only in those moments, there was equality, and even amity, in their peculiar trinity. It was as if all of them had posed as the Magdalene, all of them had posed as the Christ, all of them had painted the picture. On Tuesday Francis wrote *INRI* on the little scroll about the cross. On Wednesday he painted in five fallen nails at its foot. On Thursday he drew a white dove, tiny and hopeless as a distant cloud. And on Friday, he put the catchlight in the Christ's eyes, which could have been a single tear. And with that small bone-white dot – all colours, she remembered, and none – he was finished.

That day, that last day, the three of them stood together for the last time and looked at the triptych in its entirety. The first panel, the *noli me tangere*, was a beautiful pastoral scene, the Magdalene in red, the Christ in white, the garden in green, verdant and glowing. Mary stared up at her Lord, pleading for one last touch; Jesus refused, stern and tall, already gone from her.

In the second panel, Jesus and the Magdalene could have been wed. Yes, she wiped his feet with her hair, yes, she knelt once again while he sat; but there was a beautiful equality in their being, the way they touched, the way he looked at her, the way she looked at his foot. The alabaster jar was beside her on the floor, but it was the only costly thing in the scene; there was a rough wooden table and chair, a chicken scratching at the doorway, the wood shavings of Christ's profession scattering the floor. The colour was strong and medieval, the anatomy was Renaissance; Francis had formed his own epoch. In composition and realism the thing was extraordinary – it was a masterpiece, and they all knew it.

And then came the third and last panel, the crucifixion. And that was when one of the trinity became excluded, and three became two once more. For there was Mary Magdalene kneeling, there was Jesus on the cross, breathing his final breaths. The two of them looked at each other, and outside of their gaze there was nothing and no one else in the world.

Annie knew, at last, with absolute clarity, why she had dreaded the completion of the painting so much. She knew as surely as she knew the end of the story in the panel what would happen next. For she could see – and it was like looking at someone naked – what was there, what Francis had captured all too perfectly in that look between the Magdalene and the Christ. It was there for all to see; there for Francis to see. Love, pure, searing love.

She had known, when she had looked at him on the cross that day, that it was true what Francis had said, that the rainbow man was in love with her. Now she made an even more shattering discovery: that she was in love with him, too. Had she realised it when he'd been so kind to her about the child? Or when he had taken her to Fiesole and kissed her, and unlocked once again who she really was, the Annie Stride who had been kept in a casket and brought here with the luggage from London? Or had she loved him since she had first set eyes upon him in the Uffizi, standing there staring like the David? In any case, the thing was done, and it was now enshrined in wood and paint for all to see.

Francis, of course, had known it all along.

'My dear,' he said as he'd done once before, but differently this time – not with a playful threat, but low and grim – 'now it is time to say goodbye to *l'uomo arcobaleno*.'

She looked at the rainbow man then, her face a copy of how the Magdalene on the panel had looked her last at Jesus, his face a copy of how Jesus had looked his last at the Magdalene. 'Goodbye,' she whispered.

He took up his coat of many colours from across the chair, shrugged it on, and was gone.

Francis had turned his back, and was cleaning his brushes and singing an air as if nothing had happened. But something *had* happened. She had to follow the rainbow man. Of course she must. It was inconceivable, now, that she should live without him. She stepped towards the door. 'If you go,' Francis said, without turning, 'do not come back.'

Her footsteps stuttered, and with the stumble it was as if she saw the gutter below her, waiting for her return, embracing her with a muddy ditch just her size, there all the time to cushion her inevitable fall with the other detritus of human life. Francis had said that the rainbow man loved her, and the painting told the same story, and Francis's paintings never lied. But would he marry her, and keep her in a golden villa and gowns of silk and green gardens? She steadied herself, straightened, and lifted her chin.

Instead of heading down to the garden door, she climbed the stairs, slowly and decorously and with perfect deportment, like the lady she now was. As she stood on the landing, the sun was going down outside the wide windows, drowning in its own blood, just as it had done that long-ago night on Calvary. She watched as the rainbow man emerged far below, having reached the lane, walking fast towards the city. She followed him with her eyes for as long as she could, until he was a speck of black, the absence of colour. It was only then that she realised she'd been wringing something in her hands. It was the red cloak of the Magdalene, the red cloak that she would no longer need. There could not be another painting of the Magdalene, not after this one.

She folded the cloth, too neatly, too carefully, and placed it on the windowsill. As she did so, it struck her that, alone of all the seven colours of the rainbow, she and the rainbow man had never talked about red; and now they never would.

Chapter 17

One year and six months ago
Modelling is the easiest money I have ever made.

The good man is called Francis Maybrick Gill, and he lives in a fancy house on Gower Street. All he asks me to do is put on a white dress and sit in a chair holding some white flowers. He never touches me once.

I sit there all afternoon, in a green room with big windows, trying to stay as still as possible. He is kind to me. 'Are you tired, Mary Jane? Are you hungry, Mary Jane?' He lets me rest in between times; and if I say I am hungry, his maid brings me a slice of game pie and a glass of porter. The pie is the best thing I've ever tasted.

Then when the sun goes down he puts his pencil down, too. He lets me see his canvas. The pencil-line girl looks just like me.

He asks me to go back the next day. I agree at once, and return to Annie at the Haymarket stinking of those old flowers of his.

Francis never spoke of the rainbow man again.

Things went on as before. The surface waters of their counterfeit marriage were smooth again. They kept no company, and Francis was still away from home in the evenings. And Annie, despite the rainbow man's disturbance of the waters – a pebble thrown into the mirrored surface, the radiating ripples of his love for her, her love for him – had maintained her position as Signora

Maybrick Gill and was still the mistress of the Villa Camellia. She'd made her choice. She'd got what she wanted, but had never felt more trapped and lonely here in her eyrie.

When Francis had first brought her to Gower Street, she had felt the luxury of being left alone, untouched and unsolicited. Her days were sweet just because she did not have to talk to a man or touch a man in order to eat. To be provided for, and for nothing to be asked of her in return, was a luxury in itself. It was a luxury she had looked forward to, become used to, then bored of. Her former profession, with all its dark and obvious drawbacks, had seen her in constant company, even if it was of the lowest kind. Now she had less company than the camellias, which crowded their fragrant heads together like gossiping schoolgirls. And yet she knew it was not general company she lacked, but the company of one particular man.

She would recall every detail of her time with the rainbow man: the conversations, the companionship, the kiss. How he'd first told her about blue, and then how they'd gone on to discuss every other colour; not just what it meant to him, but what it meant to her. How he'd unlocked the real Annie Stride, colour by colour, from her past experiences, until he knew the whole spectrum of her. Every colour save red. They'd been parted before he could get to the crimson that Francis used so lavishly.

She had little to distract her from this new and overpowering feeling. She had the garden during the day, but despite its beauty, she was dull there, and every yew walk and herb garden reminded her of when she had walked there with another. She did not paint or sketch or play music or ply a needle – she had tried, but the results were hopeless. She had the Dante, but could not concentrate on the text. In the evenings she would dine alone, then go to the loggia and look at the lights of the city, where Francis was without her. But she no longer wondered where he was, and what he was doing. She only thought that somewhere in those streets the rainbow man walked in his motley frock coat, his bottles swinging and singing.

She watched in a desultory fashion when Francis's new colourman came up the road, his coloured coat in regular checks instead of shreds and patches, his bottles, not swinging from his shoulders but ranked neatly in an attaché case. He was small, and bald, and unimpressive, and gazed at her owlishly over a pair of gold pince-nez. He, too, introduced himself as Signor Arcobaleno; it was clearly a title, not a proper name. But he was not *her* rainbow man, whatever his profession might be. She would not ask *him* about red. She would not ask him anything.

In the evenings, she picked up the Dante to read to Francis. She tried to make everything as it was before, to summon again that burning feeling when she'd gone alone to bed, when she'd longed for him to touch her. But it was gone, quite gone. She was grateful to Francis; she would be eternally grateful. But love? She had to acknowledge, now, that she did not love him; had never loved him. So she was more affectionate, more attentive, than ever before; as though love, like the pianoforte or needlepoint, could be achieved by practice.

Francis did not paint her now, even though he had the colours to do it. She was used, by now, to the ebb and flow of his artistic passion. He shut the studio, and soon the smell of paint, and of her rainbow man, was quite gone from the house. She would wander in there sometimes, in the quiet afternoons, to finger the crimson gown. Red, the colour of the robe – the only stripe of the spectrum that she and the rainbow man had never talked about – seemed to represent loss. She would lift up her eyes to the hills, to that high vantage where, wreathed in cypresses, stony and squat, sat the convent of Mary Magdalene.

She knew that Francis would now be torpid and placid and might sleep a lot more; that he might wish to spend more time with her at the Roman theatre or on drives into the hills or in the tea salons of Fiesole. She endeavoured to enjoy these days and his company, understanding him, nurturing him, as if they were married in truth. This was her penance, she felt, for her transgression; she was at pains to be the perfect wife. They did not, ever, take trips into Florence, but she knew he still went there in the evening sometimes, seeking inspiration; he was making, he said, a study of a number of churches by sunset. These trips seemed to unsettle him, however; he would come back agitated, and ask her to read to him, no matter how late the hour. One night he seemed particularly het up, and could not content himself; he could neither sit nor stand. Pacing the loggia in some private passion, he asked to hear a particular canto of the Dante. 'It reminds me of the camellias,' he said.

She found the place. '"The Angel other, that sees and sings the glory, of him who inspires it with love, as it flies, and sings the excellence that has made it as it is, descended continually into the great flower, lovely with so many petals, and climbed again to where its love lives ever, like a swarm of bees, that now plunges into the flowers, and now returns, to where their labour is turned to sweetness."'

Francis came to sit beside her and clasped her hands; she dropped the book. 'Should I stop?'

He touched her cheek, and looked at her in quite the old way. 'It has been dull for you here,' he said. 'No wonder you sought company with another. I am at fault.'

Annie was touched. She tried to frame in her mind an assurance that the rainbow man had meant nothing to her, that she was glad he was gone. But she could not be St Peter and deny him; the words stuck in her throat.

'I have caged my bird; she is mine, but she no longer sings.' He sat forward and took her hands, eyes shining. He was quite the old Francis again. 'How would you like a change?'

Without waiting for an answer, he leapt to his feet and clapped his hands. 'Pack your things. I have a wonderful notion, and there is not a moment to be lost. You and I will take a very special excursion.'

His excitement, and the precipitate nature of his planning, reminded her sharply of the night they had left London. She felt, suddenly, wary of him and his caprice. But now, as then, she had no alternative. She did not want to go away from this place, the place where *he* was, her beautiful rainbow man. But she had nowhere else to go but with Francis, unless she wished to return to her old life.

She stood and took his hand. 'I will follow you to the ends of the earth, as long as we are together.' It was a ridiculous, melodramatic thing to say, but she thought that if she said it fervently enough, it might be true.

'It will not be necessary to follow me so far,' he replied. 'Only to Venice.'

PART THREE

Venice

Chapter 18

One year, three months, one week and five days ago
When I am sitting for Francis, he tells me stories to pass the time,
for sitting still for hours can, I learn, be tedious.

He tells me the plot of a book he is reading; it is about a working
girl called Marguerite. A man called Armand falls in love with her
but she gives him up, at the request of his father, so that his sister
can marry without disgrace. She dies at the end, of consumption,
but I like the story.

'Do you?' he says when I tell him so. 'Why, Mary Jane?'
'Because it shows that some working girls have honour.'

Venice was like a toybox, a cardboard wonder of doll's houses.

The palaces looked so improbable, with their pastel paint and
their delicate windows. Annie expected that the citizens of Venice,
doll-like themselves in their silks and their masks, did not enter
their houses through doors, but flicked a little brass catch for the
whole frontage to hinge open in one great piece, revealing at once
all the toy rooms inside.

It had taken the better part of a day to get here from Florence.
Francis had given Michelangelo the weekend off in favour of the
ferrovia; the new railway. He had bought them a compartment to
themselves, a little glass car with broad windows and comfortable
seats with antimacassars and lamps and a table for their refreshment. There was even a strip of looking glass under the sconces.

In it Annie hardly recognised her own reflection – gone was the girl who'd floated about the garden of the Villa Camellia barefoot and loose-haired, in a Chinese bed gown. Now she was Signora Maybrick Gill once more, an English lady and the wife of a respectable artist.

Francis had bought her a gown for the occasion of flame-coloured satin, almost exactly the same shade as her hair. The bodice was sewn with brilliants and she wore a cape of fox fur with the mask attached – the impotently bared teeth reminded her of her old friend, Jezebel's dog; bold in the face of death, which had already claimed him, his defiance come too late. She wore white gloves to the elbow, and her hair was elaborately dressed. Nezetta had proved to be rather good at hair, and had entered enthusiastically into the business of getting her little mistress ready for her pleasure trip. She had fixed amber combs and cinnamon feathers into the complicated strawberry-blonde plaits and buns she had created, soothing Annie like a difficult horse with a constant rosary of Tuscan, and had stood back satisfied after a full hour of currying. Francis, whose toilette had taken a little less time – even without the assistance of a valet – was nonetheless immaculate in tails, just as she had seen him that first night on Waterloo Bridge, the Bridge of Sighs.

So Annie had watched the city she now called home recede, as the train took them north. The rhythm of the wheels on the railway and the warmth of the sun sent her into a lolling sleep against Francis's shoulder. It seemed only a second later that she woke with a start; it was twilight, and they were crossing a lagoon that was a dark mirror under an apricot sky. Night was coming.

From the station, they walked the maze of dark streets and bridges. Francis navigated them as surely as a blind man; he had been here, he said, many times, and Annie reflected again how little she knew of him. Now and again there were glimpses of a broad waterway that curved like the Thames. But never did the

Thames see such houses standing sentinel on her banks with their stone windows cut into doilies. Nor would Venice, she was sure, exchange her treasures for the dreary wharves and mudflats of Wapping or East India Quay. She was certain this shining city had no shady corners for working girls, but she was wrong. 'Look,' said Francis. He pointed up to a side bridge, crowded with people, and a sign affixed to the wall: *Ponte delle Tette* read the black writing. 'It means Bridge of the Tits,' said Francis.

Annie was just deciding whether to laugh when she realised that the little crowd was a knot of gaudy whores, and that not one of them was clothed from the waist up. Each of them flopped their ample breasts over the parapet to tempt the passing boatmen. 'Even here,' she said.

Francis nodded. 'They say in London,' he remarked pleasantly as they walked, 'that you are never more than ten paces from a rat. I expect whores are the same. They are never far away.'

She looked at him sharply. Since he had directed that bitter speech her way in the presence of the rainbow man, she had developed a new wariness of his tongue. But there seemed to be no guile in the statement. On the contrary, he did not appear to be directing the remark at her at all; he was musing on the ways of the world, and including her with him as one of the lucky ones.

Just as she was becoming footsore in her elegant buttoned boots, the dark little alleyways opened out into a large square, with a grand white marble edifice in one corner, a snowy portico supported by broad pillars pasted with playbills. The Ponte delle Tette receded like a nightmare.

'Now for your treat,' he said expansively. 'A treat indeed, for myself, I admit, as much as for you.'

The playbills read *La Traviata*. Annie, who still struggled with Italian, translated it as something to do with falling. 'What is the play?'

'Not a play; no Shakespeare, I assure you.' He smiled. 'No, an opera, based on my favourite play, which is based on my favourite book.'

Annie was puzzled. 'D'you mean the Dante? The *Divina Commedia*?' She had a notion that made her proud of herself. 'Is it to do with man's fall from grace?'

'No; although it is greatly to your credit that you might think so. This is not about a fallen man but a fallen woman.'

'Is that what *La Traviata* means? The fallen woman?'

'Yes.' He gave her his arm up the broad stone steps, and inside the door. There was a great press of people, bright silks for the ladies and dark opera cloaks for the gentlemen, and a number of Venetians in masks, as if they were such a theatrical people they made no distinction between on and off the stage. There was golden light coming from above, reflected by the brilliants of a dozen chandeliers. She was inside the doll's house.

They walked through the glittering company and Francis surrendered his little card tickets to an usher in gold livery, then led her up a stair to their box. 'Napoleon sat here once, with his Empress Josephine,' he said, but Annie hardly listened as she stepped forward in a dream to look out at the theatre proper. She let out a gasp. It was a jewel box of tiers, painted in a light turquoise, gilded with curlicues and lilies in rosy gold. Overhead arched a turquoise sky, and instead of a sun there was an immense chandelier, hung with crystals like diamonds and encircled by cherubs. The cherubs seemed to fly around her head and the chandelier turn about like a glittering cartwheel. For a moment she could not steady herself. Not quarter of an hour ago she had watched a gaggle of tuppenny whores dangling their tits from a bridge. Now she was sitting in the seat of an empress.

She let the fox fur slip from her shoulders. She did not know how an empress behaved; the only empress she knew of was Victoria; by all accounts a dour and plain thing. She imagined how

Napoleon's empress would have acted – she was sure that Josephine, too, would have worn jewels and furs when she sat in this very place, settling herself on the gilded chair as on a throne, peering at the programme. 'Would you tell me,' she said, still being Josephine, 'a little of the story?'

'It is an adaptation of *La Dame aux Camélias*. The French writer Alexandre Dumas wrote the play, adapted from his novel of the same name, as a tribute to a woman he had loved. She was a great Parisian beauty called Marie Duplessis.' He crossed his legs. 'She was also a prostitute.'

They are never far away. 'A working girl?'

'Yes, but of a particular kind. She was a courtesan, a lady who bestowed her favours on rich men in return for an apartment or jewels or fine gowns.'

'Still a working girl,' said Annie, thinking of the girls on the bridge. 'We . . . *they* are all the same, no matter how high and mighty or mean and lowly.' Then she remembered. 'Did you read an extract of the book to me once? In London, when I was . . . indisposed? About a young lady, and some flowers?'

He touched her nose. 'Clever girl.'

A bell rang, the lights dimmed, and the orchestra began to play, softly at first, then a waltzing, lilting theme that lifted her leaden heart a little. Francis had been right. She had needed this diversion. Here, where he had never been, and could not be expected, she could try to forget the rainbow man.

The opera opened on a dazzling party, which revolved around a woman in a dress as red as the Magdalene's. Annie recalled seeing Adelaide Neilson giving her Isabella at the Adelphi, and thought now what she had then – that this lady was too old and too fat to play the young heroine; but she forgot her reservations when she noticed almost at once that the lady wore a white flower in her hair. She bent to Francis's ear. 'She is wearing a camellia.'

'Yes,' he whispered. 'That character, Violetta, is based upon

Marie Duplessis. Marie used to wear a white camellia in her hair every day of the month, save for the five days for which she was . . . indisposed.'

Francis was so polite, it took Annie some moments to realise what he meant.

'And then?'

'Then she would wear red.'

Annie was interested. In the East End, the girls would wear ribbons round their throats when they were in their bleeding time. She herself had worn such a choker. Most of the bastards would take other pleasures during those five days, but some would come sniffing like scorpions after the blood. One of them had told her he liked dollies in their bleeding time. 'Nice and slippery,' he'd said. 'Like jellied eels.'

She dismissed the memory and tried to concentrate on the action on the stage, her eyes following the little white blob of a flower. She could almost have sworn that she could smell that detested sickly scent even from this distance, as if the eyes and the nose conspired together. She watched as Violetta took the flower from her hair at the end of the first act, and gave it to one of the suitors who were buzzing round her like bees. She bent to Francis once more. 'What is she saying?'

'That he should return when the flower is wilted. He takes it to mean tomorrow.'

Then Violetta sang alone and the song was suddenly gay – like a butterfly flitting from flower to flower.

'This is her hymn to joy. She is saying that she wishes to enjoy each day – that she wishes to drown in pleasure.'

The metaphor gave Annie an uncomfortable recollection of Mary Jane's end, and she watched soberly for a while. The audience, too, after the rapturous applause that had followed the first act, subsided into a sullen silence as fortune turned on Violetta. The courtesan realised that her lover Alfredo might be the man to save her, singing her refrain *Ah, fors'è lui* – which Francis translated as 'perhaps he is the one' – but then began to cough, and clutch dramatically at her chest.

'Is she sick?' whispered Annie.

'Yes,' he said. 'She has consumption.'

Now she watched with dread; she thought she knew what was going to happen. She had heard so many working girls develop that terrible cough – first a tickle, almost as if they were clearing the throat, then a bark like a dog. Then they would bring up blood onto their sleeve, and soon they were in their cold grave instead of a warm bed. How cruel that death should separate the lovers, how terribly cruel!

But her expectations were confounded. It was not death that parted the lovers, but Violetta herself. In the second act, the lady with the camellias gave up her life of pleasure and luxury to retire to a house in the country – a house that, by the look of the sumptuous set, was not unlike the Villa Camellia. There she lived simply with her Alfredo, sustaining herself on his love instead of her endless whirl of parties. But then Alfredo's elderly father came to visit Violetta when his son was not at home. Annie watched their sung exchange with misgiving. Francis's breath was warm in her ear. 'He is appealing to her. He says that he has a daughter who is an angel – Alfredo's sister. The sister is engaged to a man she loves, but her fiancé will call off their marriage if Alfredo persists in this disgraceful union with a prostitute. Violetta agrees to give Alfredo up; to sacrifice her happiness for that of another woman.'

Annie no longer watched the flower. She watched Violetta. She seemed neither plump nor histrionic now, but noble, as she regretfully agreed to break with Alfredo in order that his sister should not be divided from her love. Annie had heard enough heart-rending music-hall songs to know what was coming. This was not the Whitechapel Empire, but the rules were the same; all the girls in the songs made pathetic ends: Polly Perkins from Paddington Green would expire, my darling Clementine would be lost and gone forever, Violetta would die alone.

She watched as Violetta became once again queen of the social whirl, this time attached to her latest lover, the wealthy Barone Douphol. The discarded Alfredo, unaware of her honourable reasons for rejecting him, shamed her in front of the whole company, accusing her of being addicted to luxury. And then the cough returned, and blossomed, as Annie had known it would: the tickle, the bark, the blood. The doctor was called, came, could do nothing. *The doctor has come and gone.* He was powerless in the face of such a fateful colour. The red camellia, the Magdalene's cloak, the flower of blood on the kerchief, the baby on the bed sheets. All those things seemed connected and collected in that last pitiful aria, as Violetta twisted on her deathbed. Even Alfredo's penitent presence could not save her; it was no consolation to Annie that Violetta died in his arms. She was not alone at the end, then, but he was.

Annie felt for Francis's hand, and clutched it. She meant, then, never to let it go again. She could not, would not return to penury – she could not beggar herself, even for love. The whores on the Ponte delle Tette had frightened her badly. *They are never far away. Never more than ten paces.*

At the orchestra's final dramatic note Francis stood to applaud frantically. She could see that his cheeks were wet with tears. The wider audience did not seem to share his enthusiasm – the applause was scant, and many patrons were already making for the exits. 'It may be the first and last time it is performed,' Francis said, dabbing his eyes with his gloved fingers. 'So I am glad we were here.' She looked at him askance. 'Sometimes we take the most precious things for granted, and do not feel the lack of them till they are gone,' he said. 'Don't you find?'

She tried not to think of the rainbow man. She forced herself to imagine only what life would be like without Francis, and clutched his hand tighter. 'Yes,' she said soberly.

Down in the auditorium Francis gently eased his hand from her grip. 'Wait for me here, dearest, and do not move,' he said. 'I have a small commission to complete.' She stood for a moment alone, under the painted sky where the rosy cherubs obligingly held up the crystal chandelier above her head.

She looked about her; and as if she had summoned him, the rainbow man was suddenly there, on the other side of the prosce- nium, still and staring. For a full moment their eyes met, and in the ebb and flow of the crowd he could be clearly seen, with no one between the two of them. The apparition seemed to reproach her with his eyes for the Devil's deal she had made, to choose wealth and security over love. Then the emptying audience closed around him again.

She blinked, suddenly icy cold, and craned around the crush of people, between shoulders and over heads, standing on tiptoes to catch another glimpse. But like a phantom, he was gone.

She shook her head; her senses were playing havoc tonight. If the mere sight of a camellia could bring that detested scent to her nose, those same eyes could easily conjure a spirit. It had not been him – he had not the rainbow coat he had worn as a colourman, not the military jacket he had worn in the Uffizi. This man had been as tall as he, and as broad, but he was clean-shaven, and immaculate, his long hair slicked back with pomade, his white tie knotted perfectly at his tanned throat. In the dark cloth of his hanging sleeves she could not have sworn if he'd had one arm or two. Only his eyes had recalled the rainbow man, dark as night and deep as damnation.

She flicked open her fan and wafted the apparition away. She would not let the rainbow man's memory turn her from her purpose. Francis was to be first in her heart from now on. So when he returned to her side, offering his arm, saying that he wished to show her something very particular before they found their *pensione*, she took it eagerly, saying, 'Oh yes, yes! *Dear* Francis, show me at once!'

The city was strange to Annie – to be so hemmed in, after a month on the hilltop, was strange; to be in the heart of a dark city and yet to constantly cross bridges over still water was yet stranger. The elegant citizens walked arm in arm, laughing and talking, the water plashed gently at the foot of the palaces, nibbling away at their foundations. There was not a horse and carriage to be seen, for there were no roads, just silvery water paving the narrow alleys, and a dozen bridges to be crossed in as many moments. There were many cloaked and masked characters in the alleys, and she found herself interrogating every face. Once again, she had to make a concerted attempt to put the rainbow man from her mind,

On their way they began to see little shops with gewgaws of bright glass and gilded masks and picture postcards, but Annie had not the leisure to stop and press her nose against the window as she had used to do in Cheapside. Francis led her unerringly to the biggest square she had yet seen, enclosed on three sides by pillared colonnades concealing arches of shadow. Here a great tower loomed over them like a jade-topped spear, there was a gold-domed cathedral and a white stone palace frilled with battlements as delicate as lace. It looked familiar. Francis stopped in the middle, scattering the roosting pigeons, which rose around them like smoky spirits. 'Do you remember?' he said.

And, quite suddenly, she did: the night they'd been to the Vauxhall Gardens, and seen this very square recreated in plaster and clapboard and gaudy paint. She remembered the harlequin sliding down the high wire with the jumping jacks at his heels. That same night they had seen Mother in the shadows, and Mother had pretended to know Francis. Tonight, she'd had a similar jolt: those bare-breasted whores. *They are everywhere*. She clasped

Francis's arm tighter – the muscle and bone of his arm in the cloth was a touchstone against the ghosts.

'St Mark's Square,' he said, gesturing with his arm as if the whole place was in his gift. 'Ruskin called it "a treasure-heap". In the church lies the saint himself, clothed in gold.'

'Is that what you want to show me?'

'No. I want to show you a place, not a person. Then, when we are before it, I have something to ask you and something to give you.'

Annie walked with him across the great moonlit square, her heart beating slowly and painfully in time with her footsteps. Above their heads the bells of the great tower tolled portentously. She knew what Francis had to ask. The subject matter of the opera, the conversation after. Had he even led her past the Ponte delle Tette on purpose, to underline to her, once and for all, how much better a future would be with him? Yes, she knew what he would ask. And she knew what her answer would be.

They walked all the way to the lagoon, where the dark sea nibbled at the city, and along a promenade to a broad white bridge open to the lagoon. The breeze brought the first breath of autumn from the ocean and ruffled her fox fur. There, at the crown of the bridge, Francis stopped and turned her around by her shoulders.

Set back from the promenade, far overhead and spanning the canal between two great palaces, was a covered bridge, like a stone rainbow, carved with curlicues and with two square windows like eyes.

'This,' said Francis, 'is the Bridge of Sighs.'

Annie had to lean, for a moment, on the parapet before her, the cold stone hurting her ribs, pushing the air out of her lungs with an involuntary sigh of her own. This, then, was the *real* Bridge of Sighs, the bridge after which Waterloo Bridge had been named. She gazed and gazed at the stone, suddenly transported back to that freezing January night when she'd leaned on a parapet like this one, the stone crushing the breath from her, the breath that she'd thought would be her last. Then she'd climbed up, and spread her arms like angel wings, only for Francis to catch at her sleeve and pull her down to earth. That same night, she'd seen the painting of Mary Jane, named for that bridge, and for this.

In her mind Mary Jane and Violetta became one, the fallen women, dead and gone. Violetta had had her chance for happiness; she could have married Alfredo and settled down, but she gave him up for honour. Violetta had been a fool. Annie would not make the same mistake. She would not renounce Francis for the sake of his soul or his reputation. He had no sister with a marriage to save, nor would Annie Stride have given a fig for it if he had. Her badge of honour, if she'd ever had it, had been ripped from her sleeve in the upper room of the Old George at the age of thirteen, and she would not wear its colours now.

She knew exactly how she would answer Francis when he asked her, as she knew he would, to be his wife. When he gave her, as she knew he would, a betrothal ring to seal the sacrament. She would wear it with pride. No one here knew her history; she would reconstruct, back in Florence, that honour she had once lost. She would not be such a fool as to refuse him, for if she did, how could she remain under his roof at the Villa Camellia? She would have to quit his house, and then what? Return to England? Or work the streets of Florence? Francis might not represent the love she felt for the rainbow man, the true love that was immortalised on his triptych of the Magdalene. But he represented her best hope for the future.

'I wanted you to see this bridge.' His voice came low and gentle. 'I wanted you to see how far you have come. Your air, your beauty, your voice – you have blossomed here. You are an exquisite young lady, Annie.' She turned to him, his eyes on a level with hers, his handsome face unsmiling for once, the grey eyes sincere. 'I have something to give you, something I wanted to give you here in this very place.'

He had one hand behind his back, concealing something; concealing the ring. She took a breath as if she were to take a plunge; a breath that was the opposite of a sigh, a breath like the one she had taken that night on the parapet of Waterloo Bridge. How odd that she should greet death and a new life in the same way. Her stomach lurched with some flat feeling that felt a little like resignation. She eased her fingers from her left glove and held out her hand. She closed her eyes, not able to face this beginning, this end.

A sickly-sweet smell assailed her nose, and her fingers met not a hard circle but something soft and velvety.

She opened her eyes. He had given her a camellia; bone-white and overblown, its petals wilting slightly. 'It is the very one from La Traviata's hair,' he said. 'I secured it for you after the curtain call.' He fitted its stem between the finger and thumb of her outstretched hand. 'I hope you know what it means.' He took her face in his hands – his fingers were cold. 'I want you to be mine,' he said. 'In *every* way. Do you understand? When we return, a new chapter will begin.'

She looked into his eyes, and read his meaning there. 'Yes,' she said. 'I'll be whoever you want.' She had meant to say she would do whatever he wanted, but the words seemed to choose themselves. She had uttered them many times to the bastards. So she was still a whore after all.

Chapter 19

One year and three months ago

Every day when I go to Gower Street Francis makes me put on the same dress – the white muslin with little sprigs of flowers. It is quite old-fashioned but he insists upon it. With his money you'd think he could give me a nice frock, silks or satins. This one isn't even as nice as the ones Annie and me used to dress-lodge in. I know Francis well enough now to be cheeky, so I ask him about it. 'Why d'you like this old dress so much, then?'

He is painting and frowns at his brush. 'I don't like it, Mary Jane,' he says. 'I love it.'

'Why?' I ask.

Still he doesn't look up. 'It belongs to my mother.'

'Where's she? Isn't she missing her frock?'

Now he puts down his brush and walks to a little cabinet. He unlocks it and takes out a white jar. He puts it in my hands. It is heavy and cold to the touch.

'Careful,' he says, and takes off the lid. Inside is grey dust. 'This is my mother,' he says.

Then I understand. I hand the jar back. 'I'm sorry.'

He takes up his brush and starts painting again. 'So am I,' he says. 'So am I.'

Annie went into the garden as soon as they returned to the villa in Fiesole, looking for a red camellia. A red camellia would give her time to think. His *lover*. She was to be Francis's lover, at last. It was something she had once longed for, and now she'd been granted it, she no longer wanted it.

Last night, in Venice, at the *pensione*, respectably lodged in their separate rooms, there had been no chance for Francis to attempt to begin their new relations; but tonight would be different.

Francis went to rest after the train journey, but Annie slipped into the Chinese gown, and down the stairs into the garden. She needed to discover how she felt, now that she was here, back in Florence.

She wandered down the garden alleys, the warm sun already dispersing the chill of early autumn, diaphanous dew riming the lawns, and contemplated the future. No marriage. No ring besides his mother's, a ring that spelled his regard but not the sacrament of marriage; not a life-long commitment, nor any protection for her if he should die. What of property, what of children? Without marriage, was she not still just a whore? And if that were true, how far had she actually risen from the gutter? If she was in love with Francis, none of this would matter – but she knew now that she was not.

She needed some time to think, to get used to the idea of this new phase of their relationship, and the red camellia represented that time. She was sure, knowing Francis as she did, that he would follow the rules, the rules of Marie Duplessis, the rules of Alexandre Dumas, the rules of the camellias themselves. Red camellias meant the bleeding time. Red camellias represented five days of grace.

So she searched the garden for red, the red of the Magdalene, the only colour she had not discussed with the rainbow man. At length she found what she was looking for, clustered behind a fragment of statue beyond the stone seat where she had sometimes sat with the rainbow man. She picked one with difficulty, for the stems were unexpectedly wiry and strong. She still hated the flowers, but had a grudging respect for how hard she had to work to pluck them; they were both beautiful and tough, just like a working girl. Heart thudding, she twined three into her hair, so he could not miss them, and walked back into the house.

Francis was sitting on the loggia, reading a Florentine newspaper. He folded it swiftly upon her approach but not before she glimpsed the headline. It read: *Girl found dead in the Arno*, but just then Annie was too agitated to concern herself with someone else's tragedy. She sat down on the chaise longue, and he saw the flowers at once. 'I would like to paint you,' he said, 'just like that.' He came to her and pulled her hair over her shoulders, ruffling the golden mass. 'In your Chinese gown, with the camellias in your hair. I will call it *The Girl with the Crimson Camellias*, a companion piece to the canvas I painted in Gower Street.' He touched the bloom behind her ear. 'Crimson, too, is the perfect colour. Like a fool, I would have chosen bone again.'

It was time for her performance – the overture was ended, the audience hushed. She looked down. 'I did not choose them for their colour,' she said, 'but for their message.' She looked at him from beneath her lashes, feigning modesty. 'Our union must wait for five more days.'

For a heartbeat, she thought he would be angry; there was a flicker in his eye, just as soon gone. He pursed his lips until they disappeared, then said kindly, 'Then we will employ the time well. Stay where you are; the light is perfect. I will be back.' He kissed her lips, and she tried to feel what she had once felt just a mile away, in a field of poppies.

For five days Francis painted her as the Girl with the Crimson Camellias. He worked outside, and he worked fast. It was as if he had just the span of her bleeding to complete the work, as if she would change her colour when the flower did, as if she herself had chameleon blood. And in a way, it was true: she was a chameleon. This girl was very different from the Girl with the White Camellias. In London, when she'd posed with the white blooms, she'd been buttoned up and virginal in white muslin. He'd practically used only one hue of paint on the entire canvas: bone. She'd held the bouquet of flowers up before her like a bride, demurely hiding her breasts, her hair bound up, her face uncertain. Then she'd been indoors, in the Scheele's green studio in the first spring light. Now she was a different creature – she lounged al fresco on the chaise on the loggia, in nothing but the blue Chinese peignoir. At Francis's instruction she wore no stays or corset. Her naked body was fully visible beneath the sheer gown, a half-moon of breast falling from her neckline, a dark, inviting shadow at her groin. Her hair was loose, her mouth half open and wanton, the red camellias tangled in her abundant, tumbling hair.

She wondered if, now that he had decided to claim her as his lover, as his plaything and possession, he was testing the boundaries of what he could make her do. She was to fulfil his fantasy, anticipate their time together. Uncannily, when he spoke, she found their thoughts marched in tandem. 'The Girl with the White Camellias had never known the touch of a man. But the red – a man has just left her bed, just left her body, and she is ready for more. Show me that, Annie. How long is it since you had a man? You must have thought of it. Think of it now. Think of our union. I want to see your desires writ on your face.'

She tried. She tried to look at Francis as if he wanted him. But it was only when she let her gaze drift unfocused and allowed her mind's eye to transform Francis's dark shape into the rainbow man that she felt her body heat. Thinking of him upon her, within her, his mouth and fingers everywhere, she found she could do what Francis wanted. She licked her lips and parted them, she arched her back so her hard nipples thrust upward and the peignoir fell away, revealing her naked breasts. She let her legs loll open, showing the sudden slick of wetness between them. She did not care, at that moment, if Gennaro saw, or Michelangelo, or Nezetta. In fact, the thought of them watching her excited her. *If you would come to me now, my rainbow man,* she thought, *I would let you take me right here in front of all of them. I'd let them all watch, even Francis. Especially Francis.* She wanted, badly, to touch herself, to relieve this aching desire, but she knew that if she did, the moment would be over, and she would no longer look how Francis wanted her to.

Francis worked fast, breathing hard. Seeing that she was transported, he did not speak until the sun went down and her incandescent body grew cold. When he told her at last that they must stop, she could see that he was hard for her, as he had not been since they first came to the villa. He left her hurriedly, and she was sure he had gone to find some private relief of his own.

Alone with the canvas, she peered at the work and detected a new style in his painting. He was not concerned, here, with realism; he had captured the very essence of her, and his brushwork was, in some places, clearly visible. This work was genius, but quite a different genius to the pious perfection of the poplar panel. It was rough and passionate and wanton. She looked like the embodiment of lust. She wondered then, with a sudden qualm, what Francis would do to her in bed.

On the fifth day, she picked the last of the crimson camellias. By tonight, she would be in his bed, and he knew it, too. After their morning sitting, he took the last flower from her hair for his buttonhole, a gesture he performed with great significance, like an actor. He had found a home for his triptych of the Magdalene and must visit a priest in Florence to finalise the sale, taking Michelangelo and the carriage. 'By the time the flower fades, I will be back. Till tonight,' he said, and kissed her hungrily, a prelude to what was to come.

Annie had had so many men, in so many ways, and she detected something new in Francis she had never known before, a darkness when they kissed, a glimpse down the pit. There was some unknown depravity there; something outside of the workaday lusts of the bastards. For the first time, she was afraid.

She could not settle to anything that day, but spent her afternoon in the garden as she always did. She took the Dante with her, trying not to recall that this was where she had first seen the rainbow man, trying not to remember that he had loved Dante, that he had called the poet the father of the Italian nation. And then, after months of tolerating Dante – and not understanding, if the truth be told, what all the fuss was about – the poetry suddenly kindled before her eyes; and one passage, unexpectedly, expressed exactly her feelings for the rainbow man: *Love, that can quickly seize the gentle heart, took hold of him because of the fair body taken from me – how that was done still wounds me. Love, that releases no beloved from loving, took hold of me so strongly through his beauty that, as you see, it has not left me yet.*

She closed the book and fixed her eyes on the ochre road. She told herself she longed for Francis's return, but it was the rainbow man she looked for. The day ended and the sun lowered, and she watched Nezetta and Gennaro walk arm in arm back to their village, for their son had not yet returned with the carriage. By nightfall she had to acknowledge that she dreaded Francis's return. If she lay with him tonight, nothing would materially change – the world already thought them married, and when the rainbow man had kissed her, he had believed she was Francis's wife and presumed, no doubt, that they already lay together. But in herself, she felt that once she gave herself to Francis, that bridge between her and the rainbow man would be broken forever. So many times she had lain back, or forward, or against a wall, and let the bastards take her – but this time it would be different. Now that she did not have to give her body for money, she had hoped that she would keep it for love.

The clouds gathered over the hills behind her, bunching and bruising in the purple of the Medici and the indigo of the Indies. Ahead of her a rainbow appeared over the gilded dome of the Duomo, taunting her. Was the colourman somewhere under its arc, touting its seven colours in his harlequin coat?

But she was not to be allowed her Florentine reverie; the elements had no sense of romance, and the clouds burst and doused her in the most English of ways. She snatched up the Dante and clutched it to her beneath the folds of the Chinese gown as she ran up the cypress path and past the fountain, its surface pocked and ruffled with droplets. Her hair was drenched, and weighed down almost to her knees; the gown sopped and dragged at her legs. Leaving wet footprints, she padded to the library to return the finished Dante to the shelf, and found that the buckram had left a red stain on her fingers.

She stood, dripping, before the silent books. She did not know how long Francis would be in town – some of his artistic meetings could run to midnight and beyond; and when he was not painting, and there was nothing for him to rise for in the morning, he did not keep an early bedtime. Thunder rolled overhead, and she began to fear for his safety in Michelangelo's rickety carriage on the open road. What if he never came back? The thought chilled her – but then she found her own concern oddly comforting. If she feared for him, if she wanted him to return safely, perhaps she could bring herself to love him a little, couldn't she?

She decided that now she had finished the Dante, she would seek out Francis's favourite book. She could not recall the exact title, but had no trouble recalling its subject – it was about camellias. A lady and some camellias. She sensed that she would enjoy it more than the Dante – it was what Francis called contemporary literature, like her beloved Mr Dickens, and what was more, it was about a working girl, just like her. For like it or not, that was what she still was. She was no one's wife. True, she was not walking the streets any more, but she was a working girl for all that. She had climbed to the top of the tree, as she and Mary Jane had always dreamed, and was a courtesan now, the consort of a rich man. She was Violetta.

Methodically, she searched the shelves, climbing all the sliding dark-wood ladders except one, which seemed to go nowhere, propped uselessly against an endcap. But she could not find the book.

The rain lashed at the windows of the glass door to the garden. The storm was gathering, the cypress trees bowing with the wind to almost touch the ground. There was nothing to do now but wait for Francis. Should she go to his chamber and arrange herself, as she'd been used to do when the richer bastards hired her for the night? Should she take off her clothes and drape herself temptingly over chaise longue or pillows? Or would he like to take her as she was, as he'd painted her for the last week, in the Chinese peignoir with the dying crimson camellias in her hair? She had forgotten, almost, how the game was played.

She wandered out of the library and up the stairs, past her own chamber and along the passageway to Francis's. She stood with her hand on the door, hesitating – it seemed strange to enter there, his sanctuary, and wait for him; presumptuous, despite his quite clear invitation. She dropped her hand and looked around her. There were other rooms here, rooms she had never really explored since the very first day she had come to the villa. She remembered then, suddenly, that night in Gower Street when she'd found Francis's cabinet of curiosities, with his stuffed dog standing sentinel and the other dead animals ranged on the shelves. Now, she looked in each room, but they were all neat bedrooms, clean and tidy and prepared for the company they never kept, the guests that never stayed; Francis's mother, bidden by his letter, had not come.

This time there was no hidden room at the end of the

passageway; only a blank wall. She frowned. It seemed shorter, somehow, than the passage in the other direction – truncated. Annie often thought in pictures, and now one suddenly dropped into her mind; she recalled the house from the garden as if she was watching a stereoscope in a sideshow, the photographs falling into their wooden frames, click, click, click. She saw the villa as it would appear on a postcard, black and white, with a slim white border and black typewriting along the bottom: *The Villa Camellia, Fiesole, front elevation.* Seven windows along the upper floor, above the loggia. Click, went the postcard. *The Villa Camellia, Fiesole, back elevation.* Six windows on the upper floor. Click. Seven windows at the front. Six windows at the back.

Click. The idea slotted into Annie's mind.

Somewhere in the Villa Camellia, there was a hidden room.

Suddenly cold, she walked slowly down the stairs again to the library. This time she did not put on the light. She went to the foot of the ladder that seemed to go nowhere. She climbed to the top of it, her hand cold on the iron of the terminal bracket. As she stood on the highest step, lightning flashed briefly, illuminating the great room. Then it fell dark again, and she saw a line, a golden line, almost as thin as a hair.

Light coming from somewhere.

Light coming from a room.

Heart thudding, she pushed at the shelf of books within the rectangle of that golden hairline. The shelf did not budge and she felt suddenly foolish – the solid, immovable oak of centuries mocked her. Then she saw, suddenly, *La Dame aux Camélias* at the far left of the shelf, the gilt tooling on the spine brighter than that of the other volumes. Another image clicked into her mind, in the slideshow stereoscope of her life. The Porcellino, the golden boar statue in the market in Florence, water pouring from his mouth into the bowl of the fountain; all of him a dull bronze save his snout, which was brightened to gilt by the hands of a thousand pilgrims coming to touch it for luck. The book was bright because it had been handled the most.

She eased her fingers around the spine of *La Dame aux Camélias* and pulled at the volume. It did not come free in her hand but cocked backwards with a faint click, and the whole shelf swung inward.

In front of her was a room, low-lit by lamps, with a window at the far end and shelves lining one wall. She honestly thought for a moment that she had stepped into a dream and was back in Gower Street, for on the shelves – and this she could scarcely believe – were the stuffed animals from Francis's cabinet of curiosities in London. There they were, all the creatures from his Fallen Woman series: the big black dog with his bared teeth, the green adder, the black cat, the sacrificial lamb curled up in death and the scapegoat with his horns wrapped in a red cloth. All still and staring, the lamplight playing on their glass eyes.

Her mind worked slowly, her thoughts treacle. Francis, then, had brought these stuffed creatures all the way here; he had carried them in those numerous trunks on the train and the boat, packed them carefully along with his paints and varnishes, just to languish in this room. But why?

She moved into the room, turning up the lamps, and the animals watched her. At first she thought they were the only things in the room; that he had recreated his cabinet from Gower Street exactly. But then her heart stopped as she saw, out of the corner of her eye, a white figure watching her. She swung round, but it was all right; it was just a dress, hanging as it might in a wardrobe; sleeves wide to embrace, hem trailing the floor. Heart thudding, she walked towards it, and fingered the stuff of the frock. White sprigged linen, the skirt stiff and stained. It was the dress she had worn in Gower Street, to pose as The Girl with the White Camellias. Not so strange, she told herself – attempting to calm her racing heart. Perhaps Francis had brought his collection with him in case he wished to reprise his London cycle of paintings here in Italy, and needed the same costumes, the same cast of inanimate characters. But then she realised that there were other objects here; that he had added to his collection. Here were the crimson camellias she had worn in her hair all week – a red wreath of them, in varying stages of decay. They were placed carefully in a circle around the final object; perhaps the strangest of all. The white alabaster jar.

She walked to it and picked it up – she had held it for so long, throughout all her sittings as the Magdalene, but now it felt cold and unfamiliar. She lifted the heavy lid, the lid she had knocked from its position once before – the one time, she recalled, when Francis had become really angry with her. She held her breath, dreading, suddenly, what she would find inside – but as before, there was nothing there but grey dust.

She must have been standing clutching the heavy jar for some minutes, for it warmed to her hand just as it used to do when she held it for all those hours of sittings. She set it back down carefully in the centre of the camellias, sensing with a strong instinct that Francis must not know she had been there. She had already turned to go when she caught sight of a series of long map drawers set below the shelves.

She laid her hand on the handle of the top drawer and pulled. It slid open smoothly to reveal a painting. The painting was on canvas, stretched but unframed, with rough edges where it had been cut from the easel. It was of a young woman. The woman was unremarkable – she was quite naked, and lying on a chaise longue – but the room was singular. It was Francis's studio in Gower Street.

Annie would have known the room anywhere – the tall, chapel-like windows terminating in crystal lilies, the chaise upholstered in wine-coloured velvet where she herself had posed as Lucrece, overlooked by the very stuffed owl that even now watched her from the shelves. But the feature that put the matter beyond doubt was the Scheele's green walls; the vivid, expensive colour that had given such character to the room.

Now that she had established the location of the painting, she looked closer at the girl – doubtless one of Francis's former models – with the professional curiosity of a rival. She no longer felt prurient or intrusive; for all that the girl was naked, there was nothing here to shock, certainly nothing that would shock one of Annie's experience. She was passably pretty – perhaps a little older than Annie herself, with curling auburn hair. It was not a bad pose, but a little too relaxed. Then she saw why: the model was asleep, fast asleep, her mouth slack, her body soft.

Annie felt a little superior – as a mere amateur posing as Lucrece, she had learned enough to know that even if you were feigning sleep, you should keep a certain amount of tension in your body, to make the pose more aesthetically pleasing. She almost smiled. She was no longer afraid. There was nothing odd about the room – Francis obviously kept the properties from all his paintings here lest he should need them again; and these canvases were stored here because he did not think them quite suitable for the eyes of the servants. Perhaps he did not think them suitable, either, for the eyes of the woman he wanted Annie to be. At any rate, this secret room in the library was obviously a quirk of the house that he had discovered and decided to use for storage; nothing sinister about that.

She continued to look through the map drawer. Below the first naked girl was another, and another, all sleeping, all in the same pose, all in the Scheele's green studio. She put them back carefully – she did not know why Francis had felt he had to hide such innocent nudes. Had he not told her himself, on her first night in Gower Street, that he was a student of the nude, and found his models in all reaches of society?

She opened the second drawer and could see almost at once

that here was even less to trouble her. These were studies of the same girls, the blondes, the redheads, the brunettes, all in the studio at Gower Street, all quite finished and varnished, the canvases stretched and completed then cut from the frames. Here, though, they were clothed, and depicted in different poses: sitting, standing, kneeling, or leaning on the Scheele's green wallpaper or by the tall arched windows. In these clothed studies, she was interested to see her old friends, the stuffed animals from the shelves. Here the owl perched on the windowsill, there the cat peeped from beneath a petticoat. One kneeling girl held the sparrow curled in her hand.

She closed the map drawer and opened the final one, the third, taking out the uppermost painting. To begin with, she saw only the white dress and the armful of white camellias, and thought it was herself. Then she saw the fall of dark hair, and the face, and her heart stopped.

It was Mary Jane.

She had to put her hand out to the wall to steady herself, her thoughts racing. What did this mean? When had Francis met Mary Jane? Annie knew, of course, that he'd painted her dead body for his Bridge of Sighs picture, but he had not mentioned that he had known her when she was alive. Had they been acquainted? They must have been, for there Mary Jane was, living and breathing in the Scheele's green studio. Annie searched the dear face for answers, but Mary Jane's wide dark eyes looked out at her sightlessly, her face shuttered and closed.

It was the flowers that gave her the answer. She looked at the white camellias in her dead friend's arms, and the scent of the dying red camellias on the shelf behind her, scattered about the alabaster jar, rose to her nose, nauseating her as they'd always done.

As they'd always done. Slowly, slowly her numb mind pieced the puzzle together. She'd hated the scent since she'd seen the camellias on Francis's hall table, the very first time she'd smelled them. The first? No. For now her sensory memory prodded her; just as the smell of a fir tree can conjure up a Christmas long past, or a cut lawn recollect a favourite summer, the scent recalled to Annie the memory of Mary Jane coming in late to their lodging house in the Haymarket, lit up from within, saying she had met a man.

And smelling of camellias.

The realisation brought with it both satisfaction and a sinking dread. *That* was why she'd always hated the smell. That sweet, innocent floral scent was forever tainted, for it had been how Mary Jane had smelled the last time she had seen her. It was, to Annie, the smell of death.

Heart thumping slowly and painfully, she searched further. Here were more studies of Mary Jane, fully dressed, always with the camellias, holding a single flower to her nose, gazing from the window with a blossom in her hair, or with such armfuls that a few petals fell to the floor. Then, below that, at the bottom of the drawer, there was a single nude. Like the other girls, Mary Jane was draped on the chaise longue, eyes closed.

Annie gazed at the painting guiltily. She had never seen her friend without clothes – when they washed, it was piecemeal, and when they slept in the same bed, it was too cold to be without clothes. Mary Jane, she knew, never let the bastards see her naked, for she would not show her brand to anyone except Annie. Even though Francis was an artist, even though he might have beguiled her with appeals to artistic truth and presence and realism and all the other fancy words he'd taught Annie, Mary Jane would never have agreed to this. She'd said, many times, that she would never let a man see her brand so long as she lived.

So long as she lived.

Annie's heart seemed to stutter. She looked at the painting again. Her friend's eyes were closed and her rosy mouth gaped slightly. Her abundant hair, black and straight with the blue sheen of a magpie's breast, fell to the floor, and her arm lolled down to the rug, the 'M' brand clearly visible.

Mary Jane was dead.

She had been dead in Francis's house. She may have been found under Waterloo Bridge, but she had been dead before she had even hit the water.

Annie dropped the painting as if it burned her, and wrenched open the other drawers. She pulled out the nudes – three, five, ten – with shaking hands. She could see her model's instinct had been correct. They were too relaxed – a slack mouth, a silver trail of drool, a flopping breast, legs falling open. Unguarded, unflattering.

The girls were dead.

All of them.

A crack of lightning right overhead made her jump out of her skin; and a second crack took her to the window. She thought that one of the trees had been struck, but the dark waving cypresses still stood sentinel, none of them cloven by lightning or set afire. But through the rain-chased glass she could see a light far down the road.

The tiny swinging light of a carriage lamp.

She grabbed the nude of Mary Jane, rolled the painting as fast as she could and stuffed it into her sleeve. Even in her hurry she would not leave her friend here to be gloated over as a souvenir, as much of a trophy as the stuffed animals. She shoved the map drawers back into place, turned the lamps down to the low glow that she'd found, and slipped out of the bookshelf door, not waiting to click it shut behind her. She stumbled down the wooden ladder, her boots slipping on the wrought-iron footplates, then ran through the dark library, down the passage, through the ivory atrium. There she wrenched open the heavy door and ran out into the rain and the night.

Chapter 20

One year, two weeks and three days ago

Francis asks me if I will pose for him in the nude. 'I assure you there is nothing salacious in my request,' he assures me. 'To me there is only purity and innocence in the naked body; Eden before the fall. What do you say? Will you do it?'

I don't even have to think about it. 'Never in this world.'

'I will pay double,' he says.

I have no modesty – how could I have? The issue is the brand on my arm; M for Mary Jane, M for Magdalene, M for Malefactor. I have sworn never to show it, and I will not break my vow. 'Even you don't have enough money to change my mind.'

He strokes his chin and studies me, intrigued.

'That is your final answer?'

'If you want a different answer, ask a different girl.'

'Very well, Mary Jane,' he says, and begins to paint again. He does not seem angry, though; more . . . amused.

Annie ran upwards, ever upwards, for downwards meant the approaching carriage and Francis.

She ran into the hills, scrambling and sobbing, soaked with the driving rain and shivering like a greyhound in the thin Chinese peignoir, which twisted around her legs, hampering her flight. She fell many times, muddied and scratched as the rain turned the red clay into bloody sludge. As she tumbled, she had no mind for herself, only for the painting rolled in her sleeve, as if it was Mary Jane herself she held.

When she was high enough, she forced herself to stop and turn. She watched the dark, moonlit hump of the Villa Camellia as the little light drew into the driveway, was detached from the carriage and carried into the house.

Then that light kindled more lights.

She knew the house well, and, heart thudding, tracked Francis's passage through the villa as the lights came on one by one. Atrium, staircase, his room. Passageway, library; and then the seventh window. The secret room, the cabinet of curiosities.

How quickly would he discover that Mary Jane had gone? For a moment she regretted her impulse to take the painting. What more could he do to Mary Jane now? Annie had given herself away; she had let him know that she had been in his cabinet. She forced herself to watch as the lights were extinguished again one by one. The rain fell, her heart slowed. Perhaps he had not discovered anything was missing; perhaps he had decided that she had gone to bed, and that he was safe. For a moment all was quiet. Then she watched in horror as a small light detached itself from the dark mass of the villa and began to mount the path up the hill. Towards her.

She ran.

She had no notion of where she was going as she fled from the light below, until she spied a light above. From some long-past Sunday-school memory a line of text unfurled in her brain.

I will lift up mine eyes unto the hills, from whence cometh my help.

She ran ever upwards to where the little light nestled in the hills, climbing towards it blindly, dashing the rain from her eyes, her brain two steps behind her feet; until at length she realised that the light represented salvation indeed: it was the light she had seen so often from her chamber, and from the loggia in the evening. It was the convent of Mary Magdalene.

There was a pathway, and a flight of broad steps cut into the hill, and as she scrambled up them with the last of her breath, she heard the horrid tread of other footsteps behind her on the stair. How could he have gained on her so fast? The sound gave her the last reserves of energy she needed, and she pushed herself on, muscles screaming, lungs bursting, and flung herself at the barred gates. She hauled on a rope and a bell clamoured out into the night, giving her whereabouts away, but she didn't care. Subterfuge was past; it was all a race now – *if they did not admit her before he gained on her . . . if they did not admit her before he gained on her . . .* Please, please, *please*, she mouthed like a prayer.

After an eternity, she screamed out in appeal, 'Let me in, in the name of Mary Magdalene!' She had not meant to say it – she had thought to say 'Open Sesame' or something very like it – but her charm worked. A benign face appeared at the bars, lit by a hurricane lamp, and the gates opened. The footsteps sounded on the threshold behind her and she flung herself inside. 'He's coming,' she gasped, and turned to help the figure in the habit slam the gate and turn the key with not a moment to spare.

Safe now, but half mad with fear and fury, she screamed though the bars in her best Bethnal Green accent, the accent she'd changed for him: 'Fuck you, Francis Maybrick Gill!'

The following figure lurched out of the dark and threw himself at the gate, drenched and breathing hard, dark hair plastered to his head. But it was not Francis.

It was the rainbow man.

Annie was silent. She couldn't quite believe what she was being told, but at the same time she knew it was true. She just had to take a minute, to stand back from the whole incredible picture that was being painted for her, just as Francis used to stand back from his canvases.

To begin with, she'd been hysterical. She'd thought that Francis had, with the superhuman speed of Spring-heeled Jack, chased her up the hill to this sanctuary and sprung out of the dark to kill her. She had blessed the bars between them, and had clung to the elderly nun who'd admitted her, sobbing and screaming. Then she'd collapsed to the ground as the nun had spoken to the rainbow man in low, rapid Tuscan, incomprehensible under the howling tempest. Sodden papers were passed through the bars and back, then Annie had watched as the figure in the habit had unlocked the gate and let the rainbow man in.

Now she was sitting in the office of the mother superior, with a blanket about her shoulders and a cup of broth in her hand. There was a small but merry fire in the grate, the wind outside had dropped, everyone spoke English, and she could begin to comprehend what she was being told.

Even then she had to get the mother superior to repeat what she'd said. Only from the mouth of a woman of God would she believe it. She would not believe it from the lips of the other person in the room, the tall, dark man who occupied the third chair in the room.

He was a rainbow man no more – now he was in all in black, just as she'd first seen him watching her in the Uffizi. He sat bolt upright, with military bearing. He wore a long black coat with a double row of dull brass buttons, black breeches and a black cravat. His black hair was slick with rain, with just a few curls beginning to dry and form about his temples. His black eyes were deadly serious, his face pale and shuttered. He stayed silent while the Mother Superior spoke.

Patiently, from behind her walnut desk, the elderly nun clasped her hands on her blotter and explained again.

'This is Sovrintendente Lodovico Graziani, of the Guardia Civica di Firenze. He means you no harm; I can assure you that I checked his credentials personally before I allowed him through the gates. You are quite safe. He is here to protect you.'

Annie still did not understand.

'Who are the Guardia . . . Civi . . . What did you say?'

'The Guardia Civica di Firenze. The Florentine Civic Guard. They are the guardians of the city, under the command of the Grand Duke of Tuscany.'

Annie felt suddenly helpless and tearful. 'I'm sorry . . . I just don't understand.'

'We are the police,' he said, speaking for the first time. 'The Florentine police.'

She looked at him.

'In London,' he said gently, 'there is a Metropolitan force to police the streets; your bobbies, your peelers, your bluebottles; call them what you will. In Florence, we have the Guardia Civica. In London, there is also a new division of detectives, who solely investigate murders. I know this because my good friend is a detective – a friend who once fought by my side in Milan, and saved my life.'

Annie's mind felt treacle slow. 'Why are you telling me this?'

He ignored her question. 'You remember I told you a story,' he went on, stern as a schoolmaster, 'the story of a man who had fought with me during the tobacco riots for the forces of Young Italy, a blonde giant with side-whiskers? You remember I told you he went back to London to fight another battle? You remember I asked you if you knew him?'

'I do know him, don't I?' said Annie slowly.

'Yes, you do. His name is Inspector Charlie Rablin, of the Metropolitan Police. He came to Gower Street one night in June to ask some questions of the householder. In the course of his questioning, he began to sense that something was not quite right. As he left, he saw you on the stairs. It was in his mind to take you with him there and then, but he did not, for he knew that in the morning he would return, bringing more men, to question the artist Francis Maybrick Gill further about a spate of recent murders.'

Annie looked from the speaker to the mother superior behind

her desk. The nun nodded once, as if to corroborate the account, and he continued.

'In the morning, Inspector Rablin returned, but Maybrick Gill was gone, and you with him.'

'To Florence,' she whispered.

'To Florence,' he said.

He stood and walked to the window, looking out through the old stone arch and the glass quarrels to the light of the city below. 'But the trail did not grow cold. The inspector made enquiries at Dover and found out where Maybrick Gill was heading. Then he sent an electric telegraph to a friend at the *ufficio* of the Guardia Civica in Florence. To me.'

Annie shook her wet hair out of her eyes. 'It seems like a peck of trouble for one girl.'

'Charlie is a good man. He could not forgive himself for leaving you at Gower Street. He had no reason to believe,' he looked down, 'that Francis Maybrick Gill meant you harm. He had no reason to believe that he had anything to do with the multiple murders of young women; but he had evidence to suggest that Maybrick Gill had befriended and painted a number of the women of the street who were later found dead.'

'What were their names?'

'I beg your pardon?'

'I need to know their names.' She had to be sure.

He took a soft leather notebook from his coat, and unwound the string that held the covers. As if he were a parson in church, he read the names respectfully. The list went on and on, a dozen, a score; Annie closed her eyes, and saw the portfolio of girls in Francis's cabinet of curiosities. Mary Jane's portrait, complete with asylum brand, was still rolled in her sodden sleeve. He read twenty or so names she did not know, and last of all, one that she did.

She opened her eyes again and addressed him by name for the first time. 'Signor . . . Graziani?'

'Yes.' His face was as stern and solemn as ever.

'Are you even a colourman?'

He did not quite look at her. 'My father was. And his father before him. And I, too, before I took arms in Milan.'

'But after?'

'After, no. Then I joined the Guardia. And when the Maybrick Gill case came along, I was chosen by reason of my experience to become his colourman. I did what I needed to do in order to get close to him.'

He'd done what he'd needed to do. He'd drawn her in admirably – befriended her as efficiently as Francis had; all that blather about colour, and rainbows, and the hues that made up her memories; all those confidences she'd shared with him of her early life – Christ, she'd *relived* them – were just so much theatre, as much of an illusion as the sideshows in the Vauxhall Gardens. And he had kissed her; a counterfeit kiss from his counterfeit character. *He'd done what he'd needed to do.*

'I suppose I will never learn about red, then,' she said irrelevantly.

'You will learn of it in time.'

'I'll not learn it from you,' she said sharply. 'I showed you my true colours. You lied and lied.'

'Perhaps. But few of us are really what we seem, Signorina Stride.' There was no pretence, now, that she was a married woman. 'Francis Maybrick Gill was not what he seemed. He was a predator, Annie. He chose his models carefully. They were all like you,' he went on, more gently. 'Every one. Girls who had been abused by men all their lives. He would draw them in in the same way, by offering them the first act of kindness or chivalry they had ever known. He would call them madam, instead of the ugly names they'd always been called. He would leave them be, ask nothing from them, these women from whom so much was asked. Then he would meet them again by chance and offer to paint them. He would make them feel beautiful.' He looked down at his hands. 'Whether or not he was a murderer, he was certainly a predator. And then, when he came to Florence, girls started disappearing here, too. Pretty girls, Annie. Girls from the street. But still we had no evidence.'

She swallowed. 'He is a murderer. And I found all the evidence you need, at the Villa Camellia.' She told him, low-voiced but clearly, about the secret room; the cabinet of curiosities and the pictures of the murdered girls; Francis's gallery of the dead.

He listened until she had finished, saying nothing. Then he said, softly, 'The picture you took, of your friend. It is evidence. I need it.'

She slid the painting from her sleeve, unrolled it and handed it to him.

'I will look after Mary Jane,' he said, and this made her want to cry. Only now did she glimpse the rainbow man again, the man she'd liked, the man she'd come to love; but their friendship had all been pretence, a charade to catch a killer. The tears brimmed and fell, and the mother superior stood up.

'No more,' she said sternly. 'This young lady needs rest. No more questions till tomorrow. Annie, our postulant, Sister Rafaella, will show you to your chamber.'

The figure in black stood, too. 'I will call again tomorrow,' he said. 'You are completely safe here. Mother Superior has instructions to admit no one but myself until Maybrick Gill is apprehended.' He must have seen Annie's face. 'We will find him.'

He took his leave of the mother superior with a little bow, and then gave the exact same nod to Annie. So correct, so formal. *Touch me not.* She thought of the kiss he'd once given her, so gentle, so real, and did not think she'd ever been quite so unhappy in her life.

But Annie had the resilience of the young and strong. She slept until noon, and when she opened her simple wooden shutters, the sun was shining and Florence was still laid out below.

She had awoken to find the young nun who had shown her to her room the night before sitting in a chair by the bed reading a prayer book. When she saw Annie stirring, she jumped up and smiled. Annie smiled back. Through a combination of Tuscan and mime, she understood that she was to wash; the young nun brought a brass can of boiling water, which she poured into a rough earthenware bowl. She assisted Annie with the steaming flannel until she was pink and clean. Then she helped her to exchange the homespun gown she had slept in for a simple long-sleeved black dress, and tied her hair up in a plain white linen headcloth in a practised fashion, hiding all of its beauty under the veil.

Annie followed the young nun to a refectory with pointed windows and long scrubbed-pine tables, where the nuns sat in neat rows. There, alongside them, she ate sausage and fruit and bread and drank strong unsweetened coffee from a glass. The nuns ate in silence, while one of their number read from a bible at a lectern. The rosary of Latin words was comforting – she understood one word in ten, but the music of the language was balm to her shredded nerves. Here she had found sanctuary; here she could just think of the next mouthful, of her next sip of coffee. She could enjoy her clean body, the plain, comfortable clothes, her scrubbed face, the hair bound up so not a strand showed. She felt she had assumed a new role in that series of women that she had played. She now belonged to the order of Mary Magdalene. There were three other young women in white scarves, so she was unremarkable. She was hidden in plain sight; no longer a famous stunner, nor a great beauty. She was invisible in this flock, one of many, and at the moment, while she absorbed the shock of the night before, that suited her very well.

After the meal and a prayer Sister Rafaella took her to see the mother superior. On the way through the church, the young postulant stopped to point to a frescoed wall. On it was depicted a lamb holding a flag over its shoulder, in a style Annie thought she knew.

The eyes seemed to live, the fleece seemed to grow. 'Giotto,' said the girl, as proudly as if she had painted it herself – and Annie was suddenly back at Santa Croce, standing shoulder to shoulder with Francis, looking at other Giottos, and he was telling her that Giotto had been a shepherd. She shivered, and passed on.

The mother superior was sitting at her desk, writing letters with a modern-looking ink pen, not, as Annie might have expected, a quill. She laid the pen by and stood to take Annie by the shoulders, examining her with eyes the colour of sage, with almost no lashes.

'You look a little better for your rest, my child.'

'I feel it, signora.'

'You address me as Reverend Mother.'

Annie did not warm at once to the elderly nun, with her 'my childs' and her reverences. She reminded her of those smug, self-satisfied dodgers in Whitechapel, those parsons or pamphlet-eers who'd associate themselves with fallen women in order to feel holy. They would happily visit the underworld, a world they could leave after an hour or two without a backward glance, so they could natter about it in their parish to thrilled gasps. She supposed it was a thrill for this unworldly do-gooder to have such an unworthy creature under her roof. But Annie was still, in some ways, Francis's creature, and had not quite sloughed off the varnish of good manners he had applied in Gower Street, so she said what was due. 'Thank you, Reverend Mother, for sheltering me here.'

'What else would I do? This convent was founded to shelter women, in the name of Mary Magdalene.'

Annie was not having this. 'There was an asylum in London, in her name, that worked the women to death.'

'Then they took her name in vain,' said the nun sternly. 'Here, happily, that is not the case. If you want to work, you may work. If you want to pray, you may pray.' She tucked her hands into her sleeves, giving her an odd appearance. 'Some come for a short time, some stay forever, but all of us revere our personal saint.'

Annie looked into the lashless eyes. 'She was a saint? The Magdalene?'

The eyes creased briefly at the corners. 'Why, yes. Made so by the Church many centuries ago.'

Annie felt as if she'd been told that the baker's boy was a baronet. 'She can't have been. She'd been in and out of bed—'

'Annie.' The mother superior smiled sadly. 'You have lived in a world of liars for so long that you cannot recognise the truth. The Lord embraces all his children. Our common past cannot keep us from His grace – it hardly marks you out here, for it is one that we all share.'

Annie's mouth dropped open. 'Even you?'

The sage eyes twinkled. 'Even me. I worked the streets of Florence for many years, before the blessed Magdalene spoke in my heart, and showed me my salvation.'

Annie's resentment melted away, and she looked at the nun with new eyes. Then she shrugged. There was no one, now, to tell her not to. 'She climbed a long way up from the gutter.'

'Indeed. And on the way, she was a penitent – after the death of our Lord, she withdrew from the world, much as we do here.'

So Annie was, once again, following in the footsteps of the Magdalene. Just at the moment, she did not ever want to leave. She could happily stay with these women, happily stay away forever from men who murdered and lied, and gave the kiss of Judas.

But it was not to be.

'The Guardia Civica who was here last night – Lodovico Graziani – he has come again. He tells me that his division are dedicated to tracing your . . . former friend, before he may sin again.'

Sin, thought Annie. That was one way to put it. The do-gooder's shorthand for murder.

'He would like to ask you some questions. Are you ready?'

'No.' She felt suddenly physically sick at the thought. One Yuletide, after a particularly profitable December, she had eaten too many comforts and had felt this way. Odd, that too much evil should give you the same symptoms as too much sweetness. She pressed her hands beneath her ribs where the feeling seemed to reside, and groped behind her for the wooden bench with the other. She felt as if Francis, the evil of him, had entered her like an incubus. How could she have lived so long with a murderer, dined with him, modelled for him, taken evenings at the theatre and at concert halls, let him kiss her and nearly – dear God, *how nearly* – sleep with her? How often had she held the hands that had killed Mary Jane? Mary Jane and how many others?

She sat down and put her head to her knees until the terrible feeling subsided. She sat up again, weak and dizzy, to face the old nun. The mother superior did not put a comforting hand on her shoulder, did not offer her water. Instead she turned from her and walked to the stone window to look down at the old city.

'Down there – Francis Maybrick Gill may be down there now, hiding in those shadows. I do not know. What I do know is that there will be women, young women, women like you, who do not see him lurking there; who do not hear his footfall, who do not see him coming.' She turned back to face Annie. 'Are you ready?'

Annie twisted the Regard ring from her finger and crossed to the window. She threw it out, and turned back before she could note where it went or hear it land. 'Now I am.'

Sovrintendente Lodovico Graziani, as she supposed she now must think of him, was waiting for Annie in the cloister. The mother superior had arranged that they should meet there during mass, when the convent's inhabitants crowded into the little church and they would be alone. For a moment they eyed one another as they became acquainted with these new versions of each other – he the detective in his black and his brass buttons, she the novice in her habit and headscarf.

In the little convent garden, with the bees skimming across the lavender heads and the sunlight striking the old stones, they were on familiar ground. As they walked amongst the herbs, the scent rising from the bruised leaves under their feet, they might have been back at the Villa Camellia, wandering the gardens, talking of colour. Only now, the discourse was more serious. Now there were no lies spoken. No pretence. The temple curtain had been rent, and now there was only truth, stark truth.

From habit, they started to stroll side by side, as they had done many times, but there was a new energy between them. On her side, now that she was safe, it was a growing resentment; on his, she knew not what.

'Are you going to teach me about colour?' she asked tartly.

Just audibly, he sighed. 'I told you, I *was* a colourman. I learned what I knew from my father and grandfather, as if I was in a schoolroom. Then I taught it to you. Those were facts I told you; scientific, incontrovertible.'

'So the colours were true. What about the rest? Were you even at the tobacco riots?'

'Yes, and I met Charlie Rablin there.' He tugged at his empty cuff. 'There is no arm in this sleeve – I did not sever it for the purpose of deceiving you.'

She was chastened, but persisted. 'But you told me lies.'

'Yes,' he said gently. 'It was never my intention to deceive. I am heartily sorry for it. I did not set out to lie, especially not to you. But I did what I had to, to stop Maybrick Gill. I have four sisters, I have a mother. Those were not lies; my family were not inventions. I want them to be safe; I want *every* daughter of Florence to be safe.'

She felt stupid and selfish and petulant, none of which she wanted to be; but she couldn't help her plaintive question. 'What about *me*? What about *my* safety?'

'It killed me to leave you there,' he said emphatically. 'But I had no choice. To take you away would have been to alert him, and we had to make him feel secure until we had built our case. But I was always watchful of your safety. That's why I agreed to model for him – do you think I harboured a secret desire to see myself depicted as Christ? No; I stayed to guard you, and I endured all the discomforts that he engineered for me. Even when I was turned from his door, I watched the house as much as I could – I even neglected my other duties to keep my vigil. How do you think I came to follow you here? I saw you leave and run up the hill.'

'You were at the Villa Camellia last night?'

'Yes. In the gardens where we used to walk. I was watching the house. I had come to take you away – finally I had reason to – but you fled before I could liberate you. But this is all wrong. We are beginning at the end; it would be more profitable to begin at the beginning.'

He took his notebook from his coat, the book of soft leather bound with string, the book with the dead girls in its pages like pressed flowers. He opened it, took out a pencil and licked the lead.

'Let us begin. In London, when you first came to know him, did Francis Maybrick Gill have any diversions, any interests?'

'Besides his painting? None. His entertainments were general; we would go to the theatre, to concerts, to public parks.'

And then she remembered.

'We went to the Vauxhall Gardens once – pleasure gardens, you know, a low place. I made him go; I was trying to show him my world. We strayed from the path, and ran into a woman from my past – Mother, we called her, the madam of our bawdy house. She greeted Francis like an old friend.' She remembered his shock. 'He was put out of countenance; he seemed truly afraid and upset, for the only time in our acquaintance.' Light dawned. 'I suppose it was because Mother *did* know him.'

'Oh, I'm sure she did.'

Annie was shocked into silence. How well did Mother know

Francis? How many times had she seen him at the Gardens, in the Strand, at her house? How many of her girls had gone to him and not returned? How much had he paid her to turn a blind eye, to write off a girl's life in return for a banknote? She recalled, with a sick qualm, that Mary Jane had told her that the only reason Mother had taken her back from the Magdalene Asylum was because she had lost two of her girls that summer. No wonder Francis had looked so sick in the hansom cab, so anxious to put the bowling miles of carriage ride between themselves and Mother. A word or two more, a couple of little details, a few specifics, and the old bawd would have unmasked him there and then.

'And at home?' asked Lodovico, filling the thoughtful silence.

'He would try to improve me: my speech, my thought processes, my knowledge of art and culture. He would have me read to him in the evenings, as part of my education, but I never saw him read a book, except one. It was one that he read to me when I'd lost a child. The child.' She remembered how they'd spoken of the baby, and the rainbow man had embraced her in the garden the day Francis had made her cry. Now he merely nodded.

'Do you know what the book was?'

'Yes. It was *La Dame aux Camélias*, by Alexandre Dumas. In Venice he told me it was his favourite book.'

'We will come to Venice later. Let us remain in London for now. What of friends, acquaintances?'

'He had none. He knew Mr Ruskin and Sir Charles Eastlake – they seemed to be patrons or sponsors to him. He said they came to Gower Street, that last night, but I knew it wasn't them.'

'How did you know?'

'Lizzie Siddal. Another model that went about on the arm of an artist. I met her at the Royal Academy, the night of Francis's exhibition. I was wearing a peacock coat, his mother's coat. Francis was very careful not to introduce me to anyone. Perhaps he was ashamed of my low origins; perhaps he felt that if I were in character I would retain some mystery. But Lizzie made herself known to me, and I did likewise. Then she said: "They don't care what you think. Not they. Not high-and-mighty Sir Charles Eastlake, nor low-and-mighty Mr Ruskin." So you see, I knew it wasn't them that night at Gower Street – I know now, of course, that it was your friend Charlie Rablin and his deputy.'

'Yes.' They walked in silence for a moment, their footsteps crunching on the gravel. 'And now let us turn to the servants at Gower Street. Could you acquaint me with the household?'

'There was a little maid-of-all-work, Minnie, her name was. She was there for my first night, then she disappeared. Francis replaced her with his mother's maid, from Norfolk.'

'Name of?'

'Eve.'

He made a note. 'Who else?'

'There was a cook, Mrs Hoggarth, but I never saw her leave the kitchen. Upstairs there was a butler, Bowering.'

'If the cook kept below stairs, the butler, I think, might have been an accomplice. I would be surprised if he is still at the house.'

She thought of the smooth and silent Bowering. 'Done a flit, you mean?' Now that Francis was gone, she revelled in the return of her Bethnal Green idioms.

'As you say. Anyone else with whom Maybrick Gill was acquainted?'

She frowned. 'He would pass the time of day with other artists when we took the air, or if we attended an exhibition or entertainment. Rossetti; Millais; Holman Hunt.'

'Do you think he knew them well?'

'He seemed to know the status of Rossetti's relationship with Miss Siddal. And he mentioned Holman Hunt another time. He was talking about mummy brown, a pigment the rainbow man

'. . . you . . . sold him.' She'd almost forgotten that the benign and colourful rainbow man and the stern civic guard walking beside her were the same person. 'He said it was made from . . .'

'. . . mummified cats.' He almost smiled. 'I do know as much as I told you, and more. The haematite in the mummies makes that rusty red-brown.'

'Yes. Francis said that when Holman Hunt found out what the paint contained, he buried his own tube in the garden. I asked him what he would do with his; he said he would paint with it. The notion that it was made from dead cats didn't seem to—'

She stopped abruptly.

'What is it?' He turned to her on the path.

'Death,' she said, and a chill passed over her body. 'Death was his interest.'

'Go on.'

She was not sure she could. The notion gathered certainty about her head, like a dark miasma. 'All the paintings,' she said slowly, 'featured something that was dead; I noticed it at the Royal Academy. All except one – the painting of me and the armful of flowers; he called it *The Girl with the White Camellias*.'

Lodovico considered. 'The camellias were dead, if they were cut flowers.'

She looked at him with something akin to admiration. 'I never considered that. And,' she said with a catch in her breath, 'in *The Bridge of Sighs*, the dead creature was Mary Jane.'

There was a brief silence; this time, Annie was the one to break it. 'Francis kept the animals, you know,' she said. 'I saw them in his cabinet of curiosities at Gower Street, and he brought them all the way to Florence – they must have travelled with us on the boat, somewhere among the trunks and packing cases.'

'I know,' he said soberly. 'I saw them at the Villa Camellia – in a secret room above the library.'

'He loved them because they were dead. He could not let them go. It all fits,' she said. 'He was in love with death. In his favourite novel, the heroine, Marguerite – the Lady with the Camellias – is dead before the story even begins. And in the Dante – well, all three books of the *Divina Commedia* deal with the afterlife: *Inferno*, *Purgatorio*, *Paradiso*. Every character the poet meets is dead; he alone walks back into the world.' She recalled her mornings in Florence with Francis, as he glutted himself on centuries of art. 'Francis always liked the crucifixion better than the nativity. He was a true Pre-Raphaelite. He liked his art to bleed, not to live. When we first came here, we stood on the Ponte Vecchio, and he said then, he said . . .'

'What did he say?'

'That everything of interest in Florence is dead, and there's nothing so wonderful as death to make one feel alive.'

Lodovico nodded grimly. 'And so to this summer. The killing summer. The murders were the talk of the town,' he said. 'That was the reason Francis was keeping you out of the city. You could not have been in Florence and avoided the headlines, the gossip, the Guardia Civica everywhere. In London, you call your police bluebottles. Here we are known as *corvi*, crows, because of our black uniforms. We have been flocking to the city all summer, circling and settling, trying to spy a murderer.'

She nodded. 'And all the time, the murderer was him. That was what he was doing, all those evenings of absence. Little wonder he did not take me with him.' The sick feeling, the feeling of too much evil, returned.

'I was as guilty as he. I thought that so long as you stayed at the Villa Camellia, away from the river, you would be safe. All the young ladies in London were drowned in the river, and all the young ladies in Florence in the Arno – of that there can be no doubt. I could have warned you explicitly, could have taken you away from the villa. At that time we had no absolute evidence that Maybrick Gill was the killer. But I had no right to let you run such a risk, for the sake of other women's lives. I owe you an apology.' It was formally given, but heartfelt.

'You are already forgiven,' she said, 'for if you risked my life one day, you have repaid the sum in the ledger by saving it the next.'

He inclined his head. 'Then when Maybrick Gill took you to Venice, I thought I would lose you forever . . .'

'So you followed me there. That *was* you in the theatre.'

'Yes. I think Francis knew that the net was closing. He left Florence in a hurry, just as he left London. He must have realised that we were close to him.'

'But he came back,' said Annie. 'He came back to Florence.'

'Yes. And that I still don't understand. I thought he'd felt the noose tightening. But then he returned and acted as if nothing had happened; as if he no longer thought he was in any danger.'

'I don't think he did feel the net closing in,' said Annie slowly. 'I think he went to Venice for a very particular reason. He wasn't running *from* anything; he was running towards something.'

'What?'

'The opera.'

'*La Traviata?*'

'Yes,' she said slowly. '*La Traviata is* the Girl with the Camellias. The camellias are the key to everything, and have been since the beginning. The very first time I went to Gower Street, Francis had a bowl of white camellias on his hall table. The smell troubled me, even then. Then, to complete his series on fallen women, he painted me as a woman holding a bouquet of white camellias. I did not realise at that time how she fitted, but now I do. He'd already given me the answer. When I'd been ill at Gower Street, he'd read to me from a book. It was a passage about a woman and some flowers. I now know that book was *La Dame aux Camélias*, the story of a dead courtesan related by her lover. The courtesan wore camellias in her hair every day, and her story was later turned into an opera. Directly after we'd seen *La Traviata*, Francis asked me to be his mistress. He marked the occasion by giving me a camellia from the hair of the leading lady, Violetta. After we returned to his villa, a place he'd named after camellias, he had me read a particular passage of Dante, and even that seemed to recall the flowers.'

'Can you remember it?'

'A little. It was something like: "The Angel other, that sees and sings the glory, descended continually into the great flower, lovely with so many petals."' Annie pleated her skirt with her fingers. 'Now I know why I could not tolerate the smell of camellias.' Her voice broke. 'It was how Mary Jane smelled, those last times she came home.'

Lodovico looked in his notebook. 'Mary Jane Stoddard, wasn't it?'

'Yes.' Tears began to leak from her eyes. She took a breath, and steeled herself to ask the terrible question. It was a question she did not want to ask, but she had to know the answer. 'How did she die? Would it have been quick?'

'We don't know.'

She shot him a look through the tears.

'I am in earnest. We don't. All the young women were found under Waterloo Bridge, drowned, and they had all been seen last in Maybrick Gill's company. It was the coroner's man who first threw suspicion onto Maybrick Gill. He was always there when the young women were fished out of the river, and he always appeared at the inquests, too, to listen to the details of the condition of the bodies. They always . . . forgive me . . . showed signs of rough sexual congress. Maybrick Gill was always immensely respectful, and would always tip the coroner's man a coin for the coffin.'

Annie remembered, that first night in the Royal Academy. 'He told me as much himself.' Then, it had endeared him to her. How much had changed!

'There is more. He paid the same coroner's man for information about where the young ladies would be buried. Further enquiries told a grisly tale: he paid the sexton of St Leonard's churchyard to open the paupers' grave.' He paused, as if he could not quite bring himself to frame the words. 'He bought their bones.'

The horrible realisation dawned, like a dreaded day. 'Jesus,' she said. 'He made paint from them. From the very girls he killed. I watched him doing it . . . I liked watching him . . .' She swallowed down bile. 'He always had plentiful bone meal. I assumed it was from Smithfield.'

'It seems not,' Lodovico said briefly.

'So there *was* death in every painting after all.'

'Yes. He literally painted with his victims.'

She could not speak. If Lodovico noticed her distress, though, he made no comment.

'There may be some small comfort. The post-mortems found water in the lungs consistent with drowning. But there were no signs of a struggle, so he cannot have thrown them off Waterloo Bridge – they would have resisted him. We believe he may have drugged them. Traces of laudanum were found at Gower Street, though it is, as you know, a common medicine.' He looked at her with sympathetic eyes, then dropped his gaze to his boots. 'We do, however, have reason to believe that he also used laudanum to abort the pregnancies of his models.'

The evil in the pit of her stomach rose to her throat. She could not bear it.

She turned on the gravel path and ran from the herb garden. From somewhere behind her she could hear Lodovico saying, 'Annie? Annie?'

She went behind a wall, out of his sight, and threw up and up and up.

Chapter 21

One year and six days ago

Once again I am in Francis's green studio, posing for him.

'You're from Norfolk, aren't you, Mary Jane,' he says.

'That I am,' I say, broad as you please. 'How did you know?'

'I recognised your accent when we first met in the Burlington. I am from Norfolk, too.'

'Whereabouts?'

'Holkham. My family have the great house there.'

I sit up, bolt straight. 'I'm from Holkham, too!'

He smiles half a smile. 'I knew it.' He waves his paintbrush at me to get back in position. I comply. I don't know why it is pleasing when you meet someone from your home, it just is. Now I like him even more. Then it dawns. 'So you are the boy from the big house?'

'Yes,' he says. 'Why? Do you think we were acquainted as children?'

It is a joke. Of course the likes of me wouldn't have known the likes of him. 'No. But I heard your mother read the lesson once in church. She was beautiful. Had a voice like caramel.'

He looks fond and distant. 'Yes. Yes, she did.'

Then I begin to remember things: gossip of happenings at the big house, madness, suicide. 'Wasn't there some scandal? Must've been when you were a boy.'

He freezes, his paintbrush suspended in mid air. And I know

then I've made a mistake. Now, I think, he'll tell me to go. But
after a moment he continues to paint. He does not speak for a time,
and then he says, 'No more stories.'

A soft knock at the door of Annie's cell.

After a long, long moment, she composed herself, and opened
the door. Lodovico stood there, saying nothing. She sat on the
bed; he stood. 'Yes,' she said. 'He did it to me. When he saved
me, I was pregnant. After a night at his house, I was not any
more.'

He said nothing for a time, then sat beside her on the little bed.
She felt the weight of him depress the mattress, but she did not
look at him.

Then, gently, 'Did he give you anything that first night? Anything
to drink?'

'Yes,' she said. 'A posset.' *A recipe of my mother's*, he had said.
Had his mother used laudanum, too?

Lodovico looked grave. 'It seems certain, then, that this was his
method. We don't know why he did this, but between Florence
and London we have various theories. That he might not want
the stamp of another man upon a woman he regarded as his; that
pregnancy might make his models too gross to paint.'

She was confused. 'But how do you know what he did? And
Charlie Rablin? How can you tell such a thing from a body? All
the women in the pictures were dead.'

'All the women in London, yes. But there was one young woman,
in Florence, who escaped from him.'

She looked at him, wide eyed.

'This was early summer, before I had received my telegraph
from London. She came in one night to the *ufficio* and made a
report about an English gentleman to an officer at the Guardia.
She said a man had befriended her and taken her to his *pensione*,
then attempted to drown her in his bath while violating her.'

Annie gasped, remembering the luxurious bath at Gower Street. 'What happened to her?'

'She passed out, and claimed she'd woken up on the banks of the Arno.'

'So he did kill at home,' she said slowly, 'and then dumped the girls in the river. He must have done the same in London.' She could not bear to think of Mary Jane.

'The officer was young and stupid, and not long in the force, having joined from the army. He was disinclined to believe a young woman of her profession. He turned her out on the street as a fantasist, and she has since disappeared.'

'Dead?' Annie whispered.

'I don't know.' He looked stricken, and suddenly, she understood. 'The young officer. It was you, wasn't it?'

He clasped his hands before him as if in prayer. 'Then I got Charlie's telegraph and realised what I'd done. I pray every night that she is still alive. I could not protect her, and I could not protect you either.'

'You tried,' said Annie. 'But I was never safe at the villa if he killed the other women at Gower Street. And I'm sure he did.'

'What makes you say that?'

'In the portfolio, the women were all pictured in the studio at Gower Street. It has a very particular decoration, in Scheele's green. The nudes were all on the divan, and the background was the Scheele's green wallpaper.'

'But he did paint the women in the studio. They posed for him. That was never in dispute.'

'But not in the nude. The nude women were dead.'

'How can you be sure?'

'I've modelled,' she said simply. 'I know the difference between a relaxed attitude and unconsciousness. And there's another thing.' She told him about Mary Jane's asylum brand – the M of shame. 'So you see, she would never show it, even to the bastards – her clients, that is. She would only be so unguarded in death.' She swallowed the tears that threatened to rise in her throat. 'I think he painted them clothed, then killed them, painted them nude and dumped the bodies. I just don't know why.' Then she remembered. 'You said you could not move against him earlier because you had no evidence. Do you have some now?'

He nodded. 'Yes.'

'The paintings I found?'

'They certainly strengthen our case. But they are evidence of the deed, not the motive. No, we have other evidence as to motive, which I received from London just yesterday.'

'What was it?'

He took something white from his pocketbook. 'A letter from Charlie Rablin. Its contents sent me straight to the Villa Camellia to rescue you.'

It fluttered palely in his hand like a flag of surrender. The very sight of it made her shiver. 'Tell me.'

In answer, he passed her the letter. It was typewritten, so there was not even an illegible hand to soften the news; the content was stark and legible and dark as pitch.

To: Guardia Lodovico Graziani, of the Ufficio della Guardia Civica, Firenze

Dear Lodo,

  Hope this finds you well as it leaves me.

  I have much news for you on the matter of Francis Maybrick Gill.

  I hardly know what to make of it myself so will not trouble you with my poor conjectures but only lay the facts before you. I will give you news of London first, before we take the Norfolk road.

  In Gower Street we attempted to question Maybrick Gill's butler, one Jeremiah Bowering, but found, as you suspected, that he'd absconded from the property shortly after his master's departure for Florence. I troubled the local force of Dartford in Kent for news of his whereabouts, as his mother's house is located in those parts; but as yet no news.

The cook and maid-of-all-work were still in residence and keeping house as best they could. The cook, one Ina Hoggarth, knew nothing; since her sphere lies below stairs, the only truth of which she could inform us was that she had not been paid since April last.

The maid-of-all-work, however, who goes by the name of Eve Richardson, seemed a likely girl; she has spent her short life listening and watching, and so has much to tell.

She said that she was brought to Gower Street from the Holkham estate in Norfolk in response to an appeal for a reliable girl to keep house. I asked her if such communications were commonplace, and she said she thought they were not – that the young master and his father were estranged, and not in the habit of correspondence, and that the letter regarding a new maid had been directed to the house-keeper of Holkham Hall, not the earl. The housekeeper, who was obviously a sensible woman, with her head screwed on, as you might say, had not troubled the old master with the request; the father being as old as he was, and having one eye upon the future Earl of Holkham, she displayed an obliging intention to keep the son sweet. So the girl was sent to Gower Street. I asked her what had happened to her predecessor, and she said that it was her impression that the girl before her – Minnie – had died after a short illness.

Annie stopped reading, the letter slack in her hand, her eyes on the landscape, unseeing. Minnie, that mouselike, obliging girl, dead?

'Can it be true, that Francis dispatched her?'

'I think so. She saw something she should not – the blood on the bed sheets. You'd clearly lost a child.'

'I told her as much,' said Annie, remembering the gore, the horror. 'I said, *my baby.*'

'As you say. For all she knew, it was Francis's child, and she might have talked. By the time the new maid, Eve, got to Gower Street, you were merely an artist's model living in his house while he painted you. Not perhaps acceptable in polite society, but not out of keeping for the bohemian Maybrick Gill affected to be. You did not share a room, nor a bed. There was nothing much to shock. But Minnie knew enough to damage his reputation, a reputation that his killing spree relied upon.'

Her hand shaking a little, Annie read on.

I asked Eve, as you prompted, for information about Maybrick Gill's mother, and here she could tell me nothing – she had never met the woman, but remembered Miss Stride asking her the same. There we left the inhabitants of Gower Street, and travelled to Norfolk.

The earl received us at his seat at Holkham Hall, a very grand place, you may be sure. He admitted us reluctantly, but only because I compelled him with the weight of the law, and spoke as little as an oyster. He would say nothing of his wife beyond the fact that she had passed on some years ago.

So we took ourselves off to Holkham, a prettyish village that lies on the estate of the same name, and there you may not be surprised to learn that half an hour spent in the public bar of the Hart's Head told me the better part of what I needed to know. Villages always talk, collectively, in a way that lone widowers do not.

There, over my tankard, I learned the sad history of the family at the big house. It seems that when Francis Maybrick Gill was a boy, he was devoted to his mother and she to him. But when he was thirteen, his father took up with a mistress, who, it appears, was a former prostitute. Lady Holkham endured the situation for some years, and then, overcome by misery and humiliation, took her own life. Apparently she jumped from an ornamental bridge over the lake on the Holkham estate.

Annie looked up at Lodovico with wide eyes.

'Read on,' he said.

The village had it that young Francis blamed his father's mistress for his mother's loss, and could not forgive his father. He demanded an income against his expectations, and took himself off to Town to make his way as an artist. A matter of particular interest was that, so the folk in the public house told me, he took with him none of his own garments, but only the dress his mother had drowned in: a white sprigged muslin.

She looked up again. 'The white sprigged muslin,' she breathed. 'It was the gown he made me wear to pose as the Girl with the White Camellias in Gower Street. It was too small for me, stiff and stained from the water. All his girls wore it in the pictures, and he kept it in his cabinet.'

'So he did,' said Lodovico. He consulted his notebook. 'We found it there, and it is now at the Guardia. Will you read on?'

She nodded.

Perhaps even more significant was the fact that Maybrick Gill took his mother's ashes with him when he left. I heard tell that half the village heard him screaming at his father as he rode down the drive that he did not trust him to look after her in death any more than he had in life. The ashes, it is said, were kept in a white alabaster jar.

Annie dropped the letter to her lap. 'The jar! It was an urn. No wonder he was so precious with it.'

'Was that the same jar with which you posed for the panel with me?' asked Lodovico.

'Yes. I once knocked the lid off by mistake.' She remembered the day, and Francis's anger. 'It was the only time he raised his voice to me.'

'What did he say?'

'He told me to have a care; he did not curse or strike me, but it was the way he said it. It could have been Mary's myrrh after all – you'd have thought it was priceless.'

'To him, it clearly was; and now we know why.' He tapped the letter, and she read the postscript.

I am undertaking further investigations both in London and Norfolk, but thought it best to furnish you with these details, being as how they provide what we in the law might call 'motive', and may also supply you with some clues as to his whereabouts. Please send news of your own investigation by return, or send an electric telegraph upon Maybrick Gill's capture.

I will write again soon,

Yours, etc.,

Charles Rablin (Charlie) – Inspector of the Metropolitan Police

Annie was silent; the plainsong of the nuns drifted from the chapel. She felt, for a fleeting moment, a reluctant shiver of sympathy for the young Francis Maybrick Gill; raised alone in a vast house by a grieving father, with every comfort that a boy could need except the loving heart of a mother.

She handed the letter back. 'The jar?' she asked, seized by a sudden notion. 'When you searched the villa, was it still there?'

Lodovico flicked open his notebook again. 'Yes,' he said. 'We have it safe at the Guardia, too.'

'So wherever he is,' she said slowly, 'he is without his mother. She was always with him. He spoke of her as if she still lived. I even asked him to invite her to visit.'

'Little wonder she did not come.' It was uttered without humour.

'God knows what desperate acts he will be driven to without her,' Annie said. 'Clearly it was the loss of her that unhinged him.'

Lodovico folded the letter into his pocketbook. 'And that, I suppose, is when he began to want to kill.'

'Do you think he intended to kill *me*?' Still, after all she'd been told, and after all she had divined on her own account, she could scarcely believe it.

'In all honesty, I do not know. He kept you alive for longer than any of the others; he showed every sign of attempting to build a life with you. Had you any sense of his wanting to marry you?'

'Once, I had. But when it came to the point, in Venice, he did not ask me. He merely gave me a camellia, just like the one I held in the picture in the Royal Academy.'

'Camellias again.' He nodded thoughtfully. 'And – may I ask you – did you and he live together *as if you were married*?'

He seemed on tenterhooks for the answer, as if her reply really mattered. For just a moment, she thought him jealous; and she was glad. He had played games with her to get to Francis, while her feelings had been real. She was sick of delicacy. 'You mean, did he fuck me?'

The ugly word rang around the cell, shaming her. But he looked at her without reproach. 'I do mean that, yes.'

'No. He never touched me in that way. He never even kissed me . . . that is, it was only once. But one kiss can be shared without engaging the affections of either party, can it not?' She was goading him again, but she did not care. She wanted him to be reminded of that moment in the poppy fields of Fiesole. Surely, even to draw her in, and glean his precious information about Francis, there had been no need to go so far?

His eyelids flickered; he had registered the slight. But he returned to his theme. 'And had you any notion that the status was about to change?'

'Yes, I must say that I did. He told me in Venice, under the Bridge of Sighs, that he wanted me to be his mistress.'

'And you agreed.'

'Yes.' Her answer seemed to pain him; he seemed so genuinely distraught that she felt she had to explain. 'You saw the opera. La Traviata gives up her lover and dies in penury. In the absence of marriage, or any other genuine attachment, this arrangement with Francis seemed to me to represent my only chance of security. And there hasn't been a lot of security in my life, Signor Graziani.'

He opened his mouth to speak, then pursed his full lips. He rose from the bed and began to pace, as if tormented. He asked his question as if he could not bear to hear the answer. 'So when you returned to Florence, you became his lover?'

'No. I wanted a little time.'

'You were afraid, perhaps, of the act of love?'

She laughed mirthlessly. 'No, not that. I've spent half my life on my back.'

He flinched. 'Were you afraid of him, then?'

She remembered the hard kiss Francis had given her, the darkness she had felt. 'I was beginning to be.'

'Is that why you did not want to lie with him?'

She had begun by being honest; she might as well continue. 'I did not want to, because I did not love him.' She might have added that she loved another, but she did not want to pay him the compliment. She was sure that his former regard for her was no more than play-acting as part of his investigation. She would not be taken in again.

He looked at her searchingly; she saw a flicker of relief in his eyes before he looked away. 'Did you tell him you did not love him?'

'No.'

'Then how did you reject his advances without giving offence?'

'I had the camellias do it for me. Francis told me that Violetta, the heroine of *La Traviata*, was based on a woman called Marie Duplessis, the lover of Alexandre Dumas. Marie would wear a white camellia in her hair every day of the month, except for the five days when she was bleeding, and then she would wear crimson. I found a bush of crimson camellias in the garden – by the stone seat.' Again, she could hardly look at him; it was where they had sat together.

'I know it,' he said quietly.

'I found enough of them to give me respite. It seemed to be a rule that he would follow; he did as the flowers told him. I suppose,' she said with a catch in her breath, 'he must be mad.'

'Oh yes,' said Lodovico calmly. 'Of that there can be no doubt. He is insane. And after those five days were over?' he asked, breath bated, as if her answer was the most important one she had yet given.

'The fifth day' – could it be true? – 'was yesterday. I ran in from the storm and found the secret room above the library. Then, as you know, I fled.'

'As did he,' mused Lodovico. 'He must have known you had seen his cabinet of curiosities, and that his sins were discovered.'

'Yes,' said Annie. 'I didn't properly close the door in the wall. And even if he had missed such a slip, he would know at once that I had been there when he saw that the picture of Mary Jane had gone. When I was standing on the hillside, I saw the lights come on in the villa one by one – the secret room was one of the first places he searched.'

'And now he is out there somewhere. Doubtless he has hidden himself close – he cannot have gone far as yet.' He sat beside her once more. 'Let us go over your excursions again.'

In the shady cell, with Florence framed in the window like a golden painting, Annie told Lodovico about every place she had visited with Francis in the old city. The Uffizi, the Bargello, San Marco. Santa Croce, the Ospedale degli Innocenti, the Belvedere. The Accademia, the Torre del Gallo, and the little white church at San Miniato.

At length he sighed and stretched. 'We have searched these

places, and have men posted at San Miniato and the Uffizi. It seems incredible that he would calmly view paintings and artefacts at such a time. Yet he cannot, I think, return to England; and on the information of the agent at Cook's, he has not bought a passage on the boat. What are we missing? Is there anywhere else in Florence he might hide?'

She thought for little, then said suddenly, 'Why must it be Florence? Why not Venice? He seemed very much attached to the place. He knew it well – he could have walked those streets blind-fold, and they were like a maze. He took me there for the opera, and it was there he chose to ask me to be his mistress. It is a place of great significance.' She smote herself on the forehead so smartly that he jumped. 'All my chatter of camellias. It was the bridge all along. The bridge is the key.'

'The bridge?'

She turned to him. 'His mother threw herself from a bridge when his father took up with a prostitute. He is taking revenge on working girls, on all of us, and the bridge is part of it.'

He glanced at his pocketbook. 'You mean the bridge from which his mother jumped? In Norfolk?'

'No,' she said slowly, piecing it together as she spoke. 'I mean the Bridge of Sighs. The painting of Mary Jane dead in the Thames was the first Maybrick Gill painting to be exhibited in the Royal Academy – it launched his career. It was called *The Bridge of Sighs* because it features Waterloo Bridge, a favoured site for suicides – the bridge is high, and the river runs deeps and fast. You told me that all the victims were found under Waterloo Bridge – it was a way for him to make their murders look like suicides.' She took a deep breath. 'That night, the very night of the exhibition at the Royal Academy, he'd pulled me down from the parapet of Waterloo Bridge. I was ready to end it all, just as his mother had done.' She had never spoken the words before, and they tried to choke her.

Lodovico sat unspeaking, the shock written on his face.

'It all comes back to the bridge,' she said, hurrying on. 'I think he is at the Bridge of Sighs.'

'In Waterloo?'

'No, the *original* Bridge of Sighs. I think he is in Venice.'

His dark eyes seemed to kindle; he got to his feet.

She stood, too. 'I want to come with you.'

'No,' he said, 'on no account. You will be safer here. I could not bear for you to be in danger again.' He took her face in his hand. 'You see, I love you, Annie. What Francis saw in me, what he painted, it was real. I know you will not believe me, and I do not blame you. But every glance, every touch, was the truth. It was not a Judas kiss I gave you. It was real. Why do you think I haunted the house? Why do you think I risked my career – my colleagues thought me obsessed. Why do you think I put up with Francis's goading, his humiliations? Yes, I wanted to catch him, but I wanted to be with you, to *save* you.'

She took the hand that lay on her cheek. 'You want to save me; but I want to save others,' she said. 'I once told Francis that I didn't believe in self-sacrifice, but I was wrong. If you want someone worth having, you have to let me do this. I've been a worthless paper whore. A shade. I cannot remember the last time I did something for someone else. On the streets of London I cared only for my own fate and Mary Jane's. Now that I've spent some time here, under the protection of Mary Magdalene, I've begun to feel . . .' she struggled to find the words, 'as if *every* woman is my business. And in order to save more women, women like Mary Jane, I have to offer myself as the sacrificial lamb. Francis has been badly frightened now, and might never reveal himself again without the right inducement. I am sure I am that inducement. I am sure he will come for me.'

There was a silence, and the crickets rasped outside the window as the nuns sang their offices.

'Very well,' Lodovico said. 'But with one proviso. This time you will not leave my sight. I swear I will never let harm come to you by his hand.' He took a pocket watch from his coat, looked at it, then put it away. 'We can make the six o'clock train.'

Chapter 22

Exactly a year ago

Next time I go to Gower Street, the sitting is very long. Now that I've said no to posing nude, Francis has been painting me as the heroine from his book, the woman with the camellias. White dress again, white flowers. For some reason, he is frantic to finish the painting today. At sundown, it is done, and I look at it, and I like it. It looks like me, but more so, somehow.

I am exhausted, so he asks me if I would like a bath. I turn to him with wide eyes. 'A bath? You got a hip bath?'

He smiles. 'No. A full bath – you can lie down in it.'

I don't need to hear any more. I follow his maid upstairs and she prepares the bath for me. I take off the white sprigged dress and lay it over the back of a chair. I step into the bath; the water is beautifully warm and I sink down into it. Bliss.

Then Francis comes into the bathroom, bearing a glass. I don't bother to cover up, except for the top of my arm, which I clasp with my hand.

'I am sorry to interrupt you.' He averts his eyes politely. 'I brought you something rather special – a wine from my father's cellars in Norfolk. It is my mother's favourite.'

He sets the glass down on the marble shelf by the bath. It is crystal, with a golden rim. The wine in it is an amber colour; it must be Madeira.

'I hope you enjoy it,' he says, and tiptoes from the room as if I am sleeping.

I lie back, as close to happy as I've ever been. This is the life. After the bath, I'll go back to the Haymarket for the last time and tell Annie the news: that Francis has asked me to move in with him. I'll tell her that I am not abandoning her; that I will be in a better position to help her. Maybe I can get her a maid's job here; Francis seems to treat his maids well. It would be fine if she could live here, too; be safe and not have to work on her back. Pleased with the thought, I drink down the fine wine Francis has given me. It is strong and sweet. I feel terribly sleepy. I try to set the glass down, but somehow I can't reach the shelf. The glass tinkles to the floor.

Then suddenly Francis is there, looking down at me. The water ripples between me and him, distorting his features, and I realise I must be under the surface; I must have slept for a moment, and slid down. I try to pull myself up, but suddenly he is in the bath with me, his weight pressing me down. I thrash and cry out, but I only speak bubbles. The water sploshes over the side. Francis is on me, he is in me, thrusting frantically. Then I know no more.

When I come to, the bath is cold; freezing.

I open my eyes and I can see only murk where there was clean water, weed where there were lavender heads. Instead of a chandelier overhead there is the moon. I float, revolving in the icy water, and a great shadow passes overhead, blotting out the moon.

It is Waterloo Bridge.

I open my mouth to protest that I can't swim, and the water comes in.

Annie knew she would have to see Francis one more time.

She thought a great deal about him on the train journey, watching the sun go down as they sped north and experiencing a whole spectrum along with the sky. Fear and revulsion were uppermost, and hatred for what he'd done to Mary Jane; feelings compounded by the realisation that it was exactly a year to the day since she'd lost her. But she was to learn that these feelings could coexist with gratitude and regret. She had spent so long feeling indebted to him that she could not, despite his actions, break the habit. She thought of his kindness and his generosity and his constant smiles, and even his genius as a painter, for no one could argue with the brilliance of his Magdalene triptych. The piety of his painting seemed completely at odds with the colour of his soul. Perhaps he was one of those wolf-like creatures of sensational literature who changed with the moonrise into someone else entirely.

Fear, like shoes or coats, wears out with the wearing of it, and during her time at the convent she'd begun to relax and regain her self-possession. She did not really think, there, that Francis could breach the walls and murder her. For one thing, the convent was like a fortress, with its vertiginous walls and high windows and iron gates. For another, there was no benefit in her murder; she had no secrets she could spill that were not already known to the authorities. If he were in Venice, he would be hunting fresh meat.

She thought of Francis's hand pulling her back from the parapet. He had saved her. Perhaps, to him, that had made her different. He was still playing God, but he had given life instead of taking it. Perhaps, in saving her, he had thought he was in some way saving his mother. Then, in that terrible summer of his boyhood, he had not been able to prevent his mother taking that plunge into the lake. But as a man, he had been in time to reach out a hand to Annie. Perhaps that marked her out from all the others – he had not engineered their meeting; he had intervened, he had been Fate's agent. He could have let her drown, but he had not.

She thought of the affection with which he had spoken to her, the way he had bestowed his mother's ring and her peacock coat upon her. Had he done as much for the other girls? She thought not. She was sure there was unfinished business between Francis and her, something connected with his mother, and one more meeting would resolve the puzzle. And with the thought of such a meeting, her fear returned; chilling, bowel-shrivelling terror.

She looked at Lodovico where he sat opposite her. Since his declaration of love they had not even touched, and now that they were flanked by strangers, there was no opportunity to. He sat with his head back on the antimacassar, looking at the shell-like lamps in their sconces above her head. He appeared calm but ready, a coiled spring. She could see the pulse beating in his throat. He had not looked at her in company, had not spoken to her on the journey at all. But she knew, now, that he loved her, as she loved him, and that they could make some sort of future together. She wanted nothing more than to continue as they were, to live a quiet life with him. But things could not carry on like that, not forever.

Perhaps for a while, for a very little while, they could have pretended that it would all end well. They would have spoken about Francis, his imminent capture, his probable capture, his unlikely capture. There would be no news of him, or some news of him, news of him having absconded to Rome or Sardinia or even Tunis. The matter would be quietly dropped, as he became another city's problem.

But she would have had to live, then, with the knowledge that he was at large. It was not the thought of grey eyes watching her from the shadows, or the prickling at the back of her neck that told her she was being followed that she feared. It was that she could not walk the streets of Florence with a quiet heart knowing that he walked the streets of another city, even the sun-baked streets of some distant empire, haunting hotter shadows and seeking foreign rivers in which to dump his victims. How could she look at the Arno on a summer's day? How could she admire the perfect arches of the Ponte Vecchio? How could she pass Dante's statue and tolerate his accusing stony stare or walk the galleries of the Uffizi and face the anguish of multiple Magdalenes? She could not make a life on those terms. In the end, she'd known what she had to do. She must put herself in harm's way. She must place herself on the altar, and hand Francis the whetted knife.

At Venice station, the scream of the whistle and sigh of the steam gave voice to what she felt – a sudden sharp agony that she might not see Lodovico again.

He leapt to the door of the compartment and slid it open for her, touching his hat as she passed him. Her instructions were to act as if she had been travelling alone, seated in a carriage with strangers. She nodded her thanks. He met her gaze with his dark eyes, and smiled – actually smiled – for the first time ever in their acquaintance. His face was transformed, from stern avenging angel to a countenance that was strangely mortal – he could be a lover, a husband, a father, a genial family man. The thought made her heart shrivel within her. That smile only quantified just how much she had to lose. She stepped down onto the platform. Now, although Lodovico had promised he would follow her like a shadow, she must pretend she was on her own.

She left the station, hardly registering the stunning view of the Grand Canal at night. Consulting her Cook's guide, making sure she could be seen, she stood for some moments, setting down her heavy attaché case, making much of its weight. Then she engaged a gondola, as she'd been instructed, and gave loud English directions to the Bridge of Sighs.

As she settled back in the crimson cushions, she watched the golden palaces slide past, lit from within by candle and crystal, round windows watching her like eyes. She realised then that ever since she'd fled the Villa Camellia, she'd felt Francis's eyes on her. She'd never really left him behind; he was with her constantly. If tonight went to plan, she'd never have to suffer his grey gaze again. For now, she craved it, she wanted him to be watching, and was sure he was; on the almost deserted water a black gondola followed her boat, far back at a distance, silent and black as a shadow.

As they drifted past the great square where Francis had taken her, that night of *La Traviata*, she could see the white marble of the Bridge of Sighs glowing above in the moonlight. She paid the boatman, and stepped ashore with her heavy burden, her step unsteady on the wooden jetty. As she gazed up at the arc of stone, she realised, as she had not before, how like a rainbow it was, bleached of all colour, original as bone. She thought then of Lodovico as she had first known him, as the rainbow man. She wondered if he was close; and hoped against hope that he would not fail in his part.

And now she stood in the moonlight, in the small hours of the night, the stone of the balustrade crushing her ribs, the moon reflected in the lagoon. She knew she had been right. This was the closing of the circle, a circle as perfect as the full moon that floated in the night, illuminating this last act. Francis had found her on one Bridge of Sighs. And here, on the other, he would lose her.

The bridge was deserted; it was too late for tourists, too early for market-goers. In the moonlight, it looked like the set at the opera house, slightly unreal. Annie had her costume; on her instruction, she had had a particular dress brought from the sequestered Villa Camellia: the white sprigged muslin that Francis had chosen to paint her in as *The Girl with the White Camellias*. The dress that she now knew had belonged to his mother, the stains it bore, the lake water that had dragged her down to her death. Everything was stage-managed, everything perfectly planned. She might have been Isabella on the stage of the Adelphi, or Violetta at the Fenice.

The scene: A bridge in Venice. A moonlit night.

Leading actress: Miss Annie Stride.

The stage was set. All that was needed was a leading actor.

And all of a sudden, he was there.

'So you do believe in self-sacrifice after all.'

His voice was the same as ever, smooth, low, cultured. She had heard it so often, in the many months they had lived together. But only now did it have the power to chill her to the bone.

'And now, we end as we began. I knew you'd understand. You were always special.'

She didn't turn around, and he leaned on the balustrade next to her, his sleeve almost touching hers, in a dreadful parody of how they had stood on their first morning in Florence.

'Bridges are good places for leave-takings. Mary Jane, and all the others.' It was the first time he'd referred to the other girls. It was a confession.

'Your mother, too,' she said, trying to keep her voice light. She had to broach the subject, and she bated her breath for his reaction.

But the anger did not come. 'Of course,' he said, almost conversationally. 'She was the forerunner.' He looked down at the silvered water. 'I did it all for her. Do you think she is grateful? Do you think she loves me now?' For a moment his voice grew querulous – for a moment he was a lonely, frightened little boy.

'I am sure she does,' Annie said soothingly, forcing herself to comfort him.

'They needed to be punished, you know.'

'Who?' she asked, knowing that she had to spin out their discourse.

'Whores. Whores like my father's. The whore who killed my mother.'

He dug his fists into his eyes, and rubbed them as if he was just waking up.

'What was the darkest moment of your life, Annie?'

She hesitated. She knew the answer very well, but doubted her ability to speak it out loud.

'Quid pro quo, Annie. I'm sure I taught you that little Latin tag. Something for something. You know my story now. It's time I knew yours.'

Still she was silent. She started to shake.

'Very well. Then I'll be on my way, before that handsome policeman of yours turns up.'

So he knew about Lodovico. He turned to go – she must stop him.

'It was in the upper room of the Old George,' she said.

He halted.

She spoke to his back. 'In Bethnal Green,' she said. Perhaps it would be easier if she didn't have to look at a human face when she said the words.

But he turned. 'What was the Old George?'

'A public house.'

'Who took you there?'

'My father. He lived there, practically.'

Francis walked forward slowly, like a panther stalking his prey. 'How old were you?'

'Thirteen.'

He was close now, his grey eyes silver. 'And what was waiting for you there?'

'A crimson room. All velvet, like the inside of a mouth. Mirrors and chandeliers, too. I thought it was ever so smart.' She could see it as though she had never left it; as, in fact, she never really had.

'And what else was there?'

'A man.'

'An old man? Or a young one?'

'An old one.' She remembered him well, in every detail. The silver hair, the jowls, the pocket watch. The sunken, mean little eyes, never leaving her body. The loose wet lips, moistened by a purple tongue. And worst of all, the breeches, already unbuttoned at the groin, ready.

'And rich, too, I'll be bound?' asked Francis softly. She nodded. He trod closer, his eyes too fixed to her.

'So your father procured you – an untouched virgin – for a rich man, to earn himself some drinking money.'

This time she did not nod.

'Oh,' he said, 'worse than that?'

He looked, and he must have seen it written in her eyes, for a wicked flame kindled in his. 'It was your *father* who ruined you,' he said slowly, savouring his terrible utterance. 'While the rich man watched, and pleasured himself.'

She closed her eyes, and tears leaked from beneath her eyelids. She cried for that poor little innocent girl who, despite her cruel childhood, had never dreamed the world could be so dark. She heard Francis's voice; light, urbane, his poise recovered.

'I can understand that you cannot appreciate the love for a parent after what happened with dear old Dad.'

She had to hold on to the stone balustrade with her hand to steady herself. To have it spoken of like that was intolerable. It would have been better if he'd hit her.

'Did you want to kill him, Annie? I'll wager you did.'

She opened her eyes. Whatever was there seemed to please him. 'So you *do* know. You know how it feels to want to kill. You see, *my* darkest moment was when Mama jumped from the bridge. That's when I first wanted to do murder. I spent the next ten years taking my revenge for her.'

'Was it only for her?' she asked rashly. She had taken a body blow, and wanted to hit back. 'I think you enjoyed what you did. You didn't just kill them, you *fucked* them, too.' She was tired of his silver-tongued lies. It was time for plain speaking.

He tutted. 'Oh, Annie. So vulgar. Mama wouldn't like that.' He wagged an admonitory finger at her. 'But I admit, my revenge had its pleasures. Only when they were dying, of course,' he said fastidiously, as if his desires were the most logical inclinations in the world. 'To be candid with you, I've never had better. A living whore could never match a dying one.' His tone was confiding. 'The muscles of their woman's parts, they *grip*, you know, like a vice, in the throes of death.' He sniffed. 'Besides, to do it when they were alive would have been disrespectful to Mama.'

He cupped her cheek, and she had to force herself not to flinch.

'And then you came along. You were different. You were worthy to wear her coat. I gave you her ring. As I moulded you, I realised you were not one of them. You were worth the trouble. You took my instruction, you became a superior young woman. If you had not found my cabinet at the Villa Camellia . . .' He checked. 'Clever Annie; was it the windows? Seven at the front, six at the back?'

'Yes.'

'If you had not found the cabinet, we would have been together that night.'

Her skin chilled. 'While you drowned me?'

'Of course.'

He took her hand, and she had to steel herself to let him, fighting her instinct to snatch it back. Was this the moment he would dispatch her? There was no one on the bridge to stop him. Where was Lodovico?

Francis's hair was silver in the moonlight; his eyes had a catchlight of bone, just like the one he used to paint in her eye to bring it to life. But this time the catchlight meant her death. 'Come along, my dear,' he said, his hand gripping hers. 'It is time. I have taken a room nearby. With a bath.' It was as if they were married indeed, and he had engaged a room for a wonderful overnight trip. 'Somewhere you and I can be *alone*.'

He knew. He knew that Lodovico was watching them. She had been so fixated on the bridge, and so sure that Francis would dispatch her there, where their story had begun, and where the watching Lodovico could intervene. She had forgotten that Francis killed his victims first, and then dumped them off the bridge later.

If he dragged her to some *pensione* where Lodovico could not follow, she was lost. She must keep him here; and she knew just how to do it. She must play the ace in her sleeve.

'I am very sorry I did not become acquainted with your mother.'

'She would have liked you,' said Francis softly. 'Not at first, of course; but once you became the woman I made you.'

'Let's find out.'

He laughed a little. '*What?*'

'Let's ask her.' She stooped to open her attaché case, and took out the heavy burden she'd been carrying since Florence. She set the alabaster jar precariously on the stone parapet.

Francis's eyes opened, moon-wide. 'You brought her here? Mama?'

His eyes were suddenly black and blank, like the dull dead eyes of his stuffed creatures. His gloved hands shot out from beneath his cloak and fastened about her throat.

She could not breathe; could not cry out. She could only hope that Lodovico, wherever he was, could see what was happening, and not mistake their hold for an embrace. Francis's face was so close to hers, an observer would take them for lovers. Fiery spots danced before her eyes. She clawed at the hands at her throat and loosened the iron grip just enough to hiss, 'No, Francis, you mustn't hurt me in front of her. She wouldn't like it.'

His grip relaxed just a fraction, and he looked confused, suddenly a boy again. The large urn glowed between them in the setting moon, white as bone.

'After all,' choked Annie, fast losing consciousness, 'Mama . . . is what matters . . . isn't she?'

The little boy nodded his head.

With the last of her strength, she reached out her trembling hand to the parapet. 'Let's . . . see . . . how much.'

Heavy as it was, it only took a little shove. The urn fell, time spun out, stretched taut like a cello string. Then there was a splash.

The iron hands were gone from her throat. Afterwards, she had a memory of seeing Francis's appalled face for a split second, eyes and mouth wide; then he was moving. Spring-heeled Jack, he leapt the parapet and jumped into the water, crying 'Mama!' as he fell.

Annie ran to the parapet and craned over, her ribs cracking on the stone. The black blot of a boat separated from the shadow of a bridge, and she heard someone shouting her name. It was Lodovico, waiting as planned. She ran down the steps and along the bank, jumping into the boat as it lurched and turned. In the water she could see a dark, floundering mass, and in the centre of it all a smooth curve of alabaster. Lodovico moved to the bow of the boat and held out his arm, shouting in Italian. Then he cried, indistinctly, 'The jar, man! Let go of the jar!' But Annie knew that he wouldn't.

The waters darkened Francis's opera cloak, his arms locked tight around the urn. As the waters swirled about him, it seemed to Annie as if he embraced a skull. For one fleeting moment she saw his face, peaceful, eyes closed, no terror, no struggle. Lodovico grabbed the sopping cloth and began to haul, a shoal of dark fish. She could have knelt, she could have helped. But she didn't. Instead she took hold of Lodovico's shoulder and bent to his ear. 'Let him go.'

He turned, his locks plastered to his face, his features dripping. 'What?'

'Let him go,' she repeated. His eyes locked with hers, and, never breaking his gaze, she put her hand over his icy fingers and deliberately prised them, one by one, from Francis's waterlogged cloak. The dark cloth fell back over the side of the boat, and the mass boiled and bubbled, subsided and disappeared. The black water closed over Francis Maybrick Gill.

They did not speak for a long, long while. Soon there would be noise, and whistles, and the Guardia would come with their dredgers to drag the lagoon for a body. But just now such things seemed unbearable; there had to be some moments of quiet.

They sat on the marble dock, feet dangling towards the water, Lodovico's cloak thrown around both their shoulders. Tacitly, they faced away from the white palace and out into the lagoon. Neither one of them could look at the bridge again. Dull-eyed, they stared at the grey dawn creeping over the sleeping silvered city. After a long time, Lodovico spoke.

'Why did you let him go?'

'He would have hanged anyway,' Annie said. 'Better that he drowned, as his victims did. Better that he should know that moment when the breath runs out and the water rushes in.' In that dark London world that she had once inhabited, it was common knowledge that the noose could be quick. A drop of the trap and a snap of the neck. Francis did not deserve such a death; to allow him a quick dispatch would have been to betray Mary Jane and all those other tragic working girls. And she had wrought another revenge upon him – he would not get to lie with the ashes of his mother as he had wished; Annie had taken such a solace from him. 'Are Lady Holkham's ashes safe?'

'In a casket at Santa Maria Novella. I charged the priest to say a mass for her.'

She nodded. However much of a monster Francis had been, his mother did not deserve to have her ashes used as bait to trap him. The Guardia had emptied the jar before they had given it to Annie together with Lady Holkham's dress.

The bells were beginning to toll the first offices of the day. They watched the sun rise over the city, painting the horizon with crimson.

'Red was the last colour,' she remembered, her voice muffled by the cloth of Lodovico's cloak.

'Red is always the last colour,' he said. 'It is made from blood.'

Epilogue

When Annie Stride walked into London's Royal Academy for the third time in her life, she was not dressed in a whore's rags, nor a magnificent peacock coat. She was wearing a voluminous journey cloak, with the hood drawn up over her head to shadow her face. The cloak concealed the travel clothes of a respectable married woman, and the clothes in turn concealed something else – below the stays and the stomacher and the petticoats was a rounded little bump; a bump that was barely showing yet but that made itself known to her by a tiny fluttering of butterfly wings, which every time had the power to stop her in her tracks, compel her to lay her hand on the precious place, and smile. But despite her delicate state, she was unaccompanied.

The exhibition was an unusual one; it was a retrospective of the work of promising artist Francis Maybrick Gill, who'd met with an unfortunate accident while painting in Venice last summer. It was January once again, and almost exactly a year since Annie had been brought here to see the first Maybrick Gill ever to have been accepted by the Academy; his famous *Bridge of Sighs*.

Once again she stood in front of that painting, looking at the dead eyes of the floating Mary Jane, and the white sprigged muslin spreading like angel wings under Waterloo Bridge. She wanted to say something terrible and biblical about vengeance, but instead she said: 'Don't worry, he's dead.' She now spoke English so little that when she did, her Bethnal Green accent was back, stronger than ever. She embraced it.

She moved further into the great room, to where Francis's Gower Street paintings hung. She was Eve in her green gown holding her apple. She was Jezebel with her braided hair and her turquoises. Then Rahab, in her simple homespun with her hair loose as a bride's. There she was as the Whore of Babylon, the only picture in profile, her white hand holding a golden chalice, the sacrificial lamb curled at her feet. And there, Lucrece, a huge horizontal canvas; she reclined in a white toga, her strawberry hair tumbling to the floor. There was Manon at her fatal card game. Then the kneeling Gretchen in her prison.

She walked on, and in the next room were the paintings of Francis's Florentine period: the Magdalene series, every one featuring the alabaster jar. All the paintings from the Villa Camellia were there, save the enormous poplar triptych, which had mysteriously disappeared.

And on the very back wall, his last painting: *The Girl with the Crimson Camellias*. There she was – wanton, reclining, replete – with the red blooms in her hair, her breasts exposed, her lips parted above and below. And hanging next to it, its companion piece, *The Girl with the White Camellias*, in which she stood, virginal and unsure, clutching a bouquet of the white flowers like a bride, in the dress that had belonged to Francis's mother. The paintings together offered a titillating tableau – they were so obviously the same girl, but in the white painting she was fully dressed and erect, and in the red, practically naked and reclining. Annie was reminded of the naughty stereogram she had seen at the Vauxhall Gardens, of the woman gradually stripped of her clothes in successive photographic plates.

A small crowd had gathered about *The Girl with the Crimson Camellias*. She was not surprised; people were always drawn to whores, even the gentry. Francis's father, she remembered, had chosen a whore over his wife, and with that preference had begun this whole sorry tale. The noble patrons of the Royal Academy this evening were no different. They hung around the painting the way the bastards had hung around the Haymarket, their scandalous, delicious whispers hissing around her like the serpent in Eden.

She stood a little apart from the salacious knot of people, keeping the lonely *Girl with the White Camellias* company. She had been in the gallery so long that her husband came to fetch her. He had allowed her to come in alone as she had asked – against his natural instinct to protect – but he could only take so much. 'I was worried about you,' he said, offering her his arm.

She took it gladly. She and Lodovico had married at the convent of Santa Maria Magdalena, with all the nuns in attendance. They'd spoken their vows on the altar steps, before the convent's latest acquisition: Francis Maybrick Gill's miraculous triptych *The Life of the Magdalene*, which the groom had had conveyed there from the Villa Camellia before his division could inventory the dead artist's possessions. In the panel, the bride and groom were depicted as Mary and Christ.

Annie had asked the mother superior about the painting on her wedding eve. Even in her dizzying, incandescent happiness, she had her doubts about whether it was worthy of its new home. It was a work of genius, decidedly. But it had been created by the Devil incarnate. And it was profane for another reason: it had within it, as all Francis's pictures did, the white pigment made from the bones of his victims. But the nun had, surprisingly, been decided, even after this dreadful disclosure. 'Whatever Francis Maybrick Gill was,' she'd said to Annie in her cell, 'he had a substantial gift. Should all his paintings be destroyed because he was a murderer? If that were the rule, our entire cultural landscape might look very different. Should the paintings be buried, or burned, because they contain vestiges of human remains?

Florentine churches hold many treasures of dubious provenance; doubtless children of the sun died to dive for pearls or mine gold for our precious reliquaries. Should we therefore not display such treasures, or should we hope instead that their sacrifices now inspire devotion? Can we not venerate these women? Is it not possible that this man, in all his evil, managed to produce work that celebrates womanhood?' She'd taken Annie's cheek in her hand. 'I agree with you that Francis Maybrick Gill behaved like the very Devil, but if this panel has the power to inspire devotion to God, then it belongs here.'

And so the vows of bride and groom were observed by their mirror images in the faces of Christ and the Magdalene.

And now Signora Annie Graziani lived in Florence, in the midst of the constellation she'd loved so well from the hill. She had settled into Lodovico's little house by the Arno, where they were treated to daily visits from Nonna and Nonno Cilenti, Nonno and Nonna Graziani, Mamma and Papa, Lodovico's four sisters Cicilia, Buona, Lisabetta and Tomasia, Buona's little boys Enzo and Rafi, and Lisabetta's new daughter Caterina. Annie found the whirl of family life charming, and the novelty of so much company showed no signs of wearing off. Still, she treasured her private time with her new husband, their precious moments alone together, and their nights in the little attic room overlooking the river. From her bedchamber she could see the Ponte Vecchio. Now there was a bridge that she loved, a bridge that did not mean fear and death, but home. She could brush her hair at sundown, and look on the bridge, and she did not sigh, but smile.

Now she turned to her husband and the father of her unborn child. 'Were we right to allow this exhibition?' she asked him, watching the little crowd around *The Girl with the Crimson Camellias*, the undoubted star of the show. 'Does he deserve to be admired by posterity? Does he deserve a spotless reputation?'

'No,' he said frankly. 'But they're good, Annie, they're *all* good.

In fact they're wonderful. And something good had to come of all this.'

Annie wondered if he was right, if the mother superior had been right. How could the work of that monster be a celebration of women? How could a man who killed women venerate them?

'When I was here last,' she said, 'I asked Francis why there was no dead creature in the camellias picture. He never answered. Then, in the convent, you suggested that the camellias themselves might have been the dead subjects.'

'I remember.' Lodovico placed his arm around her waist, as if protecting her against the memory.

'Now I realise that the dead subject in the picture was not intended to be the flowers. It was the Girl with the Camellias herself,' she said. 'It was me. I was to have been dead before these pictures were exhibited together: the red and the white, the crimson and the bone.' She shivered to think how close she'd come, and Lodovico drew her to him.

In response to the shiver, the baby kicked again, and quite suddenly Annie thought of Francis's mother. The alabaster jar had been recovered from the Venetian canal, clutched in Francis's cold dead hands. She had asked that his body be dumped in murderer's quicklime, but that Lady Holkham's jar – with its contents returned to it – be returned to his father's estate, so that some vestige of that lady could rest in the family mausoleum. If only she could have lived, to love her son, would he have become such a monster? Annie felt a sudden, and wholly unwanted, pang of sympathy for Francis Maybrick Gill. She took Lodovico by the hand and led him from the gallery.

In the carriage, she thought of all those women she'd been, all those other selves hanging on the walls of the Royal Academy. And now, as the hansom cab bowled over Waterloo Bridge to catch the boat train, she saw several young ladies, their cheeks a little too pink, their clothes a little too bright, their bodices a little too low, strolling in the freezing air and greeting the little crowd of gentlemen that had gathered with painted-on smiles. From Mary Magdalene to the Girl with the Camellias to these girls on the Bridge of Sighs. A long and inglorious tradition – the oldest profession in the world.

As it was in the beginning, is now, and ever shall be.

Annie turned to Lodovico. 'Let's go home,' she said.

Acknowledgements

First and foremost, I must thank my Three Musketeers – Sacha, Conrad and Ruby – who have supported me through what has been the most challenging of years. Additional thanks to Sacha for hauling me out of plot holes and suggesting some nice gory touches for this novel.

I also want to mention my father, Adelin Fiorato, who passed away earlier this year. I think he would be pleased that I am writing once again about the art of the Renaissance, a subject to which he dedicated most of his life.

Huge thanks as ever to Teresa Chris for being the most steadfast of agents, a loyal friend, and the most enormous fun to go to lunch with.

My gratitude to everyone at Hodder & Stoughton, particularly Emily Kitchin for her enthusiasm and expert editing, and to Jane Selley for her eagle-eyed copy editing. Thanks, too, for an amazing cover – clearly artists don't just live in the past. Thanks also to Ilaria Imperoli for checking my Italian.

For the research for this book I was very fortunate in my home city of London, where Victoriana is all around you. London also houses some of the finest museums and galleries in the world if you want to dig a little deeper into Victorian life. I am particularly indebted to the Tate Britain, where I spent a very early morning completely alone in a vast room full of priceless Pre-Raphaelites. I must also thank the Wellcome

Collection and the Hunterian Museum at the Royal College of Surgeons, for an insight into some of the darker aspects of this novel.

Alongside the darkness I hope there is beauty in the book, too. If you want to meet Annie Stride, you'll find her in John Everett Millais' *The Bridesmaid*, which was the inspiration for her look.